MADS RAFFERTY

DEADLY OCCUPANTS

ISBN:978-0-6458037-7-8

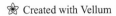 Created with Vellum

Trigger Warning

Please read with care.
This book touches on the following topics and themes.
Mentions of suicide, off-paper sexual assault, on-paper
mentions of inappropriate touching, violence, and gore, grief,
and loss.

Secrets don't stay buried with the dead.

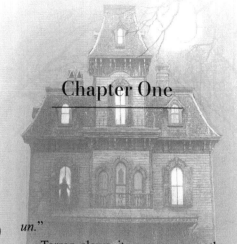

Chapter One

"**R**un."

Terror claws its way up my throat with a piercing scream. The sound erupts, blasting throughout the house, nipping at my heels as I run down the dark hallway and out the front door.

With tears streaming down my face, I crane my neck behind me to see if I'm being chased.

My eyes grow impossibly wide, a terrified gasp escaping my mouth as my gaze connects with a shadow lingering in the corner of where I stood moments before.

Panic seizes my lungs, suffocating me under the weight of my terror until I smash into something so hard the sudden jolt rips another shrill cry from me.

"What the fuck, Blair?"

I don't realize my hands are trembling until I clutch Phoebe's arms. "There's a man in the house!" I exclaim, feeling the phantom memory of his hands as they caressed my skin.

Our tour guide, a woman in her late thirties, rounds the

corner with a frown etched onto her face, no doubt having heard my shrieking. "What do you mean someone's inside?" Sally looks at me as if I'm speaking another language. "It's just us for the night, hon."

Trying to swallow past the lump in my throat, I dare turn and face Campbellton's most notorious haunted house. The stories I've heard of the mansion over the years resurface, sending ice down my spine.

The legends of this house have been whispered throughout America—the world. People travel from all over to visit the small town of Campbellton, North Carolina just for the sheer thrill of touring its sinister halls.

I'm, however, lucky enough to only live a two-hour drive from the house of horrors. And with a best friend who is obsessed with the criminally insane and anything that makes you scream, it was not a question of *if* but *when* she would drag us to its doorstep.

"When I walked back from the bathroom, someone grazed their fingers down my back and then whispered in my ear to run." My voice cracks at the end, giving way to how much the chilling gravel voice frightened me.

The house in question from the street appears as nothing but a house in dire need of a facelift, shrouded by the colorful leaves of fall. The bustling yard, however, looks as if it's trying to hide the house from the street, its trees leaning inward as if trying to warn those who pass to not even dare a peek.

Sally's eyes spark. "I see he wants to come out and play."

My eyes connect with Phoebe's round ones as we exchange a glance. Sally brushes past me, ignoring my quivering form still clinging to my friend. The woman practically bursts with excitement as she bounds up the front porch steps.

In unison, Phoebe and I turn to Evie and Violet.

The former is the said obsessed of all things spooky and she looks just as excited as Sally did a moment before as she claps her hands, bouncing on the balls of her feet, her long blonde hair swishing with the movement. "I knew the drive would be worth it!"

The latter, with her stunning mix of Asian and Caucasian features, cuts her eyes to the perky blonde beside her. "Our friend just got a pat down from a ghost and you're...clapping?" Violet drawls dryly.

Evie rolls her eyes. "You guys knew what we were signing up for."

"I didn't sign up to be groped!"

Evie's blue eyes glow with excitement as they remain glued to the two-story house, ignoring me completely. "I hope it's still inside."

My expectations were low coming here. I've heard the rumors and copious amounts of ghost stories, but I never truly believed a word of it. I only came because Evie practically forced us all to swipe our debit cards and sign the waivers. Which, might I add, I'm now regretting... Perhaps a house truly can inflict physical harm upon you.

When Evie brought up the idea of doing a ghost tour instead of a housewarming I jumped at the chance.

It had felt like a no-brainer to walk through an old, run-down house for the night as opposed to dealing with drunk frat guys wrecking our house for a housewarming party. We may not have expensive furniture but it's all ours, and I don't want our first memories of our off-campus place to include cleaning puke out of the carpet.

Sputtering out a laugh devoid of humor, my jaw drops out of exasperation as Evie, as peppy as ever, skips through the front door.

"Is she insane?"

Violet smirks, her sleek black hair swaying across her shoulders as she chuckles. "You're talking about the girl who's studying to cut into people. Of course there's something fundamentally wrong with her."

"Girls, hurry up! You're wasting precious minutes!" Evie screams from somewhere inside the house.

Shaking my head, I protest, "I am *not* going back in there."

Phoebe sighs, the rush of air blowing across my ear, reminding me I'm still clinging to her. Letting go, I take a step back as she relents, "Either way, that psycho will cause us physical harm if we don't go in."

"I love a good fright like anyone else but I'm beginning to believe there's actually something wrong with that house."

This feels nothing like the fake haunted houses the school puts together. There are no actors or props—this is real, and whether anyone believes me or not, I know what I felt. Those were fingers that slid down my back.

Violet cocks a hip as the fall night air whips across her face, parting her bangs. "I'm sure it was just your mind playing tricks on you."

"Playing tricks?" I gasp. "My mind didn't conjure up another hand and grope my—"

"If you chicken out, I'm going to be pissed," Evie says from the doorway.

Gritting my teeth, I hold my hand out to Phoebe, part of my body's tension uncoiling as her ebony skin slides against my ivory. I don't bother holding out my hand for Violet; she would rather pluck out her eyeballs than be forced to touch another human with affection.

With her free hand, Phoebe pulls her cardigan tighter around her body, her features smooth and relaxed as no doubt the science against the paranormal swirls through her mind.

I wish I had Phoebe's black and white thinking right now.

Violet struts in front of us onto the porch, her all-black ensemble blending with the night's darkness. "Let's get this horror show over with."

Evie frowns, a hint of disappointment shimmering in her blue eyes. "You all have the worst spooky season vibes. It's a full moon *and* Halloween night... Do you know how hard it was to get this tour? I had to book seven months in advance." Craning her neck behind her, she lowers her voice to a whisper. "I practically stalked Sally. You should be grateful you're touring the house and not a prison to visit me."

Sighing, I try to shake off the fear from the house and instead allow Evie's words to conjure guilt in my brain. I may not be able to summon strength right now, but guilt will make my feet walk. At least, until I tip my head back and peer at the two-story house.

It's old, so old I'm worried the front steps will crumble beneath me and send me tumbling. Paint is peeling off the front woodwork, shutters hang half off their hinges, and in every window my gaze roves over, I expect to find someone standing within the shadows.

Goose bumps line my arms and the hair on the back of my neck stands up as I lock my gaze on the front door. It feels as though the house is staring back at me, gleeful at what it finds at its entrance.

Walking up the three rickety stairs, I join them on the porch, Phoebe close on my heels. Even just standing on the porch makes my body shudder.

There is something *wrong* with this house.

Evie's eyes, as blue as the ocean glance over us nervously as she chews on her bottom lip. No matter that she had this planned months before any of us knew, Evie has always done things wanting to share the joy she feels with others.

Despite what some may think, she is a walking ball of nerves—not over the house, but our reactions. It's why she's looking at *us*, not the house. It's what forces me to say, "Thank you for getting this tour for us. It will be fun."

Evie's brows rise in shock. "Really?"

I shrug, my bright red hair swishing against my stomach with the movement. "Really. It will be a fun experience."

I'd say just about anything right now to get the sad, anxious look out of her eyes.

My support makes the nerves fall off her and within an instant, she's bouncing up and down with excitement, taking my free hand in hers she yanks me into the house.

The moment my feet cross the threshold, regret hits me like a freight train.

With the house submerged in darkness, the shadows clinging to the walls make me question what I'm seeing, and the icy chill that fills the halls makes me shiver. No matter how tightly I wrap my arms around myself to preserve heat.

Do it for the girls.

After all, they're all I have.

Phoebe closes the door behind us with a resounding click and taking one glance at the girl I've grown up with since birth, the one who is more a sister than a best friend, I know without a shadow of a doubt that she feels it too.

The house is alive and watching.

Sally walks us through to the left, into what appears to have been the parlor. Couches older than the house itself sit facing each other and when Evie plops onto the fabric three-seater, clouds of dust shoot up to greet her.

Sally tucks her short blonde hair behind her ears as she motions for us to join her. I was shocked when she introduced herself as our tour guide. I'm not sure what I was expecting but an older, sassier version of Evie was not it.

Looking at the shadows clinging to the corner of the room, I ask, "Can we turn on a light?"

"No," Sally and Evie respond in unison.

"The light deprives your senses. We want you to be open to feeling the energy of the house," Sally explains with a lilt to her voice as she tries to wave away dust mites.

A grim expression crosses Violet's features as she enters the room. "I think the house needs more than just an exorcism," she mutters under her breath.

Sally snaps her head up as we snicker. "That word is to never be uttered in this house. You will regret it if you do."

Chancing a glance toward Violet, I watch her confidence slip, her humorous mask cracking as she slowly lowers herself to the couch, sharing a conspiratorial glance with Phoebe and me as she for once, doesn't clap back with a retort. Evie, either oblivious to the tension or purposely ignoring it, leans forward to help Sally take equipment out of a black industrial bag.

My gaze roams the room as we wait. I can't help but notice that the two clocks sitting in the room are frozen at the same time.

3:13.

Evie gasps, snapping my attention towards her as she squeals in delight. "Oh my god! I've only seen these in TV shows!"

We all lean forward, ignoring the dust that rises as we try to glance at what elicited such excitement from her.

"What the hell is that?" Violet mumbles, her nose scrunching.

"It's a spirit box! It scans radio frequencies, allowing EVPs to come through."

"Care to explain what an E blah blah blah is? We don't watch *Ghost Hunters* religiously," Violet chides.

"Electronic voice phenomena," Sally explains, not lifting her head from the various gadgets she places on the wooden coffee table.

Evie flicks a switch and a sound so abrupt and jarring blares from the handheld rectangular device. The sudden disturbance makes me yelp, smashing my palms over my ears.

Static.

One that carries a thousand voices as channel after channel flips through the device so quickly that no words come through at all, as if the signal has been lost on a TV.

Phoebe cocks her head as she studies the machine, all while Violet openly disapproves. "That thing is meant to communicate with us?"

Evie chuckles. "No, Vi, the device doesn't talk; the ghosts talk *through* it."

"She's not helping prove she's not psychotic," Violet murmurs, her collection of necklaces jangling as she leans backward.

Phoebe leans into my personal space, her voice a low whisper. "If anything, we'll hear a radio talk host."

Biting my tongue to hold in my snort as Phoebe pulls back smug as ever, her brain no doubt working through a thousand reasons to dispute the mechanics of the device.

Evie ogles the device as it blares white noise while Sally walks around, placing clear white balls that light up to the touch in the corners of the room. She leaves one on top of the mantel above the fireplace, directly in front of what used to hold a picture frame. The paint around the area is dim compared to the otherwise rectangle spot. Sally moves from corner to corner until lastly, she places another clear white ball on the coffee table before us.

Sally plops down in the chair perpendicular to us and grins. "Who's ready to play?"

"*Blair.*"

A deep male grumble of a voice spills from the spirit box, the static stopping to allow the sound through. My eyes snap open wide as my heart plummets. Phoebe grips my forearm so tightly that her nails embed half-moons into my skin. She glares at the machine, as if her stare can erase what just happened.

Violet's lips barely move as she whispers, "Did that just...?"

My chest constricts. "It said my name."

Evie's shoulders slump. "Damn, I wanted them to play with me."

"By all means, Evie, take their attention away. I don't want it!"

Blue and red lights flash in the corner behind Sally, making us all jump out of our seats. Rushing for the edge of the couch we all hold our breath as we watch a small hand-sized cat ball rock back and forth until it finally comes to a stop and the lights disappear, plunging us into darkness once more.

Sally cocks her head. "Are one of you girls a psychic or medium?"

Drawing back with my hammering heart I shake my head, the other girls seemingly doing the same, even Phoebe, who looks as if her faith in science is wavering. Sally's eyes land on me inquisitively as she searches for what seems like my very soul, and as she does, a name comes through the spirit box once again.

"*Blair.*"

The word isn't a rumble or a plea, nor is it drawled with a playful tone.

It's a growled demand.

Sally's lips twitch upward into a saccharine smile. "I think you have a new friend, Blair."

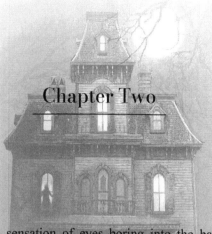

Chapter Two

The sensation of eyes boring into the back of my head doesn't waver as I say sternly, "Absolutely not."

To say that Sally is disappointed at my response is an understatement.

It's been hours since my name was growled through the spirit box and in that time, nothing has happened. I suppose Sally thought she was in for a night of horror but to my utter delight, nothing has growled, hissed, whispered, or touched me since the parlor.

However, the rooms we entered emanated such a horrid energy, it's kept the hairs on my body standing on end because despite it being quiet since the parlor, I know it's still here, whatever *it* is.

"No," I say again, half tempted to stomp my foot in protest, especially as Evie whines.

"Come on! We only have forty-five minutes left, and the ghosts have only been acknowledging you. Please, Blair," Evie pleads, clasping her hands together as she begs.

"I refuse to be bait for your entertainment."

Violet nudges me with her shoulder, a sly smirk dancing across her cherry red painted lips. "Maybe it has a crush on you."

I roll my eyes at that. "I don't care. I'm not going up there."

Phoebe crosses her arms. "What happened to no more peer pressure?" she aims at Violet.

Violet clicks her tongue. "I think peer pressure can be a healthy method for character development."

Phoebe narrows her eyes. "If anyone knows about character development it's Blair, who let me remind you studies psychology, which we should all be grateful for because if anyone goes into that attic, they'll need therapy."

I quickly flash my best friend a thankful smile for her support before Evie draws my attention and says, "It's not even that haunted. Just walk up the attic stairs and see if anything happens." Her gaze slides to the swinging string that pulls down the attic ladder.

Throwing my hands in Sally's direction, I whisper-yell, "She just said it was the most haunted room in the house!"

Sally made us sit in every room, holding our breath as we waited for any one of her devices to go off, with no luck. The only time the house has had any activity was with me, which I cannot deny. However, we can feel it, whatever it is, following us from room to room. Silent as a cat, stalking us like we're its prey.

It's waiting to pounce, and I refuse to be captured.

Sally holds out her hands, each one containing a rectangular device. "EVP recorder or the EMF meter?"

"Is neither an option?" I ask as politely as I can.

I don't want to touch either device with a ten-foot pole.

The EVP recorder is one that supposedly picks up on voices that the human ear cannot, and the other lights up red when the electromagnetic field changes, supposedly indicating a presence in the room.

Sally has expressed numerous times that everything within the universe is made up of energy; therefore, so are ghosts. Whether a ghost lights up the device or a faulty wire, I don't want to be touching it either way when it glows red.

Biting my nails, I repeat, "No."

Phoebe pulls my hand away from my mouth, forever trying to help me break the bad habit. However, the situation warrants some nail biting.

"I love you, Evie, but you will have to physically carry my dead body to make me go up those—"

Thump.

Snapping my mouth shut, we all lift our heads to the ceiling, and I watch in horror as another thump rings throughout the room, right as the floorboards sink beneath weight, making dust rain down upon us.

"On second thought, maybe you should go up there," Phoebe whispers.

Gasping, my head snaps in her direction. "Traitor!"

She shrugs sheepishly. "It would be an amazing piece to write for the paper and I need something against Trevor. He's been published three weeks in a row. This would be front page worthy!"

"Throwing your friend under the bus for an article. Nice, Pheebs," Violet chuckles.

Phoebe points a conspiratorial finger in her direction. "Do I need to remind you about last year and how you wanted to practice tattooing on us? At least my damage won't be permanent."

"Is everyone forgetting that trauma is permanent psychological damage?" I whisper.

"This is the first time we've experienced activity since the beginning of the night and it's while we're trying to convince you that it only wants *you* to go up there… I think it made its point," Evie says, trying to sound sorry, yet the gleeful gleam in her eyes gives her away.

I throw my hands in the air. "Does no one care about my well-being?"

"No," they ring out in unison, chuckling when my face falls.

Phoebe wraps her arms around me. "We're just kidding, Blair. We'll stand on the stairs while you go up there."

"That doesn't make me feel reassured," I say, frowning.

"Just think of it as a life experience," Evie says brightly.

Violet snickers, failing miserably to hold her laughter at bay. Evie plows ahead, ignoring her. "This is a once-in-a-lifetime opportunity."

"To be mauled," I murmur.

Gazing at the four sets of eyes waiting expectantly, I realize they aren't going to move until I go up there. I always want to make my friends happy, they mean everything to me but this…Sighing deeply, I force out, "Only if Phoebe goes with me."

"Done!" Evie squeals.

"Absolutely not!" Phoebe protests. She shoves away from me and rushes to Violet's side. "It doesn't want me like it wants you!"

I point to her. "I now win the battle of who would leave whom in a slasher film. You are officially the worst friend ever."

"You're the one who wants the article," Violet points out. "Front page, remember?"

Her eyes grow impossibly wide beneath her deep-brown bangs. She knows what she's doing; she's done it since we were kids. The sad, puppy-dog eyes would look childish on anyone else, but not on Phoebe. Her features are impossibly soft, making her appear almost angelic.

It also makes it impossible to say no to her.

Hence why I advert my gaze to my shoes. "I'm not moving until one of you comes with me."

Evie jumps beside me, using her long lean legs to practically leap across the room. "I'll do it! Do you want me to record in case anything happens?"

At the same time I say no, Phoebe says yes.

My eyes narrow as hers turn pleading.

"I need an article on the front page if I want any chance of snagging an internship at one of the large newspapers. You know Trevor keeps stealing my article ideas, but he hasn't done this tour. They'd know he played dirty."

After everything Phoebe has done for me, the least I can do is this.

Licking my lips, I steel my spine. "Fine, but I'm not doing dishes for a week."

She raises her hands in surrender. "Deal."

Phoebe slaps her phone, open on her camera settings, into Evie's awaiting hand, as Violet passes me Sally's gadgets. "I'd take both if I were you."

The two devices in my hand rattle against one another, the plastic of one grazing the metal of the other mingles with the sound of my hesitant footsteps as Evie clings to my sweater behind my back. There are only six steps needed to reach the attic, yet they're the most daunting steps I've climbed in my life.

My heart hammers wildly inside my rib cage as I peek over the attic floor and am greeted with darkness. Shapes and shadows float through my vision and before any can move, I halt on the step, squeezing my eyes shut tightly.

It's just a normal attic, I chant to myself.

With clammy hands and a boulder lodged in my throat, I open my eyes again, allowing my sight to adjust as boxes and old furniture swim into focus.

Storage—that's all it is. Junk.

Except the moment my sneakers touch the landing of the attic and the EMF in my hand shines a bright red light across my face. A scream rushes up my throat, the EMF crashing to the floor as I drop it, the light fading as I do.

Evie grips my clothes tighter. "What is it? Did you hear something?"

My chest heaves. "The EMF went off."

"It could just be faulty wiring," Violet calls out in support. "This house is ancient," I hear her mumble quietly.

"Or a ghost."

"Not helping, Evie."

Picking up the EMF once more, I don't release my breath until seconds pass without its red light shining in my eyes.

"Faulty wiring," I whisper to myself. "Just faulty wiring."

My sweater grows taut as Evie clings to me tighter. All the bravado and excitement that was once bubbling through her body drains the moment we step onto the landing and are plunged into something that feels far more sinister than the halls below.

"This is a lot scarier in real life," she whispers.

My heart pounds so frantically I can hear its beat in my ear as if a band has taken up residence in the canals. Licking my dry lips, I expel a shaky breath, quickly transferring the equipment to one hand to wipe my sweaty palms.

Once we're in the middle of the rectangular attic, we instinctively back ourselves against the wall, as if whatever has been following us through the house can't touch us because of it.

Evie and I stand in silence for so long that we flinch when Sally's sudden voice booms up the attic stairs.

"Anything happening?" she calls out.

Evie chokes out a breath as if laughing at how scared she is. "Nothing yet!"

"How long do you think this stuff has been up here for?" I ask.

I feel Evie's arm brush against my own as if she shrugged, but I'm far too scared to take my eyes off the room before us. "Who knows, it all looks ancient."

"How come Sally never told us the stories of the original owners?" My gaze flicks between the hole in the floor where the stairs are and the piles of boxes. "I mean, all their belongings are still in the house and we've still yet to hear of what happened to—"

Thump.

Evie gasps alongside me as we fly into each other's arms.

"What was that?" Sally asks, a hint of excitement in her voice.

My legs begin to tremble, but not from fear. It's as if we were suddenly plunged into an ice bath. My teeth chatter as I ask, "Why is it so cold?"

Evie yanks one of the devices out of my hands, fumbling with it until she presses record.

"Don't talk," Evie murmurs.

She hands the device back to me before quickly pressing record on Phoebe's iPhone. You can barely see anything, even with night mode activated.

I'm about to swear profanities. The last thing I want to do

is be silent in a room with something thumping around. But then her eyes grow wide, and I turn to watch a box begin to slide across the floor.

Evie lets go of me as she backs away, taking step after step, but I stay rooted to the spot.

I've never froze in my life.

Not when the police knocked on my front door and announced that my parents were dead, and not when my sister joined them just a short two years after.

Yet, as a large cardboard box slides toward me, wobbly and janky in its movements with no one around to push it, I freeze.

Utter terror assaults my body, forcing it to shut down.

Evie starts to whisper-yell my name, practically hissing like a cat as she tells me to move away from it, but as my chest heaves my ears begin ringing. All sound evades me as my eyes stay transfixed on the box until it suddenly comes to a halt.

The hold against my hearing lifts, sound flooding in once more, but it drowns out the screams from below and behind me. It can only focus on the heavy footsteps thumping across the old hardwood floors.

I can see where each thump comes from as dust floats toward the ceiling in their wake. The steps are so heavy the ground shakes beneath me, but no matter how much I scream at every molecule in my body to move, it doesn't.

Not even when the steps grow impossibly close, and I hear it growl my name.

"Blair."

My body doesn't move until three claws slash down and scratch me so hard my mouth is set free from its frozen stupor. Just in time to scream as my worst nightmare appears before my very eyes.

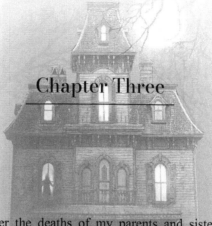

Chapter Three

After the deaths of my parents and sister, I know what it feels like to be coddled, and yet I've never hated it as much as I do now.

"Please let me help you," Phoebe pleads, guilt shining in her round brown eyes.

My usually stoic best friend stares at me with such horror etched across her face it makes emotions that I don't want to feel rise. I need her to go back to my science loving friend. I need her to not believe what happened tonight.

"I just want to be alone," I croak.

Six words.

The same six words I have been uttering to everyone since Evie pulled my trembling, crying body down and out of the attic.

To say the car ride home was silent was an understatement. It was layered with thick tension and guilt as everyone felt horrible for forcing me to go up those stairs.

And it was all for nothing. Phoebe went to watch back the footage Evie recorded, only to find the video had been corrupted. The entire screen glitched green rays for the entire seven minutes and eighteen seconds.

The same went for the EVP. Not even my screams could be heard on the recording, just static.

With my hand clutching my bathroom door, I relent, "You can stay in here tonight but please, Pheebs, let me at least shower alone." Swallowing thickly, I admit, "I need to wash it off me."

The feeling of it hasn't left me. As if it left its essence within the gouges it carved out of me.

Her eyes fill with guilt and pain as she worries her bottom lip. "I'll get us some food."

I don't tell her I'm not hungry. I don't voice that what I witnessed tonight was so horrific I'm afraid my appetite will never return. I don't utter a single word because I need her to leave. I need to see for myself what it did to me, not only mentally but physically.

I heard their whispers as they all argued, trying to blame someone for what happened, trying to make sense and reason of it all. But no one is to blame but myself. I could have said no and not gone up there. I could have stood my ground but the need to make the small group of people left in my life happy won out.

Sally was right about one thing... It wanted to play with me.

After Evie declared that she saw nothing after the box stopped moving and that she didn't know why I was screaming hysterically, I knew that it had only targeted me. For whatever reason, it wanted me to see what it showed me.

Wanted me to *experience* it.

Stepping into my bathroom, the sound of the door clicking shut intensifies the trepidation buzzing through my veins. Moving in front of the mirror, the girl that stares back at me is not one I recognize.

I've always had fair skin, but this is on another level. All the blood has drained from my face. Even my usually bright red freckles, smattered across my nose and cheeks, are dull and lifeless.

And my hair, typically thick red strands that are bouncy and full of waves all the way down to my mid-waist, is now dull and flat.

As if the very life was sucked from me.

Tears spring into my eyes as I trace my movements in the mirror.

The way my hand shakes violently as it moves toward my shirt. My lips as they part to suck in a deep breath. My eyes that grow comically wide as I lift the hem of my shirt.

As my jade-green eyes fall to my stomach, the first tear drops.

Three long slices run down my abdomen, each one an angry red welt crusted with dried blood.

My eyes slam shut as the image of what it showed me flashes through my mind.

Knock, knock, knock.

"Blair?" Phoebe calls on the other side of the door.

"I'll be out in a minute!"

Taking a steadying breath, I lower the shirt over my stomach, concealing the memory of that *thing* attacking me.

Opening my bathroom door, I find not only Phoebe waiting for me but Evie and Violet too. I lift my hand to silence them as they all open their mouths.

"I never want to mention it…ever." Looking each of them in the eye, I show them just how serious I am. "It never happened. Okay?"

"But…"

"No. It never happened."

For my own sanity, I need to pretend like it never happened, that it never showed me what it did, and that it never touched me.

"Please," I beg, emotion clogging my throat.

The girls look at each other before Evie whispers, "Okay, it never happened."

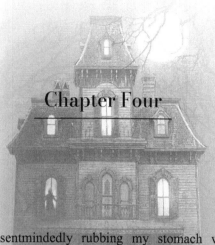

Chapter Four

Absentmindedly rubbing my stomach where the three long gashes reside, I throw my head back on a groan as I find Phoebe's lecture hall door shut. The quiet timbre of her college professor's voice floating beneath the doorway.

She is going to kill me.

Not unless these scratches become infected and take me first.

Guilt gnaws through my chest as I stare down at Phoebe's communications assignment in my hands. If it was anyone else, I would call it bad luck and chalk it up to the universe teaching them a lesson on organization. But Phoebe is not the one who needs to receive that lesson.

I've known her since we were in diapers and, usually, Violet or Evie are the ones having their ears chewed off for being late or missing assignments.

Come to think of it, I cannot remember a time when Phoebe was ever late.

She's punctual to a fault.

Last night spooked her. It spooked *all* of us.

No one has been the same since the attic. We've all been slightly dazed and distracted—the girl's unusual melancholy due to their guilt and concern, whereas mine stems from my foundation of beliefs being shaken, making me question *everything*.

I don't doubt that their experience, with my name being growled and the video footage being tampered with, has made them pause. Although Evie has always believed, I think believing and experiencing are two separate things, and watching that box move on its own in the attic shook her.

My hand drifts towards my stomach again without my consent.

"Mr. Somersby's class gives you a stomachache as well?" a deep voice drawls.

Jumping, I whirl, my eyes landing on a male leaning against the wall. I don't know why I didn't notice him… In fact, the more I stare, the more I wonder how I haven't come across him before.

He's tall…impossibly tall, with broad shoulders, honey-kissed skin, and a chiseled jaw. Yet it is none of those features that steal my breath away. It's his eyes, a dazzling light blue that seems to sparkle despite the bright luminescent lights hanging overhead.

Several moments tick by and all I can do is gawk. Which in turn makes a devilish smile spread across the handsome stranger's face. A lone dimple appears, stealing my breath in the process.

He is the most beautiful man I have ever laid eyes on.

Shaking my head, I force down every tingling sensation wreaking havoc through my body until I'm able to lock it all away inside my heart.

I wish more than anything at this moment that Phoebe was here with me. For once in my life, I have nothing to say.

"A stomachache?" I force myself to ask.

That was what he said, wasn't it?

He chuckles, the sound a deep purr that races through every particle of my being until goose bumps line my arms and legs.

Breathe, Blair. Breathe.

He kicks off the wall, nodding his chin toward the closed door behind me. "Mr. Somersby. Just hearing his voice alone makes my stomach clench."

My brows pull low. "I'm sorry, I have no idea what you're talking about."

His eyes flick down to my hand, the one that's still resting on my stomach. "The moment you locked eyes on the door you grabbed your stomach and looked like you were in pain."

My eyes widen of their own accord. "Yes! Stomachache! Every time." I chuckle nervously. That is a far greater reality than the truth of last night.

Yanking my hand away I clear my throat, desperately scrambling for anything to say. I've never wanted a conversation with a stranger to last longer as much as I do now.

"I take it you're late too?"

I fight the urge to close my eyes and berate myself. Of course he's late—we're both locked out.

His smirk rises an inch. "Unfortunately, yes." He cocks his head. "But you're not late, considering this isn't your class."

He slowly comes closer, until he's leaning one shoulder against the wall in front of me and giving me his undivided attention. It's not until the cold wall meets my shoulder do I realize that I'm mirroring his movements.

My chin rises. "And how do you know this isn't one of my lectures?"

His gaze lowers, and he does nothing to hide his sparkling

blue eyes as they sweep me head to toe. He drawls roughly, "Because I would have noticed you the second you walked through those doors."

Heat singes my cheeks, and I shake my head to make my hair fall over the crimson skin. "My friend, Phoebe, takes this class. She left her assignment at home; I was just trying to drop it off for her." I let the deep sigh I've been holding in tumble from my lips, and I can't help but notice his eyes track the movement. "As you can see, though, I didn't make it in time."

"Do you always run around making sure your friends don't forget their assignments?"

I cock my head. "Are you always late to class?"

"Touché." He grins. "I'll make you a deal."

My brow quirks. "A deal?"

"I'll slip your friend's assignment into Mr. Somersby's pile."

"And what do you want in return?"

"A date."

My heart skips a beat while simultaneously falling. His dazzling blue eyes spark at my shock. I've never met someone so forward before. It's unnerving.

But then I find my lips moving before I can stop the anxiety clawing its way up my throat.

"Very presumptuous of you to assume I'd want a date."

His brows rise high, soaring quickly as he fails to hide his immediate reaction. But then it's gone, the cocky smile he was sporting before making an appearance again.

"I think a date would be a fair trade-off for your friend's assignment. After all, I'm the one putting my neck on the line." He leans forward, so much so that I must tilt my head backward to keep our eyes connected. "I'll sweeten the deal for you, though."

Now it's time for my brow to quirk. "And how will you do that?"

"I'll make it two dates."

Before I can stop myself, a loud boisterous laugh escapes me.

"You are sure of yourself, aren't you?"

"No, I just wanted to see what it would take to make you laugh." He grins. "Was definitely worth it."

I couldn't stop my blush if my life depended on it. "Is that right?"

"Mm-hmm." His gaze flicks behind me for a moment before his blue eyes collide with mine again. "I wouldn't mind making you laugh like that again."

"You sure are going through a lot of trouble for a girl you only just met and over an assignment no less."

He shrugs. "Up to you and how much you like that friend of yours."

Biting my lip, my gaze lowers to the paper in my hands. I already know I'm going to say yes. It's been months since I've met anyone that I've been attracted to. I just don't want him to know that.

"One date."

"Deal."

The swiftness in his confirmation snaps my head up.

His tongue darts out, licking his lips before a megawatt smile spreads across his face. One that completely steals my breath.

Sliding his hand into his back pocket, he pulls out his phone. He types quickly, giving me a reprieve to study his features without embarrassment.

As his fingers move the veins in his arm protrude, drawing my gaze to the biceps that strain against his T-shirt. My fingers twitch by my side and I have the deepest desire to reach out and trail my nails along his skin to see if I can elicit goose bumps within him like his stare does to me.

He truly is handsome—beautiful even. As if he was created by the Greek gods themselves.

He's a contradiction.

On one hand, when he smiles it's full of charm and a softness that makes me want to fall into his arms. But there's an edge to him. A ruggedness in the sharp lines and angles of his bone structure.

Violet is the artist in our group, and yet when I stare at him, I find myself wanting to pick up a pen and draw.

Until he's sliding his phone to me, the screen open on an empty contact page.

Swallowing thickly, I don't dare move my hands. If I do, he'll see the slight tremble running through them. It's been years since a man has elicited such nerves from me.

It's exhilarating.

He ducks his head until he catches my eye. "It's one of the conditions of the deal. I have to have your number."

"We negotiating now, are we?" Tensing my muscles, I pray for steady hands. "And do I get to know where this date will be?" I ask, hoping to distract him as I type out my number with a hammering heart.

His eyes track my features as if he's memorizing every detail. "No, I think I'll keep that a surprise."

Handing back his phone, his fingers graze mine, making an electric current spark between us, jostling the breath from my lungs.

I'm out of my depth.

His eyes widen a fraction as if he felt it too.

"I love surprises, but I have conditions," I force myself to say.

The dimple makes a reappearance. "Go on."

"You have to text me beforehand with a dress code. I don't want to turn up in heels if you're going to pull me through mud."

He throws his head back on a laugh and the sound…I feel it all the way down to my toes, as if it was made for my body. Singing to every drop of blood my heart pumps.

"What dates have you been dragged on?"

I grimace, trying and failing to hide my repulsion. "You don't want to know."

"I think you'll find that I want to know everything about you."

The doors behind us clang open, ricocheting off the walls before students pour from the room. My eyes snap to the emptying lecture hall.

How long have we been standing here talking?

Leaning forward, he takes the assignment out of my hands. "I'll hold up my end of the deal. Will you hold up yours?"

"Yes," I breathe.

His voice lulls me into such a trance I don't see Phoebe walk out of the room until her arm is locked in mine and her worried gaze searches my empty hands. "Please tell me it's in the pile."

I open my mouth, only to be cut off.

"It's in the pile," he drawls, placing the assignment behind him.

Phoebe's eyes bounce between us, and I can tell the moment she picks up on the thick tension, the crackling of energy that's sizzling between us because a knowing smile spreads across her lips.

"And you are?"

He straightens, running a hand through his shaggy brown

hair, making his biceps bulge again. "Your friend's next date."

I can practically *feel* her squealing on the inside. "Oh? And how did this happen, Blair?"

"Blair." My name tumbles from his lips, rolling off his tongue as if he's said it a million times and loves the taste of it in his mouth.

I squeeze her arm in warning before she can say anything more and start pulling her away. "I'll keep up my end of the deal. Don't forget my terms!"

He smiles, that lone dimple shining. "I won't."

I force myself to turn away, letting the image of him standing there smiling down at me imprint on my brain.

Phoebe squeals. "I need details. Every single little detail of how you—"

Spinning, I crane my neck, Phoebe's words rolling off my shoulders as I find that he hasn't moved an inch, and his eyes bore into mine.

"You didn't tell me your name!" I call through the bustle of students rushing to their next lecture.

"Xavier."

"Xavier," I breathe, finding that I'm just as in love with the taste of his name as he was with mine.

Phoebe pulls me away, breaking our locked gazes as she shakes my focus back to her. "Holy shit! Please tell me you know who just asked you out. I know you're a hermit, but you can't be that much of a hermit."

I frown. "I'm not a hermit."

Phoebe claps her hands. "Focus! Xavier fucking Hendrix just asked you out. How did this come about?"

"Should I know what Xavier fucking Hendrix means?" I frown, quickly cutting in before she can speak. "And if you know who he is, why did you pretend not to?"

"So much to learn, B." She rolls her eyes, shaking her head. "Yes, you should know who he is. First of all, every girl in the vicinity of Avalon College knows who Xavier is and would claw your eyeballs out if they found out you're going on a date with him." She waves her hand around at the bustling students. "Everybody knows him; he's practically royalty around here." She snorts. "Scratch that, he *is* royalty."

She lifts her hand, ticking off each point on her fingers. "He's captain of the hockey team."

My heart pinches at that, longing filling it for the ice I refuse to step foot on.

Phoebe goes on, not noticing my grimace. "A law major. The most handsome guy on campus—the most popular one at that. A senior. His family comes from old money, which, if you ask me, is always a recipe for disaster…except!" She stops in the middle of the hallway, not caring about the students trying to walk around us. "He is quite literally *the* nicest guy. He's practically a puppy."

My eyes narrow. "How would you know if he's nice?"

She links her arm through mine, pulling me out of the building. "He's the TA for my class, which quite frankly makes no sense since he's majoring in law but that's beside the point." She waves her comment off. "Mr. Somersby is one of the strictest professors here, and yet even the devil himself melts into a puddle for Xavier. That, and Garret is on the hockey team with him and he talks about his good deeds all the time." She snorts. "Even Garret has a crush on the guy."

If this is coming from Phoebe—the most practical, intellectual, and matter-of-fact person I have ever met—it means something. To me at least.

She gasps. "And to think you two would have never met if I didn't forget my assignment!" She throws her head back on a deep laugh. "I am totally claiming matchmaking credit."

I held up my end of the deal, now it's your turn

How is your Friday night looking?

A little busy if I'm honest

Bailing on our deal now are we?

I'll move a few things around

Does 7pm work?

I'll be there and I'll be the one wearing....?

Delivered

As promised

Something warm

And maybe bring a pair of gloves

Chapter Five

"**B**lair has a date with Xavier Hendrix," Phoebe announces the moment we walk through our front door.

Groaning, I drop my bag right as I hear a door swing open upstairs, shortly followed by footsteps padding against the hardwood floor.

Not a moment later, Evie comes bouncing down the stairs, her blonde hair swishing as she screams, "Shut up!"

Violet pops her headphones off her ears and sits up on the couch, pointing her Apple pen in my direction. "Have you seen her? Of course he asked her out; she's stunning."

My cheeks burn. "Thanks, Vi."

Evie flaps her hand around in the air as her cheeks begin to turn an ugly shade of purple.

I grab her by the shoulders and give her a shake. "Breathe, Evie! Breathe!"

Her chest deflates as she takes a deep gulp of air. "How? When? I need every single second spent with him delegated to me…right now!"

Evie's blue eyes seem to sparkle as Phoebe talks animatedly with her hands, reciting to Evie everything she managed to pull out of me on the car ride home. Along with the text messages he sent the moment we left the building.

Clearly not needed for the conversation, I veer left, entering the kitchen and swiping several cans of soda from the fridge before joining the girls in the living room. Taking a seat on the far end of the plush white couch, I catch the tail end of my own love life.

Violet swipes one of the Cokes I placed on the coffee table and sits back, her cunning, sleek eyes never wavering from mine as she sees everything.

"I give it three dates before she freaks out," she drawls before taking a sip of her Coke.

Evie and Phoebe whip their heads in her direction, openly scowling before Phoebe whisper-yells, "Don't jinx her!"

Violet shrugs before returning her focus to the drawing on her iPad. "I'm not jinxing it. I'm just calling it how I see it."

Evie rolls her eyes. "You can be such a pessimist sometimes, Vi."

"More like a realist, Miss Barbie."

"I don't take that as an insult."

"Wasn't meant to be."

Phoebe rubs her face with her hands, agitation lining every inch of her features. "Can you stop? You're both going to freak her out before she even goes on the first date."

My nose rises in the air. "I don't freak out."

Except I totally freak out.

But if your loved ones continued to die on you, I wouldn't judge you for being scared of adding to the growing list.

Phoebe crosses her arms as her eyes take on a stubborn gleam. "Okay then, name the longest relationship you've had."

I roll my eyes. "You know I haven't had one."

She raises her hands in the air, surrendering. "And that's fine, to each their own. There's peace in solidarity, self-love, blah blah blah. I truly don't care so long as you're happy, little Miss I'm-obsessed-with-fictional-men. But what's the highest number of dates you've gone on with someone?"

"And friends with benefits doesn't count!" Evie jumps in, pointing an accusatory finger at me as she plops down beside Violet, ignoring the slight scowl that seems to always be glued to the artist's face.

"Even those didn't last longer than a few weeks," Violet mutters under her breath.

I throw my hands in the air. "What happened to celebrating and being excited about this date? When did it turn into an interrogation about my love life?"

Phoebe's hand slaps down onto my shoulder. "Babes, it can't be a love life if you never go on more than two dates with a guy."

Scowling, I mutter, "I've gone on more than two dates."

"With the same man?" Evie asks hesitantly.

My mouth drops open to refuse their allegations, but nothing comes out. Only a horrible little squeak, and then my jaw slowly closes. How have I never noticed that I've never gone on more than one—

I jump to my knees. "HA! John Bennett, sophomore year of high school! We went on four dates." I sink back down, smug as I take a sip of soda.

"I don't think it counts when you had braces," Violet chimes in, not lifting her head from her iPad.

My chest constricts, squeezing tightly.

I wasn't focused on boys in high school, when both my parents died. Two of the people I loved most in this world, the ones that were meant to be there for me for my graduation, homecoming…everything. *Gone in the blink of an eye.*

Of course I wasn't thinking about dating. I had to focus on surviving.

Then Isabella died...and by that point, my fear of losing people had sunk its claws into me without reprieve.

Something on my face must give way to the whirlwind of my thoughts because Phoebe takes one glance at me before saying, "You know what, we got off track. You have a date with the one and only Xavier Hendrix. That's all that matters."

Evie claps her hands. "I say we celebrate!"

Violet's eyes take on an animated glint. "We can finally watch the new *Scream* movie!"

My jaw drops open. "Since when—"

"Yes! Please! I've been begging you all to watch it for months. It came out in March for Christ's sake. Jenna Ortega did amazing, truly one of my favorites from the franchise," Evie says quickly.

It always amazes me how fast she can talk, and how many words she can spew in just a matter of seconds. She's lucky we all have great hearing, otherwise she'd constantly be repeating herself.

Phoebe leans toward me, fake whispering. "I think they planned this. They've officially joined forces."

Violet rolls her eyes, chuckling as she shuts down her iPad. "Evie practically glued my eyes to her phone to show me the trailer last week. It doesn't look half bad."

My eyes narrow. "Still suspicious."

Evie brings her hands together, faux pleading. "I beg of you. It is a true slasher film masterpiece. And it's still Halloween vibes!"

"It's November."

She lifts her nose in the air. "Halloween isn't over in my mind until Thanksgiving."

By the skeleton, ghost, and orange décor still bursting with life in her room, I don't doubt her. It wouldn't surprise me if we had to drag the pumpkin and ghost-stitched pillows and throws from her room at Christmas.

Evie's an enigma.

She's as bright and chipper as they come, dedicating her life to becoming a surgeon to save people's lives, and yet she has such a fascination with horror…

On the other hand, that's why I love her.

You can always count on Evie for the unexpected.

Sheepishly shrugging at Phoebe, I relent, "I'll watch it if we can order from Francesco's Pizza."

Phoebe throws her head back with a groan. "Why? Why does our best friend have to be obsessed with blood and gore?"

"It's more the suspense," Evie shoots back, already off the couch and running for her purse and shoes.

Honoring the rule in our house, Evie doesn't so much as utter a goodbye as she runs out the door. Probably too frightened we'll change our minds if she takes too long.

During freshmen year of college, Violet and Evie met when they were assigned as each other's roommates. Despite the vast differences in their personalities, they got on like a house on fire and so Evie's true crime passions came to the surface.

Violet relented to her pleas for horror in exchange that whoever is forcing the other to watch a certain film must do the food run. So it's no surprise that Violet began to cave into Evie's crime and horror suggestions.

Grabbing her iPad, Violet mutters, her hips swishing in sync with her sleek black hair at her nape as she walks out of the living room, "I say we have fifteen minutes to get ready before the storm blows through the door again."

"Fifteen?" Phoebe exclaims, her brows rising in shock.

I deadpan, "Pheebs, do you not remember when *Halloween* was released on streaming services?"

Her brows pull low, her rich ebony skin glowing in the faint candlelight. "No."

"She had already ordered the food and bought the movie. She wasn't desperately pleading to convince us, she was desperately trying to keep us on her timeline."

"Seriously? Why don't I remember this?"

"Probably was on a Friday," I chuckle.

"What do Fridays have to do with my lack of memory?"

Violet walks back in, now dressed head-to-toe in Nirvana pajamas. "You have Mr. Somersby on Fridays. You're always too flustered to realize it's the weekend."

Phoebe grimaces with disgust. "Ugh. He's worse than Trevor and *that's* saying something."

"It'll be worth the hard work if he writes you a letter of recommendation."

Phoebe sighs dreamily. "New York Times. Could you imagine if I made it? Because landing a job there *is* the definition of making it."

"Of course you will. I don't doubt that giant brain of yours will get you into whatever job you want."

The girl's conversation fades into the background as my cheeks flush crimson at the Professor's name and the reminder of what happened that comes with hearing it.

Thankfully with the low lights, courtesy of the gazillion candles Violet has lit, no one notices my blush. Just thinking of that entire interaction makes my body ignite. I don't think I'll ever be able to hear the professor's name without bursting into flames.

My body has never reacted so primally to another person before. Sure, I've met attractive guys, especially throughout my first year of college. With such an array of different personalities attending the large college, it was eye-opening to discover what I found attractive in a guy.

But this is different.

Just thinking about the way he said my name has my stomach clenching.

Snap.

My eyes pop up to Phoebe's amused grin, along with her fingers in my face. "Care to share your daydream with the rest of us?"

Violet snickers. "I want whatever put that look in her eye."

Phoebe's lips twitch, her smile spreading with the passing seconds. "It's called Xavier Hendrix."

Jumping from the couch I rush from the living room, excusing myself to change into my pajamas. The girls' laughter follows me all the way upstairs and down the corridor. The high-pitched chuckles feel as if they're snapping at my heels as I pass the girls' doors, two to the left and one to the right. Their voices don't abate until I reach the last door at the end of the corridor and shut myself within my bedroom.

After all I had lost, I never considered myself a lucky person. That was until we moved into this house.

On move-in day last month, the girls and I drew straws on who would get which room. I suppose the universe finally took pity on me because I pulled the longest one, earning myself the master bedroom.

At first, I rejected it, feeling as if Violet should have the room, being that her mom snagged the house for us. But she refused, saying it was only fair and if we switched rooms the straw system would crumble.

She didn't have to tell me twice or twist my arm to convince me. The master bedroom came with the only ensuite and after watching many movies and hearing roommate horror stories around campus, I knew the absolute carnage sharing a bathroom with three girls could create.

The next day, I purchased flowers for Violet's mom as a thank-you and I wasn't the only one—we all bought her a small gift.

Being a real estate agent, she had access to most listings in the area before they went on the market, and not only did she show them to us first, she made the application process quick and painless.

Every time I enter my room a small voice pipes up in the back of my head that flowers weren't a big enough thank-you gift.

Today is no different.

It's gorgeous. My queen-size bed sits to the left, while the ensuite is in the top right corner and a walk-in wardrobe in the back right corner. My entire book collection sits between the two, taking up the entirety of the wall space. My desk is off in the corner, along with bean bags in the middle of the room for reading.

After sharing a tiny double dorm room with Phoebe last year, the enormous space feeds the freedom that I so desperately craved.

Quickly rushing to the walk-in closet I take off my shoes, ripping off my clothes from the day as quickly as I can. Shoving them into my dirty hamper, I chuck on my closest pajama set, which so happens to be the matching Halloween set Evie bought for all of us.

She will burst with happiness the moment she sees me.

Chuckling down at the black pajamas with white skeletons my feet stop mid-stride as I find my desk lamp turned on, casting a bright orange glow over my laptop and psychology textbooks.

Frowning, I walk over to it and flick the switch off.

I don't remember turning it on when I walked in.

My mind runs on a loop, playing over the moment I entered. I could have accidentally left it on from today's early morning study session. Mr. Emerson, my psychology professor, loves having classroom debates on the subject matter after he's taught us. It's his form of a quiz and I like to be prepared. I just don't remember if I left the lamp on or not.

"Blair, if you don't come down in thirty seconds, I'm going to drag your ass down here! Naked or not, I do not care!" Evie bellows from the direction of the living room.

Shaking my head, I leave the lamp, chalking it up to my brain needing a break from all the studying and assignments professors have been shoving down my throat.

Once down the hardwood stairs, I round the corner to find the iconic *Scream* logo staring back at me from the TV, along with four large pizzas stacked on the coffee table, accompanied by two steaming garlic breads.

Evie shrieks when she sees my skeleton pajamas, matching the ones she's adorned. She throws her arms around me and exclaims, "I knew you were a Halloween lover!"

Chuckling, I give her a quick squeeze back and plop down into the corner of the lounge. My stomach grumbles as the aroma of pizza stuffs itself down my nose.

Evie passes out the pizzas. Meat lovers for Phoebe, Hawaiian for me—which I'm thankful hasn't started a pineapple war in the house again—vegetarian for Violet, and pepperoni for Evie.

Scream begins to play, casting shadows across our faces, and even the candles seem to cower, the flames shrinking as cries erupt through our speakers. The sound of metal grazing metal rings throughout the room as the killer stalks its victims in a corner store, and then the inevitable sound of when the blade meets flesh and bone.

The moment Ghostface plunges its knife into its first victim I scream, the gory details making bile rise in my throat. Violet and Phoebe's screams join mine, but a lone chuckle of glee and excitement flits through the mix, tumbling from Evie's manic lips.

Shaking my head, I whisper, "You're sick!"

"This is my seventh time seeing this. The jump scares don't frighten me anymore." She shrugs, her eyes taking on a childlike wonder as they remain glued to the screen.

I'm about to throw another retort at her in the hopes of it distracting me until the killer corners Jenna Ortega, who's injured and trying to scramble away on her hands and knees. The camera cuts to the infamous Ghostface mask. The killer raises their arm, covered in billowy black robes, the large butcher's knife glinting as it rises…

And then darkness claims us.

Screams erupt for another reason entirely as every light in the house goes out.

Fear tinges the air as not only the TV is turned off and the glow of the kitchen light removed but the candles have been blown out. All thirteen.

A hand smacks down onto my forearm, Phoebe clutching me with a death grip so tight her nails dig into my skin, hard enough that I feel one pierce the skin.

"What the fuck was that?" Violet screams.

Her fear-tinged voice validates the worry rushing through

my veins. My chest rises and falls faster with every passing second until I'm outright hyperventilating.

"Guys don't worry, it's just a power outage," Evie says, trying to calm us. Yet even I can hear the shake in her voice.

"Since when do power outages blow out candles?" I whisper under my breath. As if whatever caused the darkness can hear us. But that's a stupid thought because it's just a power outage...*right*?

A white light erupts from the other side of the couch, flashing in my and Phoebe's eyes, before Evie lowers her phone's flashlight, not being able to hide the slight tremble in her hand.

"Maybe a large gust of wind knocked the power out and the air came in through the kitchen window," Phoebe offers. Forever the one to have her mind working overtime.

"Can we just focus on getting the power back on?" I ask.

Phoebe wraps her hand around my shoulder. The other girls don't know, because quite frankly, I feel embarrassed about it. But Phoebe has known me since we were born. She knows my fear of the dark.

Some might call it irrational. I, however, don't.

Shadows hide secrets within the depths of their darkness.

Violet douses us with more fear. "The breaker panel is in the basement."

Evie groans, yet it's almost too high-pitched to be considered one. "Why did we move into a house with a basement?"

"Oh, so now we blame the house?" Violet huffs.

Phoebe snaps, "Everyone shut up, we all sound like babies. We just need to flick the switch on and off. It's probably a circuit trip from all our electronics."

Violet waves her hand to the living room entryway. "Off you go then."

"I'm not going alone!" Phoebe cries.

"Pfft, well, I'm not stepping foot in that hellhole. Evie forces us to watch all these horror movies…you expect me not to learn a thing or two?"

Phoebe's eyes grow impossibly wide. "Are you saying you think someone's in the house?"

"No!" Evie and I exclaim at the same time.

During senior year of high school, Phoebe wrote her journalism piece on home invasions. Her brain took in one too many statistics and ever since she's a walking encyclopedia of how often bad things happen in your own home.

"We will all go," I say pointedly at Violet, my brow quirking. "Strength in numbers, right, Vi?"

She mutters explicates under her breath but stands.

Squeezing my eyes shut, I count to ten in my mind and try to take a deep breath with each count. Reaching ten, I stand, pulling Phoebe with me.

This is ridiculous, it's nothing more than a power circuit trip and we're all freaking each other out because of the horror movie.

The candles though…

Clearing my throat as if I can clear the thought, I ask, "Are we ready?"

"Fuck no," Violet quips.

Evie takes a steadying breath. "Just rip the Band-Aid off," she whispers, and then we're moving.

Nobody tiptoes or walks slowly through the dark corridor —we run. Hand in hand with Evie leading at the front, her tiny iPhone light bobbing up and down. She doesn't so much as pause at the basement door; she bulldozes right through it, not stopping to consider our clammy hands or racing hearts. Or that the basement plunges us into a different type of darkness, one so vast and deep that even the temperature changes.

The basement feels as if it plunges us into an ice bath. I

can't see my breath puff out in front of my face but that's because I cannot see *anything*. Evie's flashlight has dimmed so dramatically that I can't even see my own hand in front of me.

I'm so focused on trying to see *something* that I miss the moment Evie's flashlight goes out. One minute her phone is lightly illuminating her shoes and in the next, we're thrown to the wolves of darkness.

The screams that tear from our throats matches the ones during the horror film.

"Turn the light back on, Evie!" I cry, terror clutching my heart.

"I'm trying!"

"Well try harder, it's bloody freezing in here!" Vi hisses, as if the light has something to do with the rooms temperature.

Ice scuttles down my spine, making goose bumps line my arms. Violet and Evie bicker back and forth as she tries and fails to turn on her phone's flashlight, screaming profanities about her phone dying when it was eighty percent charged. But I don't care about a word they say.

Not when I feel as if the dark is watching me. Except where I cannot see, it can see *everything*. Down to every ounce of fear that resides within my soul.

I squeeze my eyes shut, trying to convince my mind I have some semblance of control over the dark. Yet instead of my eyelids encasing my mind in darkness, I'm transported to a memory, one that I wish I could erase. And suddenly, I'm not in a basement.

I'm in an attic. Surrounded by piles of boxes and junk.

I don't need to look to know which attic, especially as one of the boxes begins to move, jerkily, sliding across the floor toward me.

"Blair," it hisses in my ear.

A whimper tumbles from my lips, tears springing to my eyes. A growl explodes in front of my face a second before what feels like rusty nails slash down my abdomen.

"Watch the truth, Blair!" it bellows.

My stomach begins to pool, crimson blood dripping through the tears in my shirt as I'm shoved forward onto my hands and knees. Down here, I can see copper-red hair flit between the boxes.

My head shakes, a scream rising in my throat.

No, it can't be… It's impossible.

Then the figure steps forward and everything I thought I knew changes within the blink of an eye.

I'm screaming.

A shrill piercing scream full of terror, but my mouth is closed, and my throat doesn't hurt.

My eyes snap open to find we're bathed in a bright luminescent light with the TV blasting upstairs. The movie resumes from where we were, the TV blaring as the killer plunges their blade into its victim, stealing the very breath and life from them.

The girl's features have turned deathly pale around me. We all tremble and no one dares to take a step or move an inch.

My hand, however, slides to my abdomen, checking to make sure it was just a memory and not a reoccurrence. For once I feel relieved as my fingers gently run over the healing gashes.

Evie's swallow is audible before she licks her dry lips. "See? Circuit was tripped for a moment."

I don't call out the way her voice shakes, nor the fear as her phone turns on by itself in her hands after failing to do so the entirety of our time in the basement. Or the fact that no one is standing in front of the breaker…having being that no one turned it on or off.

"I think I've had my fill of horror movies for the night," Phoebe whispers beside me.

Silence falls over the room until the screaming picks up on the TV again and we all seem to freeze further. Our muscles tense as we wait…for what, I'm not sure I want to admit to yet.

"Anyone want to watch reruns of *The Bachelor*?" I offer, knowing I'm not going to be able to sleep alone in my room tonight.

"Yes."

"Absolutely."

"I'll heat the pizza up."

Rushing from the room, we all clamber to leave the deadly cold basement and the fear that stuffed our hearts. I don't think I breathe until Evie turns off *Scream* and we fill the house with lights.

Picking up my box of leftovers I place it in the fridge, my appetite long gone. "I'll leave the rest of my pizza for lunch tomorrow, just please no one eat it."

Agreeing in unison, everyone walks around the kitchen in a daze, all seemingly reaching for their comfort foods and yet when we sit down in the living room, no one eats a bite. And as the hours pass, no one says goodnight or heads upstairs to their respective room.

We all fall asleep with every light glowing in the living room and kitchen.

And Violet never once reaches to light her candles.

Chapter Six

Waking up with a kink in my neck, a foot in my face, and drool dripping down my chin I'm surprised that I slept through the night. Squinting at the rays of sunshine trickling in through the windows, I find my phone face down on the plush carpet.

Quickly picking it up I press the home screen, only for the dead battery sign to appear for three seconds before vanishing.

Groaning, I look around the room, trying to find another phone or clock showing the time, only to find nothing but Evie and Violet still asleep to the world around them.

Trying to massage the kink out of my neck, I make my way upstairs, my back spasming as I do so.

As comfortable as the couch is for movie nights, it's clearly not meant for four adults to sleep on. To say that last night's sleeping arrangements were cramped is an understatement.

The house doesn't feel as terrifying in the daytime and after a sleep spent squashed on the couch between my three best friends, the fear I felt last night no longer lingers. What is horrifying, however, is the time as I plug in my phone and watch it come to life.

10:30 a.m.

Groaning, I flop back on my bed, throwing my forearm over my eyes, hoping the move can block out the list of responsibilities flying through my mind. The most daunting is the assignment from Mr. Emerson, my psychology professor.

With the work he's assigned us, I would have thought I accidentally signed up for a criminology class.

This semester, we are learning all about the various personality disorders that come with serial killers. Mr. Emerson got creative with this semester's project, assigning us not only a three-thousand-word essay on our chosen personality disorder but the task of creating a serial killer, their profile, and the childhood that formed them.

Mr. Emerson is lucky I love to read and have hundreds of romance and thriller books up my sleeve because if not, I can guarantee my writing would make him want to pluck his eyeballs out.

Putting my love for fiction to use, I'll submerge my mind into a murder mystery and research my chosen personality disorder.

Sociopath.

It isn't until my stomach violently grumbles three hours later do I realize how immersed I became in my research. I rub my hands over my face, trying to unsee the endless papers and forums filled with studies of sociopaths.

Placing the pen in my hand down, I look next to me at the

list of traits and facts that categorize a person as a sociopath. Researchers believe the difference between psychopaths and sociopaths is that sociopaths are made, whereas psychopaths are genetically "born that way."

Once I started comparing the two personalities I couldn't stop.

Sociopaths lack remorse and yet in some cases can feel empathy toward another, but psychopaths feel nothing. Sociopaths are charming and deceitful while psychopaths are manipulative to another degree, going so far as mimicking others and learning social cues as they pretend to feel. And, although sociopaths can feel, the emotions are typically bouts of rage that are shallow and fleeting.

Psychopaths have no ability to form true, meaningful emotional attachments, and yet sociopaths can form close attachments to one or a few individuals.

Some studies believe that sociopaths act more impulsively and erratic compared to the meticulous mind of a psychopath, and yet various serial killers with sociopathy would detest those findings.

The list goes on and on and on…for three pages.

But the more I stare at the growing list, the more the pounding in my head grows.

Closing my laptop and notebook I push back from the desk and quickly snatch my phone before heading downstairs in search of Tylenol and lunch, hoping that the painkillers and leftover pizza will cure the statistics-fueled headache.

I tip my hat to those who devote their life to this, who have to see the gruesome scenes in person and face the serial killers and their heinous acts. I would never be able to do it; I certainly don't have the stomach for it. I'd much rather pick up the pieces of those they hurt in their path.

My mouth is already salivating for the food, except when

I step into the kitchen, I find a pizza box lying open on the kitchen island, empty.

"No, no, no."

Yanking open the fridge, I confirm that the pizza box was mine. I knew I would have to get used to accidental food stealing, items going missing, and the general lack of privacy that comes with sharing a place with so many girls, but I don't think I truly prepared myself for how frustrating it can be sometimes.

Taking a quick picture of the remnants of my Hawaiian pizza, I fire it off into the group chat.

I may seem petty, but there's nothing worse than looking forward to food all day only to find it gone when you go to eat it. My mind built up the item on a pedestal, and now nothing sounds as good.

Placing the phone down on the counter I search the fridge and cupboard, already knowing that my luck for the day has run out. It's Saturday and usually, we do the group shopping on Sunday.

"Dammit," I mutter under my breath, knowing I'm going to have to leave the house.

Jogging back upstairs with my phone in my back pocket I head for my closet, only to stop the moment I cross my bedroom door.

Sitting open on my desk is not only my laptop but the notebook I was writing in, flipped to the second page of my psychology notes.

Frowning, I slowly walk over and openly gawk.

Am I losing my mind? I could have sworn I shut down my computer and closed the notebook.

Rubbing my eyes with the palm of my hand, when I pull away, I expect the sight to be changed but I still find the items open, my screen blinking brightly back at me with the latest

Safari browser open.

Sociopaths vs. Psychopaths: Understanding the Mind of a Serial Killer

I scoffed when I clicked on it; not all sociopaths and psychopaths turn into serial killers. The diagnosis isn't a gateway to murder, but the most prolific serial killers in our history almost always are diagnosed with one of the disorders, and people tend to picture them when they hear the words *sociopath* and *psychopath*.

I don't blame them, I'm guilty of doing it myself.

Shaking my head, I shut the laptop and close the notebook.

I'm tired, *exhausted* even. I slept horribly last night and obviously researching serial killers and their disorders is getting to me.

Forcing myself to walk away so I don't think too much about it, I quickly shower and throw on the nearest boyfriend jeans I can find, pairing them with a fluffy white sweater and sneakers.

I'm almost out the door when a faint orange glow catches the corner of my eye. Turning, I find my bedside lamp on, glowing faintly across my pillows and duvet. My eyes practically bulge out of my head as I stomp towards the bed.

"Old houses and their stupid electrical circuits," I growl under my breath.

Our electricity bill is going to be through the roof unless we can fix this. Quickly texting Violet, I tell her about the electrical problems. I don't want to come back here to find my things burnt to a crisp because of an electrical fire.

Notifications buzz through my phone. Clicking out of my and Vi's text thread, I open the group chat.

F.R.I.E.N.D.S >

Did someone forget I called dibs? 😩

Violet
IB | I love being vegetarian best alibi

Evie
WTF!

M | Wasn't me, I hate pineapples 🤢

Phoebe
P | I swear on pizza itself it wasn't me

My frown remains as I descend the stairs and leave the house. Throwing open the driver-side door, I jump inside my black Jeep Wrangler and throw my phone and purse across onto the passenger seat.

Someone had to have eaten the pizza, but it will get me nowhere to point that out if they continue to lie. Besides, I'm turning hangry, and it's in the best interest of my friendships that I don't respond.

It takes me fifteen ravishing minutes of my stomach grumbling along to the beat of my Taylor Swift playlist until I pull into Ruby's Diner.

Ruby's Diner has been our holy grail since freshman year. It's the cheapest food in town and surprisingly the best. It doesn't give us food poisoning like the run-down diner on the corner of Main Street and it caters to Vi's vegetarian needs, so it's been our perfect go-to spot ever since we discovered it.

With adorable red booths, white-and-black-checkered tiles, and stunning pink and blue dresses for the waitresses, the entire vibe of the diner is thrilling. Ruby's transports you through decades and right back into the fifties.

The tense muscles in my forehead finally ease as I find

our signature booth free. Sliding into the leather seat the kink in my neck dissipates and the weight of the research falls off my shoulders as Daisy rounds the corner.

Her blonde hair is held up in a high ponytail and her blue eyes widen with joy when she sees me. If it weren't for Evie's long hair, the girls could pass as twins. Daisy and I met freshman year and without knowing it, I pointed her in the direction of this job. It was an innocent conversation, one where I babbled on and on about how obsessed I was with their chicken paninis. The next day when Phoebe, Evie, Violet, and I came in for lunch, Daisy was serving us and thanking me profusely.

I know how difficult it is to weasel your way into a job in a college town. Juniors and seniors tend to get first pick, usually because they worked there the previous year. No sense in hiring someone new when you know who already works.

It's the luck of the draw around here—and how good you are at hearing gossip about which seniors are leaving for internships in the city.

Daisy doesn't offer me a menu as she asks, "The usual?"

"Absolutely."

With a smile, Daisy leaves to submit my order of one chicken panini with pesto, cheese, and avocado, with a side of fries.

I've had the panini for over a year now and I'm still not sick of it. I don't have to be a psychology major to know it's a hyperfixation food for me.

Settling into the corner I pull out the paperback in my bag and turn to my marked page. The romance book has had me hooked since the moment I picked it up. A blessing and a curse, since it is extremely hard to put down the book you're reading for fun to swap it with the textbook that's been glaring at you mockingly, screaming profanities about whatever assignment is due.

It's the one thing I miss from high school—the freedom and time I could spend reading without feeling guilty for not studying.

Half an hour and twenty-one pages later, Daisy slides my food onto the table and without missing a beat I scarf it down, my stomach praising its thanks.

I mentally thank whoever ate my pizza because this is far greater.

No sooner have I eaten my last French fry, Daisy walks up to my booth with the check and a to-go cup.

This girl is heaven-sent.

The moment my hands wrap around the warm cup the smell of pumpkin and spices rises to greet me.

"Ugh, thank you. I seriously don't know what I ever did to deserve you, but this is exactly what I needed," I say, tapping my phone against the card machine. A ping rings out as the transaction goes through.

Chuckling, Daisy avoids my compliments, instead asking, "Are you guys going to the Halloween party tonight?"

Frowning, I pack up my bag and stand. "It's November. Why is everyone still celebrating?"

She shrugs as she follows me to the door. "Honestly, no clue. It's annoying, purely because I'm running out of costume ideas."

I chuckle. "I gave up after having to create two, I'm always jealous of the people who are creative enough to keep going. But sadly, I'm not going. I've got a psychology assignment I have to work on."

And I have a date, although I don't want to go around flaunting that. I hate jinxing things.

"Don't remind me." She grimaces. "I have a biology

paper due Monday that I haven't started. Procrastination at its finest, although I do work better under pressure."

"I wish I could say the same, but I think I'd break out in hives if I didn't allow myself enough time," I reply, a tad bit too honestly. "But! One of the other girls might be going; you should text them."

"I will!" She smiles. "Drive safe."

"Thanks, Daisy."

Stepping into the late afternoon breeze, fall weather sweeps across my face and puts my body at ease. There is nothing better than fall, the way in which the earth seems to hug us, cocooning us in its cozy grip.

Fall is the season for reading.

Fall is the season for pumpkin-spiced drinks.

Fall is the season for sweaters.

Fall is my definition of peace, the utter epitome of relaxation.

That is what I feel at this moment, with my belly full of my favorite comfort food, my upper body snuggled in my sweater, and a pumpkin latte sitting in my cup holder.

Until I turn my key in the ignition, and nothing happens.

"You have got to be kidding me!"

Dropping my head onto the steering wheel, I yelp when it honks back.

With my foot pressed against the brake, my hand keeps flipping, turning the key back and forth. Maybe if I do it a hundred more times, my car will want to wake up.

Everyone told me Jeeps are unreliable, and now I can't help but agree. Granted, she hasn't failed me until now, but in truth, the only reason I kept the car is because it belonged to my sister.

The last thing I would ever do is throw something she cared about away.

It would feel like throwing *her* away.

Jumping out of the car, I pop the hood open, as if I'll ever know what anything under it means. It isn't until I'm staring at all the different parts that look like a junkyard maze do I truly realize how out of my element I am.

Sighing deeply through my nose, I give up and pull out my phone, intending to Google the number of my insurance company or a tow truck. Honestly, I don't even know *who* you contact when things like this happen. My dad passed away weeks before my sixteenth birthday, and I never received the car breakdown lesson. But I'm momentarily saved by that rather embarrassing Google search when a deep timbre voice, one that sends tingles down my arms, calls out to me across the parking lot.

"We have to stop meeting like this," Xavier drawls.

I bite the inside of my cheek to stop the megawatt smile that threatens to escape. "Meeting like what? A damsel in distress?"

His eyes rove over me as if checking for injuries. "I was going to say with you in stomach pain, but what happened?"

Frowning, I quickly look down to find my hand on top of my stomach again, cradling the three long gashes that surprisingly have started to scab.

How many times do I touch the scratches without realizing it?

Snatching my hand away, I try to ignore my flaming cheeks that no doubt match my hair. "My car won't start."

"Want me to take a look at it?" he offers and before I can accept, he's already lowering his backpack to the ground and staring at the engine.

"Please do. Truth be told I have no idea what I'm looking at."

Standing behind him anxiously, I can't help but watch the

way in which his biceps flex as his hands rove over the car. The way he bites his bottom lip gently as his brows pull low in concentration. His jawline is all sharp edges, and I want nothing more than to run my fingers through his unruly brown curls.

Xavier's voice jolts me from my gawking.

"W-what?" I stutter, wanting nothing more than to smack myself for looking so stupid as I didn't retain a single word he said.

His lip twitches as a heated look takes over his face. "Looks like your car battery is dead."

My head snaps to my car. "*How* is that even possible?"

"When was the last time it was serviced?"

"Three months ago." My hands flail in front of me. "The car battery was replaced then."

He shuts the hood and leans against it, crossing one ankle over the other as he folds his arms across his chest. I never knew it was possible but the muscles in his arms seem to double in size.

"You were probably given a faulty battery. You have insurance, right?"

"Yeah, I do."

Why does electricity seem to hate me?

"I'd offer to jump the battery for you"—he points over his shoulder to a sleek black truck—"but it looks like some of the wiring has been fried and I'm not particularly in the mood to be electrocuted."

"No, no, that's okay. Umm…" I look around nervously. "I don't suppose you know who would be able to fix it without being electrocuted?"

A smile spreads across his face and not just any smile, but the most perfect smile I've ever seen. One that's so dazzling and bright it makes my own lips tug upward.

"My buddy works at the local mechanic shop and they have a tow truck. I'll call him. He owes me a favor, so it'll be on the house."

"Are you sure? I don't want to impose."

His phone is already in his hands, my words ignored as those blue eyes connect with mine.

His smile doesn't drop, those sizzling eyes never leaving mine as he drawls, "Hey Dylan, remember when you borrowed my truck for a week and you said you owed me? I'm cashing in my favor."

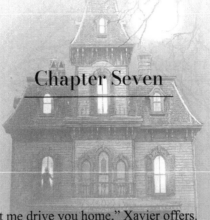

Chapter Seven

"Let me drive you home," Xavier offers.

Shaking my head, I back away. "No! You've done enough. You have successfully saved the damsel in distress."

If it weren't for him, I would have been a baby giraffe wobbling through the mechanic industry, praying not to be ripped off. Now my sister's Jeep is safely tucked behind the mechanic doors, waiting to be fixed. Xavier was right—the new battery had been entirely drained and some of the wirings had been fried.

Although now I don't have a car for a week or two.

He grins, following me every step I take. "Come on, take me up on the offer. I have a perfectly safe truck right here and I need to know where you live so I can pick you up tonight."

My eyes flick back and forth between his, noting how the ring of gold that shines around his pupils seems to glow in the faint afternoon sun. Swallowing thickly, I think about the ride in his truck here to the mechanic, the way his arm rested on the center console and the heat wafting off his body in waves.

Yet despite how feverish I felt, my entire body was covered in goose bumps.

I know I'm getting in that truck—he truly doesn't have to ask me twice—but I don't want him to know how eager I am to spend as much time with him as possible. Or how the way his truck smells divine, like the sandalwood scent I get off him when I'm standing close enough.

It's as if my years of being unaffected by men have come at me with a vengeance. As if my body stored up every ounce of hormones it could in preparation for Xavier. Nobody has affected me in this capacity. I'm struggling to come to terms with that fact myself, so there is no chance in hell I'm allowing him to know that tidbit of information.

That is precisely the reason why I stand here silently and shake my head with a small smirk.

His eyes spark with the challenge. "I'll let you choose the music."

"It's a five-minute drive. That's one and a half songs."

Half of the ten minute "All Too Well," Taylor's version at least.

He clicks his tongue. "Fine, what's your favorite treat?"

"Now we're talking." Grinning, I hold my hands behind my back and rock on the balls of my feet. "Impossible to choose from, but at this moment, I'd have to say gummy bears."

He clicks his tongue. "Okay, if I promise to get you gummy bears for tonight will you let me drive you home?"

Pretending to ponder over his offer, I pick my bag up from the floor and circle him, walking backward in the direction of his truck. "Deal."

That dimple makes a reappearance, along with my erratic heartbeat, as his warm hand brushes my shoulder and takes my bag off me.

Quirking a brow, I tease, "Giving me the full gentleman treatment?"

Following me to the passenger-side door, he opens it, gesturing for me to enter. He doesn't speak until I'm seated, buckled in with my bag resting at my feet.

That's when he leans forward and whispers, "Is that what you want?"

The question makes me pause, not because of the words, but because of the intensity with which he states them. How he seems to hold his breath as he searches my face for any sign of my answer.

Do I want him to be a gentleman?

Licking my bottom lip, his eyes snap to the movement, tracking my tongue.

Deciding to answer honestly, I whisper, "Yes."

And he does just that, the entirety of the five excruciating, heat-filled moments. Holding to our deal, yet again, he allowed me to pick a radio station to settle on and asked me questions about my classes. It isn't until he pulls up in front of my house that I realize I didn't get to ask him a single question about himself.

He whistles. "Nice place. How did you guys manage to swing this so close to campus?"

"My roommate's mom is a real estate agent."

"Ah, you got shown the houses before they were listed?"

My cheeks flush. "Something like that."

I force myself to open the door, praying I don't tumble or trip sliding out of the giant truck. Relief threatens to swallow me whole as I land both feet on the grass without embarrassing myself.

Turning to Xavier, I find his eyes sparkling down at me. "I'll pick you up at seven?"

I dip my head, my blush creeping up to my ears. "Yes please."

"Don't forget to dress warmly."

"I won't."

"See you soon, Blair."

Again, he says my name like a prayer that's been answered, making my blush deepen.

"Bye, Xavier," I sing.

Turning, I quickly jog up the front porch steps and let myself in, noting how I don't hear the rumble of his engine pull away until the front door closes behind me.

He remained a gentleman until the end, but I don't have a moment to blush, giggle, or smile over that tidbit because the house is plunged into darkness again, the setting sun glowing faintly through the windows and the TV blaring the *Scream* movie from last night that we never finished.

Didn't Evie get her fill of all things frightening?

Shaking my head I mutter under my breath, "Evie and her horror." Picking up the remote, I flick the TV off and call upstairs, "Evie! You left the TV on again!"

Yet as I walk up the stairs, no one calls back and answers me.

"Evie?"

The moment I reach the top step I lean forward for the light switch and turn it on, only for it to flicker for a moment before burning out.

I throw my hands in the air. "You have got to be kidding me."

My hand is halfway to my bag, reaching for my phone, when my bedroom door swings open, making a scream tear from my throat as Evie jumps out.

"Date night starts in three hours!" she squeals.

My heart pounds against the hand I lay on my chest. "What the fuck, Evie?"

"Why are you standing in the dark?" she asks.

"Why are you in my room?"

"Touché."

Stepping past her, I thought I would be entering my room but instead—

Evie jumps in front of me with her hands held up. "Okay before you freak out…I have it under control."

"Did you dump my entire wardrobe out?" I ask, looking at the mountains of clothes.

She tips her head from side to side. "Technically…yes."

"Why?" I say, resigned to the state of my room. "I won't know where anything is."

"That's where you're wrong! I sorted it all into piles." She rushes around the room pointing to various mounds of clothing. "Streetwear chic, cozy chic, sensible chic, trending chic—"

"Let me guess…winter chic?" I ask when she gets to the last one overflowing with coats.

She rolls her eyes. "Fuzzy chic."

Hanging my head in my hands, I count to ten. Evie means well, she always does. Her mind just works in mysterious ways. Lifting my eyes, I find her worried expression and before she can climb into a hole of self-criticism, I say, "Xavier told me to dress warmly and to bring gloves."

Evie beams. "Fuzzy chic it is."

Phoebe materializes with a bag of Takis, her steps unheard before she practically throws herself into the bean bag beside me. "Evie, why does it look like a Goodwill in here?"

She wags her eyebrows. "Date night."

Phoebe hums. "Makes sense." Plopping Takis in her

mouth and chewing around a mouthful, she waves to the door. "You left the TV on again by the way."

Evie frowns, not taking her eyes off the fuzzy chic pile. "I didn't turn it on."

"It was playing the slasher film from last night," Phoebe deadpans.

Stealing a chip, Evie ignores us as she pulls out one of my favorite coats.

I turn to Phoebe, puzzled. "I turned it off when I came home a few minutes ago."

Phoebe stops chewing for a moment. "But I only just came in and it was blaring. I'm surprised you guys didn't hear it."

I glance toward the door. We really need to get the wirings in the house checked.

Evie yanks out another black coat lined with white fleece. Phoebe exclaims, "Oh, that would look so good!"

Jumping up, I take the coat and start roving the piles looking for my best boyfriend jeans.

Evie practically bounces with excitement. "What do you think he's planned?"

I'm always shocked when my mind reminds me Evie was never a cheerleader. Her entire personality screams peppy, as if dialed to bubbly twenty-four-seven.

Sorting through the pile of denim chic, I find my favorite light-blue, high-waisted jeans and throw them on the bed. "Honestly no clue, but I dare say nothing outside."

"Why?" Phoebe asks, her mouth full of chips.

Snatching a white bodysuit, I eye the piles of clothes for a sweater. "Because he said to wear gloves and it's not snowing now." I turn around. "Speaking of, does anyone have any?"

Phoebe stops digging in her Takis bag. "You live in North Carolina and you don't own gloves?"

Evie is already skipping out of the room. "I have the perfect pair!"

Rolling my eyes, I turn back to my new wardrobe space. "I used to borrow Issy's and after…"

I don't need to finish the sentence. Phoebe comes to stand beside me, her Takis forgotten. "Maybe you can pull out a pair?"

"No," I say sternly.

It's one thing to use her car; it's another to take her clothes. It's all that's left of her and if something were to happen to her stuff…I would never be able to forgive myself.

Phoebe must hear the steel in my tone, or perhaps my eyes have taken on an unshakable gleam, but she backs off, helping me rake through the clothing items. It isn't long before she's pulling out a soft emerald cardigan.

"This will look stunning on you," she says softly.

Evie shoves her hands between us, flapping a pair of mittens. "These match it perfectly!"

Snorting out a laugh, I take the items. "Thanks, Evie."

"I get credit for the sweater," Phoebe exclaims.

Considering Phoebe lives in sweaters and vests it doesn't surprise me she picked out a good one.

Evie squeals as she throws herself into the piles of clothes. "I can't believe you're going on a date with Xavier!"

Phoebe follows her lead, giggling as she bounces from the impact. "You should have seen how smitten he looked."

I fall beside them and can't help but giggle myself. "He really looked smitten?"

Phoebe props her head up with her fist, her tone taking on a whimsical lilt. "He stared at you like you hung the moon."

I snort. "Hung the moon? Really, Phoebe?"

Rolling her eyes, she relents, "Fine…like you were the last slice of pizza and he was a starved man."

Evie and I throw our heads back with a laugh. "For a writer, you have a very unique way of explaining things."

Now it's Phoebe's turn to roll her eyes. Throwing her arm over her face in dramatics, she splays back on the clothes. "Don't remind me about writing."

I grimace. "Trevor?"

"Trevor," she growls before narrowing her eyes. "Nice diversion."

"What can I say, it's the psychologist in me."

Evie snorts out a laugh. "Go get changed so we can approve."

Groaning, I pull myself up and snatch the clothes off the bed, trying and failing to ignore the nervous flutter taking flight in my stomach.

From: cemerson@acmail.com

Subject: Midterm Assignment

As we're approaching three weeks from the due date
of your midterm assignment— which, as a kind
reminder, goes toward 30% of your final grade—I
want to reiterate that if you have any issues or
questions, please feel free to email me or visit my
office during student hours.
With that being said, enjoy diving into the minds of
the criminally insane and what makes them tick.

Sincerely,
Mr. Emerson

Chapter Eight

A familiar truck engine roars through the neighborhood, eliciting squeals from the girls beside me. I'm not sure who's more nervous, myself or them.

The answer comes to me when I hear the engine cut and footsteps clack against our porch seconds before a light rasp of knuckles hits our front door. Because while the girls look excited for me, my stomach sinks, bottoming out as nerves like no other squelch my heart.

I don't even realize I'm not moving until firm hands give me a light shove toward the door.

Taking a shuddering breath, I shoo the girls around the corner, and I don't pull open the door until I'm sure they won't come out again.

The second the door opens to reveal Xavier, clad in dark-black jeans and a form-fitting white T-shirt, my nerves simply fly away, flapping with excitement, transforming from a caterpillar to a butterfly.

He leans against the doorframe, one of his legs kicked over the other as if he had all the time in the world to wait for me. Xavier's eyes give a slow perusal that I feel every inch of the way and the moment that glorious smile stretches across his face, that lone dimple popping out to wink at me, I have to hide a full-body shudder.

"Blair."

The way he says my name as if starved for the word— famished for *me*—makes me sigh.

"Xavier."

He kicks off from where he was leaning, turning to the side as he gestures in the direction of his truck. "After you."

My heart goes haywire. Which is odd considering I was sitting in the truck just a few short hours ago, but there was no pressure, no date. This time, I feel the weight of Xavier's stare across my skin like he's a starved man.

I move to shut the door behind me, but Xavier beats me to it.

With nothing left to do with my hands, I practically fly into the truck, craving the scent of sandalwood that I know will smack my senses.

Before my hand can wrap around the door handle, Xavier's large tan hand is there, gently pulling open the door. "Have somewhere to be?" he teases.

"No," I squeak. Quickly shaking my head, I stutter, "I-I mean, y-yes?"

His brow lifts but he doesn't say anything.

"Are you going to buckle up?" he finally asks.

My eyes widen. "Yes!" Quickly snatching my seatbelt, I click it into place, trying to laugh off my nerves. All the while, Xavier stares at me with that knowing bashful smile, which is not helping matters.

He's *too* handsome.

He chuckles darkly to himself as he closes my door and the sound sends chills down my spine. He rounds the hood, and as I peer out the passenger window, I see the girls' faces pressed against the living room window.

I doubt they can see me but just in case, I start to shoo them but they all cheer, clapping and smiling as they give me thumbs-ups.

The sound of the driver-side door opening snaps my gaze to the front.

Before pulling away he leans into the back seat, coming so precariously close to me that his aftershave assaults me. Sandalwood tinged with a mix of *him*. It's a heady scent, one that makes me feel like a lunatic considering I try to inhale as deeply as I can.

Pulling back, he says, "Close your eyes."

"Is this the part where you cuff and blindfold me?" I blurt out.

I'm thankful for the dark interior of the car because if it weren't for its shadows, he'd be able to see my cheeks flush as crimson as my hair.

I have to get my nerves under control. I'm about to consider chastising myself further but he throws his head back with a deep belly laugh.

"As much as I want to dive into that question, no." A short bark of laughter flits between his lips again as he shakes his head and repeats, "Just close your eyes and hold out your hand."

A small thrill hums through my bloodstream at the fact that I made him laugh.

Sighing deeply, I make a show of closing my eyes and cupping my palms.

The sound of plastic crinkling fills the car before something relatively heavy is plopped into my awaiting hands. As my fingers wrap around the contents, I know just by the feel what it is.

My eyes fly open to find a rainbow of gummy bears, adorned by an adorable pink bow, sitting in the palm of my hand.

A smile erupts across my face.

"Thank you," I whisper, not daring to peek up.

This is hands down the cutest thing a man has ever done for me, which just shows the type of men I've dated before.

How low have I set my bar?

"It's perfect, Xavier."

Finally daring to lift my eyes, I think they betray me, because if I didn't know any better, I could have sworn his cheeks were tinted pink.

He clears his throat, his voice coming out gruff as he turns the ignition. "Have any guesses as to where we're going tonight?"

Settling comfortably into his leather seat, I let my head fall back onto the headrest and throw out, "Amusement park?"

He bites the corner of his cheek as if to stop himself from laughing. "I may be handy at most things but even I can't build an amusement park in twenty-four hours."

"Touché."

The closest amusement park is an hour's drive away. I suggested it purely to try and get a sense of how far we're driving today. But as he takes all the roads toward campus, I begin to doubt the guesses I was about to throw at him.

If he takes me to a frat party...whatever was brewing between us will die quicker than he can blink.

Except he doesn't turn on the street that heads toward the frat houses.

All thoughts fly out of my head as he pulls in front of the sporting facility.

Turning to him, I find a cheeky grin plastered across his face and a devilish glint gleaming in his blue eyes.

The moment my gaze locks on his, the air in the car thickens, pulsating with the tension brewing between us. The type of tension that knocks the very breath from you.

His voice is like a whip, striking the silence in the air.

"Have any ideas yet, Blair?" he drawls, his voice lulling my heart into a steady rhythm.

Needing to break the seriousness of whatever is brewing, I throw out, "If it's a contest of who can pump more weight, I hate to break it to you, but I can barely carry my textbooks."

His lips twitch but he doesn't cave, doesn't laugh. He simply pulls a key from his back pocket and asks, "Do you skate much?"

My eyes spark as memories rush through my brain, the endless hours Isabella and I spent on the ice.

Xavier sees it, the moment exhilaration rushes through my bloodstream.

He jumps out of the car and rounds the hood, opening my door with a devilish grin. "Question is, who's the better skater?"

"You may be a hockey player, Hendrix, but you have nothing on my moves," I tease, skating around him in circles.

His brow quirks, a competitive glint dancing in his eyes. "Oh? Is that right?"

Flipping, I start to skate backward, the blades feeling like a second skin as I feel the smoothness of the ice glide beneath me.

"Go on then, prove me wrong," I sing, turning to skate sideways, holding out my hand as I wait for him to demonstrate.

While Isabella never took up figure skating, choosing to skate just for the hell of it without pressure, I was an addict when it came to the ice. I forced my parents to put me into classes at five and I never looked back.

Isabella used to call me Bumblebee for how busy I always was. I was either on the ice training or goofing off with her. Off the ice, my time was spent studying and hanging out with Phoebe.

My entire world revolved around ice skating and what I could fit into the hours outside it.

That was until my parents died.

Then nothing was the same. I didn't even want to put my skates on again. Especially not after Isabella. She had coaxed a few skating sessions out of me during the holidays and I could feel it, the love and passion for the sport being renewed. That door cracked open to take a peek to see if it was safe…if it was time.

Then she died two months later and the door slammed closed.

I thought it had sealed shut.

I'm not sure what it was—Xavier's carefree grin, the excitement in his eyes as he handed me the skates, or perhaps the fact I didn't want to trauma dump on him on our first date —but I took the skates from his hands and pried open that door.

I was janky at first, as wobbly as a newborn horse, but after a moment my body began to glide, muscle memory kicking in, and then my heart soared at the freedom that was coursing through its vessels.

Being that Xavier is on the hockey team, I don't doubt

this is his go-to for dates...but I find I don't care in the slight-est. Not as the wind rustles through my hair and my feet glide against the fresh ice.

My heart soars with the renewed vigor of falling in love with skating once more.

Phoebe will be so thrilled when I tell her. She's been trying to get me to skate for months.

The surprise on Xavier's face as I began to not only skate but *figure skate* was priceless. I wish I had a camera to capture it. If the look he gave me was anything to go by he certainly didn't expect for me to be a natural skater let alone a talented one.

Then he proceeded to shake himself out of his frozen stupor and chase after me, flying down the ice rink like I was an opponent he had to capture.

He bows deep at the waist as he skates past. "What do you want to see, Your Highness?"

Snorting, I shake my head. "Double two-foot spin."

He rolls his eyes before scoffing. "You taking it easy on me, Blair?"

"Trust me, you'll thank me later for taking it easy on you," I breathe, his body's warmth singeing my skin as I skate precariously close, only to pull away as quickly as I arrived.

Xavier's eyes spark at the dance we seem to have started.

Before I know it, he's behind me, his hands settling gently on my hips as his breath puffs down my neck, making my skin pebble.

"How much trust do you have in me?"

The breath I was holding whooshes out in a huff. "None at all. I barely know you."

In one quick movement, he lifts me off the ice and spins me, quickly catching me in the air before he gently puts me back down again. His hands slide up my body until they rest precariously close to my chest, his large palms stopping at my rib cage.

"For now."

Before I can berate him for a magnitude of safety issues —he could have dropped me on my ass, for starters—he's off again. Sprinting down the end of the rink until he turns, sliding across the edge as he launches himself into a double spin.

My mouth gapes open.

The move was almost elegant—as elegant as it could be on a six-foot-three hockey player, but elegant nonetheless. I certainly didn't expect it.

Clapping slowly, I skate over to him as he mock bows, clutching his chest.

"I'll accept your formal apology on our second date."

My eyes shine. "Someone's feeling cocky," I tease. The nerves that had consumed me at the start of the night fell away the second my skates touched the ice and confidence I haven't felt in a long time awoke.

He shrugs. "I feel I deserve a second date after that turn."

My brows flick up. "Is that right?" We skate toward each other, meeting in the middle and as we pass, our eyes lock. "And what will my prize be if I nail the spin?"

He clicks his tongue. "Anything you want. You name it and it's yours."

Is it stupid that I want to blurt out *him*? That all I want is to hold his attention on me for eternity? When his eyes are on mine it's as if I'm the only thing that matters in this world, and it's a glorious feeling.

My lips part, my body warming despite the ice.

I want more than just his eyes on me, and as his gaze flicks down to my parted lips, his dazzling eyes heating at the sight of me licking my bottom lip, I think he knows exactly what I want.

"How about this?" he says, his voice guttural and gravelly as if he just woke up. "I'll go again, and if I pass whatever you throw at me"—he closes the dwindling gap between us, knocking the breath from my lungs as he cups my cheek and lifts my head—"I get to kiss you."

My heart pounds a ferocious beat as I can do nothing but stare into his fiery eyes.

His palm slides down my cheek, over my jaw, and across my neck, coming to rest on my collarbone as I whisper, "Deal."

Xavier rips away from me, a deep groan leaving him as if it physically pains him to do so. But there's a light in his eyes, a determination that wasn't there before.

He skates backward to the end of the arena. "Throw everything you got, Blair," he calls.

My entire body is alive and wired, humming with anticipation. I want nothing more than to have his hands on me again. To have those lips pressed against mine.

I want to know what he feels like. If he'll be slow and gentle, or passionate. I want him to pour the heat that's shining in his eyes into the kiss.

I want it all.

It's why I'm half tempted to throw out something easy, but he can't know how badly I want him. He can't know that just a simple touch of his skin against mine steals the air from my lungs. He cannot know that his nearness makes my brain disappear and my heart take over.

And that's why my heart cries as I call out, "A double lutz."

He cups his palms over his chest, right above his heart. "Setting me up to fail, are we?"

"You called yourself the best skater, so skate," I tease.

He points at me, that lone dimple appearing as he grins. "You're on."

"Stop talking and start turning! Delay techniques won't work on me, Hendrix."

Instead of snapping another retort, he turns, gliding into a long diagonal skate toward the corner of the rink. He turns, skating backward, and with my heart in my throat, he launches off his back foot. With his arms tucked tight, he spins quickly in the air, landing on his opposite foot with a flourish that shocks me beyond repair.

I can't help it, I squeal.

But the excitement that rushes through me is short-lived as Xavier's eyes lock on mine and he takes off, practically shooting off the ice toward me.

"Xavier," I breathe.

Before his name is even out of my mouth, he's upon me. At first, I'm frightened he'll crash into me but as his hands grab my waist, he plucks me off the ice and wraps my legs around his middle. All thoughts of his double lutz are long gone.

"I win," he growls.

He smashes his lips against mine and everything fades. The worry of being in the air on ice disappears and all I can feel is him.

The kiss is intense, so much so I'm surprised fireworks aren't going off. His tongue dances across my lips, begging for entrance, and as I do, he groans, my moan mingling with the deep timbre that fills my mouth as we collide.

He holds me to his body, cradling me as if I'm the most precious thing in the world.

The heady feeling is all consuming, all powerful.

And it never stops—the rush, the adrenaline, the lust that

consumes me.

I never want to pull away, and as Xavier holds me to his body tighter, I presume neither does he.

Heat pools in my belly and as if my body is dunked in a bucket of desire, my hips start to move, moans and groans tumbling from our mouths as the kiss begins to move further than just a kiss.

It's no longer a want, it's a *need*.

One that I think only he can fulfill because I have *never* felt this way.

Xavier suddenly rips himself away and as my eyes snap open to see his face grimacing in pain, I gather myself and pull in deep puffs of air.

When he speaks his voice is so low, so gruff, a jolt of desire strikes me, especially as he says, "I'm not rushing this. You're too precious to rush."

"Okay," I say breathlessly, my body whining but my heart melting at his care.

Xavier pauses and a thousand thoughts seem to fly through his mind. His eyes grow pained as he lets me down slowly, especially as every inch of my skin is flush with his on the descent back to the ice.

Wonder and awe fill my voice as what he did bombards my mind. "How?"

Xavier doesn't let me go; he simply wraps his arms around my lower back and keeps me flush against him. "You never asked how I got into hockey. My mom used to be a figure skating coach." My eyes spark and Xavier notices, that grin popping out in full force. "She forced me into it before I switched to hockey."

"You played me."

He bites the inside of his cheek. "And I'd do it all over again just for that kiss."

I think it's clear who the best skater is

You barely tested my skills!

Guess we'll have to have a rematch

What a shame

Now that I know your skating history, it'll be a fair competition

What do you want if you win?

Delivered

You

Chapter Nine

My bladder threatens to explode at any moment, but I can't move.

My entire *being* is working against me.

It feels as if my limbs would rather tear from my body than do what I say.

And it's all because of the shadow standing in my doorway.

It's been watching me sleep, I know that truth within the marrow of my bones. The prickling sensation at the back of my neck is because of its watchful gaze that hasn't left since the moment I entered its front door. I can always feel its presence, even though I try to shake it off.

As the shadow grows it takes with it all my sense of control. The only part of my body that moves is my chest as it rises and falls rapidly, my heart hammering wildly inside, screaming at me to run.

But I can't.

Because it's far too late to run. I'm already trapped within its claws.

A lump lodges itself in my throat, rising impossibly high,

threatening to drag the contents of my stomach with it. The shadow moves, spreading across the hardwood floor, and doesn't stop until it reaches the edge of my bed.

Shadows reach for me, falling over my feet as a sharp claw pierces the blankets covering me and pulls.

My mouth drops open to scream, but no sound leaves my lips. In the next breath, the shadow crashes over me until nothing but its darkness consumes my vision and its hand wraps around my throat.

Squeezing mercilessly, the shadowed hand begins to rise along with my body as it lifts me from my bed. Not stopping until its growl brushes across my ear. This close, its foul odor makes me grimace.

My body tries to gag, the natural instinct flaring, but my throat can only wheeze as the shadow growls against my ear.

"You're mine now, Blair."

Awoken violently by the sensation of falling, my body jolts as I crash against the mattress, my limbs flailing as I bounce up and down.

Scrambling backward until I collide with my headboard, my hand clutches my throat, expecting to find the skin bruised and tender

The sheets are scattered on the floor. *As if they were ripped from the bed.*

I shake the thought away.

It was a nightmare. I tossed and turned and kicked them off.

A nightmare, I chant, trying to calm my terrorized heart.

Licking my dry lips, it takes my heartbeat several minutes to settle before I reach over and flick my bedside lamp on. My shoulders relax as I find the room free of shadows and hands wanting to squeeze the life from me.

It's been a while since I've had a nightmare.

I forgot how unsettling they are. Especially as I look down to find my body covered in sweat, the fitted sheet beneath my limbs drenched with perspiration.

Evie's incessant horror and slasher films are finally taking their toll on me it seems.

Groaning, I drag myself from the bed and begin to strip the sheets. I started having nightmares after my parents passed. Usually, they entailed a horrible car wreck. Despite never witnessing the crash that took their lives my mind has created a very vivid image of what it could have looked like.

Once the nightmares began alternating between my sister's death and my parents' car wreck, they were frequent. Although, it's been several weeks since my last.

I thought the date I had with Xavier would have kept the nightmares at bay, considering how much fun I had. I suppose ice skating could have brought one on, despite enjoying the reunion with the ice. Memories and fears could have unlocked as my heart opened up to the old love.

But the one I just had was…new.

Rolling the sheets into a ball I plop them beside my laundry basket, a task I'm leaving for myself tomorrow, and head toward my ensuite. Stripping my clothes, I place them in the hamper and step under the scalding water.

Muscles in my back and neck begin to loosen, uncoiling from the tightness of my dream.

I wash my sweat-soaked hair, lathering shampoo in the red strands until I'm convinced not a drop of perspiration is left on my body. With my head tipped back, my eyes closed as I rinse the suds, my heart suddenly skips a beat.

A prickling sensation falls over me.

A girl knows intimately the feeling of being watched. I can remember the first time I had leering eyes set upon me, the way it makes the hairs on the back of your neck stand on end, while something within you screams to turn and peer back at the eyes locked on you.

Intuition is strong in everyone, but not as strong as a woman's ability to know when someone's unwanted attention is placed upon them.

And this moment is no different.

Goosebumps spread down my arms as I hear the shower door creak open.

My eyes fly open. A piercing scream strikes through the bathroom. Mine.

Standing in the shower, with half my hair covered in suds, I cannot do anything but gape at the open shower glass door.

My eyes flick to the bathroom door to see the lock firmly in place and the bathroom empty except for me.

Yet the shower door stands wide open before my very eyes. A door I had closed myself, one that had remained shut until I closed my eyes.

"Hello?" I call out, only to chastise myself.

This isn't the girls' doing; they wouldn't violate my privacy for a prank, and if it's not them, whoever it is certainly won't announce themselves.

Have I not learned anything from Evie's movies?

Swallowing heavily, I lean back, hurriedly washing the remaining suds from my hair without taking my eyes off the open shower door. I am *not* touching the handle, nor am I going to move it.

I do not care if the cold air freezes me.

Without checking that I washed my hair sufficiently, and without my eyes leaving the glass door, I search blindly behind me until my hands latch on to the faucet, quickly turning until the water ceases, plunging me into silence.

Standing stark naked, I have never felt so exposed…so vulnerable. I am no stranger to anxiety; I have experienced it many times in my life, especially after my family's tragic deaths, but this… My heart does not listen to me when I try to calm its erratic thumps as I step out of the shower.

The nightmare has clearly spooked me.

"It's just an old house. The doors creak and the wood groans," I mutter to myself as I reach for my towel. "The bathroom is slanted, and the door rolled open. Nothing more."

Saying the words out loud does nothing to squelch the fear that overrides my body. Because I know I closed that door and I know this bathroom isn't slanted. I could put a ball in here and it wouldn't roll.

And this certainly is not my brain working against me in the wee hours of the morning.

Despite all that, I force myself to believe the words. Because if I don't…I will never sleep in this house again.

Terror is not a word I throw around often, but it's what consumes every part of me as my hands shake pulling on a fresh pair of pajamas. It's an emotion that floods my veins as I reach for the locked bathroom door.

Turning the knob, the resounding click of it unlocking is so loud throughout the space I stop breathing for a moment. Holding my breath as my ears strain to hear if anyone is on the other side.

When nothing scuttles or thumps, I pull the door open. With my heart in my throat I quickly swing it open the rest of the way and take one step into my pitch-black room before gasping for air that's abandoned me.

Quickly rushing back into the bathroom, I slam the door with a startled cry. My body trembles so violently it takes me three attempts before I successfully lock the bathroom door once more.

The room was not covered in darkness when I left it. It was bathed in a faint orange glow from my bedside lamp.

One that I did not turn off myself.

I don't dare step foot in my bedroom until four hours later when the sun shines, illuminating the space. Those painfully slow four hours were spent trying to calm my breathing as I was on the verge of hyperventilating at every creak and groan in the house.

They were also spent trying to come up with a logical explanation as to why the shower door opened on its own and the lights turned off themselves. I was only able to come up with one plausible reason, but as I tiptoe out of my room and look at my lamp, I rule it out.

The switch has been flicked off.

This isn't because of an electrical circuit. Electrical circuits don't flick switches.

Am I going insane? I must be.

Yet crazy people don't question if they're crazy, and that is the mantra I mutter to myself under my breath as I make my way downstairs. Seems I wasn't the only one who had a terrible night's sleep.

Phoebe's eyes flutter closed, the arm propping her heavy

head sliding down the kitchen island. Even Evie's peppy attitude has vanished. There's no energy in her today as she drags her feet across the floor and yanks the freshly made coffee from under the machine.

Violet drops her bowl, cursing under her breath. The sound makes Phoebe's eyes fly open and land on mine.

"Coffee anyone?" Evie asks with a yawn.

"Abso-fucking-lutely," Violet mumbles.

"Yes," Phoebe groans.

"Bad night?" I ask.

Phoebe holds up her hand with a wince as if just the sound of my voice sends a marching band through her skull. "Don't even sta—"

"Ugh!" Evie groans. "Who keeps taking my mug?"

Phoebe physically recoils at Evie's noise level.

Violet rolls her eyes. "No one is taking your goddamn mug, Evie. We have been doing this every morning!"

"Someone is taking it!"

"If you accuse me of taking the stupid mug one more time, I will throttle you," Violet hisses.

"What mug?" I whisper to Phoebe, apparently not quiet enough.

Evie whirls on me with bloodshot eyes, deep purple bags underneath them. "My heart mug."

When all I do is give her a blank stare, Evie throws her hands in the air. "The 'you will always have a place in my right ventricle' one? It's medical humor and my mom gave it to me as a graduation gift. I drink from it every morning, but someone keeps taking it."

I raise my hands in surrender. "It's not me."

Evie arches her brow, swinging her gaze to Phoebe.

"I don't like medical humor," Phoebe mumbles into her bowl of untouched cereal.

Evie frowns, her eyes growing heavy as she stares at the kitchen island.

Giving her shoulder a quick squeeze, I move past her, snagging a cup of coffee. "It will turn up, Evie. It probably just got lost in the move."

She shakes her head adamantly. "No, I've used it since moving here. Every morning, I search for it without luck and then I get home after class and it's sitting on the middle of the island."

I frown, my gaze moving toward Violet and Phoebe. They look just as perplexed as I am. Grabbing the nearest mug I pour the freshly made coffee, my gaze searching for the creamer.

Turning, I lean against the counter and look Evie in the eyes. "I swear to you, it's not me."

"Me neither," Phoebe mumbles around a mouthful of cereal.

Evie swings accusatory eyes to Violet.

Violet scoffs, annoyance etched across her face. "I told you it isn't me! Between classes and my apprenticeship at the tattoo shop, I don't have time to move your stupid mug around."

Evie stomps away toward the stairs. "Well, someone in this house is moving my stuff and I am over it!" she screams, slamming her bedroom door for emphasis.

My feet stay rooted to the kitchen tiles as my heart beats wildly.

Evie *never* loses her temper. She's studying to become a doctor for a reason. Evie doesn't create harm, she heals.

Just thinking about her abnormal behavior makes the eerie sensation from last night return, and my neck prickles with discomfort. I crane my head, as if I'll find someone else standing in the kitchen staring at me.

Breaking the silence, I whisper, "Have any of you…experienced anything weird lately?"

Violet's eyes cut to mine, narrowing into slits. "Not you too."

Avoiding her sizzling gaze, I turn back to the coffee, stirring it absentmindedly before shrugging. "Well, there have been a few instances that—"

"Like what?" Phoebe cuts in, asking far more gently than Violet.

Turning, I find her eyes open, her expression wary. As if the moment I utter the words and share what's happening, it becomes real.

"Lights turning on and off on their own, objects moving…" Taking a deep breath, I steel myself for my next words. My hammering heart makes the mug in my hand quiver. "Last night, my shower door opened on its own and when I got out…the lights in my room were turned off."

"What do you mean the shower door opened?" Violet asks, setting her coffee down.

"I was rinsing out the shampoo in my hair and I heard it creak open so—"

Violet cuts me off. "You didn't see it open?"

"Well, no, but it was just clo—"

"It's an old house, Blair, things are bound to squeak. Your elbow probably knocked it open. And the lights are without a doubt faulty wires. I've already called my mom about it."

I turn to Phoebe for help, but this is the moment she chooses denial. The walls around her come down, her belief in science and facts cementing that nothing strange is occurring.

Violet rises without another word and rinses her mug before climbing the stairs. Her door slams a moment later.

Phoebe reaches for my hand. "I think the haunted house

has you spooked, B. What happened up there terrified you, and I have no doubt it's taken its toll." Standing, she walks around the island and wraps her arms around me. "We're safe here. Nothing is happening."

Gasping, she pulls back, holding me out with her arms. My heart starts careening, thinking she might've seen something, before she says, "Oh my God, how did the date go? I can't believe we forgot to ask! You got home so late, we all fell asleep waiting. Tell me everything and don't leave out a single detail!"

And just like that, talk of lights turning off by themselves, doors mysteriously opening, and the eerie feeling of my nightmare are put on the back burner.

To: cemerson@acmail.com

Subject: Assignment Clarification

Mr. Emerson,

Would you be able to schedule time aside for me to
come in? I would love some clarification on the essay
aspect of the assignment.
I've completed my research and yet am unsure
which direction you would prefer us to take our
essays in.

Blair

From: cemerson@acmail.com

Re: Assignment Clarification

Blair,

I have a spare moment tomorrow morning at 10:15.
Please let me know if this would suit.

Best,
Emerson

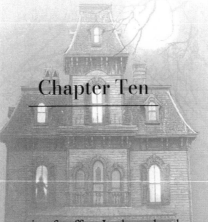

Chapter Ten

Taking a sip of coffee, I rub my hands over my eyes as if the action can restore my energy and make my eyelids feel as if they don't have a thousand grains of sand rubbing against my eyeballs.

Lifting my head I read the clock—2:18 p.m.

This assignment will be the death of me. Metaphorically, of course.

Mr. Emerson did end up answering my questions, yet not the way I originally planned. After accidentally walking in on another female student in his office crying, I backtracked quickly and emailed my list of questions.

It was far too awkward to wait in the hall for Mr. Emerson, and obviously the other student needed tending to more.

However, when he responded to my email with all my answers an hour later, I no longer had an excuse to procrastinate the assignment further.

Trying to understand someone who does unspeakable things to human beings makes my stomach recoil. It's also opened my mind to the possibility that one day, I may be a therapist treating someone who has psychopathy or sociopathy.

People always say that those who go to therapy are the ones healing from the wrongdoings of those who truly need the therapy. But I'm not naïve enough to believe my doors will never open to someone mentally deranged.

Could I keep a straight face if someone shared thoughts of wanting to hurt another?

I fist my hand against my chest and truly regret my last cup of coffee as I try to massage the buzzing of nerves in my body. With my heart rate already spiked, my heart lodges itself into my throat with a scream as a tap comes from the window in front of my desk.

My hand flies to my mouth, slapping over my lips to try and squelch further sounds from escaping as I jump up.

Laughter comes a moment later. Giggles, from tiny little humans.

"Oh my God," I breathe.

Peeking my head over the windowsill, my eyes snag on a little boy crouching beneath my window with his hand over his mouth, trying to stifle his laughter. A little girl who not only mirrors his crouch and stifling giggles but his blonde hair.

The little boy hands what I'm assuming is a small pebble to the girl, and as she cranes her neck and pulls back her arm, I back away.

I fake a scream as another tap, louder this time, raps against my window.

I smile for the first time today as their giggles rise with my scream. All thoughts of serial killers and girls crying in professors offices fly out of my mind at the sound of those innocent chuckles.

Ding dong ditch. However, I don't believe they got the

"ditch" part of the game figured out yet. Nor the ringing of the doorbell.

Footsteps thud outside my bedroom door, the sound rising as someone runs up the stairs. I turn my head in time to watch Evie practically explode into the room, a baseball bat clutched in her hands.

"What is it? Is it a rat or an intruder?"

Stifling a laugh so the kids don't hear, I pry the bat from her hands. "Some kids are playing ding dong ditch against my window," I whisper.

Her shoulders visibly deflate. "God, Blair, you screamed bloody murder!"

"Sorry, I thought I was the only one home."

She shakes her head. "I just got back and walked through the front door right as you screamed. Jesus, you know how to give a girl a heart attack." Her ease quickly vanishes as she pauses. "How are they playing ding dong ditch against a window? And why not ring the doorbell?"

My eyes practically roll into the back of my head. "Who knows what goes through their little minds. They're not even—"

A loud *thunk* cuts me off, another pebble flying. I snort. I'm surprised the window hasn't scratched or cracked yet.

"Aren't they supposed to run?" Evie teases at hearing their laughter.

I snort. "I don't think they've figured that part out just yet."

Evie creeps up to the window, waiting, her hand hovering over the opening. Until another pebble hits the glass again and she yanks open the window.

"Gotcha!" she yells.

Their little screams slice the air, so deafening I slap my hands over my ears, as they sprint off for the main road.

"You just gave those poor kids a heart attack!" I sputter around a laugh as she closes the window.

She shrugs, a wicked smile grazing her lips. "Someone had to teach them the running aspect."

"Better us than Mr. Lumberg on the corner."

Evie visibly shivers. "Ugh, he gives me the creeps."

As our laughter dies, I notice the purple bags around Evie's eyes and the tension that slowly creeps back into her shoulders as she looks around my room.

"Are you doing okay, Evie?"

Her outburst this morning was so out of character that I haven't been able to shake it from my thoughts.

Groaning, she plops down into my bean bag and smacks her hands over her face. "I'm so embarrassed, I practically threw a tantrum. I don't know what came over me. I just got so angry…and over what? A mug? I'm never angry."

Taking a seat on the bean bag beside her, I pry her hands away from her face. "Don't be too hard on yourself. You're human. You can't be a walking pep club at all hours of the day." I shrug. "You just had a bad day, the girls understand."

"I screamed at Violet."

"Violet, especially, will understand. She frowns more than she smiles," I joke, earning a small chuckle from Evie.

Her laughter dies. "I slammed a door."

"And screamed at children."

Her eyes widen, growing as round as saucers. "Oh my God!"

I throw my head back with a laugh. "Evie, relax, I'm kidding! Everyone slams a door in their life and screams at kids. It's *normal*."

In some situations, like this one. Otherwise take it from the girl studying psychology and the ramifications parents have on their children's minds—screaming at children leaves its mark.

"Not for me." She shakes her head. "I've felt so strange since Campbellton."

My head rears back in shock. "The ghost tour?"

Biting her lips, she dips her head. "I know it's normal to be angry every once in a while, but not for me. I never raise my voice and slam doors. I may like horror films, Blair, but I don't like living in them."

My chest tightens. "Why do you feel like you're living in a horror movie?"

"I can't describe it and that's why it's so frustrating! I can feel the difference, not just in myself but in the house." Her eyes dart around as if the walls are listening. Lowering her voice to a whisper, she leans forward. "You can't tell me you don't feel it too. It *feels* wrong."

It's on the tip of my tongue to choose the route that Phoebe and Violet have, to choose denial, to spew the same speech they gave me about wiring and old houses...but I can't.

"I feel it too," I whisper. I look at my open ensuite door. "Last night my shower door opened on its own and then when I came out here, I found all the lights I turned on had been switched off."

Evie's eyes widen as her jaw falls open. "Violet keeps yammering on about old electrical wiring, but I woke up the other night to get a glass of water and found the TV had turned itself on."

"Let me guess, the movie was playing *Scream*?"

"Yes!"

"When I found you in my room before my date, I came home and it was playing on its own... I turned it off but when Phoebe came home after me she said it was playing."

Wrapping her arms around herself, she shakes her head. "Violet and Phoebe can crap on all they like about coincidences and old houses but the longer we stay here, the stranger things are."

"I tried talking to the girls about it this morning, but they wouldn't listen."

"I say we burn Palo Santo."

Frowning, I ask, "What the hell is Palo Santo?"

Tucking a blonde strand of hair behind her ear, Evie pulls out her phone and starts typing rapidly. "I've been researching how to remove a spirit from your house and this forum—"

I cut her off. "I-I'm sorry, did you just say *spirit*?"

"Yes! What else would be doing this?"

Splaying my hands in front of me helplessly, I whisper as if to not offend the house. "I don't know. I thought we were just talking about bad vibes!"

Ghosts, spirits, whatever Evie wants to call them—it's another thing entirely to admit to.

My mouth drops open, wailing as my stomach bleeds, the sight before me shredding my heart in two.

"Look at the truth, Blair… It will be yours soon." A foul odor surrounds me as a claw drags down my cheek. "You're mine now, Blair."

My eyes snap to the attic, watching in horror as the shadow lifts the blade and brings it down, dragging it across—

Evie's voice drags my mind back. "According to the forums I've joined, our haunting seems to be poltergeist activity…"

My eyes drop to see my hand covering my stomach.

The scratches are nearly gone—thank goodness for no scarring—but I can still *feel* them.

Goose bumps rise along my arms and legs, ice scuttling down my spine. I *feel* eyes boring into the back of my head. Anger pulsing against my body in waves. My heart takes a nosedive. We're not alone anymore.

"Evie, stop," I whisper.

It could just be the kids returning, watching us through the window, but I know it's not.

"Someone suggested we sage the house, but then they got reprimanded and said to use Palo Santo. Something about sage only clearing the energy, allowing our fear to replace it and attract more. Palo Santo cleanses the energy and replaces it with positivity energy."

Evie's words go in one ear and out the other as the hair on my arms rises.

"Evie," I warn.

With her eyes glued to her phone, she is utterly oblivious to the change in atmosphere, the way goose bumps line her arms, and how her hands tremble from subconscious instincts between fear and the sudden plunge in temperature.

"Apparently all you have to do is open your front door and windows, keeping the back door closed and locked. Start from the front door and light the stick, walking around the room and wafting the smoke in the air."

A breeze falls across my neck, fluttering the hair at my nape. My eyes widen. Evie closed the window after the kids ran off and I didn't turn on a fan.

The breeze falls down my back in a slow caress and I can do nothing to stop the whimper from tumbling from my lips as tears spring to my eyes.

But Evie is hyperfixated.

"You go from room to room, saying a mantra of... I honestly need to look that part up again but once you return to the front door, all you have to do is say—"

A sharp pain slices down my back, making me lunge forward and snatch the phone from her hand. "Stop!"

Evie's face pales, her usually tanned honey skin turning ashen.

It only takes her a moment, a split second to see why I was pleading, why I was begging her to stop. Her eyes bore into mine, as if not daring to focus on whatever caused the shift in the air.

I don't dare turn around and ask her if there's a scratch down my back.

I do *not* want to know. *Ever.*

Quickly rising to my feet, I look around, finding nothing amiss in my room. Nobody is lurking in the corners, my bathroom, or the hallway. Yet the *feeling* of it is so strong that Evie stands at the foot of my bed, shaking.

"What is happening?" I whisper more to myself.

BANG.

The sound of the front door slamming has Evie and I jumping toward each other, both of our screams mixing in the tense air, until a familiar voice calls out from below.

"It's just me! Wow, you guys are on edge." Violet chuckles. "Can you guys come down here? I have a surprise."

Evie turns to me. "Do we tell her?"

Shaking my head, I snatch my phone from my desk, my assignment and serial killers long forgotten as I run out of my room like my ass is on fire. "God no. She will try to institutionalize us." I lower my voice to barely above a whisper. "We'll do the Palo whatever thing you mentioned when they're not home."

"Are we sure it's a good idea after what just happened?"

"I think we need to do it *because* that happened."

Because it wouldn't have gotten mad if it wouldn't affect it.

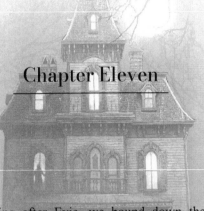

Chapter Eleven

Trailing after Evie, we bound down the stairs to discover Violet buzzing with excitement in the living room. Her cheeks uncharacteristically turn a bright shade of pink as she faces Evie, blocking an item behind her on the coffee table.

Pulling her hands from behind her back, she holds out a mug with a diagram of a heart.

"I'm sorry."

Evie snatches the mug with a gasp. "Why would you take it?"

Violet frowns before quickly shrugging off Evie's accusation. "I didn't, I found it on the kitchen table. That isn't my peace offering…this is," she says, stepping aside to reveal an old record player.

Another gasp flies from Evie's mouth. Clutching the mug to her chest she steps toward it, gazing at the vinyl player with such awe I'm surprised she doesn't begin to cry. "Vi! If you didn't steal the mug, why did you get me this?"

"Clearly someone is messing with you, and it isn't me, but I shouldn't have spoken to you how I did this morning."

Evie's bottom lip wobbles before she wraps her arms around Violet's small frame. "Thank you. You didn't have to do this."

Violet visibly stiffens, her shoulders hiking up toward her ears before Evie jumps back like she was burned. "Oh! Sorry Vi, I just got swept up in the moment."

Violet ignores her, turning to the vinyl player as she tries to brush off the affection.

"I found it at a junkyard, so no big deal but the guy said it's still in great condition."

Evie leaps up the steps, calling over her shoulder, "I'll grab my dad's collection and test it out!"

Then it dawns on me why Evie stared at the record player as if it hung the moon and I have to hand it to Violet, she knows how to pull Evie's heartstrings.

Evie's dad gave his entire vinyl collection as a gift to Evie, stating that she needed to refine her taste in music. The comment and gift came a short few days after he caught us all singing "WAP" by Cardi B in his backyard. To say Mr. Prescot was mortified is an understatement.

However backhanded the reasoning for receiving the collection, Evie saw through it for what it truly was. Her father adores his collection and had spent twenty years building it, and Evie believes he gave it to her so she could have a piece of him while she was away at college.

I wait until I hear her bedroom door click shut before turning to Violet.

"Vi, have you been messing with her?" I ask quietly.

Despite pleading her innocence to Evie, I haven't been moving the mug and neither has Phoebe. It's not something she would do.

She shakes her head, raising her arms in innocence. "I *swear* to you, it isn't me."

"Then why get her the record player?"

It looks more like a gift bought out of guilt, though perhaps a part of me is just desperate for her to be the one moving things around the house. Because I know Evie's mug isn't the only thing to go missing.

Makeup products, jewelry...pieces of clothing. It's all been moved only to reappear hours or days later.

"You know how sentimental she gets over her stuff; I had no right to insult her by calling it stupid." Vi shrugs. "I felt bad for making *her* feel bad."

Staring into her brown eyes I see the truth shining in their depths, making my heart plummet.

"If it isn't me, you, or Phoebe...then who the hell is moving her stuff around?" I whisper as Evie's feet pad down the stairs.

"That is what I would like to know," she drawls, the worry that was etched across her face dropping the instant Evie rounds the corner. Pasting a strained smile across her cheeks Violet helps Evie set up the record player.

Evie cheers. "Oh, he is going to love this. I cannot wait to send him videos!"

"Maybe then he won't think we're terrible influences on you," I snicker.

She rolls her eyes. "He doesn't think you guys are a bad influence."

Violet and I look at each other before we burst into a fit of laughter. "Evie, your dad once cornered me in your kitchen trying to get me to join your church. He said I could benefit from Sunday mass."

Evie ignores us and continues tinkering with the record player as if we're not even speaking.

Evie's dad is infamous in our group for trying to convert us to Jesus. I have no qualms about what religion people take to; I think it's a beautiful thing to believe in a higher power, so long as they don't try to shove it down my throat. Now don't get me wrong, Mr. Prescot does shove it down our throats, but he is the most kindhearted man I have ever met.

Every time we visit, he makes sure to have our favorite beverages and snacks available. He offers to carpool us all despite having our own vehicles and the man still lays a small piece of candy on Evie's pillow as a nighttime treat any time she stays there.

Over the holidays we all took turns staying at each other's houses, for those to meet the parents we hadn't yet previously.

When we stayed at Evie's house, we all walked into her room at night to find four pieces of candy waiting for us, one on each of our pillows. Adorable doesn't begin to cover Mr. Prescot.

Now despite how kind and soft-hearted the man is, it has become a running joke of who Mr. Prescot believes needs to be saved by Jesus the most.

Unfortunately, Evie takes the cake every time as she doesn't take to the religion. Yet he doesn't look at her differently, he may invite her to Sunday mass every weekend, but he loves his daughter and doesn't hold her beliefs against her despite his strong ones and I think that's a beautiful sentiment to his personality and nature.

"You guys know what he's like; he invites everyone he comes across to Sunday mass."

Violet snorts. "Do you remember the time I turned up to your house with blue streaks?"

Evie's eyes bulge. "Oh my God, I thought he had a heart attack! I was seconds away from dialing 911."

Chuckling, Violet pulls a random vinyl from the pile and

hands it to Evie. "What about the time I told him I was an atheist?"

I point an incredulous finger at her laughing form. "That was just cruel."

Rolling her eyes, she relents, "I must admit, I was PMSing that day, but—"

The most horror-inducing sound fills the room.

My shoulders hitch of their own accord as the vinyl spins wildly, moving just as frantically as the melody.

I've always heard people talk about classical music with a lilt to their voice and a starry expression. Always preaching how it sings to your soul and moves your heart, but this... This is not beautiful, nor is it heavenly.

It's as if hell itself created it.

Violet smacks her hands over her ears. "God, Evie! What the hell kind of music is that?"

Quickly removing the needle, the music ends abruptly, right as it soared to a climax. The music may have stopped but the energy it elicited lingers like a foul odor.

"I think I've found *Scream*'s new background music," I say with a shiver.

Evie ignores my jokes as she picks up the record, turning it this way and that. Shock lines her face.

Violet visibly shudders. "That was the most horrible sound known to man. Why on earth would your father listen to that?"

"He doesn't."

"What do you mean he doesn't?" I ask cautiously, my eyes never wavering from her now pale form.

The vinyl in Evie's hand begins to tremble, wobbling violently before Evie drops it, allowing it to clang to the living room floor. She snatched her hand away from it as if the vinyl burnt her.

"Nobody touch that thing!" she hisses.

Reaching out, I gently grab her arm. "Hey, it's okay. It's just a creepy song."

Jumping out of my touch, she spins to face us with tears pooling in her eyes. "That is not my dad's!"

"I'm sure you just didn't notice it when your dad gave you the collection," Violet counters.

Evie wobbles before she starts backing out of the room. "I went through all of them, Vi. I know that wasn't in there and my dad would *never* have something like that."

With my heart pounding wildly in my ears I quickly jump in to calm her. "It's probably Garret's! I know his roommate has a record player and he could have put it in your room as a joke to spook you."

Her feet stop retreating, but the tension in her shoulders still lingers.

Clinging to the small opening she's given me, I push on. "Let's go out for dinner and have a night away from the house. It has everyone on edge."

Evie's blue eyes slide from me to Violet. "Can you come with me to my room to grab my shoes and bag?"

"Of course," Violet says, not missing a beat as she follows her upstairs. She turns and gives me a conspicuous glance before disappearing.

Perhaps the conversation and events of what happened in my room put her on edge. I certainly don't blame her, and she has been on high alert for some time now. The stress has probably begun to weigh on her heavily, waiting to bubble over.

Truth be told, I believe its weight is beginning to suffocate us all.

Strange things are occurring within the house and it's because of that that when I text Phoebe, telling her to meet us at the diner for dinner, I don't ask whether the record is Garret's or not.

For once, I don't want to know the truth.

An hour later my phone buzzes across the booth table.

Nestled between the watchful eyes of Phoebe and Evie in our signature booth at Ruby's Diner, I quickly snatch my phone.

Oohs and *aahs* ring out around the booth, the loudest one coming from Garret, who slings his arm across Phoebe's shoulders. The candlelight dances across his ebony skin as he wiggles his brows.

"How's Hendrix doing, Blair?" he teases with a knowing smirk.

Up until an hour ago, I have been able to dodge Garret's ribbing in regards to my and Xavier's date. Being that he's on the hockey team with him and dates my best friend, it was only a matter of time before he started to tease me endlessly like an annoying older brother.

Garret and Phoebe have been dating since they were fourteen years old. I know...cue the eye roll of jealousy. However, they're adorable and as thick as thieves since childhood. Not as close as we were of course, but he was always there for her. Waiting for her to give him the slightest lick of attention.

After the stunts he pulled on both of us to get her attention in middle school, he deserves all the teasing thrown at him.

Hence why his continued mischievous banter at every

notification from my phone has awarded him a smug smirk, along with a fry thrown at his face.

Phoebe rolls her eyes. "He's just excited to finally have something to tease you about."

Throwing another cold fry at his head for good measure I turn to an exciting new text from Xavier.

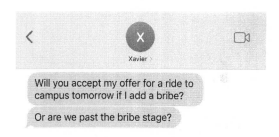

Violet whistles. "Look at the blush creeping over her cheeks!"

"He texted her!" Evie brings her hands in front of her chest in a praying motion. "Please go on a second date."

"Don't pray for the second, pray for the third," Phoebe snickers.

Garret grimaces. "Should I warn Hendrix about her tendency to…?"

"Run before the exchange of any emotional connection?" Violet finishes.

"Absolutely not! No warning is necessary," I declare.

My thumbs are not speed texting a response because of their dramatics, nor is it because Evie pleaded for me to see him again. It's because every time his name pops up on my phone, butterflies swarm my stomach, along with a small smile of joy.

And that kiss.

God, I want his lips against mine again. I've never had a

kiss feel as electric as his. I could practically feel the energy sizzling between us.

With his blue eyes, lone dimple, and luscious lips in mind, I hit send.

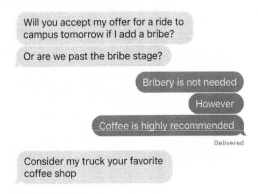

Phoebe knocks her shoulder into mine. "B!"

Lifting my head, I take in the copious sets of eyes locked on me.

"Care to share with the class?" Violet retorts.

"How's Cat doing, Vi?" I ask instead.

Evie bites her bottom lip to hold in her chuckle as Violet's cheeks grow pink.

Violet has had a crush on her fellow employee, Cat, since the day they started the tattoo apprenticeship together in the summer. She has yet to work up the nerve to ask if she's interested.

I quirk a brow. "Care to share the text messages you've been typing under the table?"

"Or why you lock your phone whenever someone enters a room," Evie mumbles under her breath.

Seems I'm not the only one who noticed.

Flipping her shoulder-length black hair behind her, she

lifts her chin. "Point taken."

Garret claps his hands together. "As much as I love all the tea being spilled tonight, I have an assignment due and have to get back."

"Ugh, Garret, rule number one of girl dinner…" She eyes him with an accusatory glare. "Never bring up reality."

My stomach sinks. Until now I had completely forgotten about the record player and Evie's freakout. That must also fall under her category of reality because even though Garret has been here the whole time, neither Evie, Violet, or I have dared ask Garret whether the vinyl belongs to his roommate.

I don't think any of us want to hear the answer.

Garret flicks a thumb in my direction. "Xavier is very much real."

She rolls her eyes. "Sex and love don't count. Assignments and work, however, are a no-go."

Speaking of assignments, with everything going on recently, my psychology assignment slipped my mind. Nothing like throwing yourself into researching sociopaths to distract you from the house terrorizing you.

Violet leans forward, placing a twenty down on the table to cover her portion of dinner. "She just wants to continue procrastinating her reading assignments. One of her teachers assigned two hundred pages."

Garret's brows narrow. "That's not horrible."

"Every *day*," Evie grumbles.

Thick brows shoot into his hairline. "Surely there's not enough material to assign two hundred pages a day," he sputters. "Never mind material, who has the hours to read that many pages for one class?"

Evie folds her arms across her chest. "You would think so! But no, every day she sends a new link to our email along with notes on which parts were her favorite." Sighing loudly,

Evie moves to let everyone else slide out of the booth. "She likes to make sure we all know she has read the material and can quiz us at a moment's notice. She also likes to pretend her class is the only one we attend."

Garret shakes his head. "Damn, I'm glad I went into finance."

After thanking Daisy and each of us leaving a tip we stroll out to the parking lot, each of us entering our respective cars. Jealousy sizzles in my veins as I jump into Phoebe's car, sequestered to being a third wheel.

Fifteen minutes have never felt so long before.

The second Phoebe parks on the street I'm flying out of the car, fleeing their incessant hand-holding, whispers, and giggles. However cute they may be, no third wheel wants to feel like they're intruding on something that is no doubt leading to activity behind closed doors.

Violet snorts. "I told you to ride with me."

"I cannot wait for my car to be fixed," I grumble under my breath.

Which is…not *entirely* true. Knowing that Xavier is picking me up tomorrow morning has made the prospect of being carless much more enjoyable than I first anticipated.

Evie rounds her car, all of us walking up the short flight of stairs to the front porch. "I think they're cute!"

"Oh, they're adorable. But in the passing years, I've become almost like a piece of furniture blending into the background." I lower my voice to a whisper as they cross the street. "They somehow always forget that I'm around."

Violet's smirk is saccharine. "Dirty talk?"

I point an accusatory finger at her. "Do not start."

"Don't start what?" Phoebe asks, coming to stand beside me on the porch, Garret close behind her.

"Nothing," we say in unison.

With a perplexed expression, she turns to Garret. "Are you coming up?"

"And that, ladies, is our cue," Violet drawls. "Night!"

Snickering, Violet and Evie barge their way through the front door, leaving me outside with the two love birds on the porch. Violet closes the door with a fit of laughter at leaving me to fend for myself.

Which, a moment later, is replaced by Evie's blood-curdling scream.

Garret, Phoebe, and I all but barge into the house, finding Violet and Evie standing side by side, their complexions ashen.

Skidding to a halt, my eyes widen as they lock on what has the pair trembling.

"What?" Garret yells, his eyes roaming the living room for any threats. "What is it?"

"What has gotten into you guys?" Phoebe asks, her hands fisted in Garret's T-shirt.

"T-the TV," Evie stutters out.

"What about it?" Phoebe asks, her brows narrowed.

Swallowing thickly, I push past the bolder in my throat as I whisper, "It wasn't on when we left."

It shouldn't come as a surprise to us. It's happened before but…not like this. We were always in separate rooms; our denial had the opportunity to pin the blame on someone else.

Not with this case.

We three girls never turned on the TV. We all left at the same time and locked the front door to a quiet house.

No amount of denial can blame it on one of us forgetting to turn it off.

And again, it is no random program playing on the screen, nor the static of a blown circuit.

It's *Scream*…the moment Ghostface brings the knife up and plunges the blade into its victim.

The scene we were in the middle of watching when the power cut.

The exact one that continues to turn on by itself.

And this time, Violet doesn't utter a single word about wiring or circuits.

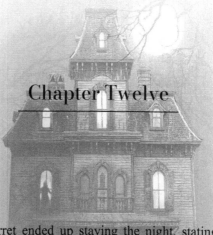

Chapter Twelve

Garret ended up staying the night, stating that we should call the police because of the obvious signs of an intruder. Nobody rebutted his statement, yet nobody agreed either. Evie begged and pleaded for everyone to stay in the living room like the first night the power cut out, but most were too scared to stay in the room with the TV that tends to turn on and off by itself.

That and if I didn't know any better I'd say Violet and Phoebe are pulling away. I understand that most of the activity in the house occurs when we're all together but the thought of us drifting apart because of the oddness of the house sends a pang to my chest that no matter how much I rub the ache, it won't go away.

While Violet locked herself in her room and Phoebe had Garret to cling to for safety, Evie slept in my bed, tossing and turning the entire night as nightmares seemed to plague us both.

At least I can feel like I still have Evie to turn to. The only one beside myself who seems to not be clinging to denial.

Every muscle within me aches and screams as I ease

myself out of bed the next morning, tight from trying to stay as still as possible last night, as if that would protect me from whatever is happening in the house. Trying to stretch out the kink in my neck, my head swivels to the empty spot beside me. I find the sheets cool to the touch.

It's Monday morning, and Evie has classes bright and early. Which in turn makes me think of my own classes and groan. The sound sends a pounding headache slashing through my skull.

With heavy joints and aching muscles, I drag myself to my desk and swallow back two Tylenol pills, praying for the medicine to kick in sooner rather than later.

And then a thought sends natural adrenaline through my body.

Xavier is picking me up.

The thought of Xavier whisking me away from this house, hearing his voice, and getting into his car which is full of his intoxicating scent sends a warm buzz through my bloodstream. So much so that I practically fly through my morning routine.

I don't notice how much faster I'm getting ready until I'm bouncing down the stairs a half hour earlier than usual.

With my eyes glued to my phone screen as I enter the kitchen, watching the clock tick by another painfully slow minute, it's the smell that gets me first.

My nose scrunches as a gag makes its way up my throat.

Covering my mouth and nose from the rotting odor, a loud humming rings past my ear. Flies, many of them, swarming so close it makes me squeal.

"Oh God, what is that?"

Coughing and sputtering, I find the source in the middle of the kitchen island.

Takeout containers lie half opened, the spoiled food

tipped across the counter from boxes with a recognizable, fifties red logo—Ruby's Diner.

I don't remember seeing anyone with a takeout container last night. The food must be from a previous visit.

Taking a quick photo, I send it off into the group chat, letting them know that whoever left this owes me dinner, most preferably a chicken panini.

I put on cleaning gloves and start sweeping the food into a trash bag. The atrocious smell stuffs itself down my nostrils, solidifying my thought that this food was from a past visit—most likely weeks ago by the decay.

Quickly throwing the bag into the trash can out front, I run back inside and spray a heavy dose of Lysol in the air, then peer down at myself. The last thing I need is to get into Xavier's beautiful new black truck smelling like *this*.

Clicking open my phone, I quickly send another text in the group chat.

Checking the time, I groan before dashing upstairs to my bedroom. I rush over to my wardrobe, rip off the sweater I had spent twenty minutes debating over whether or not to wear while doing my makeup—I suppose the universe chose for me—and put on my second option.

The light-wash denim jeans that cinch my waist and flare at the legs looks adorable paired with the cropped pink sweater. Staring at my reflection, I decide that perhaps everything does happen for a reason because the light pastel pink makes my skin look like it's glowing.

Ding.

Another incident that no one wants to come forward on.

Rolling my eyes, I pocket my phone and head back downstairs. With the smell of Lysol clinging to my hair, the memory of *Scream* playing on its own, and the intense craving for fresh air compared to the rotting smell of spoiled food wafting from the kitchen I decide to wait on the front porch, not caring how it will appear to Xavier.

Taking a seat on the front steps, I pull out my Kindle and continue reading the small-town, country romance book that helped me get to sleep late last night. I could pick up my laptop and continue my essay on sociopaths but if I never make time for reading, it'll never happen.

Being a slow burn, the more I turn the page, the higher the anticipation builds and sitting on that seventy percent mark, I am dying for them to finally kiss. Who wouldn't, between a struggling heroine and a spicy—

A large hand comes down on my shoulder, ripping a terrified scream from me.

"What the fuck?" I bark, scrambling backward.

"I'm sorry!" Xavier stands there with his hands in the air. "I called your name several times. Didn't you hear me?"

I fling my arm between us. "Clearly not!"

His lips twitch, and then his cheeks hollow out—not by much, but just enough to let me know he's trying his hardest not to laugh.

Narrowing my eyes, I point at him. "Don't you dare start laughing. You nearly gave me a heart attack!"

Crossing his lips with his finger, he mimics a lock. "Scout's honor, I won't laugh at you."

The maneuver draws my attention to his lips, the ones I haven't been able to get my mind off since our date. Until they twitch again, making my eyes fly to his.

Then he throws his head back and a deep belly laugh rumbles from his chest. The veins in his neck strain as he wipes the tears forming in the corner of his eyes.

"I don't think I've ever seen someone so frightened before. You were worse than a deer."

Huffing, I rise to my feet, snatching my Kindle off the ground, thankful that it didn't crack. "You swore you wouldn't laugh."

He shrugs. "Good thing I was never a scout."

I can't help the laugh that rises within me. "Worse than a deer, huh?" I ask as we walk toward his truck.

I must have truly been out to the world because that engine is *loud.*

"I'm beginning to wonder if you're a cat because I swear, I watched your life pass before your eyes."

I hide the blush that creeps along my cheeks, not only at his tease but at the kind gesture he makes by opening his passenger door. I turn to him once I'm buckled in.

"Maybe that will teach you a lesson about frightening a woman."

His brow quirks. "Maybe this is your sign to get your hearing checked."

"My ears don't need to be checked."

He leans in further, so close that I can see the specks of gold around his irises and the scent of sandalwood invades my senses. "I called your name five times."

And isn't that a travesty that I missed my name tumbling from those lips?

As if he heard my thoughts, his eyes snap down to mine, watching as my tongue pokes out involuntarily and swipes across my suddenly dry lips. He sucks in a sharp breath, coming to an abrupt halt.

My heartbeat quickens to a pace of insanity as he leans forward, the cords along his arm straining. His face comes impossibly close to my own, invading every inch of my personal space as his hands brush across the tops of my thighs, there and gone in an instant.

Lifting my eyes from his lips I find his gaze searing into me, filled with such heat his lids grow heavy. Until he snaps backward, putting a to-go cup between us.

"Coffee?" he offers gruffly.

Taking the cup from his hand, electricity dances between our fingertips as the aroma of cinnamon greets me.

My eyes light up like a Christmas tree. "What did you get me?"

"Cinnamon latte."

The moment pumpkins come out I stop ordering my usual drink altogether in favor of soaking up the pumpkin-spice lattes. I haven't had my usual order in weeks.

How did he know it was my favorite?

As if reading my thoughts, I watch, a sick sort of glee humming through me, as Xavier's cheeks tint a light shade of pink.

He coughs, adverting his eyes to his shoes. "I cornered Phoebe the other week on campus and asked her what all your favorites were."

I can practically feel my eyes spark with delight. That cheeky woman—of course she would have been more than happy to help Xavier.

My cheeks hurt from how much I smile. "Getting intel on your opponent?" I tease.

His head lifts finally, the blush still marring his face.

"Thank you," I whisper, scared that if I voice the compliment too loud it will break whatever intensity that hums between us.

His head dips quickly to lay a gentle peck against my forehead. His lips are there and gone in an instant and yet the touch, the *feel* of him, lingers against my skin as he says thickly, "You're welcome."

Drawing back, he closes the door before I can think of what he just did, how it made me feel, and the fact that I want him to do it again. Over, and over, and over.

Xavier clears his throat as he turns the ignition and takes off down the road, heading toward campus. I never noticed how short the drive was. I wish we moved into a house farther away. I want twenty minutes with him, not five.

"Do you have many classes today?" he asks.

"No, Mondays are my quietest days. I only have two lectures. What about you?"

He grimaces. "Opposite for me. Mondays were already a drag before I got my schedule." He looks over his shoulder before flicking his blinker on and turning.

The campus sign looms on the horizon, the ticking clock of our expiration.

We both start.

"So—"

"Do you—"

Chuckling, the tips of my ears turn pink.

"Ladies first."

"No, please, you go," I insist, not daring to admit that I had nothing to say, just the need to extend the time spent in his car.

"Do you need a ride home? And please don't say Uber."

His arms strain as he turns the wheel, parallel parking perfectly into a spot near campus.

Of course he parallel parks like he invented it. I have yet to find something this man doesn't succeed at.

"My roommate is giving me a ride." At the look of disappointment that flashes across his eyes, I go on. "We're going to the mall."

What I don't share is how we're planning to buy Palo Santo and smoke bomb our house until whatever is inside it leaves. I already feel paranoid over it; I don't need him gawking at me like I need to be institutionalized.

Putting the car into park, his hand lingers on the gear shift, close to my thigh. I can practically feel the heat radiating off him and my thighs itch to move toward his hand.

"Are you free Saturday?" he counters.

Mentally rifling through my calendar, my smile practically jumps off my face. "Yes."

Winking, he slides out of the truck. "Then it's a date."

As he rounds the hood I snatch up my bag from my feet and go to open the door, only to find it whisked open, with Xavier leaning one arm against the frame.

He's impossibly tall, so much so that he appears to be looking down at me despite the height of his truck.

"Can I surprise you again?"

When he holds out his hand, I slide mine against the rough feel of his palm and savor the warmth that floods my body.

"On one condition. You must—"

"I'll send a text with the dress code, *and* I'll have a bag of candy waiting for you on the passenger seat," he chimes in, reading my mind.

For the entirety of the day, all I thought about was Xavier.

The way his hair was long enough to show waves yet too short to allow the curls to take full formation. How he towered over me, making me feel safe and secure. The tease of his lips against my forehead this morning.

And that one dimple that always made its way to the surface as if winking its hello to me. But most of all, I couldn't stop thinking about his eyes. There was a feeling they invoked in me, one that was indescribable.

I spent the majority of my two classes obsessing over it. I haphazardly scribbled down notes during my lectures and welcomed the distraction of his blue eyes ringed with gold when my professor brought up our assignment on serial killers.

That was until the lecture finished and I walked down the steep stairs where Professor Emerson pulled me aside.

I waited awkwardly, watching as he said farewells to every student, his friendly and kind brown eyes seemingly twinkling. Anyone can see how much he loves his students; I've certainly never had a professor as invested as he is.

Hence why my anxiety was so high, my mind churning with all the reasons why he would want me to stay after class.

When he finally turned to me, he stopped so close I could pick out individual gray hairs amidst his brown ones. But all that worrying, all the anxiety, and he simply wanted to ask how my assignment was doing.

I found it odd that he singled me out but I felt proud that I could answer him and inform him I was almost done with the assignment. I was certainly proud when his eyes lit up with excitement and shock that I was going to hand it in so early.

Until, as he was walking me out of the lecture hall, us being the only two in the surprisingly deserted hallways, my heart and body froze as he put his hand on my lower back.

Very low on my back.

So much so I thought it was an accident, a simple hand brush, but it remained there, hot and heavy as a boulder. An overwhelming suffocating sensation came over me as his hand began to rub back and forth, his fingers gracing my lower backside.

Stunned speechless, I didn't shake his hand off. The only other time I had frozen like that was in the Campbellton attic, and the second that thought entered my mind, I stepped out of his grasp and excused myself.

Which leads me to now, walking dazed and confused as

thought after thought pelt me along with a heavy dose of denial.

Did that really just happen?

I'm so consumed by an overwhelming sensation of disgust that I almost don't recognize Evie as she steps into my line of vision.

Her lips move but my ears are still ringing. I have to shake my head and say, "What?"

Then suddenly I can hear, my vision clearing and color returning, although my heart is hammering wildly.

"Are you ready to sage the shit out of the fucker in our house?" Evie says again, looking at me oddly.

Can she tell what just happened? Can she tell I'm confused on whether I'm being dramatic or if my professor touched my lower back so his fingers could brush against the top of my ass?

Can everyone tell?

My thoughts simply fall away as I lock them in a box and shove them into the deep corners of my mind. Trepidation for another reason entirely builds. Everything about our house comes crashing in.

I don't have time to deal with this. I can't afford for my head to be all over the place.

I'm sure nothing happened, a simple trick of the imagination.

It was a simple accident, I tell myself.

Linking my arm with Evie's I turn my back on my lecture hall and keep my mind focused on our biggest problem. Our house.

"Are we sure we should do this?" I ask, repeating the words Evie whispered to me yesterday.

Clutching my elbow, she pulls me from the throes of students exiting the lecture hall and into the direction of the parking lot. We pass Xavier's truck as she whispers, "After my dream last night, I'm ready to pack a bag. We need to do this, Blair."

My brows pull low. "What did you dream about?"

Evie jumps into her Volkswagen, slamming her door shut with a resounding thud, ignoring my question as if she didn't hear me.

"Evie, what did you dream about?" I repeat.

She shakes her head, and I'm about to push further until I spot the silver in her eyes.

Laying my hand atop hers, I stop her from reversing. "You can tell me."

She takes a moment to breathe as if gathering herself before she turns to me with a lone tear sliding down her cheek.

"I dreamed that it killed you."

Chapter Thirteen

"**Y**ou're going to burn down the fucking house!" Evie sputters.

"The lady in the store said that the more smoke the better!" I exclaim, holding the bundle of sage as far away from myself as I can.

"Yeah, and she also said that if it catches fire there's negative energy in the house. We've gone through five bundles!"

"And we will keep going through the bundles until this bitch of a smoke turns white!" Coughing through the hazy clouds of smoke, I ask, "Are you sure you opened all the windows?"

The lady at the store helped us immensely, writing down the steps needed to cleanse our house. She assured us that the likelihood of a negative attachment being in the house was low and that old houses hold energy. We simply needed to clear out the energetic cobwebs.

Steering us away from Palo Santo, however, she said to use white sage, a type of shrub used in smudging rituals to cleanse energy and spaces to ward off evil spirits in case there was one.

I thought it was all a bunch of bullshit, but she explained that white sage smoke burns black and gray when there is negative energy present in need of cleansing and that it only burns white when it's pure. She demonstrated how it should appear with good energy in the store and until we arrived back at the house and lit the first bundle, I didn't believe it.

Not until the long stick-like bundle of leaves and shrub caught on fire, nearly burning Evie's hand in the process as dark, angry black clouds of smoke wafted up to the ceilings.

We quickly put it out, opening all the windows as instructed to allow the lower vibrational energy in the house to exit, while leaving the front and back doors closed to not allow any new presences to enter.

Since then, we have moved around the house clockwise, entering every room, cupboard, and crevice. All while muttering the chant the woman wrote down for us. Until now, all five bundles have spat out black or gray smoke, but this one finally turns an off-white shade.

"Is it turning white?" Evie whispers over my shoulder, holding the fireproof bowl we bought at the store.

I don't dare respond, as if whatever momentum the sage has found will be destroyed by my voice.

Moving down the stairs we enter the living room, watching as the smoke turns an angry shade of gray again, and yet with every word Evie chants behind me, it begins to dull, settling into a milky white.

Despite the ritual being anticlimactic I'm thankful to see the white smoke rising to the ceiling. "Now, Evie! Say the closing chant!" I say as I reach the front door.

Never in my life have I ever felt so strange, disabling smoke alarms to walk around the house and holding a stick of burning leaves as my friend chants over my shoulder. Yet with every walkthrough, we felt it. Felt the heaviness that had settled over the house grow lighter. The tension within our muscles began to loosen and the god-awful headache I had suffered for what felt like weeks finally lifted, now just a dull throb.

Even Evie whispered around our third lap that she was beginning to feel more herself.

Chanting the closing prayer, I hand the bundle to Evie, watching as she carefully dabs the sage into the sand-filled bowl, successfully putting out the flames.

We stand at the front door for a moment in silence, as if waiting for the house to clap back and say, *Gotcha*! But it never comes.

Evie breathes a deep sigh of relief. "We can never tell the girls that we did this. They would never let it go."

"I don't care if I take this to my grave, it worked. I can *feel* it." I turn to Evie. "You feel it too, right?"

Evie's blue eyes sparkle as she nods but her mouth tightens, as if afraid to voice the change, in case whatever we banished will return with a vengeance.

Clearing my throat, I ask, "How are we going to get rid of the smell before the girls come home?"

"We don't. This stuff is so potent we'll have to take them out for dinner. Do you want to text them to meet us at the diner?" Evie asks as she dumps the ashes and sand in the trash can.

My stomach clamps and my hand smacks against it to stop the rolling nausea from swelling. "Absolutely not! After this morning, I need to not see the logo for several weeks."

My fingers run over the spot where the three long scratches resided. Granted, they took longer than most scratches to heal but it has been several weeks since the incident and I'm more than happy to look at my reflection in the mirror after I shower and not find three angry welts embedded in my gut.

Evie grimaces. "No diner, noted." She purses her lips, thinking, until suddenly snapping her fingers. "How about a drive-in theater? We haven't done that since summer!"

"Can't, my car is still in the shop." And it's the only car capable of lowering the back seats to accommodate the four of us.

She groans. "I forgot. When will that be fixed?"

"No clue. Xavier hasn't mentioned it, and the mechanic hasn't called me." I shrug. "I just hope nothing more than the wiring is wrong."

That would be the nail in my financial coffin.

Despite the hefty inheritance I received when my sister passed away, handing down the entirety of the life insurance payment from our parents to me, I try to avoid using it for anything other than my tuition, rent, and schooling needs. Every time I go into the bank account, it feels wrong. I shouldn't have the money—I should have my family.

I've picked up babysitting gigs whenever I could in the hopes of feeling some financial control and freedom from the guilt. Because every time I'm forced to transfer money out of that account, I have vivid nightmares of their deaths. But due to the piling workload, courtesy of my professors, babysitting has taken a back seat in the passing weeks, and my savings from the nannying jobs during the summer has significantly depleted.

I'll have to search for babysitting jobs to pay for the repairs.

While I was deep within my thoughts, the mention of money dragging my mind down into a dark abyss, Evie was off in her little land, her mind consuming her until she beams.

"I've got the perfect idea."

An hour later, we have Violet's obsession with all things scented wax to thank for coming to our rescue. With thirteen candles lit along with the aroma of pizza filling the house, all traces of sage have disappeared.

Evie's idea had me dubious at first but then as she began running around the house waving a ginormous beach towel in the air, I joined her after seeing the smoke curl toward the windows.

With perspiration sliding down the nape of our necks and backs, our stomachs began to rumble from the exertion. That's when the idea of pizza and its lingering scent struck.

So as laughter fills the porch steps, the click of the keys turns in the knob, and Violet and Phoebe saunter through the front door, I don't hold my breath because the house is officially free of sage.

"Perfect timing! The pizza just arrived," Evie says as a way of greeting.

Violet dumps her bags in the hallway. "What's the occasion?" she asks, already taking her vegetarian pizza to what she's claimed as her corner of the couch.

"Someone left that atrocious mess for Blair to clean up. We all owe her a pizza."

Phoebe's nose scrunches in disgust as she plops down beside me. "That did look awful."

"Believe me, it smelled worse than it looked."

Evie visibly shudders. "We're eating, let's not talk about rotten food."

"Hmm, I agree." Violet turns those cutting eyes on me. "How was the ride to campus this morning, B?"

I choke on the bite of pizza sliding down my throat. With my sputtering, Violet's eyes narrow further as she assesses me.

"It was fine."

Her brow rises. "Just fine?"

Finally swallowing the lump of pizza in my throat, I wipe my mouth. "Yep, just peachy."

The girls exchange a glance before turning to me with shocked gasps.

"She likes him!"

"I cannot believe it."

"The one and only, Xavier Hendrix, has converted Blair."

Rolling my eyes at their dramatics, I grumble, "I don't know what you girls are going on about."

Phoebe points an accusatory finger at me. "Yes, you do!"

"Oh my God, she's blushing," Evie squeals with delight.

My hands snap to my cheeks of their own accord. "They are not!"

"Hot to the touch?" Violet teases.

"No," I lie.

Phoebe leans forward, her slice of meat lovers beginning to slowly fall as she assesses me. Then, her eyes widen. "Oh my God, you've fallen for him."

"I have not!"

"You absolutely have."

"Pick your jaw up off the floor and eat your pizza before it drops everywhere," I mutter, cramming another slice of Hawaiian into my mouth.

She gasps, jumping to her knees on the couch, the slice in her hand long forgotten as it drops into the box. "I knew it! You're defensive! Oh my God, you like him!"

I grab her hands, trying to yank her back down to the couch. "Stop it! I don't!"

"When was the last time she genuinely liked someone?" Violet asks Phoebe.

I wave my hand in the air as I pull Phoebe down. "Hello! I'm right here. You could just ask me!"

Completely ignoring me, Phoebe turns to the girls. "Not since middle school. Even then she refused to admit she had a crush. All the others were just…"

"Playthings?" Violet offers.

"That's cruel," Evie whispers.

Phoebe gives her a friendly pat on the knee. "Oh, you have no idea. These guys had no clue that the girl they were dating was as bored with them as she is with science."

Groaning, I slide further into the couch. "You are all horrible and incredibly inaccurate!" Although the protest comes out half assed because, well, Phoebe isn't entirely wrong. Grief is a powerful thing, and it made my heart afraid to love anyone new.

I wanted to let them in, but I somehow always said yes to the dates where I never felt anything emotionally and yet said no to those I knew deep down I would fall for.

I'm not sure how Xavier made it through the guards stationed at my heart.

But I'm glad he did.

Phoebe pats my leg without so much as looking at me. "Denial is a very deep river in B's mind."

"Okay, I'm done with this conversation."

"No!" they scream in unison.

"We need to know how the car ride went," Evie insists. Although the whine is fake, it's drawled out dramatically.

Evie already knows how the car ride to campus went. She grilled me the moment I got in her car, and she wouldn't let up until we were halfway through the mall when I finally relented.

But she can't let the girls know.

I shrug, begging the simple motion to settle my erratic pulse. "It was nice. He picked me up, the ride was short, and then he dropped me off at campus."

My words are met with blank stares, blinks, and then outright groans.

"I swear to God if you don't fess up in sixty seconds, I'll inflict bodily harm upon you!" Violet exclaims, jumping to a stand to make her point.

Rolling my eyes, my shoulders slump. "It was nice, okay? It was really, *really* nice. The moment he pulled up to campus I wanted to spend more time with him, and he even offered to give me a ride home, but I had to decline." I can't help the slight twitch of my lips. "Although he did ask me out on another date."

Phoebe holds up her hand as she chews vigorously and then swallows. "Hold up, why did you have to decline a ride home from him?"

Deer in the headlights.

That is what I imagine I look like right now as I feel the blood drain from my face.

"I-I, uh, I p-promised Evie I'd go home with her," I stutter.

Evie recovers faster than I do. "I asked Blair to help me with something." She waves her hands in the air toward me. "She's the only one studying psychology, so I thought she would know."

Violet frowns, flopping back into a seated position. "This is the first I've heard of needing help. Are you okay?"

Shit.

"Mm-hmm," Evie answers, shoveling another slice of pepperoni into her mouth.

Phoebe looks like she doesn't believe her. Violet, too. Our story is unraveling, and before I can stop myself, I spew a bunch of word vomit to save Evie and me from outright lying.

"I think I like Xavier!" I scream.

The girls' heads snap to me with my outburst, one that I didn't consciously plan. I suppose having to force the words out of me came with a higher volume and pitch. I've never felt this way about someone before, so admitting to liking him more than a friend truly has my heart twisting in agony, if only because it's just another person to add to the list of those I could lose.

It took months for me to open up to a friendship with Evie and Violet. Phoebe had to practically hold my hand the entire way, and even now I'm terrified something bad will happen to them.

Claps and cheers pull me from my thoughts, smoothing out the furrow in my brows.

"I knew it!" Phoebe sing-songs.

I tune them out as they begin gossiping amongst themselves about my love life. I've successfully ignored them, until I have a pizza halfway to my mouth and a hand smacks me across my forehead.

"Are you feeling all right?" Violet asks, her sleek black hair swaying as she stands over me.

"Uh, I was until you smacked me." Swatting her hand away, I rub my forehead. "Did you have to hit me so hard?"

Evie sighs. "She doesn't know her own strength sometimes."

Violet continues to stand over me, mirroring my frown.

"What is it now?"

"You just confessed to liking a man, a golden retriever one at that."

"So?"

Her eyes widen. "So?" She turns to the girls. "We need to take her to the hospital."

"You're being dramatic, she's fine," Phoebe chuckles.

Violet's index finger pushes into my forehead. "She likes emotionally unstable men! Hello, is no one seeing the problem here?"

"I think it's great that she finally likes someone stable," Evie counters.

I whack Violet's finger away from my head. "Guys, I'm right here! Can you maybe include me in the discussion?"

"No," they say in unison, before going back to one another.

I throw my hands in the air as Violet takes her seat again.

"Do you think she's concussed maybe?" Violet ponders.

"I am not concussed! I just like him more than a friend, okay? Can we please drop it before you all begin to freak me out to the point of no return?"

Phoebe's eyes widen before she turns to Violet. "If you freak her out before the third date, I will smother you in your sleep."

Evie chews on her bottom lip while playing with a lock of her blonde hair. "We do need to break the two-date curse."

Quickly picking the TV remote up, I put on the newest rom-com release. "Look! Glen Powell and Sydney Sweeney!"

All conversations of my love life drop the moment the girls see Glen enter the screen shirtless, and the pounding headache their incessant chatter caused settles into nothing but a dull ache as our focus remains riveted to the screen.

It isn't until a half hour has passed and Phoebe and Violet

are immersed in the movie do Evie and I share a triumphant glance. Not one of them mentioned a lingering odd smell of smoke after everything said tonight.

And for the first time since the ghost tour, we watch the entirety of the movie without the power cutting out.

How much candy would one have to require for a second date?

Depends

My candy requirements are billed hourly

Ahh moving up the corporate ladder I see

Someone has to pay for my next fix

How about I double your hourly rate no questions asked ?

Moving away from the original deal I see

No no the original deal still stands

Wear something you would while moving houses

That's oddly specific

I have a specific date planned

No hints?

Now look at who is trying to stray from the deal

I never break my promises

I was simply negotiating

And neither do I

But the time for negotiations has ended

Am I going to wish they were still open?

Not for a moment

When do you have a free day?

Saturday

I'll pick you up at 3

3 must be my lucky number

3 bags of candy and we have a deal

Delivered

I'll make it 4

From: cemerson@acmail.com

Re: Assignment Clarification

Blair,

I do hope my email cleared up all your questions. If
you need further assistance please don't hesitate to
reach out to me again.
You can reach me at this email after hours.

cemerson@acmail.com

Emerson

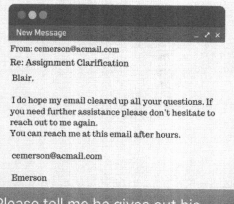

From: cemerson@acmail.com
Re: Assignment Clarification
Blair,

I do hope my email cleared up all your questions. If you need further assistance please don't hesitate to reach out to me again.
You can reach me at this email after hours.

cemerson@acmail.com

Emerson

Please tell me he gives out his personal email to all his students?!?

Violet

Phoebe

I haven't heard anything bad but mind you I don't know anyone in his classes

Evie

It's giving creepy vibes

After class he pulled me aside to ask about my assignment

He started escorting me out of the lecture hall with his hand on my back .... WAY too low

I thought I was looking into things but this is making me feel uncomfortable

Violet

trust your gut a girl always knows a creepy man when she sees one

But everyone loves him!

Phoebe

Just because the man has charisma doesn't mean he isn't trying to get close to girls he shouldn't be

I'll just keep a close eye on it

Technically he hasn't done anything wrong

Chapter Fourteen

As Saturday rolls around I'm sitting anxiously in the living room, surrounded by the girls, all as tense as I am. They helped me get ready today for my date with Xavier, pondering over my closet for hours on what to wear for "moving houses."

It was the most ridiculous description of an outfit requirement and yet when I got the text message, I couldn't stop smiling.

The girls and I settled on tight black leggings and an old gray cropped crewneck. It shows a sliver of my stomach, the black leggings molding to my curves, and it's at least a similar outfit to what I wore when we actually moved into this house.

With only putting on light makeup and letting my red hair fall loosely around my waist, it didn't end up taking me that long to get ready. Hence why we have been anxiously waiting in the living room for—I check my phone for the thousandth time—forty-two minutes.

I'd tease the girls endlessly about their nosiness if it weren't for the fact that I know they're all anxious because they want me to make it to the third date. They all cleared their schedules for the afternoon to help me get ready in case it was the last date I had with Xavier.

I couldn't stop my eyes from rolling when I found out their true motives, but truthfully, I just feel grateful to be anxious because of a date and not because of this house.

It's been almost a week of no nightmares, flickering lights, shower doors opening on their own, food being left out, and no TV turning on and off of its own accord. With every night that passes without incident, Evie and I do a silent, celebratory dance in the hallway before bed.

When Violet's voice breaks the tense silence, I almost collapse with relief.

"Now under no circumstances are you to get the ick. We need to make it to the third date."

My nose scrunches up in distaste. "What do you mean *we*?"

"I'm emotionally invested for you."

Sputtering out a laugh, I'm not surprised to hear it holds no humor. "And I'm not emotionally invested?"

Phoebe places her hand on my knee, forever the mediator in our dynamic. "She didn't mean it like that."

"Yes, I did."

Phoebe throws her hand in the air in defeat. "Fine then, dig yourself a hole."

Violet's eyes slide to mine, and her knee stops bouncing as she sighs deeply through her nose. "Shit, B, I'm sorry. I just think he's a great guy and I'm happy to see you finally going out with people on your level."

"My level?"

Evie nods. "Oh yeah, remember Jeremy? The hardcore metal guy?"

"What was wrong with Jeremy?"

Evie looks at me incredulously. "What was wrong with Jeremy?" she parrots.

"Blair…he stranded you in Charlotte for another girl he picked up at the concert he took you to."

I snort. "I can't believe I forgot about that."

"Although anyone is better than Jeremy," Evie points out.

"True," I mutter. Turning to Violet, my voice softens. "Thank you, that's very kind of you to want good things for me."

Her chin rises. "Yes, it is."

DING.

Gasps ring out, mingling with the sound of the doorbell.

"Did he come to the front door?" Evie whispers in excitement.

"That's usually what people do, Evie," Violet hisses under her breath.

I feel like adding that he came to the door last time but I can't speak.

Phoebe gives my shoulder a playful shove. "Don't just stand there! He's waiting!"

Scrambling off the lounge, I quickly survey myself in the mirror before hushing the girls' whisperings. Once they've settled, I throw open the door, only to end up gawking at the sight.

Xavier stands in the doorway in gray sweats, adorned by a tight white shirt showcasing every ridge and dip of his rippling abdomen and chest. Moving attire is suddenly my favorite. In his hands, he holds a bouquet of pink tulips.

Pink fucking tulips!

They're my favorite—always have been, and always will be. *I need to thank Phoebe later for giving him the rundown.*

His lips tip upward as he smiles down at me. My weight

leans against the door as I mask my lust and move toward nonchalance.

He does his own perusal of me, and by the heat that shines back at me as his eyes lock on mine, I'm inclined to believe he likes what he sees.

But judging by Xavier's smoldering look, I clearly didn't do a good job at masking my own once-over. Especially as his smile widens when I swallow thickly and throw out a husky, "Hi."

I can't help myself, my eyes dip lower again for a moment before flying back to his face.

What is it about men in gray sweatpants?

He bites the corner of his cheek as he holds out the tulips and a bag of gummy bears.

"Candy and flowers. You're really going all out on this one," I tease.

A deep timbre of a laugh floats from his lips, the sound dancing along my skin and making goose bumps rise.

"Just holding up my end of the bargain. I see you held up yours."

I wave my hands down at my body. "My moving attire. Care to tell me what we're doing?"

He clicks his tongue. "Nope."

Rolling my eyes playfully, I open the door up farther as I raise my voice, making sure the girls hear me. "Come in while I put these in a vase."

The pounding of pattering feet rushing through the living room has me biting the inside of my cheek to suppress my laughter. I knew they'd be eavesdropping, and now's the time as any to get the inevitable out of the way, especially since you can't get to the kitchen without passing the living room.

Pausing in the archway, I have to stop myself from snorting. Evie is holding a magazine upside down, Phoebe just lies there staring at the ceiling, and Violet is outright grinning like a Cheshire cat.

"Xavier, these are my roommates and best friends, Evie, Violet, and Phoebe."

The girls scramble up, feigning innocence.

By the smirk Xavier shoots my way, he knows they're busted.

Evie practically flies off the couch. "I'm Evie."

"Phoebe," she says with a wave.

Violet stands, approaching Xavier like her prey, and he has the good sense to straighten. She points a newly painted finger in his direction. "You so much as hurt her and you'll wish you were never born." A devilish smirk spreads across her face. "Then I'll cut off your balls and shove them so far down your throat you'll beg me to finish you."

"Violet!" we curse in unison.

My eyes are as wide as saucers as I grab Xavier's forearm —deliciously thick—but I'll ponder the feel of him after I drag him out of the lion's den.

Except he just throws his head back on a deep belly laugh and grabs my hand, linking our fingers together to stop me from pulling him away. The rough callouses on his hand tickle my smooth skin.

"I'll bring her back in one piece," he swears.

Her eyes narrow, surveying him, and whatever she finds must satisfy her because she huffs and walks back to the couch. "Very well, enjoy yourselves."

Evie practically dives for her once she's in reach, angry whispering under her breath.

Taking that as my cue, I begin to pull him away, noting that he lets me this time as I say, "Come on, the kitchen's this way."

Xavier looks around as I quickly fetch a vase and fill it with water.

"Is she always…?"

"Yes."

"Noted."

Chuckling, I gently place the tulips in the vase and pick up my bag. "She's amazing once you get to know her. She's just rough around the edges to strangers."

He gives me a gentle smile, one that makes his single dimple appear. "Fair enough. Trust is earned, right?"

My eyes shine. "Right."

I didn't notice that we had stopped walking or that we were simply standing in the hallway staring at each other as something fizzles between us, growing so taut I have the deepest desire to lean forward into his warmth.

The reality of what we're doing comes crashing down around us as Violet calls out from the living room, "Hurry up and leave so we can talk about you!"

My blush spreads from my cheeks to the tip of my ears as we quickly leave the house. Xavier's shoulders shake with quiet laughter. "Your friends are hilarious."

"I'll tell Vi you said that. It'll earn you brownie points."

Opening the passenger door once again, Xavier waits until I'm buckled in before he closes the door and rounds the hood of his car. Sliding into the driver's side, he turns on the heater and takes off.

We fall into a comfortable silence, the chatter of the radio drawl fading into the background as the drone of his tires on the highway lulls us into a calm state.

Just the mere warmth of his body heat fills the car, and every inch of me is aware of him. Aware of the deep breaths he takes, the way his eyes flick to mine every so often, and my body certainly notes the times his gaze drops to my thighs.

"Have any guesses as to where we're going?"

His voice jolts me, yanking my eyes away from where I have apparently been staring at his side profile.

Shaking my head, I stare out the window. "No idea. Want to give me a hint?"

If I turn to watch his response, I'll become trapped in... *him*, so instead I keep my gaze locked on the scenery in front of me. I have never been so mesmerized by someone before. Dangerous territory for my heart to be in, and by the pitter-patter of its frantic melody, I think it knows.

My plan fails miserably as he begins to talk, the deep husky timbre of his voice drawing my attention of its own accord. One moment I'm staring at the trees whizzing by us, and in the next, I'm looking at him. Trapped in the way his voice makes tingles race down my body.

He clicks his tongue. "Hmm, I think the only thing I could say is, prepare to get dirty."

My brows quirk. "Dirty?"

His eyes slide to mine and hold for a second before he drawls, "Very."

My cheeks tint pink as I whip my head to the front. I have to physically stop myself from shaking my head to clear my mind. It's dived off the deep end and gone straight into the gutter.

Clearing my throat, I sputter, "H-how far away are we going?"

Xavier's lips pinch as he tries not to laugh. "Not long at all. In fact..." He flicks on his blinker and pulls down a long gravel driveway. "We're here."

Straightening in the seat, I look out the window, watching the endless trees pass as I wait for any hint of what we're doing. As far as I can see, all there seems to be is hay. When I finally make out a sign, I gasp and turn toward him. His eyes are on me already.

I'm breathless as I say, "Oh, you are so on."

"Competitive, are we?" he asks as he puts the truck in park.

At my smirk, his eyes alight. "You have no idea, Hendrix."

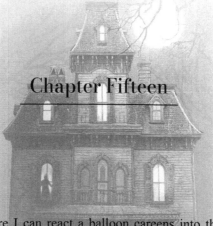

Chapter Fifteen

Before I can react a balloon careens into the side of my head, knocking me off balance the moment it pops. Pink paint explodes across my face.

"Ahhh! You are so going down for that, Xavier!"

The moment I see him try to make a mad dash for safety I pull my arm back and launch the paint-filled balloon in my hand as hard as I possibly can. His long, powerful legs flex every muscle as he leaps for a stack of hay, only to tumble as the balloon hits him square in the chest. The white shirt turns green with paint.

Peering down at himself he freezes, and with my heart in my throat, I watch as he lifts his head, pinning those blue eyes on mine. A dazzling, mischievous smirk dances across his lips.

"Sunshine, I suggest you run."

Without a moment to process the name he called me or the way it makes my heart soar, I take off running as he charges for me, his hands ladened with two balloons.

With a yelp of surprise, I turn and run.

With endless rolling hills and terrain, the owners created

several obstacle courses and mazes out of hay for paint-balling. And for those who don't want to get pelted, balloon tossing.

Our maze is full of the leaves fall has shed. The owners dumped piles in nearly every corner, allowing those in the maze to hide from their assailants.

Dashing left and then right, my stomach sinks as I turn the corner to a dead end. A large arm wraps around my stomach seconds later and lifts me off the floor.

"Gotcha," Xavier whispers in my ear a moment before he drags us backward into a giant pile of leaves.

I squeal with delight. Xavier breaks our fall, placing me on top of him, with my back to his front. The position momentarily knocks the air from my lungs as we land.

Xavier spins me around, and as every part of us aligns, I bite my lip to stop myself from audibly gasping.

"What are you doing?" I whisper.

"Shh."

Not a moment later, footsteps pound around us as the other team races by.

It's meant to be a group activity but the moment that horn blasted, Xavier and I shot off, instantly throwing balloons at one another—our supposed opponents long forgotten.

However, it seems that the memory loss was one-sided.

"I thought we weren't doing teams."

As my eyes begin to adjust to the darkness and the small streams of light flitting through the gaps between the leaves, I watch his eyes flick back and forth.

"I don't want anyone else throwing balloons at you."

Tension builds again, lighting up between us like a thousand fireworks. We just sit there, waiting to see how long the blasts will last.

Licking my lips, I note how the movement makes his lids droop.

"Who's winning?"

"I lost track," he confesses.

My brow quirks, yet his eyes are still on my lips. "Enjoy pegging me with paint?"

"No, I enjoy watching your face light up when you smile. It's as radiant as your hair," he says gutturally. "Like sunshine."

My inhale is sharp, the sound fierce as he steals my breath.

Sunshine. He thinks I'm sunshine.

He appears to be waiting—for what, I'm not sure—but all I know is that at this moment I want one thing.

Him.

Without second-guessing myself I lean forward, a thrill running through me as the corner of his lip twitches upward, that lone dimple appearing quickly before it vanishes as his lips come down upon mine.

Fireworks.

An explosion of them takes off as our lips connect.

A deep rumbling groan flows from his mouth to mine as he slides his hands up my neck, cupping my cheeks.

I thought our first kiss was amazing, but this is on another level. This is what it feels like to have two hearts connecting.

The kiss is slow, languid. Xavier takes his time as if he has the entirety of his life to do so, exploring me with such softness it makes my toes curl.

Until a true explosion occurs.

My eyes fly open as something hits my back and liquid drips down my legs. At the same time, the leaves around us burst, flying high into the air in all directions before slowly fluttering to the ground.

Xavier growls as he flings a balloon at the scraggly teen who chuckles with his friends.

Scrambling off Xavier, I crane my neck to find purple paint dripping down my back.

"Hey!" the pimply boy whines as dark navy-blue paint drips down his goggled face.

Xavier shrugs, linking his fingers with mine. "Sorry, were you preoccupied with something?"

The kid's friends snicker around him, making the teen narrow his eyes. He dips his hand into his bag of balloons. "Get him," he hisses to his friends.

Xavier and I run, taking off in a full-out sprint as laughter bubbles up from our chests.

"I think you pissed him off!" I squeal with laughter.

His hand tightens in mine as he quickly turns left. "Not as pissed as I am that he interrupted us."

With the flush that creeps up my neck and along my cheeks, I'm thankful for the pink paint mingling with my skin, concealing the way my cheeks no doubt match my hair.

Coming to a halt, Xavier drags me behind a thick pile of leaves, high enough to conceal us without having to dive into it. Squatting behind the pile, we both peek our heads out from either side. I hold my breath as pounding footsteps draw closer and sigh with relief as the group of teenagers run past us.

Drawing back, I whisper, "Thank God, it would have been horrible if—"

Yellow paint cascades down my face as Xavier pops a balloon above my head.

Gasping, I lean forward so as to not get any paint in my mouth. Xavier's face turns red as he quakes with silent laughter.

Quickly pulling out one of my own balloons, I pop it over

his head. My own laughter ripples out of my mouth as bright blue paint rolls down the entirety of his face.

He's lucky he had the forethought to put his goggles back on when we were running. I didn't, until I see the gleam enter his eyes. I scramble with my pair, shoving it down my face as I spring into action and take off.

His thundering footfalls follow me. He chuckles, dodging every one of my attempts to throw paint balloons at him. I'm laughing along with him until I turn right into another dead end. A sense of déjà vu falls over me, and I can only pray he's merciful again and pulls me into another pile of leaves to continue kissing me.

Xavier approaches from behind, his hands full of balloons.

"Any last words?"

Sputtering, I shove my hands into my pouch, only to draw up empty. That's why he was laughing—he watched me empty my entire arsenal as I ran straight for a dead end.

My mouth opens and closes like a fish out of water, a thousand snarky comments whirling through my mind as his arms rise to douse me in paint.

Until a flash of navy-blue catches my attention out of the corner of my eye.

Crossing my arms over my chest, I quirk a brow. "You seem very confident in yourself that you're about to win."

"Well, statistically, I think I already did, thanks to your little juggling act from before."

Before I can stop it, I snort, the sound making his eyes blaze with humor. I can't even make myself feel embarrassed as I scramble out of the way.

"I wouldn't be too sure about that," I say, just as the group of teens pelt Xavier with dozens of balloons.

I couldn't control my laughter even if I wanted to. My

stomach aches from the deep sound pouring out of me with abandon. Paint coats the six-foot-three hockey player until he resembles a rainbow unicorn.

Xavier searches the room until his eyes catch on me behind a pile of leaves, a hand covering my mouth as my shoulders shake. He points, the paint splashing him forgotten. "I'm giving you a ten-second headstart. I suggest you start running."

My eyes widen as he begins to count.

"One."

I jump to my feet.

"Two."

Dash out from behind the leaves.

"Three."

Dodge the paint from the teenagers.

"Four."

Run as fast as I can.

"Five."

A slight pause from Xavier.

"Sorry, you should have made a deal to ensure the ten seconds!"

Paint rains down upon me, but even the cold of it couldn't douse the heat thrumming through my body.

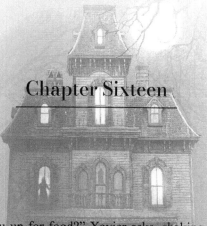

Chapter Sixteen

"You up for food?" Xavier asks, shaking clumps of paint from his curly brown hair.

"Absolutely, I'm famished."

During the hour-long session, I was surprised by my lack of exertion. The last time I did cardio that didn't involve skating was when I was fourteen and growing hips. I only have Xavier to thank for the lust and adrenaline rush to hold off my fatigue.

Except now that it's wearing off, I'm as stiff as cardboard and the more steps I take, the more I realize how much my muscles are beginning to ache. So much so that as I follow Xavier out, I'm now hobbling.

My stomach grumbles madly, not helping the circumstances.

He stops just outside the door and waits for me. As I reach him his dimple appears as he slides his fingers through mine.

"How are you holding up?"

"Cardio and I are not friends," I grumble as the muscle aches truly begin to set in. I'm ready to slump into his truck, but we keep walking right past it. I check behind me. "Umm, not to be rude, because I'm sure you know what your own truck looks like, but haven't we passed it already?"

Xavier chuckles. "Yes, we have."

"Okay and…are we going to keep walking? Because I swear my legs are about to fall off."

"Do you always say exactly what you think?"

I cock my head. "Yep, why?"

"I like it."

"Well, that's all fine and dandy, but my original question still stands."

Xavier halts so suddenly that our joined hands yank me to a stop.

He juts out his chin toward the restaurant across the road. "They have the best burritos I've ever had. I figured I could bless your taste buds with their food."

If I could internally slap my face, I would.

Xavier lowers his head as a blush makes its way across my cheeks. He doesn't stop until his lips brush across my ear, making me shiver.

"Sorry I didn't tell you what I was thinking."

Before I can respond, his lips press against the top of my head, there and gone. Then he's pulling away, rising to his full height.

Sucking in a sharp breath I try to memorize the feel of it because it made my entire body come to life as if a fire ignited within my veins.

Xavier quickly pulls me inside, letting me take a seat on the booth side as he takes the regular, wooden chair. I pick up the menu to hide my flaming cheeks, but Xavier gently lowers it, forcing me to make eye contact.

"I love it when you blush. It makes your freckles stand out."

"At the rate you're going I'm going to be permanently blushing."

He cocks his head, trying to discern my words. He opens his mouth to speak, only to be cut off by the waiter. A muscle ticks in his jaw before his eyes soften and turn to me.

"You have to try the chicken burrito with queso on the side."

"On the side?"

"Trust me." He winks, turning to the waiter to order for us before asking me to choose a side and drink.

I usually hate when men order for me, but there's something about his eyes, the easygoing way he speaks to people, that lulls me into a state of peace and makes me want to say yes to everything he says. Smiling at the waiter, I thank him before handing back our menus.

Xavier leans back in his seat. "I'm just praying I haven't hyped up the burritos to the point of disappointment."

"I must say, the queso on the side is a bold move."

"That, I have every ounce of faith in."

Smiling, I pull my eyes away from his as my body begins to heat again. Instead, I look around, noticing the beautiful artwork representing Mexican culture. "How did you find this place? It's amazing."

"You haven't even tried the food yet," he points out.

"I love small businesses; there's something to be said about a family-run shop. And don't dodge my question!"

He stretches his legs out, making his calves brush against mine. Swallowing at the heat radiating off him, I physically force myself to concentrate on his words.

"My mom found it actually."

If it weren't for the level of concentration I placed on him, I would have missed it—the tightness around his mouth and the sense of sadness behind those words.

"Are you guys not close anymore?" I dare ask.

Xavier seems to chew on his cheek, pondering his answer before he says flatly, "She's dead."

My eyes shudder closed. "I'm so sorry, I shouldn't have intruded."

He waves my apology off. "No, you're fine. It was years ago."

"When did she pass?" I ask carefully.

"I was nine."

My brows rise. "That's so young, I'm sorry."

He shrugs.

Grief is such an odd thing. Until you've experienced it, you truly cannot imagine the pain it causes someone. The loss that rips your world apart. The deaths that change who you are at your core.

"Are you close with your parents?" he asks, moving the topic away from himself.

My chest squeezes at the pity I know I'm about to receive.

"They're both dead."

Xavier's eyes snap to mine, a cloud of sadness—and strangely guilt—passing over them. "I'm sorry."

Our eyes catch as we freeze, and for a moment, something crackles between us before we both chuckle nervously.

"You hate it too?" he asks. "The sorries?"

Groaning, I ease back in the booth. "So much. I never realized before this moment how natural it is to say though."

"Me neither." Shaking his head, he leans forward in his chair. "This feels far too depressing for a second date. Why do you study psychology?"

I chuckle despite myself. "If you want to move away from family…next question."

His brows rise in surprise. "Really?"

"Oh yeah. After attending the lectures, I'm now convinced all therapists have just as much baggage as their clients."

Our laughter is halted as the waiter drops off what smells to be the most divine food. My mouth salivates as I thank the waiter, and I barely inhale enough oxygen into my lungs before diving into it. Flavor explodes across my tongue, making my face light up in surprise.

Xavier sits there, his burrito halfway to his mouth, untouched, as he watches my reaction. "It's good, huh?"

"Good?" I repeat. "It's heavenly, although it does feel…"

"The queso."

"Hmm?"

Xavier picks up his queso and shows me how he pours a dollop straight on top of the burrito and then takes a bite. Mirroring his movements, I'm delighted as I take another bite and moan.

Xavier stops chewing but I'm far too engrossed in eating the best burrito I've ever had in my entire life to focus on the way his eyes heat as he watches me eat. I've always said food is good if the dining table falls silent, and despite having a thousand questions brimming on the tip of my tongue for Xavier, we both fall quiet as we devour our food.

It isn't until Xavier is more than halfway finished before he breaks the silence. "I can't believe you've never eaten a burrito like that."

My cheeks flame. "Is it common?"

"Extremely," he laughs.

Once Xavier's finished with his food, he moves on to the bowl of tortilla chips and guac.

His head tilts to the side as he studies me. "Movies or TV shows?"

My brow rises. "Are you playing this or that?"

"Would it be bad if I was?" He smirks.

Biting the corner of my cheek, I ponder as I swallow another bite. "TV shows. I'm always sad when a movie ends. You?"

"Same. Although I'm a sucker for a movie franchise or series."

With my burrito now finished, I stare longingly at my plate, wishing I could rewind time and eat it again for the first time. Trying to squelch the yearning I pick up a tortilla chip and dip into the guac, not at all surprised when I find the guac is the best I've ever had too. "I'm a sucker for movie series."

"What's your favorite genre?"

"Romance and dystopian. There's something to be said about a make-believe world that isn't too far out of reach. What about you?"

Finishing off the tortilla chips, Xavier grins. "Horror."

We make to stand, Xavier leaving bills on the table, along with a hefty tip as we wave goodbye and thank the staff.

The crisp fall air whips across my face once we exit the restaurant. Walking here I was a sweaty, heart-pounding mess and now that my body has returned to its baseline, I realize just how chilly the air is. I wrap my arms around myself.

Xavier notes my pebbled flesh and wraps his arm around my shoulder. Gritting my teeth to restrain myself from sighing, I lean further into him, savoring the feel of his warm body.

"You and Evie would have a lot to talk about then," I continue. "She's a horror fanatic."

"Really? What's her favorite type?"

"Psychological thrillers and slashers."

As Xavier opens his passenger door, I practically fly in, my body craving heat.

He must hear something in my tone because he asks, "And you're not a fan?"

Once I started to feel like I was living in a horror movie? No, not anymore.

My eyes lower to my hands to find them fidgeting on their own. I quickly put them beneath my legs to stop.

Clearing my throat, I try to smile, yet it feels strained. "Not really, no."

"Life is scary enough as it is. Honestly, I love them because my father is obsessed. He would force me to watch every single one."

My brows rise. "That would have been terrifying for a child."

He shrugs. "It was his way of bonding."

"Are you still close with your dad?" I ask.

"I practically worship the man." His eyes grow heavy. "He stepped up after my mom died."

Laying my hand on his arm I feel the muscles bunch beneath my touch. The warmth that soaks through my fingers makes me shiver with delight.

"I'm glad you had someone there for you," I say gently.

It's a precious gift to have someone step up; my sister was an angel in my eyes. I'm not a religious person but sometimes I tell myself the angels needed her to return. It's a far easier pill to swallow than the truth of how she died.

Clearing his throat, Xavier backs away, closing the door.

The heavy energy shifts, going back to our playful flirty nature from before we mentioned our dead loved ones.

As Xavier drives in the direction of my house, I realize with stark clarity that I don't want the date to end, and that Xavier Hendrix might very well be the man to break my two-date curse.

From: cemerson@acmail.com

Subject: Midterm

Blair,

Thank you for handing in your assignment. I'm just going through it now.

With it contributing to a large majority of your grade, I feel I must give you a second chance, being as you handed it in earlier than the submission deadline.

Please visit me at my office so we can discuss this further.

Emerson

Would you like the good news or the bad news first?

Rip the Band-Aid off and hit me with the bad news

Dylan just called

More issues have come up with your car and he needs you to go down to the shop to fill out some paperwork

And go over a new price

Is it Friday the 13th?

Bad luck today?

You have no idea

Delivered

Chapter Seventeen

When I see Xavier's name flash across the screen of my phone, I jump off the couch and excuse myself, muttering to the girls about needing the bathroom before I jog upstairs.

"Hello?" I answer, closing my bedroom door behind me.

"What type of bad luck are we talking about?" Xavier says by way of greeting. "Walking into walls, bird poop, forgotten assignments? I know it isn't car issues, although I suppose you can now add that to the list."

Chuckling, I plop down into my bean bag, my gaze roaming the starry night outside my window. "The type of bad luck that has my computer crashing and losing all my assignments that are due in a matter of weeks."

The relief I felt turning in my psychology midterm early evaporated the moment I received Emerson's email. Any time his name enters my inbox now, the hairs on the back of my nape stand on end.

"Fuck, did you manage to recover the files?"

My body sags into the bean bag. "Yeah, I did eventually. The gods of luck gave me a reprieve and the technician was able to restore the files. I had to buy a new computer though."

"Well, that's not *that* much bad luck then," he teases.

"Oh, there's more."

He groans, the sound of sheets rustling coming through the line. "Lay it on me, Sunshine."

Biting my lip, I try to stop myself from smiling as I picture him nestling into his bed, calling me Sunshine while grinning. That one dimple no doubt popping out to join the conversation.

Clearing my throat, I rush out with heated cheeks, "I came home from the computer store, and someone had spilled water without cleaning it up."

"No."

"Yes." I laugh, but it's more depreciating than anything. "With my brand-new laptop in hand, I slipped and crashed to the floor. Breaking my back in the process…and my shiny new computer." Rolling over onto my side, I pop my chin into my hand. "You should have seen the salesman's face as I came hobbling back into the store with a broken laptop."

Thank goodness for the free seven-day AppleCare; otherwise, I would have been out a hefty four thousand dollars.

"Wow, you weren't kidding about Friday the thirteenth vibes." He coughs and then his voice lowers. "Is your back okay?"

My lips twitch. "Yeah, I'm okay now. Nothing that some ice couldn't mend."

"Now I feel awful about being the bearer of bad news."

Groaning, I squeeze my eyes shut. Another thing I'll have to dig into my inheritance for. I mentally chastise myself because I should be grateful that I have the funds to pay for these issues. I know I'm a lot better off than my fellow class-mates, and I don't take it for granted, but I cannot help the guilt and grief that consumes me with every swipe of my card.

"I surprisingly forgot about that for the few minutes we were on the phone." Sighing deeply, I mutter, "I swear someone hexed me. Either that, or someone is pushing a lot of pins into my voodoo doll."

The deep rich sound of Xavier's laugh barks down the line, the sound so soothing it makes my stomach clench.

"I don't think anyone has a voodoo doll of you. I can't see why anyone would even remotely dislike you."

Flames erupt across my cheeks.

"So, this all happened in one day?" he rushes on, as if I'm not the only one blushing.

"Yep," I say, popping the *p*.

He clears his throat, and despite the action, his voice still remains husky. "Care to share your bad luck with me?"

My breath stutters. This is it; I'm going to make it to the third date.

The girls are going to go feral.

My mouth opens, about to speak—

BANG.

My phone flies out of my hand as a scream pierces my room. With wide eyes, I jump up quickly, right as children's laughter floats through my cracked open window.

Placing my hand against my pounding heart, I try to slow my breathing as footsteps pound up the stairs a moment before the door flies open. Violet charges into the room with a baseball bat in her hands, giving me déjà vu from when this happened with Evie.

"What happened?" she barks.

Phoebe and Evie enter the room, hot on Violet's heels.

"Are there roaches?"

"Is it the shower door again?" Evie asks anxiously.

Adrenaline courses through me and before I can answer the girls, the children's laughter floats into the room once more. Evie's eyes light up like a Christmas tree.

"It's the ding dong ditchers!" she whispers to the girls.

Violet frowns. "The what?"

The girls argue back and forth as Evie explains the children, right as more pebbles rain against my window. Their little cackles join the fake screams we all let out.

"BLAIR!"

Oh my God, I forgot about my phone!

Scrambling, I lunge for it halfway across the room and pray there's no cracks as I turn it over. I suppose my bad luck streak has ended because the only thing that greets me is a smooth phone screen and Xavier's deep voice.

"I'm coming over there."

"No!"

The girls gasp, making me realize what I've just done. "I-I mean, you can if you want to. B-but there's no need. The neighbor's kids play ding dong ditch and it scared the absolute daylights out of me," I stutter through my explanation.

Concern tinges his voice. "Are you sure you're okay?"

"I promise, they just gave me a fright is all."

Violet's eyes narrow as Evie claps her hands and squeals. "She's going to make it to the third date! I *repeat*, she's going to make it to the third date!"

"What did they say?" Xavier asks.

My eyes widen as I motion for Evie to zip her lips, but all it does is entice them to my conversation. With the kids long forgotten they come barreling over to me, whispering and mouthing to put it on speaker.

No matter how much I shake my head no, they won't listen.

"Blair?"

"Uh, just a minute," I mutter, quickly muting myself before I turn to them with blazing eyes. "Out!"

"Why?" Evie whines.

"I swear we'll be quiet," Violet promises, still holding the baseball bat.

Phoebe crosses her arms over her chest. "Don't make me pull the childhood card."

Evie rolls her eyes. "That is such an unfair advantage."

"If you three want me to make it to a third date with Xavier then you'll leave. I'll tell you everything, but your hovering is making me nervous."

Phoebe is the first to soften, trying to drag Evie away as she says, "Of course, B, we'll wait downstairs."

Violet walks away backward, using the baseball to point at me. "We want all the details."

"Yes, yes, I promise," I say, shooing them out. "Now close the door!"

Not trusting them to not eavesdrop, I lock myself in my bathroom before unmuting the call.

"Xavier?"

"Hey."

His voice pulls a heaving sigh from my body.

"You said something about sharing bad luck?"

He barks out a laugh. "After all that screaming I think you need to take me up on my offer even more so."

"Is that right? And what is it that you're offering?"

"I'm thinking of a movie marathon tomorrow. That way, you're safe at home and you won't have any mysterious potted plants fall on you, have your wallet and ID stolen, or find gum mysteriously in your hair. Now that I think about it, it's just safer to get you off the streets and away from citizens."

I couldn't hold back my laughter even if I tried. "You think I'm a danger to society?"

"Absolutely, and I volunteer to take the brunt of the bad luck."

"That's very chivalrous of you. I'll nominate you for the community hero award." Chewing my bottom lip, dread coils in my stomach, paired with a hefty dose of apprehension. *For once when it comes to men, I don't want to say this.* "I really would love to, but the girls and I already have a hiking trip planned tomorrow and quite honestly, I have no idea how long it's going to take us."

"Ahh, I see they're one step ahead of me. I should have thought of a more remote location too."

I snort. "Let's just hope I don't fall off the mountainside."

"Please don't."

We both fall silent as his words linger, the husky way he drawled them and the full body shiver that assaulted me as he did so.

"How about a ride to the mechanic tomorrow morning?" He pauses before going on. "I'll bring coffee."

I beam. "Coffee was the magic word."

His voice lightens. "Perfect, what time do you want me to pick you up?"

If I didn't know any better, I'd say he sounded excited.

My heart rate spikes. "Is eight too early? Phoebe wants us to leave here at around nine."

"Not at all, I'll see you tomorrow at eight."

My cheeks hurt from smiling so wide. "Okay, I'll see you then."

I move to pull the phone away, except his voice stops me.

"Blair?"

"Yeah?"

"Make sure your bad luck doesn't take you out before I see you."

Chuckling, I shake my head. "I'll try my best."

I hang up, then walk downstairs and enter the living room smiling so hard my cheeks hurt. The girls grow silent until Phoebe's smile spreads.

"Oh my God, she made it to the third date."

They seem to hold their breaths as I drop down onto the couch. I shrug. "Maybe."

All hell breaks loose as the girls jump on me from all directions, squealing and cheering their celebrations.

I also note how a few bills are passed between their hands as bets are won and lost.

To: cemerson@acmail.com

Re: Midterm

Professor Emerson,

Was there an issue with my assignment?

Blair

From: cemerson@acmail.com

Re: Midterm

Blair,

Yes, are you available to drop by tomorrow?

Sincerely,
Emerson

To: cemerson@acmail.com

Re: Midterm

Professor Emerson,

I'm not available this weekend. I can come during
school hours Monday?

Blair

From: cemerson@acmail.com

Re: Midterm

I expect to see you in my office before my first
lecture.

8:45 a.m. sharp.

Emerson

Chapter Eighteen

Xavier leans against the side of his truck the following morning, adorned with a devilish grin and holding two large cups of coffee.

"I see you made it through the night," he teases.

Taking the to-go cup he holds out for me, I bite my lip as electricity sparks between our fingers. "Let's just hope I can get through this car ride without spilling or breaking anything."

Xavier taps the hood of his truck as I slide into the passenger seat. "She can handle anything you throw at her."

"Good, because I contemplated bubble wrapping myself."

Xavier chuckles, the sound lingering as he closes the door and jumps into the driver's seat. As we peel away from the curb, a flutter of white catches the corner of my eye and I turn in time to see the curtains in the living room part, showing the girls clapping and cheering.

I bite back my laughter before turning to face Xavier, loving the gray short-sleeved shirt he's wearing because it showcases his muscles flexing as he turns the wheel.

"Did Dylan say much to you about the state of it? Or are we walking in blind?"

Xavier grimaces. "Walking in blind."

Taking a sip, delight fills me as cinnamon explodes across my taste buds. *He remembered.*

"How long ago did you say you had it serviced?"

"Only a couple of months."

Checking over his shoulder, Xavier turns his blinker on before switching lanes. "You should contact the mechanic you got it serviced from. It shouldn't have battery issues yet, not when it was only just replaced. You could have bought a faulty one."

I slide further down into the heated leather seats. "And so, the bad luck continues."

"Forty-five hundred dollars!" I squeak.

Xavier frowns. "Fuck Dylan, what happened to the friends and family discount?"

Dylan wipes his hands on a rag towel covered with grease. "This is a discount, a huge one. That money is just to pay for the parts that need to be replaced. I'm not charging you for my hours."

The groove in my forehead furrows further. Now I feel even more horrible.

"Are you sure that's the issue?" Xavier asks.

Dylan rolls his eyes. "You want to get under the hood and look yourself?"

Xavier rubs the back of his neck. "Sorry man, it's just a shock that's all."

Following Dylan through the busy shop, he directs us to the reception area. "It'll probably take a week or two to order the parts in, and then from there another two to fix her."

"Jesus, okay, do you need the payment in full today?"

Dylan shakes his head. "No, only fifty percent to start ordering. Although I will need the rest when the parts come in."

I suppose I can take up more babysitting jobs to try and cover the dent this will make in my inheritance. Perhaps I can ask if our little ding dong ditchers need any babysitting. Someone clearly needs to keep an eye on them.

I hand my card over to Dylan, shaking my head as an image of my sister and my parents lying in coffins flashes through my mind. I can practically hear my heart plummet as I think of my sister. Everyone always questioned whether we were twins or not. Two years apart and you'd think we were identical. The only difference was that she was a few inches shorter than me.

Her funeral felt like an inside scoop to my future.

Dylan's voice drags me to the present as he hands back my card. "I also think Xavier is right. You should contact the mechanic you ordered from to see if the manufacturer can cover any of this. I'll document all the proof for you because it should have never been sold to you in this condition." He shrugs. "At the very least, the mechanic needs to know their parts are faulty."

Rubbing my forehead as a headache blooms, I thank Dylan for being kind and helping me out. After thirty minutes of exchanging contact details and signing endless forms, Xavier puts his hand on my back and walks me out to the parking lot, steering me in the direction of his truck.

Xavier helps me in then leans inside, resting his forearms

against the top of the door, making his shirt rise. I can't resist looking at the sneak peek of his abs.

Xavier clears his throat, the sound making my eyes fly up to his face.

"I feel awful now and like the true bearer of bad news."

My head thumps against the headrest. "No, it's not your fault. These things happen."

"I guess the bad luck continues, huh?"

I can't help but smile despite my current circumstances. "I think you were right, a mountain is the last place I should be." My eyes close as I groan. "Phoebe won't let me bail though. She'll just yammer on about sunshine and fresh air clearing my bad mojo."

"She's probably right."

"Yeah, I know."

Swallowing thickly, I open my eyes to find him staring down at me, and I quickly realize that I don't want to leave him or the safety I feel when I'm near him.

Be brave, Blair. Take the initiative.

Xavier cocks his head as he watches a war wage through my mind.

I've never asked someone out before, never gotten this far with *wanting* to spend time with a man. Although he was the one to ask me out first and it was his idea... Technically, I'm just rescheduling.

Adrenaline courses through me, my voice rising higher as I rush out, "Do you want to come over when I get back from hiking?"

His eyes spark, shining as if I breathed life into them with my words. A slow smile spreads across his lips, that lone dimple appearing as he drawls, "Absolutely."

I didn't realize I was holding my breath until it exhales from my body in a deep sigh. But my breathing is short-lived.

It picks up again as Xavier ducks his head and enters my space, not stopping until he's a hair's breadth away from my lips.

His fingers run up my cheek before sinking into my hair, and my eyes close of their own accord. My chest restricts, squeezing tight. My lips aren't the only things feeling impatient.

His breath fans against me as he whispers, "Just make sure you don't fall off the cliff before our date."

He seals his words by pressing his lips against mine, hungry, as if he's dying for my touch.

Lightning strikes our bodies as we collide. The touch and feel of him is like no other, making my heart beat rapidly as he groans into my mouth. His hold on me tightens as he tries to pull me as close to him as he possibly can.

He completely devours me.

It's intoxicating, the way his hand cups my cheek, his scent of sandalwood encasing me, and then he goes and slides his tongue against the seal of my lips, gently asking for entrance. The groan that tumbles from him as I grant him access makes my skin turn molten.

If this is what it's like to ask him out on a date, I cannot wait to do it again.

"Then he kissed you?"

Violet rolls her eyes. "You sound like a schoolgirl, Evie, of course he kissed her. They've kissed before."

Evie spins around, walking backward. "Yes, but it's more frequent now, and that kiss sounded amazing."

I do have to hand it to Evie. "It was amazing," I say, panting.

We've been hiking for what feels like hours. Well, at least more than the four hours it's been since we started hiking this mammoth of a mountain. I'd check my phone but the idea of using even a sliver of energy on retrieving it from my backpack has me gagging.

My legs practically drag as I force myself to take one step after the other. The only one of us that seems even remotely okay isn't Phoebe, who tries to hike every weekend, but Evie. She bounces with every step, beaming at the nature surrounding us.

Violet, whose been scowling at the perky blonde, glowers further. "How much longer until the top?"

Phoebe heaves, stopping to rest her hands on her hips. "We should have made it to the top an hour ago."

"What?" Violet exclaims, tipping her head back to look at the mountain peak rising between the trees. "Phoebe...did you check the level of hiking experience they recommended for this trail?"

Phoebe's lips thin into a tight line. "Yes. Of course. Everyone knows there are different hiking levels and..."

"Times," Violet finishes for Phoebe.

Silence descends, the sound of the wind rustling the trees around us filling the tense reserve until Phoebe cracks under the pressure.

"I forgot to check the level."

Violet and I groan deeply while Evie chirps, "That's fine! It won't take us that much longer to reach the top."

"We have to be down and off the mountain before the sun sets," Violet adds. "Which is in five hours."

Evie pouts. "Do we have to go down?"

"Yes," we say in unison.

"Fine, but I'm coming back!"

A shocked bark of laughter flies from me. "You do that, Evie."

Violet has already taken off, dozens of feet down the mountain when she calls, "Hurry the fuck up! I don't want to be here when it gets dark!"

We sing at the top of our lungs to Taylor Swift's "Are You Ready for It?" I chuckle as Evie uses her hairbrush as a microphone.

The energy is high after finally making it down the mountain, albeit unsuccessfully by nightfall. Going up is one thing, coming back down and trying not to fall or slide is another.

By the time we even had reception on our phones, they had already died, and that's how my heart felt when I jumped inside the car and saw the time flashing on the dash.

9:18 p.m.

I had no way of contacting Xavier even if I had his phone number memorized.

The bad luck has continued. The first time I make it to date three, and I accidentally stand them up.

Shoving the guilt aside, I focused on enjoying the time spent with my friends in the two-hour car ride it took us to get back home, and with the fast food stop, it isn't until close to midnight when we pull into the driveway.

Long past the time to invite Xavier over for our date.

Phoebe gathers our fast-food trash, dumping it into the garbage cans out front.

"I want to know how long that hike takes beginners because I actually think we flew through it."

Everyone turns to Phoebe with dubious expressions.

"Pheebs, it took us eight hours and we didn't even complete it," I say.

She waves me off, inserting her key into the lock. "I bet you twenty dollars. I'll look it up and see that it suggests twelve hours for beginners."

Violet snorts. "That's hopeful but I doubt it. We took a hundred breaks."

"More like thirty."

Phoebe swings open the front door. "Thirty breaks in eight hours is pretty good…statistically speaking."

Dumping our hiking packs on the ground I close the door behind me but don't make a move. "Phoebe, can you switch on the light? I can't see anything."

Click.

Click.

Click, click.

"I'm trying."

There's only the sound of the switch clicking back and forth in the darkness, because nothing is happening.

"What do you mean you're trying?" Evie whispers.

"I-I'm trying! Nothing is working!" Phoebe stutters, panic rising in her voice.

With my heart pounding I wrap my arms around myself tightly. "Can someone turn their flashlight on?"

At hearing the tremble in my voice, Phoebe comes to my side, wrapping her arm around me as Violet and Evie try the lights.

"All our phones are dead," Violet reminds me.

I instinctively start chewing on my nails as anxiety whirls in my chest. The feeling of a thousand bees taking flight settles, swarming my lungs until there's no more air left for me to breathe.

Phoebe rubs my arm up and down. "It's okay, Blair, it's just another power outage."

"I-I don't want to go down to the basement without any lights!" I stammer.

"God, no one does, but we can't have no—"

BANG.

A door slams upstairs, cutting off Violet's words as we all scream. My lungs cease to exist.

Thump...thump, thump.

Cautious footsteps ring out, followed by pounding as the once slow steps take off into a run.

THUMP, THUMP, THUMP.

"RUN!" Evie shrieks.

Thump.

Thump.

Thump, thump.

The moment the rushing footsteps pound against the hardwood stairs I'm spinning, turning back to the front door. Multiple sets of hands start to shove me out the door as fear makes us wail with dread.

"Someone's in the house!"

Phoebe tears across the front lawn, screaming at the top of her lungs. "Help us! HELP!"

My aching legs are forgotten as my stomach drops and adrenaline pours through my bloodstream. Forcing my legs past the point of exertion, we run for the house across the street.

Phoebe pounds on the neighbor's front door, her ebony skin ashen. "Please help us! Please! There's someone in our house!"

Tears roll down my cheeks freely as I keep whipping my

head behind me, expecting to see the assailant run out of the house. Instead, though, the front door of our house closes.

"They're still in the house! They're still in the house!" I wail.

The door in front of us swings open a heartbeat later to reveal a man not much older than ourselves ushering us inside with a phone pressed against his ear.

"I heard the screams; I've already called 911."

My chest heaves, my body shaking violently. Phoebe wraps her arms around me as we both stand shell-shocked.

"Oh my God," the man utters.

With his eyes locked on something behind us, we all turn. A light shines on the second floor of our once pitch-black house.

Violet reaches out, clutching my forearm as if to steady herself. "Blair…"

"That's my bedroom," I whisper in shock.

Someone's inside my room.

Chapter Nineteen

Red and blue lights flash, illuminating the street as not one, not two, but *three* police cars come speeding down the road, their tires screeching against the asphalt as they halt at the front of our house.

The neighbor who so kindly opened his house to us pulls us inside as who appears to be his girlfriend rushes around, handing out blankets and water. If it weren't for her, we would have all stayed rooted to their front porch, shaking head to toe from not only the cold but the fear consuming us.

Violet peers out the window, watching the officers like a hawk, as if they're the ones who broke in. I, on the other hand, have to turn away because every time my eyes slide to my bedroom window, my stomach recoils.

Phoebe continues to rattle on and on about burglary statistics. I try to zone her out but it's hard, especially as she mutters, "Home invasions happen every 30.48 seconds, equating to three thousand break-ins a day."

Trying to drown out Phoebe and her statistics, I ask, "Can I borrow a phone charger?" I'm surprised to hear my voice is hoarse.

No doubt from screaming bloody murder.

The man's girlfriend gasps. "Oh yes! Of course!" She rushes from the room and returns with multiple cords. I realize I don't know her name, nor her partner's. They couldn't be much older than us, and yet they seem more mature. Perhaps PhD students?

Shaking my head, I realize it's futile to try and get to know them. Anything they say will go in one ear and out the other. My mind is too preoccupied with the events of tonight.

"I hope you all have Apple products," she mumbles nervously.

Looking into her heart shaped face, kind eyes and brown hair I make a note to come back and thank them when my mind stops rethinking the same thought.

Someone was inside my bedroom.

"Thank you," we say in unison.

My hands tremble so violently it takes me six times to try and plug the small charger into my phone's port. Once the little Apple icon appears, I heave a sigh of relief.

But once it turns on, I stare blankly at my contacts.

I don't have anyone to call.

The only people I ever would are sitting next to me in this room.

The loss of my sister and parents opens up like a black hole inside my chest all over again, sucking all the air out of my lungs, as I'm hit with just how alone I am in the world.

Not a single family member to call.

Not even a distant cousin.

My throat constricts, my eyes burning from the unshed tears I try to hold at bay, but before I know it my thumbs are moving of their own accord as I type out a harried text message.

I'm not sure what possessed me to type the message, let alone send it.

For all Xavier knows I blew him off and now I'm texting him when something horrible happened only after two dates. We didn't even get to make it to the third.

Violet scrambles off the couch, throwing the blanket that was wrapped around her shoulders to the ground. "They're coming over here."

Knock, knock.

The couple who's taken us into their home opens the door and lets the officers inside after exchanging words in hushed tones. When the woman's eyes slide to us, a flash of surprise alighting her face, there and gone in an instant, my back straightens.

The next ten minutes are a whirlwind of activity, one I spend in a daze. Moving throughout the motions as if a zombie, not in control of my own body.

My limbs are heavy as they drag me down the neighbor's front steps and across the street, back to the house that's now filled with light from the switches that turn on when you use them.

Words are uttered, so many that it's hard to keep track of them all, especially as two sentences repeat in my brain like a chant that I cannot banish.

No one was inside the house.

No signs of forced entry.

Violet's face turns red with anger as she explains what happened to any police officer who will listen. And those who won't, she *makes* them.

If it weren't for the girls hearing and seeing all that I did, I would begin to believe I was crazy. How can someone break into your house without leaving a trace?

I know what we heard. A person doesn't just imagine someone running in their own house.

Not to mention the power failing, only for my bedroom light to shine in our faces as if to taunt us—taunt me.

A car comes screeching to a halt right as the officers try to get us into the house. Garret jumps out of the beat-up pick-up truck that he's had since high school. He doesn't stop running until Phoebe's in his arms, and the moment they touch, she crumbles like dust.

Sobbing into his shirt, she mumbles incoherent sentences, yet he's still able to piece it all together. With Phoebe in his arms, he turns to the officer. "There were no signs at all?"

The officer has the decency to look at us with sympathy. "Just the bedroom light on and the power cut to the rest of the house."

"Well, the girls were away all day today. Clearly none of them did it."

"I'm sorry, son, I'm not sure what to tell you. We found no forced entry and we've searched the residence top to bottom—twice. There's no one inside. We'll have this all on file in case another incident occurs." He digs his hand into his front pocket, retrieving a small rectangle card. "Here's my contact details if you wish to call."

Dipping his hat, he rounds up his men and the police leave just as quickly as they arrived.

The couple across the street says their farewells, giving

Garret their contact details for us in case we need any more help.

Once they leave, nobody dares step foot inside. Nobody so much as moves an inch.

Garret whispers soothing words of comfort into Phoebe's ear, embracing her in a hug that makes me jealous I don't have someone I can call. Especially as Evie clutches Violet despite her grimace. Standing on the outskirts with my arms wrapped around myself, I wish for someone to lean against.

"Are we going to stand out here all night?" Evie asks.

Violet pulls back from the blonde, relieved to not be touched. "Do you want to go in there?"

"Not particularly, but it's freezing out here."

With Phoebe still nestled in his arms Garret steps forward, his eyes locked on the house. "The cops searched every inch of it. No one's inside. I'll stay the night; we'll keep our phones off silent and all the bedroom doors have locks."

"Are we really going to go in there?" I ask nervously.

"It's too late to stay somewhere else and Garret's dorm room isn't big enough for all of us," Phoebe says softly.

Easy to say when *her* bedroom light hadn't been turned on.

I can't hide the sarcasm that drips from my voice as I say, "Well then, after you."

"B, come on," Phoebe sighs.

"No, I'm not going in there first and there's no way I'm staying in my room." I shudder at the thought.

"I don't want to go in first either!" Phoebe cries.

"We will all go in together!" Violet snaps. "Your bickering isn't helping matters." She turns to me, her eyes softening. "You can sleep in my room. I understand that you're scared, but it doesn't take away from the fact that we're *all* scared."

Guilt gnaws through me. "Sorry Pheebs, it's just…they were in my room," I whisper as if that's explanation enough. It must be, because she pulls herself away from Garret and wraps me in a tight embrace.

"It's okay. We will do what the cops said and get cameras."

"Fuck cameras, I want a German Shepherd."

We all turn to Evie with incredulous gazes.

She shrugs. "What? They train them to be police dogs for a reason! They're amazing guard dogs."

Despite the circumstances, Violet snorts, sending off a chain reaction of laughter.

"I think we'll just start off with cameras," Garret says, his lips twitching.

Evie huffs. "Fine, but mark my words, you will all regret not having a grizzly-trained beast."

Violet clamps a hand on Evie's shoulder, trying to move her toward the door. "Okay, Evie."

"Don't patronize me, I'm serious!"

"Who's going to train it?" I ask, and as her mouth opens to retort, I go on. "Who's going to stay home to look after it? Walk it? Feed it? Evie, we're in college. Dogs are like children; we don't have the capacity to take care of it."

Her features begin to falter, her hard resolve crumbling, and then I hit the nail on the head. "You're a medical student. When you start your surgical residency that poor animal would be completely neglected."

Wrapping a lock of long blonde hair around her finger, a sheen of silver glistens across her blue eyes. "Will I never be able to own a puppy?"

"Oh, for heaven's sake, you've gone and done it now, Blair," Violet mutters, rolling her eyes as she extends her arm stiffly to pat Evie on the back—like a dog, no less.

"Evie, you will have a puppy, just not when we're in college."

"Promise?"

Violet clicks her tongue. "Yes, now stop crying."

"What are you? Allergic to my tears?" Evie counters.

"Yes, actually, I am," Violet says, stone-faced.

Headlights turn onto our street, stopping whatever quip Evie was about to snap.

Garret steps in front of us all. "Get onto the porch."

Not having to be told twice we scramble backward onto the porch until we're all huddled together.

"Surely they wouldn't do a drive-by," Evie whispers.

"Who would be driving out this late on a Sunday? It's nearly two a.m.," Phoebe says.

I'm about to retort that it's a college town but my mouth snaps shut just as quickly as it opened.

It can't be.

A black truck that I know all too well breaks across the driveway, not even cutting the headlights before a familiar figure jumps out and sprints toward the house.

"Hendrix? What the hell are you doing here?" Garret calls.

"Xavier," I breathe.

My feet move of their own accord as if the wind itself is carrying me to him. He pays no attention to Garret, bypassing him immediately, and rushes directly to me. His dazzling blue eyes frantically rove every inch of me.

My arms lift as I hurry out, "I'm okay, no one's hurt."

At my words, his shoulders visibly deflate, but he doesn't stop coming for me until his front is plastered to mine and I'm wrapped in his warm embrace with my head cradled against his chest.

He rests his chin atop my head, breathless as he says, "I

came as soon as I could. I'm sorry it wasn't sooner. My phone was on silent. I'm lucky I woke up at all."

I'm not sure why—perhaps it's the shock or the adrenaline wearing off—but his words unravel me. As if a neatly tied bow had been holding me together all this time and his presence gently pulled the satin thread, making me come undone as my shoulders start to quake with a silent cry.

"I've got you, Blair." His hands rub my back in slow, soothing circles. "I've got you."

The sound of shuffling footsteps behind me fades into nothing but background sound as all I can focus on is *him*.

Quickly wiping away the tears glistening against my cheeks, I tilt my head back to Xavier. "Thank you for coming."

He leans down, brushing his lips against my forehead.

I'd melt into a puddle, but I hear Evie say, "*Aweeee*" behind me and it douses me with a bucket of cold water. I spin around in his arms, catching the devilish smirk playing on his lips as I do so.

Violet's brow quirks. "Are we ready to face this bitch now?"

"Yes," I say before I can change my mind.

"Let me just park my car quickly," Xavier murmurs. "I'll be right back."

Nodding, I let him step away.

Once he's out of earshot, Garret whistles. "That man is smitten, B." Phoebe beams beside him, nodding her head frantically.

A violent blush creeps along my cheeks. "You think?"

"Look at you, blushing," Evie squeals. "You like him."

"Shh!" A door slams behind me. "Can we talk about this when he's not here?"

At the same time, Phoebe and Evie pretend to zip their

mouths shut with an invisible lock, the pair pulling a snort from Violet.

Xavier's sudden appearance has lessened the tension, as if my bow wasn't the only ribbon he pulled loose. But all niceties and blushing giggles halt as Xavier bounces up the stairs, wrapping his arm around my waist and squeezing gently. "Okay, ready."

Then we all remember why he's here.

I'm not sure what's more daunting, having to enter the house again or knowing I'll have to tell the story to Xavier while being inside said house.

Garret steps forward, his hand wrapping around the door-knob, and in one fluid motion he pushes it open. The sound of its hinges squeaking has the hair on the back of my neck rising.

At least the police flicked the electricity back on to the lower half of the house and had the decency to leave the lights on for us.

There's no one in the house.

I remind myself of what the police said as I cross the threshold. Pulling up the mental images of the squad cars, I try to assure my shaking body of the sheer number of officers that searched the premises.

But a niggling feeling in the back of my mind knows we're not alone, and that whatever was in the house didn't go far at all.

"Hendrix, let's do a sweep ourselves, for peace of mind," Garret says, not waiting to hear his response.

Xavier's eyes flick down to mine. I'm not sure what he finds but it makes his lips thin. "I'll be quick."

As the pair disappear in opposite directions of the house, every fiber of my being is screaming for me to run, to hide from whatever targeted me and turned on my bedroom light.

Was it a message?

Are they taunting me?

Are they coming back for me?

Xavier bounces down the stairs, a frown furrowing deeply on his face. "Blair? Are you okay? You've tensed up."

Xavier comes over and wraps an arm around me and it isn't until he does that I realize he's right. It's as if I've turned to stone. Shaking my head, I swallow thickly, trying to force my muscles to loosen but to no avail. I remain rooted to the spot.

"It doesn't feel right," I confess.

Garret links his fingers with Phoebe's as he returns. "It's the fear and shock of what happened. It'll wear off over time."

Violet turns to Evie. "I'll stay in your room, leave the lovebirds to their own devices."

My eyes widen, a flush creeping up my neck as I glare at Violet.

Xavier dips his head again. "I'll stay with you if you want. I don't mind."

I swallow thickly, hating the smug expression that over-takes Vi's features as I turn my head and cling to the life raft he's offering me. "Please."

We all state our plan—phones off silent, doors locked, and lights on—so whoever it was doesn't come back and thinks we abandoned the house. The guys lock the house and do one final sweep, checking every nook and crevice before stating it's clear.

I give all the girls quick hugs before we separate into our respective rooms.

Xavier and I are last, trailing behind everyone as we climb the stairs. The memory of the stranger's footsteps thuds along to the beat of my rapid heart. I don't think I'll ever forget the sound.

Garret and Phoebe disappear into the closest room to the stairs, shutting the door with a resounding click, a second click ringing out seconds later as they turn the lock. Violet gives me a wink as she goes into Evie's room and Evie at least has the decency to try and hide her happiness about Xavier staying over. Her excited, twinkling blue eyes are the last thing I see through the slit of her door before she closes it, another resounding click ringing out, the second bedroom door to be locked.

Linking my fingers with Xavier's, I pull him down the hallway, stopping in front of my room at the end of the hall.

"This yours?" he asks, turning the handle before I answer.

"Yep," I say, popping the *p*.

He walks inside, his eyes roaming the roam. My entire personality is on display for him. The four walls don't simply contain where I sleep—it holds the core of who I am, practically bursting at the seams with it.

"Wow, this is huge. It's really nice, Bl—" It isn't until he's halfway through the room that he realizes I haven't stepped foot inside. "Are you coming in?"

I can't speak. My mouth opens but no sound comes out and I hate the bastard who broke in. I hate them for making me scared to speak in my own house. Making me fearful to step into my own *bedroom*.

Home is where you're meant to feel your safest, and what happened here tonight violated that safety and comfort.

"I checked this room myself, Blair. I promise, no one is in here," he assures me.

Perhaps it was the exact words I needed to hear or perhaps it's his voice, the way the deep timbre makes my muscles relax. But one moment I'm standing beyond the threshold, not wanting to ever take a step inside, and in the next breath my feet move, stepping through. I close the door behind me, the third click ringing throughout the house from the lock.

"I can sleep on the floor or bean bags—"

I stop his words in their tracks. "I blew you off and without even an explanation, the second I messaged, you came running. We can share a bed, Xavier."

His eyes spark when his name tumbles from my lips.

"I take it from the text that the break-in isn't the only story you have to share with me?"

With all the events that transpired this evening, I forgot about the hike. My shoulders droop. "There's a lot for us to catch up on."

Xavier takes a seat on the bed, stretching his arms behind his head as he nestles into my sheets. "I'm all yours."

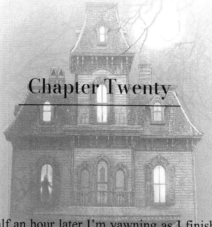

Chapter Twenty

Half an hour later I'm yawning as I finish catching Xavier up to speed on everything that transpired. The hike, our missed date, my phone dying, the moment we came home to someone in the house, and, what scares me the most, my bedroom light.

Xavier's turned toward me, propping himself up with a fist. I'm nestled into my warm sheets, wearing my favorite matching pajamas, while he stays lying on top of them.

He insisted on it.

"That's why you were hesitant to come in here."

I bite my lower lip. "It felt…targeted, you know? Why only turn on my light?"

"I understand why you feel that way, but for your own sanity, I'm going to say it was probably random."

A humorless laugh barks out of me. "My bad luck continuing?"

"I told you, you are a menace to society."

I playfully slap his arm, my cheeks flushing as my hand connects with the warm, hard muscles of his bicep. Cursing

my genetics and the vibrant red blush that I *know* matches my hair, I lower my eyes.

"I'm sorry about our movie date," I say instead, changing the topic.

"It's okay, we can do it next week." Two of his fingers slide beneath my chin, lifting my head until my eyes collide with his. "I love it when you blush. Don't hide it."

If he wanted me to blush further…mission accomplished.

His fingers trail down my neck, not stopping until they rise over my shoulder and move down my arm, the languid glide halting when he gets to my hand, only to link his fingers with mine. "How do you feel?"

If it weren't for the question I would have stared at our joined hands like an imbecile. Instead, the question draws a heaving sigh from me as the weight of it all presses down upon me. "Weirdly violated." I shrug. "This is my space, and someone invaded it without my permission."

"I wish I could say something to comfort you, but I can't begin to imagine how you're feeling," he says sincerely.

I nestle further into my sheets. "I don't even know what to say."

Silence descends as I look up at my ceiling. The night-lights I found shoved in my bedside table are now plugged in and beaming a beautiful pink and yellow glow across the room.

"Would you rather…have hotdogs for fingers or cucumbers for legs?" Xavier asks, his tone serious.

I turn my head to him with barely restrained laughter. "What kind of question is that?"

He shrugs innocently. "One that will distract you."

My lips twitch up into a smile as I say, "Hotdogs for fingers."

And Xavier continues to distract me, asking me a hundred abnormal this-or-that questions until I fall asleep to the sound of our low chuckles. With my head on his chest and his arm wrapped around me, I forget for a moment that a stranger was walking in my bedroom mere hours ago.

I'm jolted awake but my muscles don't move. Not even a twitch.

With my body locked as tight as a statue my ears strain to hear what woke me so suddenly.

Tap.

My eyebrows furrow, my mind trying desperately to place what the sound is.

Thump.

Thump, thump.

Sleep clings to my mind, covering it with its cobwebs until—

BANG.

After the last sound it doesn't take my mind long to wake up fully or to place the noise coming from downstairs. Nor does it take long to answer the question as to why my body is frozen.

Thump, thump, thump.

My breath is stolen from me, sucked into the endless tension that fills my room as heavy footsteps clunk around downstairs.

Thump.

Thump.

As the sound grows in volume it jars my body, shaking it from its immobile stupor.

My arm flies out beside me, my hand whacking aimlessly until it connects with Xavier's form. Once it does, air flows through my nose and into my lungs.

The release of oxygen comes with a swell of relief filling my chest but only for a moment, a second, because the sharp intake of breath is cut off by—

THUMP.

My chest begins to rise and fall rapidly as more footsteps ring out.

Thump, thump, thump.

A whimper of fear tries to tumble from my lips, but I smack a hand over my mouth to stop it. Without taking my eyes off the bedroom door across from me I begin to shake Xavier.

"Xavier, wake up!" I whisper as softly as I can manage. "Xavier, please wake up."

Long black eyelashes flutter as his lids open, glassy confusion marring his features before they collide with my stricken gaze.

The drowsiness of sleep is wiped off his face in an instant. "What's wrong?"

I point to the doorway with my free hand as my other puts my forefinger over my mouth, signaling him to be quiet.

My ears strain as Xavier does the same, tilting his head to the side. Three seconds is all it takes for him to hear.

Thump.

Thump.

Thump, thump.

Xavier's jaw drops, his eyes growing comically wide as his face turns ashen.

"It's probably Garret," Xavier whispers, his voice taking on a slight tremble.

"Walking around in the middle of the night with boots on?" I shake my head. "It's not him."

Thump, thump, thu—

Ding.

My phone pings, the sound making my heart lurch violently as the footsteps downstairs halt abruptly.

Scrambling to my bedside table, my fingers shake as I flick it to silent mode. It's a text from Phoebe.

Swallowing thickly, my fingers hover over the keyboard.

THUMP, THUMP.

Xavier, halfway out of bed, stops moving entirely as the footsteps pick up once more and grow closer, moving *up the stairs*.

Thump.

My chest constricts.

Thump.

My throat tightens.

Thump.

My eyes burn with unshed tears.

Xavier's horrified eyes snap to mine, and he wastes no time dragging me out of bed, physically hauling me up from under my arms and carrying me swiftly to the bathroom. He places me down on the tiled floor. My heart hammers in my ears as the steps draw closer.

Thump, thump.

Xavier moves away, picking up the bat Violet left in my room from the ding dong ditchers. His thick hands wrap around the metal right as a loud thud descends over the hallway, the footsteps stopping atop the landing.

THUMP.

Xavier stands in front of me, his back rippling with tension. He doesn't take his eyes off my bedroom door, not even for a second. Because the footsteps start up again and they don't stop at Phoebe's door, or Evie's, or Violet's empty room.

Thump.

Thump.

Thump.

The footsteps grow impossibly loud, matching the rhythm of my hammering heartbeat as I cling to the back of Xavier's shirt.

BANG.

BANG.

BANG.

BANG.

A small whine falls from my lips, making me release him to smack a hand over my mouth. The footsteps stop, right outside my door.

BANG.

Xavier freezes where we both stand in the bathroom doorway. The doorknob rattles.

Then it begins to turn.

"I thought you locked the door?" Xavier asks, not masking the fear in his whispered words.

My chest quivers, my breathing turning choppy.

"I did," I murmur shakily.

BOOM.

Before the words are even out of my mouth the door flies open, so fast a bloodcurdling scream rips from my chest as it slams into the wall.

Xavier moves quickly, pushing me into the bathroom with his hand already on the door to close it. Instead, he pauses.

"Close the door, Xavier!" I scream.

He ignores me. Then, his body begins to shake, slowly at first, a slight tremble in his clothing that grows into an avalanche of fear.

Grabbing his arm, I move to close the door myself, daring to peek at the intruder who—

Nothing but darkness stands in my doorway.

"W-where did they go?" I stutter.

My question is greeted with silence and daring myself to move, I round Xavier to find astonishment written across him. His wide eyes look past me to the open doorway.

Gently placing my palm on his cheek, I turn his head to me. "Xavier, breathe."

As if my words commanded him, he inhales sharply, the shock broken as he stutters, "T-there was no one. The d-door —my God, the door—opened on its own."

My brows furrow. "What?"

Before he can answer me, music fills the house.

My head slowly turns to my open bedroom door as if my eyes can see all the way down to the living room where the music swells, a shrill crescendo filling the house's hallways.

It comes to a piercing climax, taking with it my heart as it quickly plummets.

What Xavier said seconds before doesn't seem so farfetched, especially not as Evie's disturbing vinyl plays its melody of horror. Dread builds within me to an all-new high.

I go to move away from Xavier, but before I can take another step, he wraps his arms around my waist and stops me. "Don't go down there."

"Did you see anyone open the door?"

He swallows thickly, the words trapped in his throat forcing him to answer with a shake of his head.

Linking my fingers with his, I drag him into the hallway, my heart in my throat as I call for the girls to come out. Evie and I lock eyes and by the look on my and Xavier's faces, the truth of the situation makes her face crumble.

Shaking her head in disbelief, she breathes, "No."

"No one was in the house," I whisper.

"Of course someone was in the house!" Phoebe says dubiously. "We all heard their footsteps!"

Before I can respond Xavier chimes in, his voice full of disbelief. "They walked right up to Blair's door and swung it open but…no one was there."

Licking my suddenly dry lips, I can't peel my eyes off the staircase as I say, "We didn't even hear them retreat to the living room to turn that thing on."

Violet, a shell of herself, sways where she stands. "I threw the vinyl away."

Evie gapes. "What?"

Violet ignores her, locking her gaze on mine. "After Evie's meltdown, I threw it away. I didn't want her to get upset the next time she saw it, so I threw it in the trash." Her lip quivers and the fear I see shining in her dark eyes has me leaning back into Xavier's warmth. "It was trash day. That vinyl shouldn't even be in the house."

The music stops abruptly.

Yelps tumble from our mouths as we wait for the sound of boots, but they never come. Instead, red and blue lights fly down the street, illuminating the bottom of the stairs.

Chapter Twenty-One

fter the police leave with quizzical expressions, giving us another pep talk about no forced entry or signs of a break-in and probably believing we're crazed college students, we all stand huddled in the living room with various expressions of shock, fear, and dread.

Violet hasn't stopped staring at the record player sitting atop the mantel with the vinyl held within it. The very one she said she tossed.

"We should sue," Phoebe all but growls.

Evie and I exchange glances before I laugh nervously. "Phoebe, you can't sue Avalon Police Department."

Phoebe turns, jutting out her hip. "And why can't I?"

"There's nothing to sue over."

Phoebe sputters. "We've had someone break into our house *twice* now! And they barely glanced around the house the second time." She crosses her arms over her chest, anger flashing in her eyes. "They're not doing their job."

Garret wraps an arm around her shoulder. "Babe, they searched the house top to bottom. If there was something to find they would have found it, and besides Xavier and Blair—"

Phoebe's hand flashes up, cutting off Garret as her eyes zero in on Xavier. "I do not care what you think you saw." She softens when she turns to me. "Someone is messing with us, and the police are doing nothing to stop it."

I bite the corner of my nail, my hand instinctively raising. "Xavier said no one was behind the doo—"

"Did you see it?" Phoebe cuts me off.

"What?"

"Did you see the door open on its own?"

As her eyes narrow on my nail biting, I rip my hand away, only to end up anxiously wringing them. "No," I answer hesitantly.

Triumph flashes across Phoebe's eyes as she pivots back to Xavier. "You were half asleep; you don't know what you saw."

"With all due respect"—Xavier looks toward Garret for support, who shrugs helplessly—"I know what I saw. The door flung open on its own. There wasn't—"

"No!" Phoebe interjects. "Doors do not open on their own! You were sleep deprived."

Garret winces, peering at Xavier as if to say, *I'm sorry.*

Evie steps up beside me. "Phoebe, do you maybe think there's some truth in what—"

"No," she says defiantly.

We're going to get nowhere with her. I can see it in the set of her shoulders, the way she's squaring off as if preparing to debate for hours. Denial is a blessed thing; it can help you work through emotions your brain isn't equipped to process yet.

However, denial is beyond frustrating to those around you.

"Think whatever you want, Phoebe, but just know that when it comes for you"—I pause, watching the way she seems to gulp—"I won't look you in the eye and accuse you of lying."

Betrayal strikes. I watch the moment it happens and I instantly want to take back my words. Pluck them from the air and swallow them back down.

But I can't.

"I'm not saying you're lying," she says softly. "I'm just saying that doors do not open on their own."

"No, they don't," Evie agrees. "People and things do."

"What do you mean *things*?" Garret asks, his expression far more open than his girlfriend's.

Evie's gaze slides to Violet, who still stands comatose over the record player, the very sight of it hypnotic to her.

"I don't think it opened on its own. I think a ghost is messing with us," she says simply, returning her gaze to pin Phoebe to the spot.

Phoebe sputters out a laugh devoid of humor. "There are no ghosts in this house, Evie! Ghosts do not exist outside of your movies."

My body tenses the moment the air crackles between the two.

I *hate* confrontation. I would do about anything to be as far away from this conversation.

Evie turns to Violet. "Vi, do you think it's a ghost?" she asks with a twinge of hope, as if the unusual question will shake her but she remains frozen, her eyes wide.

Xavier lays his palm on the small of my back, no doubt seeing the change within me. "I think we need to take a step back and process everything before we jump down each other's throats."

Garret chimes in, looking relieved. "Xavier's right.

We're all tired," he says pointedly at Phoebe. "I doubt any of us have gotten more than two hours of sleep. So let's talk about this again in the morning when we're all clear-headed."

Xavier's hand begins to rub circles on my lower back. "Until then, I have a buddy who works at a security company. I'll call him tomorrow and order some cameras to be installed for you guys."

Garret dips his chin. "Luke's Dad's company, right?"

"Yeah." Xavier turns to me. "Luke is on the team with us."

The tension in my shoulders lessens at Xavier's offer. "Thank you," I whisper hoarsely.

Garret turns to Phoebe, squeezing her shoulder gently. "Cameras will be good, Pheebs."

Phoebe doesn't say anything, not even a goodnight before she spins and drags a sheepish Garret up the stairs behind her.

Bang.

Her door slams moments later, followed by the sound of her bedroom door locking.

Little does Phoebe know that my bedroom door was locked and yet it somehow still opened on its own. Locks, apparently, mean nothing in this house.

No matter that the sky is beginning to turn from black to gray, the moon making its descent as a new day begins, the fear running havoc through my body doesn't lessen.

Four hours after the police left, four hours after my bedroom door flung open on its own, and four hours after my friend's outright denial of what's happening in this house, I haven't closed my eyes for a moment.

Xavier hasn't slept either. We've spent the last four hours talking, clinging to the normalcy of conversation as we asked each other questions, and despite the past twenty-four hours weighing heavily on my mind and body, my skin prickles for another reason than fear.

The soft wisp of air that blows across my cheeks every time Xavier turns his head to talk to me and the deep timbre of his voice sends chills throughout my body.

His voice is rough around the edges, exhaustion trying to drag him into unconsciousness, but he seems to refuse, keeping his eyes on me instead. It's the most beautiful sound I have ever heard. One that replaces the memory of the vinyl playing its horrendous melody, and because of that, I keep asking question after question.

"What was it like? Growing up without siblings?"

Isabella and I were inseparable, despite our two-year age gap. My mom used to say we were best friends the moment she brought me home from the hospital.

"What people with siblings seem to forget is that as normal as it is for you to have siblings, it's just as normal for those without." He shrugs. "I mean, sure, from time to time you see your friends with siblings and get jealous of the bond and banter, but I think I get that through my teammates."

I'm thankful for the darkened sky and its ability to hide my blush. "I guess I'm just curious what it was like growing up in your house…if it was quiet."

He snorts. "My house wasn't a quiet one, especially not when my mom was around."

"Were you close with your mom?"

Xavier stiffens, but only for a moment. His body deflates with a deep sigh, growing lax beside me once more.

"No."

Turning over onto my side, I face him. My eyes trace over the silhouette profile of his face, the way his nose runs down in a straight line and curves slightly at the end. The tick of a muscle in his jaw as he clenches. The thick black lashes that flutter as he blinks.

As he turns toward me, his eyes appear to change to a shade closer to green as the nightlights glow around the room.

"I've always been closer to my dad, even before she passed." His forehead crinkles as his brows lower. "Let's just say my mother didn't win any parental awards."

My heart pinches. "I'm sorry."

He shrugs, the movement rustling the sheets beneath him. "No matter how horrible she was...I always clung to a sliver of hope that she would work on things." His swallow is audible. "It was the one thing my father and I always argued about. He was harsh but I suppose he just wanted me to see her for who she was."

"And who was she?" I dare to ask.

"A drug addict." He pauses and seems to gather himself before continuing. "No one outside our house would be able to guess, but once you were inside, it was obvious. Valium was her choice, one that she continued to pick over me."

His voice drops, making my heart ache for the pain in his admission.

"The pills made her languid, lazy. I'd always have to make my own food because she'd doze off and burn it. Could never iron my clothes when I was younger for the same reason too. It drove my dad insane, but he tried...tried to get her help and fix her but it was no use. Her depression dug her a hole she couldn't climb out of.

"I couldn't even have friends over because of how disgusting the place would be once I got home from school.

My father and I would always have to clean up after her messes after she took one too many pills." He shakes his head. "He used to say that my mother had one true love and that wasn't her son or husband, but her precious pills."

I couldn't imagine having a parent that didn't love you. I loved my parents equally; they were amazing in every way. Sometimes it feels like I was given the best because they were always going to die when I was young.

As if the short years I had with them had to be packed full of love and laughter. With memories worth cherishing until I grow old and wrinkly.

"I don't know how it feels to grow up with a parent who isn't there for you, so I'm not going to try and soothe something I don't know how to heal," I say gently. "But I do know grief and I know that no matter the person or relationship, you are always left with unanswered questions."

Xavier falls silent, whether he's stewing over my words or thinking I'm a heartless bitch I don't know. As the seconds turn into minutes, I fear he's fallen asleep, until his voice cracks throughout the room like thunder.

"I know she was a horrible mother. She was always high and never present but..." His hand stretches out, his fingers tracing patterns up and down my arm that lies between us. "Sometimes I daydream about what my life would look like with her still here. Whether she got sober...whether she left."

"The what-ifs would drive any sane person mad," I say gently.

I don't realize he was holding his breath until he lets it all out in a rush. "Do you have what-ifs that keep you up at night?"

I flop onto my back, understanding why he's changing the subject and putting a spotlight on me and yet hating it all the same.

"Every day," I answer honestly. "Losing my parents was like being violently woken from a dream. All of a sudden, I was plunged into a different reality, one without happiness or light. It felt as if my entire world turned bleak and gray."

Xavier grows impossibly still, waiting for me to continue.

I focus my gaze on the ceiling, watching as the first rays of sunshine begin to stream through the window. Mixing and mingling with the nightlight colors.

"But I had my sister." I laugh a humorless chuckle. "You call me Sunshine but...my sister was a pure ray of it. She would light up any room she walked into. Despite all we had lost, and the immense amount of responsibility thrown upon her shoulders to take care of me at only eighteen...she refused to lose her spark. It was as if she clung to it for dear life to spite the universe for taking our parents."

I snort. "Isabella and I looked identical, the only difference being that she was shorter but...it felt like she was always the tallest person in the room. Her radiance commanded attention." My chest deflates, along with my heart. "It's why it was such a shock."

My eyes burn as tears begin trickling down my cheeks. "She never put her burdens on me, which allowed me to finish what little childhood I had left." I turn my head to the side, my tears sliding with me. "Out of all the regrets and what-ifs that keep me up at night, not seeing through her bubbly ray of sunshine is the one I loathe myself for most."

My lip trembles as my voice wavers. "If I had seen through it, seen through the mask she wore, I know I could have helped her...I could have stopped her." My chest constricts. "I could have been the person she was for me when our parents died." The emotions of losing her undo me. "She was never meant to stay strong for so long... She didn't allow herself the time to grieve and it claimed her."

"Did…did she…?"

I put Xavier out of his uncomfortable misery and whisper, "She took her own life two years ago."

Xavier sucks in a sharp breath. "Blair, I'm so sorry."

That's why I decided to study psychology. For the small chance to understand why Isabella did what she did and how her own brain drove her to take her life.

I'm not sure when it happened but the tears in my eyes fill to a point of no return, blurring everything before me. Then I'm suddenly lying in Xavier's arms, his warmth cocooning me as my heart breaks for the loss I will never be able to recover from.

What I don't tell Xavier, what I haven't voiced to a single soul, is that my sadness was so suffocating, so destabilizing and all-consuming, that if it weren't for Phoebe and her family—Garret, too—I would have never made it.

I would have joined my sister.

As unhealthy as it is, the three girls in this house give me a reason each day to not let the what-ifs get to me. To not allow the hole my sister left in my heart to swallow me whole.

Chapter Twenty-Two

"Are you sure you don't want a ride to campus?" Xavier asks several hours later, lingering by his truck.

My smile is slow to lift, exhaustion making me feel as if I'm sinking into quicksand. "I wouldn't be able to stay awake for the drive, let alone classes. As much as I hate saying this, I think it's best if I stay home for the day."

Xavier's gaze slides to the house, a pensive look overtaking his features. "Are you sure you feel safe to do so?"

I carefully avoid his question, not wanting to lie. I don't feel safe in this house, and I don't think I ever will.

"The girls are staying home today as well, so I'm not alone."

It looks as if he wants to argue, as if he wants to throw me over his shoulder and take me as far away as he can from the house, but instead, he shakes his head and frowns. "Okay, but I'm calling Luke today and hopefully I can have those security cameras up and running for you by tomorrow night."

Something tight within me uncoils. "Thanks, Xavier."

He moves to leave but before he does, he spins, striding

toward me until he stops a hair's breadth away and cups my cheek. Tilting my head toward him, he captures my lips. My body grows languid, melting into a puddle as all my worries wash away for the few moments our lips are fused together.

Until he pulls back, and reality crashes down around me.

"I'll try and get the cameras as quickly as I can."

Gripping the hand still cupping my cheek, I brush my thumb back and forth. "We're all on high alert. Nothing bad is going to happen."

Yet even as I say it, I know it's an empty promise, one that I cannot keep and one that I certainly shouldn't be voicing.

Placing a featherlight kiss against my forehead, he whispers, "Text me if anything else happens."

At my nod, he reluctantly pulls away. I stay rooted to the floor, not going inside the house until his black truck pulls away from the curb, turns at the end of the street, and disappears.

I could have gone to classes today, and although I am tired, I lied about why I wanted to stay home.

Opening up about my sister to Xavier sliced open the wounds I hadn't dared peek at. The scars across my heart that I couldn't face. Although Phoebe helped me glue the pieces back together, I never healed. Not truly.

There's been one thing that I haven't been able to face since the moment Avalon's sheriff knocked on my door and told me my sister had taken her own life.

Her journal.

"Is he coming back tonight with cameras?" Evie asks the moment I walk through the door.

"He said he'd try and get them by tomorrow."

Despite everything that has occurred, the only thing I can think about is my sister's journal. My mind is hyperfixated on it. It's as if the second I admitted to myself that I was ready, the floodgates sprang open.

Isabella never left a note, and with that decision came a lot of questions, ones that I never thought would be answered and probably never will be but…perhaps her journal can give me closure.

I go to move past Evie, my mind far away, but she stops me by wrapping a delicate hand around my bicep.

"Are you okay?"

Turning to face her, I notice the deep purple bags beneath her eyes, the way her once shiny and bouncy hair is now life-less and dull. Her cheekbones are stark against her face. Has she lost weight?

"I feel like I should be asking you that," I answer honestly. "Evie, when was the last time you slept?"

She takes a step back, wrapping her arms around herself before she shrugs. "It's futile to try. Even if I do manage to fall asleep, I'm hounded with nightmares."

With the weight of my sister's grief lying heavy on my heart and the wish I make every day that I had seen the signs…I step forward, lowering my voice. "Do you want us to all sleep together maybe? Safety in numbers?"

If it meant we could get our perky, happy Evie back, I'd put up with just about anything, even Violet's snoring.

She shakes her head. "I'm okay, B. I know the dreams won't stop until it's satisfied, and I've come to terms with it."

My heart sinks, dread coiling in my stomach as I not only frown but rear back in shock.

"Until it's satisfied?" I repeat. "Evie, what do you mean by that?"

Her swallow is audible. "I'm on coffee duty. Want a cinnamon latte?" she asks, ignoring me as she trudges past and slips on her shoes at the front door.

"Evie, what did you mean by that?" I say more forcefully.

She shrugs into a coat, acting like she never heard me as she snorts. "As if that's a real question, of course you want one!" She throws a smirk over her shoulder before calling out, "Be back soon, B!"

I'm tempted to rub my eyes and see if that changes anything because *what* just happened?

I know we're all on edge and clearly sleep deprived but what did she mean by *until it's satisfied*? Satisfied with what? Our level of fear?

Trudging up the stairs with another load of questions bouncing around my head, I'm so preoccupied with the exchange that I don't register entering my room by myself for the first time since last night, and as my eyes lock on my closet door, everything escapes me.

Slowly, I approach the walk-in wardrobe. I shove my winter coats to the side and kneel, reaching for the large shoebox that I shoved into the back corner the day we moved in here. I drop to the floor the moment my fingers connect with it.

Opening the black lid, I suck in a sharp breath as I come face-to-face with hundreds of images of my sister. It's all the pictures she had taped to her bedroom door.

Isabella loved photography and loved capturing the beauty of the world around her. She was insanely talented, and she loved life...at least until the grief of our parents consumed her.

Pushing the documentation of her life aside, my hands

shake as they latch onto a white leather-bound journal. I got it for her the Christmas before she passed. I told her to write everything about college in there for me, the lessons and warnings I should know before starting. The moment my eyes landed on the intricate floral dents in the white leather, I knew it was meant for Isabella.

My mouth goes dry as I bring it out of the shoebox, my body slumping backward inside my closet, connecting with a pile of shoes and heels that dig into my back, but I couldn't care less.

The only thing I care about is the familiar handwriting that sucker punches me and steals the air from my lungs as I open the journal and read one of the final journal entries my sister wrote.

I finally know who's been stalking me for the last six months.

Isabella's Journal Entry

I <u>knew</u> I wasn't crazy.

For months I have been questioning everything. I've questioned my own sanity and my own memory and all along it was him.

I never would have thought someone was capable of this. Not him.

I haven't told anyone what happened... All those instances...

He made me think I was going insane, made me doubt what I saw and heard with my own eyes and ears. I never told anyone because he had so thoroughly convinced me that it was all in my head, I was afraid of people thinking I was insane. I've spent the last couple of months worried someone would notice and institutionalize me.

But it was never me who needed to be locked away... It was him.

He fooled me...fooled everyone.

Not for long, though. Tonight is the Kapa Nu party and once I show everyone the photo I have of him, no one will believe him ever again.

I finally know who's been stalking me for the last six months, and I won't let him get away with it.

From: cemerson@acmail.com

Re: Midterm

Blair,

Considering I offered you a second chance out of the kindness of my heart, I'm extremely disappointed in you for not showing up for our meeting this morning.

To: cemerson@acmail.com

Re: Midterm

Professor Emerson,

I apologize. My home was broken into twice yesterday and with everything that occurred, I am not attending today's lectures. I apologize for not informing you sooner; the meeting slipped my mind.

Blair

From: cemerson@acmail.com

Re: Midterm

Blair,

I'm incredibly sorry to hear. Please take all the time you need to regain your composure. I'll see you bright and early your first day back. Please stop by my office. I'll allow my second chance to remain on the table for you.

Emerson

Chapter Twenty-Three

My hand drops the journal as if it burned me.

My entire body shakes as my sister's words pour through my mind, leaping off the page only to assault me, one after the other.

Stalked. My sister said she was stalked.

Not only that, she *knew* the stalker.

Who would have betrayed her? Her friend group wasn't small in the least—she was very well liked. Especially, as it seems in these photos, in the end too. She has her arms around so many people, so many girls and guys. Picnics, parties, frat houses, campus…she was surrounded by people constantly.

I wouldn't even know where to start. Who to question.

Why did she never tell me? I never would have called her crazy. I would have believed her, I always did. So that begs the question.

Who terrified—*terrorized*—my sister to the point that she was fearful to tell even *me*?

I don't realize I'm crying until I watch a tear drop onto

the leather journal, the one that I thought she was filling with happiness and memories.

It's why I never touched it, not wanting to see all she had lost, all she had left behind.

Swallowing thickly, I will myself the strength to pick up the journal again, and when I do, it weighs my hands down. I flick through page after page, skimming journal entries to find that she didn't start writing in it until six months before her death.

Is that why she started? To document all that happened to her? She said in the last entry that she never told a single soul, but even that would drive the most sane people crazy. Perhaps this was her outlet.

A whimper tumbles from my lips, my eyes burning as they fill to the brim with tears.

Is this the real reason she took her life? Because someone made her so fearful to live, she ended it before they could?

I slam the journal shut at the thought. Hoping it will lock away the burning questions, the unsettling truth sinking into my heart, the heaviness in my chest, and the undeniable agony rippling throughout my body.

My chest practically buzzes, vibrating like a hummingbird.

Someone pushed her to take her life. Someone took my sister from me.

I need air.

Pushing away from the journal, I leave the scattered photographs and the shoebox that contained the answers I never knew I needed for over two years and jump to my feet.

I need *air*.

My chest heaves with the oxygen my lungs don't receive.

I need to get as far away from the journal as I possibly

can. The closer I am to it the more it feels like I'm being eaten alive.

What little control I thought I had has been wiped away, stolen without reprieve, and I need a sliver of it back. I need to feel in control. Otherwise, if I'm not…it will swallow me whole.

I need to drive. I need to be as far away as I can, as far away from—

My car is in the shop.

My thoughts continue to spiral, spinning out of control as the loss of my sister rips a path through my heart like never before. I put my hands against my chest, trying to ease the grip grief has on my lungs. It feels as if it's squeezing, clutching it with all its might and it won't let up.

It won't let me *breathe*.

I *need* control.

I need to feel in control of myself again, of my emotions…of my life.

Squeezing my eyes shut, I breathe in deeply for one count of four.

One…two…three…four.

I could walk across the hall to Phoebe and show her.

You leaned against her for two years; she doesn't need to be dragged back down.

One…two…three…four.

I could clean the house from top to bottom, scrub it like I wish to scrub my brain.

You only clean when you're anxious; the girls will ask questions.

One…two…three…four.

I could go knocking from door to door and try to find babysitting gigs.

The thought of using an ounce of my inheritance right

now to pay for anything, necessity or otherwise, has bile rising in my throat.

I wait for my mind to come up with an excuse, a reason why it's not good enough but the more I ponder the idea, the better it feels. I'll get out of the house, go for a walk, and get some fresh air to clear my mind.

In the process, I can try to find a new client to earn some extra cash.

The constriction against my chest lessens a fraction, as if the fist holding it lets a finger go. The second it does, I know that it's the right decision.

With one last glance back at my walk-in wardrobe, I rush from the house with my head low to make sure no one sees my red-rimmed, puffy eyes.

Because the moment I tell them…it all becomes real.

Knock, knock.

Before I notice what I'm doing I'm chewing on my fingernail. I can practically hear Phoebe yelling at me in my mind to put my hand down. I only do so when the front door handle turns and opens a moment later.

Pasting on my friendliest smile, the withering old lady that greets me returns one of her own.

"Hi, dear, what can I help you with?"

I'm perplexed for a moment before I presume she's visiting her grandchildren.

I've been knocking all afternoon, going door to door throughout the neighboring streets but with no luck. No one who has children wants to live close to a college campus, not with the parties that are hosted at all hours of the night and day.

It wasn't until I was walking home that I remembered our little ding dong ditchers. I couldn't believe I hadn't asked our neighbors yet to babysit the little rugrats. Hopefully, I can teach them how to correctly play the game.

"I was hoping I could offer you my babysitting services." At her frown, I power on, the desperation of needing some semblance of financial freedom away from my grief kicking into high gear. "I know how much of a hassle two little kids can be and being that I live next door, I was hoping to offer their parents help." Her frown only deepens, so I up the ante. "I've been babysitting for the last six years. I have experience with all ages and I have my CPR certification."

She leans against the doorway, her small frame shrinking slightly with the movement. "That's all well and good, dear, but I'm sorry to say that there are no children here to take care of."

It's my turn to frown. "Well, of course there is. They have been throwing pebbles at my window for weeks." Her brows rise and I rush to fix my error. "I don't mind in the slightest! All children should play ding dong ditch at least once in their life."

The perplexed grandma cocks her head. She's adorable for an old person, with short curly white hair and very vivid blue eyes that can't seem to stop assessing me.

"Dear, I don't know what you're going on about. Perhaps it's another neighbor's kids."

My heart plummets, only to shoot sky-high.

There are no other children. This was my last door to knock on.

I shake my head. "I've just knocked on every door within a five-mile radius… There is no one else to ask."

The more she stares the more I realize she thinks I'm insane. She goes ahead and cements that belief by taking a slow step behind her door, moving to close it.

"Very well, good luck with your endeavors."

I move before I can think, jamming my foot in the door. The old woman's eyes widen, and her hands begin to tremble.

"Is it maybe your grandchildren visiting?"

Please let it be real.

Her frown deepens as fear gives way to anger. "Not that it's any of your business but they live in Connecticut and, no, before you ask, they haven't visited in months. Now if you'll excuse me…" She nudges my foot out of the way. "I'd like to be left alone."

She punctuates her farewell by slamming the door in my face. The click of the lock soon follows.

I should move—*leave*. But I can't.

All I can do is stare at the door and gape.

If no one in the neighborhood has children…who has been throwing pebbles at my window?

Chapter Twenty-Four

"There were never any children."

Phoebe snorts. "Of course there are children, she's just an old coo-coo lady."

"Apparently, I'm the coo-coo one." I throw my hands in the air. "There were never any children throwing rocks at my window!"

Violet plops down into her seat, one hand holding her iPad and drawing pen, the other clutching a can of Diet Coke as she assesses me. Her gaze is as piercing as our neighbor's. Perhaps Vi thinks I'm insane too.

"It could have been anyone's children," she finally says.

I shake my head adamantly. "I knocked on every door today, for blocks, trust me—"

"Why?" Phoebe cuts in.

I wave my hand in the air. "Not important." A blatant lie. "What is important is that there are no kids…anywhere. This is a college town, no one wants to raise children around beer kegs and naked streakers."

"Who the hell is running naked?"

"Phoebe! Can you focus on the important details please!"

She raises her hands in surrender. "Fine, continue on with your theory that the children all *four* of us saw throwing small pebbles at your window is...what? Imaginary?" Her eyes soften. "B, I love you, but I know what I saw. I don't see people that aren't there."

"Neither did I before I moved into this house."

Silence descends at my words.

My swallow is audible. "There are no kids. Our neighbor is the only one old enough living near us to even have grand-children and she said they haven't visited in months. *Months*," I emphasize.

"No one?" Evie whispers.

"No one. Unless they popped out children when they were twelve or thirteen...which is highly unlikely."

Violet's sleek brows rise. "What do you think it was then?"

Her question shocks me and all I'm able to utter is a measly, "What?"

"What do you think it was then?"

Phoebe scoffs. "Are you seriously entertaining this?"

Violet slides her incredulous eyes to Phoebe. "I know you've chosen denial but after what has occurred in this house, I'm no longer blind. We all saw those children, but now that we want to find them they're suddenly missing and not a single person has seen children living in this area?" Violet snorts, yet it holds no humor. "I'm beginning to think the crazy ones are those who don't think this house is haunted."

Phoebe glares. "Oh, so now *I'm* the insane one because I'm trying to think rationally?"

"Guys, come on," Evie tries to interject. "There's no point in figh—"

Violet stands. "How can you experience and see all that we have and think differently?"

"Maybe because I'm not insane?"

"Phoebe, stop," Evie begs.

Violet sneers. "Call me insane one more time—"

"SHUT UP!" I snap.

Phoebe's eyes widen as Violet stumbles backward at my outburst. I've never once raised my voice at them...not at anyone. I don't lose my temper.

"This is what it wants," I say hoarsely.

"Blair's right," Evie whispers. "It continually pits us against each other—moving important objects, going against what we wish, and making it look like one of us did it."

"Do you guys hear yourself?" Phoebe asks. "You're talking as if it has a mind of its own, as if—"

"This isn't something that *isn't* intelligent, Phoebe."

Violet shrugs. "I don't care about intelligence. All I know is that too much has happened that can't be explained."

Phoebe stares at us, gaping. "Are we seriously considering ghosts right now?" She turns to me. "Ghosts."

I shrug, not being able to hide the sarcasm in my voice as I say, "I'm open to suggestions that don't include faulty wirings."

Phoebe looks at me incredulously. "Do you really believe ghosts are real?"

A snippet flashes across my mind from the attic once again without permission.

The hand around my bicep tightens as it yanks me forward so forcefully my head snaps back.

Crying out in pain doesn't stop its movements. Instead it chuckles, low and vicious as it shoves me through the opening and growls, "You're next, Blair."

Ice scuttles down my spine, the image it's showing me so horrifying, bile rushes up my throat.

"Here's a taste of what's to come," it snarls before striking.

Quick as a whip it comes down upon me, slashing my body with what feels like rusty nails. Pain burns through me for what feels like centuries.

Until it withdrawals, the sound of my tearing flesh permitting the air as crimson blood begins to drip.

With a lump lodged in my throat, I say hoarsely, "Yes."

The silence between us stretches. No one makes a sound, not as Phoebe thinks. I watch the events pass over her features, watch everything click into place, and I even see her body stiffen, a slight tremble running through her fingers.

Until something makes a door in her mind slam shut. An air of indifference surrounds her as she builds her wall of protection against the truth.

"This is ridiculous. I'm going to sleep at Garret's tonight." She walks away without a backward glance, muttering under her breath, "Fucking ghosts."

Nobody moves until the front door closes.

I should be offended, should give in to the burning sensation running across my chest at the rejection from my best friend, but I know her reaction has nothing to do with me. Phoebe isn't ready to deal with reality yet, and considering how bleak and terrifying it is, I don't blame her.

I'm also feeling slightly relieved I didn't tell her what I found in my sister's journal. She would have clung to that for the reason I'm losing my sanity.

There are no ghosts, I could imagine her saying softly. *You've suffered a great tragedy, and this has opened up old wounds… You're using the ghosts as a distraction.*

I almost snort out loud.

Violet clicks her tongue. "What now, ghost girls?"

Evie groans. "For the love of—please don't be nick-naming us or the ghost."

"Why not?" She shrugs. "Makes it less scary."

The memory from earlier floats to the surface of my mind, dancing around the edges of my consciousness as if to tease me.

I shudder. "Nothing will make this less terrifying, and certainly not a nickname."

Evie chews her lip. "Does anyone know what to do in this situation?"

Violet sniffs out a laugh. "I'm no *Ghostbusters* fan, but I'm pretty certain their techniques wouldn't work."

Refraining from rolling my eyes I let my mind take me on a path more helpful. "Did you find anything else in your research about Palo Santo?" I ask.

"Palo what now?" Vi chimes in.

"Palo Santo." Evie waves her hand in the air, dismissing Violet's question. "Long story. Besides, it didn't work."

We thought it did for *weeks*. It had us fooled.

"Was there anything else in the forums?" I ask again, redirecting Evie's attention.

She grows quiet, pensive as she thinks. I'd grab a soda while we wait but I'm too terrified to go anywhere in the house alone now.

I can't believe no one has seen those children. After the encounter with our neighbor who I now know as Mrs. Adler, I went knocking again and despite the annoyed looks I received by knocking on random strangers' houses for the second time that day, they were all more than happy to inform me they had never seen a little boy and girl in the area, nor knew any.

I'd think it was impossible—someone has to have children somewhere—but with the campus only five minutes away it isn't that shocking.

So who the hell has been throwing rocks at my window? If I was the only one who saw them, I'd be checking myself into a psych ward right this moment, but I wasn't. We all saw them—even Phoebe.

I asked for a distraction after reading my sister's journal entry and I certainly got what I wanted.

"We need to know what we're dealing with," Evie says, pulling me from my thoughts.

Violet rolls her eyes. "We know this already."

"No." She shakes her head. "We need to know who we're dealing with… We need to go back to Campbellton's haunted house."

"What the fu—"

"Are you insane?" I cut Violet off. "The absolute last place we should go is back to *that* house."

"We're already dealing with one haunted house and you want to collect another?" Violet chides.

Evie folds her arms across her chest. "The house isn't haunted…at least, I don't believe so."

"What are you getting at, Evie?" Vi says.

Evie peers over her shoulder before leaning forward and whispering, "I think the ghost followed us from Campbellton." Evie's eyes quickly slide to mine before they lower. "I think something attached itself to Blair when she was attacked in the attic."

My heart drops as they both turn to me, their eyes assessing as if the ghost is clinging to my back, digging its nails into my flesh and—

"No, that's insane. It's unrelated."

Violet shrugs before leaning back once more. "I don't know, B, I think it makes sense."

"It's too large of a coincidence for it *not* to be related," Evie says slowly.

"Can that even happen?" I huff. Evie's slow nod has my chest deflating. I cross my arms. "Then I'm certainly not going back."

"We need to learn about the house's history and who could be haunting us," Evie counters.

I scoff. "Well, it's a good thing we have something called the Internet."

Violet stands, pacing the room as the possibilities begin to suffocate the room. "No harm in seeing what we can learn first. Blair's right, everything is on the Internet nowadays, and worst case, we can call that wacky tour lady and ask her questions."

"First of all, she's not wacky." Evie holds up her finger as Violet opens her mouth to no doubt shoot off a retort. "And secondly, if we want answers, we should just go to the source."

"Why do you want to go back there so badly?" I ask, not able to hide the suspicion from my voice.

Evie frowns down at herself, a quizzical look entering her eyes. "I'm not sure."

Violet claps. "Okay that's it, everyone out. This house and that thing are getting to our heads. We can research in the library."

"I have a better idea."

"Ruby's Diner? Really, Blair?" Violet snorts. "You're addicted to the paninis."

"If I'm going to spend the next several hours researching a ghost that's haunting us and its sordid past, then I want good food."

Evie pops her head between Violet's two front seats. "Blair has a point."

Evie's complexion has already improved on the short ten-minute drive to the diner. The house truly is affecting her. Sliding my eyes to Violet, I note the small bounce in her leg and the incessant taps of her fingers.

The house is affecting everyone.

Sighing, I shove open my door once Vi parks. "Let's just get this over with."

Chapter Twenty-Five

Two and a half hours, one chicken panini, two bowls of shared fries, and a hot chocolate later, my mind isn't the only thing ready to burst.

"And I thought the house was driving me insane! I actually think this is worse!" Rubbing my temples, I tick off on my fingers. "Some claim it's haunted because it was once an insane asylum, others say murder, brothels, a motel...the mafia." Rolling my eyes, I slump back into the booth. "Nothing in any of the stories matches up... How is that possible?"

Evie pinches the bridge of her nose. "I'll have to call Sally."

"Who?" Violet asks around a mouthful of fries.

"The tour guide."

Violet clicks her tongue. "I'll get the check."

It's one thing for Violet to believe ghosts are haunting our house, it's another to get her to sit and actively listen to ghost stories for this long. Evie and I lost her twenty-five minutes in and she's been scrolling on her phone ever since. I'm not surprised she volunteered to get the check; she'd do anything to leap from this booth.

"What if Sally's version is incorrect?"

Evie sighs. "It shouldn't be. You can't work there for years without knowing the history of the house."

Frowning, I mull over our tour, my memories *before* the attic. "Why weren't we given a history of the house?"

Evie starts shoving her laptop into her bag and I mirror her movements as she whispers, "That I would love to know."

Violet saunters over to the booth, snatching her keys before throwing over her shoulder, "Hurry up bitches, we have a ghost hunter to call."

Evie chuckles. "She's a haunted house tour guide, not Aaron from *Ghost Adventures*."

"I just think she's the crazy lady that got excited whenever I was attacked," I mumble under my breath, following the girls out of the diner.

As I slide into the back seat, Evie and Violet sit in the front, a phone already lying in Evie's palm. As the last ring sounds a perky voice comes through the speaker.

"Sally's Spooky Adventures, how can I help you today?"

Evie's face lights up. "Sally! It's Evie Prescot, how are you?" Evie's glowing smile stays glued to her face as if Sally can see and will be nicer because of her peppy attitude.

Sally pauses on the other line before stuttering, "E-evie, I'm pleasant. How are…things?"

Sally is probably halfway to having a heart attack right now. When Evie pulled me out of the attic, all Sally cared about was not being sued. I wonder if she's added bodily harm to her consent forms.

Evie ignores her question. "I was actually wondering if I could ask a few questions about the house?"

"I'm not so sure if that's the best idea, all things con—"

"Considering Blair was attacked? Yes, well, I have the belief that because she was attacked you wouldn't mind helping us out... Isn't that right, Sally?"

Violet's eyes widen, mirroring my own before we both slap a hand over our mouths, trying to contain our shock.

Violet quickly mutes the call. "Way to go, Evie!"

"After all the ghost stories we heard today I don't want to go back to that house, and we need answers." She quickly unmutes right as Sally concedes.

My eyebrows jump practically into my hairline. *That* is what made her refuse to go back? Not the actual ghost haunting us?

Sally sounds resigned as she says, "What do you want to know?"

"Full disclosure?"

She sighs, her saleswoman voice dropping. "Full disclosure, but hurry up, I only have ten minutes."

"When did the hauntings start?"

What sounds like the shuffling of papers comes over the line before a chair squeaks.

"The first documented incident was in 1932."

That's not that long ago... For some reason, whenever I think of a haunted house, I think of centuries ago, and by the surprised flicker on the girls' faces I'd guess they feel the same.

Although it almost was a hundred years ago.

"We've tried researching why the house is haunted and everyone—"

"Says a different story," Sally cuts in. "I know, that's the working of the Campbellton Police Department."

A stunned silence fills the car before Evie blurts out, "Why?"

"The hauntings started after a tragedy in the house occurred involving the Merlington family." Sally's sigh is heavy before she goes on. "The case went cold and with the paranormal activity in the house increasing every year as owners came and fled, it started to become a phenomenon. The police were sick of nosy people believing they could solve the case and so they decided to—"

I can't stop the words from pouring out of me. "Spread false stories to bury the case?"

Evie's eyes widen as Sally asks, "Blair?"

My cheeks flush. "We need to know what happened in that house, Sally."

"I'm sorry, I really am, but even I don't know the case details. They've truly buried it so deep that even the locals aren't sure which story is true or false. Those that were around are all long gone."

"Do you know anything at all?" Evie asks, her patience wearing thin.

Violet bites the inside of her cheek as she pulls out her phone, her fingers moving furiously over the screen. Evie and I turn to each other with quizzical expressions until Sally's voice fills the car once more.

"There is one fact that seems to be consistent among the locals."

We wait. Even Violet pauses her typing as we hold our breaths.

"The youngest boy, Liam Merlington…" Sally pauses as if she needs to compose herself. "He witnessed such an atrocity in that house that he was said to have died from terror."

"What a load of bullshit," Violet declares, sauntering into the house.

"Do you think she was trying to scare us away from suing?" Evie asks hesitantly.

A short burst of laughter explodes from my chest as I grab us all a can of soda before joining the girls in the living room. It's as if there's an unspoken agreement to not go upstairs.

"Maybe one of the police's false stories got nestled in her head. Honestly, who knows." I crack open my can of Coke and take a sip before continuing. "I feel like we just wasted our entire afternoon."

"Not necessarily," Violet says, her head still buried in her phone.

Evie throws herself down onto the couch. "Who the hell have you been texting this whole time?"

"Zach."

Evie mirrors my frown. "Who's Zach?" I practically pout. "What happened to Cat from the tattoo parlor? You were so smitten!"

Evie hides behind her can of soda, chuckling as Violet lifts narrowed eyes to me. "One, I am not smitten. Two, I am not interested in Zach." She smirks. "I'm interested in what he can do."

Evie gags. "Not helping your case."

"Get your mind out of the gutter." Violet rolls her eyes as she puts her phone down. "Zach is a hacker I met freshman year."

"How do you just *meet* a hacker?"

"And why do we care what he can do?" Evie adds.

"You'd be surprised. A lot of gamers become coders and hackers," Violet answers, ignoring Evie's follow-up question.

Evie's blue eyes narrow. "Since when did you even game?"

"We're getting off track," she deadpans.

"Okay, put us back on track. What exactly do we need Zach to hack?" I ask, taking a sip of my Coke.

The soda nearly flies from my mouth as I choke at Violet's next words.

"The Campbellton police database. More specifically, the Merlington's files."

From: cemerson@acmail.com

Re: Midterm

Blair,

I've tried to be cordial and I wished to not speak of this over email but seeing as you've missed two of our scheduled visits, I must inform you that your assignment was flagged for plagiarism.

If you wish to explain yourself, I'll see you in my office tonight at 6 p.m. sharp.

Emerson

Chapter Twenty-Six

The more I read of Professor Emerson's email, the further my brows furrow. A quick glance to the top of my phone screen tells me it's 5:32 p.m.

"Guys, I have to go to campus really quick." Snatching my purse from the front hallway, I call out, "This isn't over though!"

The door slams behind me from the wind. Tucking myself in tighter in my coat, my thoughts whirl as I begin to seethe.

The walk to campus only takes me fifteen minutes tops and yet I spent the entirety of that time pouring over everything I wrote. Every syllable, every keystroke...it was all my own.

How could my assignment be flagged for plagiarism? How is it even possible? Did someone steal mine? Is that even a possibility?

By the time I make it to campus, my nose and cheeks feel frozen stiff as I bustle past students, hurrying to make it to Professor Emerson's office before six. This has all been a large misunderstanding that will be cleared before he marks me a zero for this assignment.

My chest is heaving from exertion as I knock on Professor Emerson's closed door.

Am I too late?

My body tenses as I hold my breath, waiting and praying that he's—

"Come in."

Sighing deeply, I open the door to find Professor Emerson sitting behind his oak desk, the white collared shirt sleeves rolled up to his forearms as he pours over the scattered documents littering his desk. He looks up, his brown eyes seeming to light up at the sight of my harried form, sending an uneasiness through me.

"Ah, Blair, I'm glad you were able to make it to our appointment this time."

It takes a special force within me not to openly frown at the man that can make or break my grade. This was not an appointment we made.

Did he forget the email he sent me?

I move to take a step forward but he halts me. "The door, Blair."

Something within me tightens with unease as I turn and close the door. The sound of it clicking into place makes my shoulders rise.

Taking a shuddering breath, I steel myself before turning. Professor Emerson makes a show of waving me to the chairs in front of his desk. My back protests at the stiffness of the material.

"You said there was an issue with my midterm paper?"

His gaze rakes over me, seemingly pausing at my jumper's hemline before he darts his focus away to the copious amounts of paperwork. Shuffling through stacks, he pulls one out that's heavily highlighted in red.

"Yes, indeed there was."

I'm forced to tip my head back as he rises from his chair and slowly rounds his desk, taking a seat in front of me against the oak, possibly trying to soften the blow by making this overly friendly.

It doesn't.

"As I stated in my email this evening, your paper was flagged for plagiarism of another student's."

My mouth drops open to dispute the horror of what just came out of his mouth but he holds up his hand to silence me.

"Don't try to lie, I've heard every excuse in the book and I do not wish to hear it again from your lips."

The way he says *lips* as if a sultry curse has my back snapping upright. "There is no possibility of that being plagiarized," I blurt. "I wrote every single word myself, and pored over the assignment for weeks. I even handed it in early."

He remains silent. I ignore the way he leans back on his hands and looks down his nose at me.

"I did not steal or copy another student's work," I emphasize.

He seems to smirk as his eyes drift over me before rising. "I've heard that line too, Miss Stevens."

The food I consumed today begins to rise as a thousand bees take flight in my chest.

"Please let me prove I didn't steal it."

"How?"

That stumps me. I didn't think he'd allow me to do anything. I thought I'd have to hand in a mountain load of extra credit assignments to earn back the grade.

"Whose work was it flagged along with?" I ask.

"You are not privy to that information, Miss Stevens."

Before I can stop myself I throw my hands in the air in

frustration. "Then how am I supposed to prove my innocence?"

Professor Emerson puts his hands between his legs, spreading them farther until they brush mine slightly. I was so focused on pleading my case, I didn't realize how close he moved toward me.

Crossing my legs, I move them in the other direction, focusing on not failing this class as opposed to how creepy he is.

"I can show you my notes. I brought my notebook which is written by hand. I detailed my research thoroughly and it supports my case."

He shrugs, his foot inching closer to mine until it taps against my sneaker. "You could have written those notes after stealing from the student."

My jaw is clenched so hard I'm surprised my teeth don't snap. "I didn't steal another student's assignment."

"It doesn't matter what you say, Miss Stevens. The fact remains that I have two students with the same assignment and only one willing to do anything to improve her grade."

My brow furrows as I try to think of anyone who had access to my laptop to be able to steal my assignment, and who would be stupid enough to not change it.

"How much is this going to affect my overall grade?"

"It doesn't have to."

At my puzzled expression, Professor Emerson sets my supposed plagiarized assignment down behind him and leans forward. So much so I edge backward.

The moment his hand lands on my knee my heart lurches out of its cage, only to nosedive into the pit of my stomach.

It was never an accident.

None of his touches ever were.

Professor Emerson leans down farther, using my frozen

stupor against me to get closer. "I'd be happy to give you the grade the assignment is worth…but only if you make it worth my while."

My eyes flare, indignation rising within me along with anger as my body is finally freed from shock. Jumping to stand, I smack his hand away and shove his chest with every ounce of strength within me. A kernel of satisfaction hums through me as he goes sprawling backward on his desk.

At first he smirks, his gaze full of satisfaction until he sees mine and I seethe, "Don't you dare ever touch me again."

Snatching my purse from the ground with shaking hands, I bolt for the door, having to try it three times before my quivering hand gets it and I rush from the room, only to collide with a soft chest.

A groan tumbles from my lips as I crash to the floor, along with the one I ran into.

"Blair?"

The familiar voice snaps my head up and when I look up at Phoebe also sprawled on the floor, I'm shocked to feel my eyes burn with unshed tears.

Phoebe's gaze furrows as she looks from me to the door that slams behind me.

Scrambling to her feet, she helps me stand. "Come on, let's get some air."

Sitting beneath a tree in one of Avalon College's many lawns, it only takes a morbid ten minutes to describe what feels like the most violating ordeal.

"Oh Blair..." Phoebe says softly. "You must report him. If he did that to you, he's surely done it to many others."

The female student crying in his office comes to mind. Now looking at the memory, he was oddly close, his voice soft and gentle as if comforting a lover.

"I absolutely will." My body shudders at the image of his hand on my knee and how it began to travel downward. "Ugh, what a perv!"

Phoebe and I fall silent.

"I'm sorry about earlier."

Peering over at Phoebe, I find her eyes on the campus buildings but her mind far away.

More than grateful for an opportunity to not think about what just happened, I say, "I understand why you want to continue staying in denial but...it's beginning to hurt, Phoebe."

Her sigh is deep and full of pain. "I know. I'm so sorry, Blair." When she lifts her head to me, there's silver lining her eyes. "The reality of it, though...I can't deal with it. It's terrifying to know that something we can't see is terrorizing us."

"I know," I say softly.

"When I'm away from the house my mind begins to process everything but then I have to go back to that house and it's just...it's too much sometimes."

I can't help but agree with her. It is terrifying, and it's even more daunting to admit that something is happening and then willingly walking back through the front doors. I can see how it's easier to deny everything and be oblivious, but it's not letting us.

As my eyes stray to the building in front of us, my heart plummets as I watch Professor Emerson casually stroll across campus, his eyes twinkling as they connect with some female students.

Despite the conversation at hand, I find myself saying, "I want to go home."

Phoebe follows my gaze before she rises and stands in front of me, blocking not only my view of him but his of me.

"Come on, I'll drive you home," she offers.

"You're still not staying the night?"

She shakes her head slowly. "I'm sorry…I just…I need a night, Blair. Just one night where I can sleep without nightmares chasing me. I need to wake up fresh and be able to think clearly."

"I understand."

My legs are heavy with sadness, almost dragging as we walk to her car.

She pauses at the hood of her car. "Do you need me to stay though? If you need me, I will, Blair, no questions asked."

I shake my head, unable to ignore her sunken eyes. Phoebe has always been there for me, and this time, she needs me to be there for her.

"No, it's okay. Go to Garret's."

"Are you sure?"

"I'm positive, and you're absolutely right, we need you level-headed," I tease, trying to make the situation lighter.

She snorts. "I think we at least need one person in that house who has slept more than a measly two hours."

Despite the terror that overcame Phoebe's features as we pulled up to the house, she still offered to stay with me. It was harder to say no this time but Phoebe is always there for me.

She can't continue to take care of me if she can't even care for herself.

With that thought in mind I declined and rushed from the car, her promise of seeing me tomorrow morning nipping at my heels as I walked inside.

With the feeling of bugs crawling over my skin and my knee burning where Professor Emerson touched me, I race upstairs, calling out to Evie and Violet that I have homework. In reality, the last thing I want to do is explain the sordid ordeal again. Once was enough to make my stomach roll with Phoebe. I'll let her tell the girls.

As I jump in the shower and begin to scrub my skin raw I can't help but wonder what Isabella would do.

She would no doubt rage for me and storm the campus buildings requesting he was fired. He should be, but the thought of explaining it to his colleagues, who are probably his friends, makes my blood chill.

Perhaps I'll just make a formal complaint through email. Get the ball rolling behind my screen until I know someone believes me... Then maybe I'll feel okay talking about it in person when they no doubt question me.

Stepping out of the shower with red skin, I'm quick to change into my pajamas and take my laptop to my bed.

With a heavy heart I begin to type.

Chapter Twenty-Seven

"Are you insane?" Phoebe exclaims.

Phoebe's eyes have remained wide since the moment she returned to the house this morning to us all bleary-eyed after another horrendous night's sleep. It didn't help matters when Violet and Evie mumbled on about the Merlingtons, police files, and hackers. It didn't take Phoebe long to piece together the string of jumbled words.

With everything that happened last night it slipped my mind what the girls were planning to do.

"You can't hack into police files! We could go to jail for this, Violet!"

Evie rummages through the cabinets. "It's already done," she says, not looking Phoebe's way as her movements become frenzied.

"We are not going to jail," Violet drawls casually.

"Yes! We are!" Phoebe turns to Evie. "Will you stop rummaging? Our friend is getting us sentenced to orange jumpsuits."

"What are you looking for?" I ask.

"My mug," Evie growls.

Violet straightens. "Again?"

"Again."

Phoebe waves frantically in front of Violet's face to grab her attention. "Who cares about the damn mug going missing? Tell whoever your hacker is to stop."

"Can't, it's too late," Violet says flippantly, her attention glued to Evie. "Did you check the dishwasher?"

"Yes, of course I did."

"The laundry?"

"Why would it be in the laundry?" I ask.

Violet shrugs. "I don't know where the ghost hides these things."

"There is no ghost hiding things!" Phoebe cries.

"Yes, there is," we sing in unison.

"This is why we're doing it! I'm sick and tired of weird shit happening in this house!" Evie jams a finger into Phoebe's chest. "Wake up and take a look around. This is not normal, Phoebe!"

Phoebe rears back. "Evie, calm dow—"

"Do not finish that sentence."

Standing between the two before things escalate, I say softly, "Do you truly believe that what's been happening—the missing objects, lights flicking on and off, the TV playing *Scream*, rotten food, intruders that aren't there, *children* that aren't there—doesn't suggest something paranormal is happening in this house?"

I saw the fear in Phoebe's eyes last night when I asked her to come home—that's not from faulty wiring.

Phoebe's eyes flick back and forth, searching mine for what, I'm not sure.

I soften, pleading. "Come on, Phoebe, be honest with

yourself. Can you truthfully say it's not abnormal? That it might be caused by something paranormal?"

With the reminder of our conversation last night I feel like getting on my knees and begging her to face reality.

Phoebe's gaze continues to bore into mine and she must find whatever she needed to because a moment later her shoulders droop and she whispers, "I don't know what to do."

"You don't need to know right now," Evie says behind me gently. "We just need you to believe us."

"I do need to know. There is a natural order to the world, problems and solutions. Problems I can handle. Problems that do not have a definitive solution and aren't backed by science…that is something I cannot handle."

"There might be," I say hopefully.

"How?" she asks, defeat written stark across her beautiful dark features.

My body almost deflates with relief that her wall of denial is finally coming down.

Violet rounds the kitchen island. "The files."

Phoebe rolls her eyes. "Our solution is not hacking confidential police files."

"It actually is," I hate to admit, my stomach recoiling at the words.

I despise doing the wrong thing. But in this moment, I push the guilt aside and explain, "The history of the house isn't known to anyone but the locals from 1932, the original officers on the case, and the Merlington family."

"The file Zach is hacking is the Merlington case containing the details of what happened to the family," Violet goes on.

"It will explain the haunting."

Phoebe stares at us like we're animals cornered in a cage,

frothing at the mouth and going feral. "Okay, and what will knowing this do exactly?"

I peer behind me to see Evie and Violet share a look. "We didn't...get that far."

Phoebe groans. "Do you guys hear yourselves?"

I feel like shaking her and her pessimistic attitude, but I know that if the roles were reversed and I came home to them all bleary-eyed and muttering about hacking police files, I'd think they were insane too. "If we know who is haunting us maybe we can perform a ritual."

"A ritual?" she asks dubiously.

"A séance," Violet explains.

"Have you not been paying attention to the movies Evie forces us to watch? We don't know what we're doing; we could very well welcome more spirits rather than get rid of ours."

"HA!" Evie squeals. "So, you do believe there is a ghost."

"Of course, something weird is happening!" Phoebe snaps. Her chest heaves as if the words burst out of her without permission. "We all know that record was never Garret's."

My head rears back. "Who told you about the record player?"

Phoebe points behind her to a sheepish Violet, who raises her hands. "I had to know if it was Garret's or not."

"I don't blame you, I just..." I shake my head, returning my focus to Phoebe. "Even knowing all that and seeing the record that Violet threw out for yourself, you doubted us?"

"I never doubted you." Phoebe shrugs. "It's hard, okay? It's challenging to see with your own eyes something that alters your entire belief system."

As much as I want to cling to the hurt of what Phoebe's

denial has caused, my armor drops as I take a step forward
and wrap my arms around her.

"You could have told us how you felt," I say gently.

*Especially last night when she was opening up. I suppose
she wasn't fully ready.*

Phoebe drops her forehead to my shoulder, her breath
leaving her in one fell swoop as she returns the hug and
clings to me. "I didn't want to face it." She lifts her head and
I'm shocked to find her eyes lined with silver. The sight
makes my heart pinch painfully.

"I'm all for trying to get rid of this thing but can we
please not do anything illegal?"

Violet grimaces. "Sorry, Phoebe, it truly is too late. Zach
is sending the files over in an hour."

Pinching the bridge of her nose, Phoebe steps out of my
arms, yet remains by my side. "What's our chances of getting
caught?"

"Honestly?" Vi looks toward Evie, who's still rummaging
the kitchen for her mug. "Close to none, he's amazing at what
he does. I'm just surprised he hasn't been recruited yet."

Some of the tension in Phoebe's shoulders seeps out of
her. "That's good but...what the hell do we do with the information? Even if we do a séance—which I'm strongly against
because, well, horror films 101—what exactly do we say to
get rid of it?"

Evie pops her head up from behind the kitchen island.
"I'll research!"

"And if we invite more ghosts into the house?" I dare ask.

We look toward each other, sharing glances before Violet
and Phoebe say in unison, "We move."

Phoebe paces back and forth.

My gaze follows her as if I'm watching a tennis match and her form is the ball bouncing between the walls of my bedroom. I can practically *see* the indentation her feet are going to leave in my rug.

She's been like this for the last seventeen minutes. Every once in a while she'll stop and turn to me, open her mouth as if to speak, and then snap it as quickly as it opened and resume her pacing. I've tried to offer words of comfort and answer any questions she might have, but she shuts me down and just shakes her head, muttering to herself under her breath.

Over the years of growing up with Phoebe, I've learned patience is what she needs. She needs space and time to compose her thoughts and feelings, to process all that goes on beneath the surface.

And that's what I master now—patience.

My phone buzzes with an incoming text.

The X was risky but after all he's seen and endured in this house, the fact that he hasn't run away says a lot about who he is and it melts my heart. Besides, a little flirting lightens the mood considering the reason why he's installing cameras.

That, and for some odd reason, I'm nervous to tell him about how inappropriate Emerson was. Half of me just wants to wait for a response to my complaint email before I say anything. The other half physically recoils when I think about the professor and his insinuations.

Another thing my mind doesn't want to think about…the privacy we're all about to lose. Cameras in every hallway and room. I'm just grateful I talked everyone out of installing them in the bathroom. I've heard enough horror stories of cameras connected to the Wi-Fi getting hacked.

Phoebe stops before me suddenly, her face ashen. "I had a dream that this would happen."

"What? What type of dream and when?"

Flopping beside me on my bed, Phoebe lays back, groaning. "The night we returned from Campbellton."

My mouth drops open. "Before I begin lecturing you, I need to know what exactly you dreamed about."

Phoebe's eyes take on a sheen as she fights off tears. "Everything! Evie's missing mug, the rotten food, your shower door opening on its own, the headaches you get, the so-called intruder, Professor Emerson, the *Scream* movie… even the children!"

My eyes widen at her mention of my headaches. I haven't told anyone about them and when they went away after the Palo Santo I didn't see a point. They returned a few days ago but I thought that was because of Isabella's journal. I thought it was my grief manifesting physically.

"Why did you never say anything, Phoebe?" I try to keep the anger I feel rising in my chest out of my voice but it's no use. Phoebe and I know each other better than we know ourselves; it's why I'm so shocked. "We never hide things from each other, not to this magnitude."

"Well, now we do," she says, her voice dripping with sarcasm.

"No, we don't." I jab my finger in her arm, forcing her gaze to snap to mine. "You're telling me now and that matters, but I swear to God if you hide anything like this from me again…"

"I know, I'm sorry, I just got so spooked! I even started researching psychics. I thought the dream was a nightmare at first but as the events continued to unfold exactly as they did in my dream…" Her swallow is audible as the color drains from her face.

I slowly sit up in my bed as I start to suspect what could make her so terrified to speak. "Phoebe, how did the dream end?"

She shakes her head feverishly. "No."

"What do you mean *no*?"

"I refuse for our reality to end the same way my dream did, and for that to happen, I cannot utter a single word." She quickly sits up, her voice growing quiet. "I even saw this, B… I saw this exact interaction. It's as if I lived for months in that dream." She shakes her head. "I don't know what happened in the end or how…only what came of it. But trust me on this, you *never* want to know how the dream ended."

The terror and conviction in her voice make something within me fear what exactly this spirit can do and if it can cause us physical harm.

My hand snaps to my stomach, the skin tingling as if feeling the phantom pain of those three long gashes from the attic.

"Blair?" Phoebe calls, her eyes flicking from my face to my hand.

"Are you going to tell the girls?" I ask, ignoring the way she's staring at me with concern.

She shakes her head. "No. They're already upset with me for—"

"Going into denial and making us feel crazy when we spoke about it?"

Phoebe's brow quirks. "Could have said it gently...but yes, and you know Evie. She would never stop asking how the dream ended."

"I'm not so sure I won't pester you," I say honestly.

Her eyes turn pleading. "Please don't, B. For your own sanity." Her bottom lip starts to tremble, her eyes filling with unshed tears once more. "I don't want it to come true. Please don't force me to say it."

Staring into her brown eyes that plead with me to drop it I sigh. "Okay, I won't ask, I promise."

After all...we all have our secrets.

I feel my sister's journal at my back, as if it has eyes of its own and is searing a hole into the back of my skull. I lectured Phoebe on keeping secrets from me and here I am keeping the biggest secret of all. The one that kept me tossing and turning for hours, my eyes unable to close without seeing the unread pages of her journal entries. It feels like I'm violating her mind but I have to know. Did someone drive her to take her own life?

Phoebe slowly rises as I gnaw on my lower lip. "What is it, B?"

"I don't know if I'm ready to say it yet."

That makes her straighten, like her body is preparing for a physical blow. "What aren't you telling me? Is it big?"

"Huge."

"Do you want to write it down on a piece of paper?" she asks, already making her way to my desk.

It's something she's always done with me. My sister wasn't the only one who kept a journal. I've always found that putting my thoughts and feelings down on paper somehow allows me to compose my thoughts. Sometimes they're like a tornado, spinning endlessly without care for what gets picked up and thrown out until I put it down on paper, into words that I can physically see. Only then does it begin to calm its chaos.

As little as nine, Phoebe has asked me to write down my feelings. She noticed the shift in me when I was asked to express myself vocally. It's almost like I shut down, the emotions overpowering me.

Until my first journal. Until I was able to compose my thoughts and structure my garbled words.

This will be the first time I say, "No."

Phoebe stops suddenly, shocked at my answer. "Why can't you tell me?"

I shake my head. "Because it's easier if I show you."

My legs wobble as I stand, my hand trembling violently as I reach for my closet door and the shoebox within. My chest rises and falls rapidly as I pull it out, ignoring the pang in my heart as my eyes gloss over her photographs.

Returning to my bedroom, it feels as if all the blood drains from my face as I hand the journal over to Phoebe, whose brows are so low I'm shocked she doesn't feel the hair against her long lashes.

She flicks through the journal, her gaze perplexed. "Why are you giving me your journal? Do you want me to read an entry?"

Still not being able to voice the words aloud, I flick to one

of the last pages written in and tap it twice with my finger-nail, which I hate to note is bitten to the quick.

She starts reading, and I hold my breath as Phoebe's eyes widen. "I-I don't understand what I'm looking at," she stammers. "What am I reading, Blair?"

Finally finding my voice, I say, "It's not my journal."

"Whose is it then?"

"Isabella's." I choke on my next words. "Someone was stalking her."

Chapter Twenty-Eight

"I think someone drove her to take her own life. Terrorized her beyond rational thinking."

Phoebe's eyes well. Isabella was like a big sister to Phoebe; we practically shared her. We both grew up with Isabella's antics, both idolized her as if she hung the moon. I know this journal entry is hurting her just as much as it hurt me.

"I would say that I can't see Isabella doing that but…"

I smile sadly. "I know, me too."

It's why it cut so deep. Isabella's death was a shock… although *shock* doesn't even begin to accurately describe it either. I never thought Isabella would harm herself. Not once did I doubt her safety, but I wish I did. Maybe she'd be here helping us eradicate a ghost instead of me clutching her old journal.

"If this is true then we—"

My head rears back. "What do you mean if it's true? Of course it's true! Isabella wrote it herself."

"B…she could have been suffering from a mental breakdown. It would explain why she did what she did," she says carefully. I open my mouth to protest but Phoebe gently squeezes my hand. "We don't know what her mental state was before, but this shows that she was in distress and clearly something was happening." She shrugs pitifully. "Her mind could have been playing tricks on her, B."

"I know it wasn't." I snatch my hand out of hers, trying to ignore the way a flash of hurt strikes in Phoebe's eyes at my recoil. "You can think what you want but it finally all makes sense to me. Someone terrorized her and I'm going to find out who."

Phoebe's eyes search mine, flicking back and forth before she relents. She simply says, "Okay."

"Okay?"

She raises her hands in surrender. "Okay."

I don't realize how tense my body is until it seems to deflate, especially as she adds, "I'll help in whatever way I can, for Isabella."

"Thank you, I think she—"

"We have the files!" Violet calls from downstairs.

My and Phoebe's gazes collide, fear, horror, and anticipation sizzling in their depths. We freeze for a second before jumping into action and racing downstairs.

"We're not done talking about this," she whispers.

"I know."

She stops me mid-step. "You could have come to me."

"I only read it yesterday morning and I didn't want to deal with it yet."

Her brow quirks. "Denial?"

I roll my eyes. "Don't start."

"I'm just pointing out the hypocrisy," she says, a sly smirk lifting the corner of her lips.

Leaning against the railing I peer below, checking that the girls aren't near before whispering, "Trust me, I know. It's why I showed you the journal, but can we please not tell Vi and Evie yet? I just...I need to find answers first."

"I understand." Her voice grows gentler. "How are you going to though?"

"I'm going to read her entries and try to piece together what happened."

"And you think you'll be able to?"

My hands lift helplessly. "It's worth a shot. This is Isabella we're talking about... I'd do anything for her."

"Guys, hurry up! We're practically sitting on gold right now!" Evie calls.

Phoebe moves to leave but stops short. "I'll help you, B, but let's promise no more secrets between us."

"Besides the ending of the dream?"

She visibly shudders. "Besides that. Anything but *that*."

"Deal," I whisper.

"Oh my God! HURRY UP!" Evie screams again.

Racing down the rest of the stairs, Phoebe and I round the corner of the living room. Violet and Evie face Evie's computer, the former a deadly shade of white and the latter practically hovering mid-air.

"Oh my God..." Violet whispers, terror filling her words.

Phoebe takes a seat beside Violet, wrapping an arm around her before thinking better of it. Violet's never shared why she hates physical affection, nor have we asked.

Evie's hand hovers over the keyboard of her laptop, her mouth agape.

"What does it say? What am I reading?" Phoebe asks, her words eerily similar to those she whispered when I handed her my sister's journal.

"The entire Merlington family was brutally murdered in their own home in broad daylight," Violet explains.

"Butchered is more like it," Evie whispers hoarsely.

Phoebe claps a hand over her mouth. "Oh God, that's horrible."

"That's not all." Violet takes over for Evie, scrolling through the document until she lands on a page with an image of a small boy in the left-hand corner.

"This is Liam Merlington, Douglas and Arabella's youngest son." Violet's voice quivers, shaking at her next words. "He was found four days later, sitting shell-shocked in the middle of his family's mutilated bodies."

"He died on the way to the hospital from dehydration," Evie says sadly.

Violet slides glistening eyes my way. "They say he hid upstairs in the attic during the murders. They don't know how long he hid for or how long he sat in their blood but by the time they found him, the blood was caked to his little body."

"T-the attic?" I stutter.

Evie's eyes grow wide. "Do you guys think…?"

"Why would a traumatized five-year-old become an attacking ghost?" Phoebe says, every word dripping with sarcasm.

Violet frowns, her head snapping back to the documents before she hurriedly scrolls.

"What is it?" Evie whispers.

Violet doesn't answer her, ignoring all of us until her fingers suddenly halt. "They never found the murderer."

"What?" Phoebe snatches the laptop, reading the document for herself.

Evie hums. "That would explain why the Campbellton police were sick of people coming into town, trying to solve the mystery."

My brow quirks. "Not enough to spread rumors. Those officers are no better than gossiping high schoolers."

Evie gasps, turning to Phoebe's pensive face glued to the computer screen. "You think it's the murderer haunting us?"

Violet rolls her eyes. "You'd have to be a sadistic bastard to cross over and haunt people."

"Are you forgetting about the dead bodies?" I say dryly.

Evie chews on her bottom lip. "I don't think it works that way, V."

Phoebe spins the laptop in our direction, tapping on the screen. "The coroner believes the uncle slit his own throat."

Evie throws her hands over her eyes as if her brain showed her the image. "Ugh, Phoebe! Too much detail!"

"You're the one who wants to cut into people!" Phoebe cries before shoving the laptop further into our faces. "They *did* find the killer, lying amongst his victims."

Violet gasps, snatching the laptop. "Oh my God, how did I miss that?"

"What would make him snap?" I ask, leaning forward to read the report myself.

The medical examiner report notes that the wounds inflicted upon the Merlington family were caused by someone left-handed, Uncle Harvey and Liam Merlington being the only two left-handed people. Detailed reports show how Harvey Merlington's wounds appear to be self-inflicted, the knife plunged into his abdomen at an upward motion, along with very jagged, unclean slashes along his wrists and neck.

Violet leans backward. "My money's on a jilted lover."

"You can be so crass," Evie scolds. "These people were brutally murdered and you're betting money? The youngest was a six-year-old little girl. Have some respect."

Violet rubs her face roughly. "God, Evie, you're right. That was messed up, I'm sorry guys."

"Don't apologize to us, apologize to the Merlingtons," Evie mutters.

Violet rolls her eyes. "They're dead, they're not going to hear the apology."

"Where did your empathy go? Did someone zap it out of you? That was a one-eighty flip, even for you."

Violet narrows her eyes before grumbling, "I'm sorry the uncle snapped and decided to butcher the Merlingtons."

BANG.

A door upstairs slams shut.

Screams rise, along with our terror as it electrifies the room, making the hairs on the back of my neck stand up.

"What was that?" Evie whispers, her voice shaking.

"Just the wind," Violet says, trying and failing to insert calm into her voice.

The lights shining on the stairs landing flicker out.

Thump.

My throat tightens, a lump of fear rising as the hallway light leading to the basement is the next to go.

THUMP.

A heavy set of footsteps land on the bottom of the stairs, making us yelp as the lights in the kitchen go out.

One by one.

And as the room grows alive and wired, I know it isn't our terror that's fueling it, especially not as the living room lights vanish. Then shatter.

BANG.

Glass flies in all directions above our heads.

"APOLOGIZE TO IT NOW, VIOLET!" Evie screams.

"I'm sorry!" Violet cries. "I'm so sorry!"

BANG.

My throat burns as another scream rips from me. The

bang was closer than the first, and it's not a door this time. It's as if something threw a chair at the wall.

Evie whimpers. "It's not good enough!"

Tears spring to my eyes as terror clutches my heart. "What did you do, Violet?"

"I didn't mean to! I'm sorry!" she weeps.

BANG.

The girls and I jump into each other, huddling into a tight ball of shaking limbs.

"Stop!" Phoebe shrieks.

BANG.

It's moved closer, as if feeding off our screams and every sob and shriek.

"Ahhh!" Violet screams. "I won't say it again, I promise! I won't joke about the Merlingtons ever again. *Please* stop!" Violet begins to sob in earnest. "Please, I'm so sorry."

Every light in the house suddenly turns on, including the ones above our heads, basking us in bright lights that force me to squint. I blink rapidly, adjusting to the sudden intrusion, and lift my gaze to the ceiling.

The lights aren't broken.

I search around us, looking for the glass that I not only heard but *felt* shatter everywhere.

"Where's the glass?" I wheeze. "Where's the glass?!"

The room fills with the sound of our harried breaths.

"What glass?" Phoebe asks, making me pale.

"I-is it done?" Evie stutters, her focus on the hallway now illuminated and quiet.

The hairs on the back of my neck stand up, and my stomach bottoms out. That's when I know it isn't done toying with us, and that it never will be.

My body feels it coming before I do.

Every door in the house opens, then closes, one by one with a piercing jolt.

Bang.

Bang.

Bang.

Bang.

BANG.

It cuts the lights once more, drenching us in darkness and making me fear I'll lose my bladder.

Bang.

Bang.

Bang.

Liquid drips down my cheeks. Surely they're my own tears, but I'm too terrified to let go of Evie and Phoebe's arms to check. Especially as the slam of the final door seals our fate.

BANG.

I'm hyperventilating now, my breaths coming out in short puffs as footsteps sound from upstairs.

Thump.

Thump.

Thump.

It starts at my room, slow and tentative at first.

Until it breaks out into a sprint down the hall.

THUMP, THUMP, THUMP, THUMP.

"Run!" Evie screams at the top of her lungs. Catapulting herself off the couch, she drags us with her.

Thump, thump, thump, thump, thump.

It's running for us.

Evie slams into the front door, yanking on the handle.

"Open the door, Evie!" I scream.

"I'm trying! It won't open!"

There's a gap between Evie's words and our screaming,

one that lasts a millisecond but feels like a lifetime, one that gives me time to feel the reverberations beneath my feet and hear the sound of its footsteps as it comes barreling down the stairs, directly for us.

Thump.

Thump, thump.

Thump, thump, thump, THUMP, THUMP, THUMP.

"OPEN THE DOOR!" I scream, craning my neck to look the intruder in the eyes, only to see nothing but shadows.

But the steps keep coming.

Thump.

Thump.

Thump, thump, thump.

Violet's eyes are rimmed with tears spilling over as she bangs both her hands against the door. "Help us! Help us! Please, help!"

"Please open the door!" I urge, feeling exposed at the back of the group. My nails dig into Phoebe's shirt as she wails, banging her fists against the front door with all her might.

Thump.

Thump.

Thump.

Thump.

The steps loom closer, but the girls don't seem to know that. They can't hear it over their screams—but I can.

And it keeps coming, not stopping until my very legs quiver from fear and the vibrations of its marching stomps. Cold as death air rushes for my face and I finally scream.

THUMP.

But no scream comes out. Nothing does but a garbled choke.

Something is wrapped around my neck, squeezing and squeezing and *squeezing*.

I try to claw at it only to end up scratching my own skin.

This isn't the first time this has grabbed me. This is eerily similar to my dream…the nightmare that has plagued me for weeks.

I'm hallucinating. I must be hallucinating.

Except as my eyes begin to pop and my neck begins to burn from my windpipe being crushed, I know it's not. Especially as the tightness turns into a tug and my feet stop touching the ground.

Higher and higher and higher I rise, until my legs are dangling a foot off the ground.

I kick with all my might, not caring who I catch in the process, but I must have kicked the girls because their screams evolve from scared to petrified as they turn from the front door to find me hovering mid-air, choking.

BANG, BANG, BANG.

Pounding fills the house, a different kind as it comes from the front door on the other side.

My body practically melts with relief, and *it* feels it. Squeezing its claws around my neck tighter in retaliation, it doesn't stop until black stars shoot into my vision.

Darkness creeps in from the corners of my eyes until searing pain spreads across my abdomen, making my eyes snap open.

Phoebe is screaming at the top of her lungs, her hands wrapped around my ankle trying to pull me down. Her face flushes, tears streaming down her cheeks and yet for some reason I can't hear what she's screaming.

Light floods the hallways beneath my feet, the chill of the night's air rushing for the skin on my back. One moment I'm hovering, my life seeping out of me with every passing second and in the next I'm falling, landing on the floor with a deadly crash. Agony shoots into every bone in my body.

Oxygen rushes through my mouth, allowing me to finally scream in anguish.

A familiar deep voice floats through my ears, gentle hands running over my body as warmth floods my bones once more. The icy chill of death and what attacked me retreats as curly brown hair comes into view, accompanied by crystal-blue eyes peering down at me.

"Xavier?" I whisper a second before darkness swallows me whole.

Chapter Twenty-Nine

The first thing I feel is the scratchy sheets engulfing my body, closely followed by the pain spreading like wildfire down my throat. Then the sounds come.

"She should have woken by now," says a gruff voice.

"She shouldn't be unconscious at all." Evie sucks in a sharp breath. "What did the doctor say again?"

"That doctor is an asshole with a god complex. Use your own knowledge and fix her."

Evie sputters. "Just because I'm studying to become a doctor doesn't mean I know anything. I can tell you how many bones are in the body, which diseases can lead to death, how the cells reproduce...but I cannot tell you why our friends aren't waking up."

Shock crashes into my body as I find my eyes sealed shut, crusted as if I haven't opened them in weeks. Trying to blink feels as if a thousand pounds are weighing down my eyelids.

The moment I get anywhere, I wince. Blinding white light pierces me, forcing me to slam my eyes shut once more.

The girls continue to bicker with each other, a deep husky

male voice infiltrating every now and then, the sound so comforting it eases my racing heart. At least for a short while, as my fingers begin to twitch and my toes wiggle, my body screaming for me to move.

"All I'm saying is that it wouldn't be bad to have Phoebe's brain right now."

"And what's wrong with mine, Vi? Too much—"

Xavier cuts them off. "I think she's waking up."

My mouth feels like it's full of cotton.

My throat is engulfed in pain.

My eyes burn as they open again.

The last thing I remember before darkness claimed me was Xavier's beautiful blue eyes. And nothing has changed. Once my eyes adjust, they land on him.

And the moment they do, he breaks out into a smile that's full of relief.

Gasps fill the room, bodies rush for me, but I keep my sight set on him.

"There she is," he sighs, as if he's been carrying the world on his shoulders.

I try to lick my cracked lips to speak, finding that I barely have any saliva. Tracking the movement, Xavier jumps up, only to return a second later with a pitcher of water.

"Oh thank God," Evie cries.

Violet stands at the end of the bed while Evie openly weeps beside me. The pair look haunted in more ways than one—their eyes hollow, dark and sunken.

Violet lifts an incredulous finger. "Don't you ever do that to us again!"

I can't help but let out a dry wheeze of a laugh. I try to say I'm not sure what I'm guilty of, but nothing except a strange, scratchy noise leaves me. Frowning, I slowly reach for the water Xavier offers as Evie scolds her.

"Can't you just be grateful?" she says between sobs.

Violet's eyes narrow but she bites her tongue.

The silence gives me a moment to pull back, for the first time noting why there is an annoying beeping sound surrounding me.

Clearing my throat, I manage in a small wheeze, "Why am I in the hospital?"

Xavier's features grow tense as Evie sucks in a breath and looks over her shoulder to Violet as if asking for help.

Sighing deeply, Violet's shoulders slump. "How much do you remember?"

I wish I didn't remember anything. However, I sadly admit, "Everything."

Violet and Evie look at each other again, giving me a moment to inspect the room—and the one person in our group clearly missing.

"Where's Phoebe?"

Tension fills the room, so thick I'm surprised I don't start choking on it. At the looks crossing their faces, I force myself to sit up straighter even as panic blooms throughout my body.

"Where's Phoebe?" I ask again, more sternly.

Xavier wraps his hand around my own. "Blair—"

The pity I find in his eyes makes me recoil and snap, "No! Tell me where she is!"

His gaze flicks across the room.

My brows furrow as they all seem to look in the same direction. Sitting straighter, I follow their movement, only to have my heart plummet.

Lying unconscious in a bed beside my own is Phoebe, with bandages wrapped around her forearms. The monitor tracking her heart rate is slow, so slow it makes my own spike, my monitor beeping profusely.

My breaths come fast and faster until I'm hyperventilating.

Evie runs out of the room calling for a nurse, her voice harried and full of terror.

I'm not sure why. Perhaps the monitor is recording my heart breaking, because the one person in this world I cannot lose is lying in a hospital bed unconscious, and all I can seem to do is scream.

I don't remember how the nurses sedated me. I don't remember screaming so hard my voice broke and no sound left my mouth. I don't remember pushing everyone out of my way as I scrambled out of my bed to hers, and I certainly don't remember shaking her so hard they were worried I'd injured her.

I don't remember any of it.

All I remember is the pain that spread throughout my body. The fear that sunk its claws into me at the very real threat of losing her.

The person I would give my own life up for.

Because it wouldn't be a life worth living if I didn't have Phoebe.

It's been two days since I woke to find I had been unconscious for seventy-two hours.

Five days since Phoebe hasn't woken.

I can barely look her family in the eye when they come to visit. How do I answer their questions? I don't know why we fell unconscious. Neither do the doctors.

Garret is harder to avoid. He knows the oddities of the

house and he certainly isn't stupid. But how can I face his questions when my own aren't answered?

No one knows what happened to us and why.

No one knows why I woke up and she didn't.

They're calling it a medical mystery.

Usually I like reading mysteries. This one, however, is tearing me apart from the inside out.

The hospital is preparing to check me out, but I can't leave her. I refuse to leave her side. It's where Xavier finds me, sitting in a chair beside her bed, clinging to her hand while Garret snores softly in the chair adjacent. He hasn't left her side either, not even to take a shower. Every time I get a whiff of his odor my mouth opens to snap a retort but then I see his sunken eyes, the puffiness of them and the redness from his endless crying, and my words fail me.

I hold my finger to my lips before pointing to Garret's sleeping form.

"Are you ready to talk about it yet?" he asks gently.

Xavier's been so kind and patient over these past few days, it's a miracle he stuck around. I don't think I could have gotten through this without him or the girls.

Now I just need my best friend to wake up.

"I'm not talking about it until Phoebe can hear."

Xavier rubs the back of his neck. "But what if—"

"I wouldn't finish that sentence if I were you, lover boy," Violet drawls as she struts into the room, barely chancing us a glance as she types furiously on her phone.

Garret wakes with a start at her loud voice. Grumbling, he sends a seething glare in her direction, one she pays no attention.

"Nice one, Vi," Evie chastises.

Violet lifts her head, suddenly sheepish as a flash of guilt shines in her eyes. "Whoops, sorry."

I pull my gaze away, keeping my focus on Phoebe, watching for any sign that she's waking up.

Beep.

Beep.

Beep.

If I could I'd unplug that damn monitor. It drives me mad to know that nothing is physically wrong with her, besides the bandaged arms. Her heart beats, her liver isn't failing, her brain isn't swollen… Medically, she is perfect.

Running a frustrated hand through my hair, I sigh deeply.

"Why does she have her arms bandaged?" I find myself asking.

I'm sure it isn't the first time I've asked. My mind seems to continue the same loop of thoughts, seemingly not going to stop its mental race until she wakes.

Silence descends.

If it weren't for the incessant beeping of her monitor, you could hear a pin drop.

I turn my head to Evie, knowing she's the easiest to crack. By the sight of her eyes widening a fraction, I know I'm right.

"Why are they bandaged?"

Her swallow is audible as she looks to Garret, as if this isn't the first time she's been questioned on this. "We think she got them when she tried to pull you down."

"Her arms are covered. In gashes of three."

My eyes close as nausea swirls.

Xavier frowns. "Pull Blair down from where?"

The girls and I all exchange glances.

I'm not sure why they haven't shared what happened with Xavier. Perhaps it's my own reasoning.

Fear.

It's also the same reason why I refuse to lift my shirt.

Why I refuse to acknowledge the three gashes I feel with every slight movement of my body. Why I refuse to look at the evidence of it maiming me in the exact same way I was in the attic of Campbellton's house.

"What happened in that house?" Xavier asks.

Violet finally lifts her gaze from her nails.

The guilt shining in her eyes is hard to miss. Despite a small voice whispering that if it weren't for her flippant comment none of this would have happened, I know that's not true—not entirely. Whatever this is, it's not a good spirit; it would have been pushed at some point, and it's been toying with us long enough for me to know it was waiting for its chance to pounce.

I was unfortunately in its crossfire.

I seem to always be, and perhaps that isn't random after all.

Because of me, Phoebe is lying unconscious.

I've never been as sure about anything as I am about this.

"She was— It ran— I think it wrapped—" Violet, for once in her life, stumbles over herself. The usually quick-witted, humorous girl is stumbling out of fear.

Evie's eyes fill with tears as she whispers, "It lifted her off the ground."

Xavier frowns, a flash of disbelief crossing his face before he slowly turns to my neck, the finger-like bruises marring the skin, the evidence of two hands that wrapped around me. Xavier sways before he takes a seat on the hospital bed I vacated.

I wonder what the girls told the hospital so they wouldn't call the police.

Considering the gashes I received in the attic, it likes to mark its prey. Whatever *it* is.

It even felt the same, an agony like no other, its claws a rusty blade inflicting the most pain possible.

I must have drowned out their chatter because when I lift my head to finally speak, Violet and Evie are in a heated debate about what is and isn't possible.

"It's the same scratches from the attic," I blurt, my voice grating, still beyond recognition despite the copious amount of medications I'm on.

Only time will heal the voice it tried to steal.

Evie is the first to look, her face turning as white as a ghost—no pun intended—as her gaze drops to my stomach, thankfully covered.

"That's impossible. How could it replicate—"

"It didn't replicate," I cut off. "It reapplied."

"You think what's in the house is what attacked you in the attic?" she asks softly.

"I don't think, I know." Avoiding Xavier's stare, not daring to see if he thinks I'm insane despite all he has seen, I go on. "The pain was identical to what I felt when I was attacked in Campbellton. It's not like a normal scratch. This *burns*, like fire in my flesh."

"What attic? And what happened?" Xavier asks.

His question results in utter silence. The girls have been dying to know and yet dread to ask. Out of fear or guilt, they've respected me not wanting to talk about it.

Xavier has no idea the land mine he just stepped on.

"Blair, I think it's time you told us what happened in the attic."

The soft declaration comes from Evie, who munches on her lip with nervous ferocity.

My and Xavier's gazes clash, the colors of the forest meeting the depths of the ocean.

"What happened, Blair?"

I swallow, razor blades sliding down my neck as if threatening to slice if I speak the truth. But the way Xavier is looking at me, open and gentle, ready to catch me no matter what...it makes the words tumble from my mouth before I can even think to stop them.

"It showed me how my sister died...and how I'll follow the same fate."

Chapter Thirty

"Tell me everything."

"Halloween night, we all drove to Campbellton and went on a ghost tour at the haunted mansion. Evie and I were up in the attic when I was attacked."

I expect shock to fill his features, but instead, it's as if something dawns inside of him, clicking a piece of a puzzle into place he's been searching for.

Evie wrings her hands. "I don't understand why it would show your sister taking her own life."

My gaze flicks to Phoebe's closed eyes. "I never said it showed me taking her own life."

Garret has the decency to ponder his words before gently saying, "But Blair…that's how Isabella passed away." The way in which he says this, as if coddling a child moments away from having a breakdown, makes me straighten my spine.

If Phoebe were awake, she'd be telling me to reveal what I found.

My eyes burn as I hold back tears. All I want is for her to

wake up, and if getting the truth out there will help solve the mystery that's happening in our house…I'll do it.

I'm hesitant for a moment. Then suddenly, my chest feels light and I find myself speaking. "I've had Isabella's journal since she passed away, but I was always too afraid to read it." Playing with the hem of my shirt, I lower my head, not daring to look at anyone as I feel their gazes pin me to the spot. "It felt like a violation of privacy, but I also wanted to know why she left me."

Quickly glancing at Xavier, I find him as still as a statue, hanging on my every word. "After talking about her to Xavier, I found it didn't debilitate me, not like how it did that first year." I shrug, feeling uncomfortable bearing my soul. "I thought I was ready. I thought it was time to read it but when I flicked to one of her last entries…"

I look to Phoebe, begging her to wake up and say what I can't.

Except she doesn't move.

Not so much as a flinch.

"Isabella wrote about being stalked."

The words tear from my throat as if they're the cure to Phoebe's unconsciousness.

Gasps fill the hospital room and I feel more than see their tension, waiting for me to fall apart. Little do they know, I already did, only to be distracted by children that don't exist and some non-physical entity that nearly killed me.

"She said she found proof of who had been stalking her for months and was going to confront them." My voice trails off, growing quieter by the second. "That was the last thing she wrote."

"And you think…?" Xavier's sentence fades, letting me fill in the void.

"That someone tormented her, driving her to her suicide?"

Quickly biting my nail, I steel myself to say what I truly believe. "At first, yes, but after taking into account what I was shown in the attic...no." Heaving out a deep sigh, I relent, "I think her stalker murdered her."

Evie leans forward, resting her hand gently on my shoulder. "That's a bit of a leap, B. I think it's more possible that whoever stalked her drove her to do what she did."

I can only imagine the emotions that flash across my face from the turmoil in my heart.

I think it's why Garret pipes up and says, "Either way, someone is at fault for her death. We know that now."

"Does this change things for you?" Evie asks cautiously.

"Of course it does. It changes everything."

Xavier finally breaks his silence. "Are you going to try and find out who it was?"

Splaying my hand across my heart, I vow to my sister, "Of course! I will never stop looking until whoever did this is brought to justice."

"Good," he says gruffly before striding across the room and taking a seat next to me. Tentatively taking my free hand in his, soothingly brushing his thumb back and forth, he asks, "What exactly did you see in that attic?"

The darkness of the attic suffocates me and suddenly for the first time in my life, I feel claustrophobic. The walls cave in on me as a box across the room moves on its own, shuffling, tentative at first, and then certain as it rushes.

Evie fades into nothing behind me as if whatever is in the room blocks her from sight.

"Blair," it growls.

A hand that I cannot see grabs my jaw, yanking my head roughly to the side as a foul odor whips across my face. Another low growl fills the air. "Watch."

My entire body tries to cower away, forcing the hand to cling to my face tighter. My body begins to tremble, my breathing turning choppy.

I'm about to force my eyes closed when a flash of red hair stops me in my tracks, sucking the very air from my lungs. Another flash of it appears, a quick blur as it moves from box to box, seemingly hiding.

The hand at my jaw drops as a shadow across the room draws my attention. It's large, impossibly so, as it towers over every item in the room. The bulky frame appears to have wide shoulders, its height not the only thing imposing but its weight. The floorboards beneath my feet vibrate with every heavy thump the shadow creates.

The blur of red moves again, trying to get away from the shadow but despite its size, it's fast. It pounces, wrapping a hand around a jean-clad ankle, making a scream pierce the air.

The sound sends chills down my spine. It sounds... familiar.

The shadow yanks and, with one hard tug, sends the owner of the red hair sprawling into the middle of the attic.

I gasp, yet no oxygen reaches my lungs. Air is not something attainable, not as I come face-to-face with Isabella.

Terror is written starkly across her features, ones so similar to mine it's as if I'm watching myself.

The longer my eyes bore into her small frame, the more I notice how different she looked in the months before her death. The last I saw of my sister, she was lovely and bubbly, a ray of sunshine.

Now she's as gray as a storm cloud.

Her cheeks are hollow, the freckles smattered across her nose and cheeks stark against her pale, porcelain skin. Her eyes are sunken and dull, the bags beneath them a predominant purple. Even her hair is no longer vibrant.

It's as if something has sucked the very life from her.

"Please," she cries, holding her hands out in surrender. "I won't tell anyone, I promise."

The sounds of the shadow are muted, as if the memory is being altered so I only see my sister, but it must say something because the little remaining color that was in her face vanishes within a blink.

There and gone as her mouth drops open to scream.

"Help! Help me please!"

Quickly scrambling, she spins onto her hands and knees, then bounces onto her feet in one fluid motion that shocks me more than anything. Isabella didn't have an athletic bone in her body and yet every instinct within her must be pushing her to fight.

She begins to run now, to a door that suddenly appears. It's filled with hundreds of photographs. I realize with stark clarity that it's her bedroom door, covered with the images that are now sitting in a box in the back of my closet.

The moment her hand wraps around the doorknob she's yanked backward, thrown to the ground. The shadow lands on top of her, pinning her to the floor.

She thrashes with all her might, kicking her legs in all directions, bucking wildly as her head shakes side to side, but all that fight is useless against someone of this size.

"I swear I won't tell anyone," she pleads, her voice cracking. "I will never tell a soul what you've been doing." Her lower lip wobbles, trembling violently as she sobs. "Please don't do this."

The shadow clutches her ankles and begins to drag her, not toward her bedroom door but another, one that leads to the bathroom.

I know before it happens what's coming.

A hand wraps around my bicep, roughly yanking me forward as it smashes through the bathroom door and shows me what happened to my sister.

As the shadow moves away, leaving nothing but my sister's corpse, the foul rotting smell assaults my senses once more. It turns to me and growls, viciously low, "You're next, Blair."

With tears streaming down my face I turn to Phoebe. The only person besides myself who truly deserves to know what I saw. Isabella was as much her sister as she was mine.

Holding my breath, I pray that the story shocks her enough to wake her.

Yet as the steady sound of her monitor continues to ring out, my head drops. My heart pinches painfully at my new reality.

Everything within me protests what I saw, repels the very words I just uttered. That someone made it look like she took her own life.

I spared them the details, but I wasn't as lucky in that attic.

It showed me every graphic moment, every last second of my sister's life, and the moment the fight left her as she took her last breath. The tears that fell freely as he pinned her down in that bathtub.

My stomach churns, bile rushing up my throat.

I flinch as a hand lands gently on my back, rubbing soothing circles up and down my skin.

"Let it all out, Sunshine," Xavier whispers. "Let it all out."

The words are my undoing.

Turning to Xavier, I crumble. Breaking down over what I saw in the attic and the fact that another life is slipping through my fingers. One I'm clutching to so painfully my body is wracked with sobs.

Minutes, hours, days, weeks later, I pull away from Xavier as Evie whispers, "This is all my fault."

Violet's head snaps to the usually cheerful blonde. "Of course it's not."

Tears streak down her cheeks. "It really is."

Her haunted eyes land on mine and something within them has me straightening.

"What is it, Evie?"

Her shoulders shake as she begins to cry in earnest, her words stuttering out of her as she blubbers, "W-what's happening in the house. It's a-all my f-fault."

"Why?"

It takes her a minute to compose herself before her blue eyes, swimming in guilt, swing to Phoebe. "I asked the house to scare us."

"What?" Violet snaps.

"Our house?"

Evie shakes her head profusely. "No! I hate what's happening in the house. I-I...I asked the spirits at Camp-bellton to scare us." She swallows thickly. "To show us a good time..."

My shoulders droop at the guilt that must be racking her. No doubt the very thing that's been eating her alive.

"Evie, I don't think this is your fault."

"But you were attacked because of me!"

I snort. "I was attacked because Phoebe wanted a good piece to write for the college's newspaper." I throw my hands in the air. "Hell, I was attacked because Sally wanted me to go up there and provoke it." Shaking my head, I hope she can hear the unwavering certainty in my voice when I say, "This is not your fault."

Her lip wobbles. "I'm the reason we went."

Violet winces. "Yes, but we all agreed to go. As for you asking ghosts to interact with us...that's a shitty thing to do, but I don't think it caused all this. If you knew what would happen you would have canceled the entire thing."

"If it weren't for the thing in the attic...I would have never found out what really happened to my sister."

And what the spirit claimed is going to happen to me next.

For the first year after my sister's passing, I wished to be reunited, to speak with her, to hear her voice and laughter... just one more time. My hand instinctively reaches for the burning gashes across my abdomen. Now I feel as if my wish is about to come true, but not in the way I had hoped.

Chapter Thirty-One

Several hours later Xavier forces me to go home to shower, pack a bag of fresh clothes, and stay with him while thirteen cameras are installed around the house, flashing a bright green light every three seconds in the kitchen, living room, hallways, basement, and bedrooms.

It's an eerie feeling to know you're being watched, one that after weeks of being tormented isn't unbeknownst to us. Before the cameras I already felt like I was being watched, my space violated every day. Now we're going to see exactly what goes on within this house when we're not looking.

Waiting for Xavier to finish double-checking the cameras the papers in my hand crinkle, the words written in the Merlington files swirling in my vision. After everything that has transpired, Violet printed off copies for each of us when we returned home, instructing us to read every detail to try and find clues as to what could be haunting us and why. I grabbed the pieces of paper and, thankful for no cameras in my bathroom, took a scalding hot shower.

When I stepped out still feeling like a shell of myself, I found Xavier waiting for me on my bed, refusing to leave me alone after all I had confessed. My gaze slides to him now as he walks around the kitchen with his phone in his hands watching the live feed.

Unlike myself, the cameras make Xavier feel safe and secure. I wish I knew how that felt. Although, he wasn't the one who watched his sibling be murdered or was attacked in his own house—lifted off the ground by an invisible force.

My hand instinctively goes to my neck.

It felt exactly like my dream several weeks before, or at least, what I thought was a dream. Now looking back at it, at the sheets I had passed off as me kicking in my sleep, perhaps I *was* lifted off my bed. After all, I woke by the sensation of crashing to the mattress, my limbs flailing as if I had been dropped.

Once we stepped foot inside, no one seemed to want to touch on what happened…as if the severity of our reality and the increased violence is too much to face. The girls have to resume going to classes, whereas I on the other hand am going back to the hospital.

I don't want to be away from Phoebe any longer than I have to.

I need to be there when she wakes up.

Not if, *when*.

There's no other reality I'll accept.

Focusing back on the papers in my hand, the horrible description of what the Merlington family went through weighs heavily upon me. I shove them into my duffel bag, leaving it as a task for my future self and as I do, my fingers brush Isabella's journal.

I've put it off for long enough.

The girls asked what else I had read, if there were any clues as to who she was talking about, and I felt like a coward admitting that I hadn't faced it yet. Not after reading that last entry. But I need answers. I need to know the truth, and the only thing I have to go off of right now is her journal.

So, with an erratic thumping heart, I slide the journal out of my duffel bag.

If I thought the Merlington's case felt heavy in my hands, that was nothing compared to this journal. The words feel as if they're waiting for me to read them, to uncover the puzzle pieces and figure out the true ending of her story.

My heart lodges in my throat as I open it, flicking to a random entry halfway in.

Taking a deep breath, I dive headfirst into my sister's life, praying that there's a life raft nearby ready to save me when her words begin to drown me in grief.

Isabella's Journal Entry

What nobody tells you is that attending college doesn't answer all your life questions. It doesn't answer the doubt growing roots in your mind, and it certainly doesn't tell you what to pursue in life.

I've never known what I want to do—ever. I'm as flighty and fidgety as a hummingbird, my wings constantly flapping, wishing to fly.

I thought that attending college would answer all my questions, especially the ones everyone seems inclined to ask you.

What are you majoring in?
What career path do you want to venture into?
What do you want to do for the rest of your life?
Cue the eye roll.

I've only just turned twenty for fuck's sake. Who wants to choose what they do for forty hours a week for over forty years?
I CERTAINLY DON'T.
I want to smack them the moment they ask. Truly, I want to hurt someone.

It's been over a year and a half since I've started college and although it doesn't seem like a lot, I've signed myself up for endless classes, taking on a workload nobody in their right mind could juggle, all in the hope that something sticks.

The only things that has are my friends.

Acquaintances is more like it but the only time I truly feel I come alive is with people. The endless parties and social mixers my roommate dragged me to in my first year made me realize how good I am with people.

I know, I know, I sound like a cocky bitch but it's true. I thrive in social settings and this is no different.

I may have clung to the lifeline of parties a little too closely though... I'm failing out of my business class. Trust me, I'm shocked too. I thought business would be smooth sailing but the moment the technicalities came into play, I realized I'm more a marketing girl than anything and well...now I'm scheduled with a tutor every Tuesday afternoon.

Now here is the real kicker, and this sounds horrible, but I'm glad I failed. Ecstatic, even.

Because the most cliché of all cliché situations happened. When I walked into the library study room to meet with my tutor, I found out he is the most stunning man to walk this planet.

Saying he's handsome doesn't even do him justice. The gods themselves might've crafted him. And when he smiled at me...I knew I was in trouble.

By the mischievous glint in his eyes, I think he knew too.

Let's just say, I'm still failing business—even more so now with him in the picture—and I'm more than happy to keep failing the class that I already know I'm going to drop in a few months.

I just want to keep seeing him every week. Is that so bad?

According to my professor, it is. I've never had a teacher so up my ass before. The emails are incessant, the check-ins are constant, and he pores over my work with a fine-tooth comb. If I didn't know any better I'd think he was failing me on purpose.

I don't mind though. Like I said, I want to keep seeing my tutor. I guess that's why I haven't tried to call out my professor.

What I do know though is that Elsie is beginning to get on my nerves. We've been living harmoniously together since freshmen year, so you'd think her bad traits would have come out sooner, but no.

Our friendship has become slightly strained in our shared room. Outside it's fine when we're not reminded of all the nitty-gritty details. But when I came home this afternoon to find my clothes rummaged through again, I lost it. The past two weeks, I've come home to something missing or moved.

It's beginning to drive me insane because she swears up and down that it's never her. I don't believe her though. How can I? All her items are pristine, never moved and never missing.

I feel a little guilty for this, but next time she's out or in a long lecture, I'm going to snoop. We live together for Christ's sake, it's stupid to take things from me and then hide them on her side of the room.

I don't want a confrontation; I just want my stuff back.

Isabella's Journal Entry

Can you die from insomnia? Because if you can I should check myself into the hospital.

I haven't slept in three days and I feel like I'm going insane.

The only time I've managed to get a wink of sleep are during my lectures and that's not working anymore. The professors are getting irritated with me.

It's not my workload. I've dropped three classes in the hopes that I'll find some time to sleep but it hasn't helped.

Every time I close my eyes there's a tap on my window, the one that's directly next to my bed. At first, I chalked it up to the tree branches but when I peeked outside, I don't think any of them could reach.

What's worse, the tapping won't stop until I open my eyes and when I do, it's followed by a sound frightenly close to nails scratching on a chalkboard.

The first time it happened, I thought I was dreaming. But it's been a constant thing every night for a week. I become physically sick now when I see my bed. I'm so scared.

I asked Elsie if she heard anything but she's always been a heavy sleeper. Not even her alarms wake her in the mornings—it's usually me having to shake her.

Speaking of Elsie...I didn't find a single one of my missing items on her side.

It was never Elsie going through my things.

Chapter Thirty-Two

"**R**eady to go back to the hospital?"

The sudden break in silence makes me flinch, my hand flying to my chest as if to stop my heart from flying out of its cage. Xavier's suddenly there, towering over me.

"Jesus, Xavier! You scared the crap out of me!"

Chuckling, he plops down next to me. The moment his eyes lock on the journal in my hands, all humor fades in an instant. "Is that hers?"

Sighing deeply, I close the journal. It's one thing for me to be violating her thoughts, it's another to let my—whatever Xavier is becoming—read it. "Yeah, it is."

If he's fazed by me not allowing him to see any of it, he doesn't mention it. It looks as if he's more understanding than anything.

"Do you want to talk about it?"

My eyes move to the journal as if a black hole sucked me in. Gnawing on my lower lip, I frown. I do want to talk about it, but something within me doesn't want to. It feels wrong to speak about what she was fearing with someone who is a stranger to her.

What a horrible thought that is. She will never meet him, the boy who is slowly capturing my heart.

Shaking my head and the depressing thought away, I peer back up at Xavier, to the open blue eyes full of kindness and patience. I know Xavier would be able to say all the right things in this moment, to soothe the array of emotions bombarding me and the truth spilling from the pages. The horror that my sister endured before her death.

But it feels wrong.

I need Phoebe.

The thought has tears springing to my eyes.

"No, it's okay," I say finally, noting that he doesn't seem offended or dejected. Craning my neck, I'm shocked to see that I've been poring over her journal entries for hours. The clock in the hallway reads 11:21 p.m.

A featherlight kiss presses against my head.

Turning back, I find a hint of worry in his eyes. "How about we get out of the house for a bit? Grab some breakfast, my treat." He finishes his offer with a dazzling smirk capped by his dimples.

My brows quirk. "It's nearly midnight…you know that, right?"

"The best time to eat breakfast," he says with a grin.

The tension in my shoulders evaporates until Phoebe comes crashing into my mind.

"I want to go back to the hospital. I don't want to be away from her."

He slowly dips his head, chewing on his lip before he suggests, "How about we pick up breakfast and take it to the hospital? We can eat it in the hall…give Phoebe's mom a moment with her."

I don't see why not. "Okay, sounds good," I say.

There's a tirade of emotions bombarding me as I quickly pick up my duffel bag and follow Xavier out to his truck, wondering in the back of my mind if Violet and Evie will be safe on their own.

On one hand, I'm hurt, so deeply pained that Isabella never came to me with what was happening. That on those nights she couldn't sleep, she felt as if she couldn't call me. It makes me wonder if she stepped into too much of a mother role and was fearful of crossing a line.

Then another part of me is afraid of what I'll read next. As the journal entries go on, the torment someone was clearly inflicting her with continues to escalate.

I'm waiting for the journal entry of her realizing she was being stalked.

Because taps on a window you can brush off. Even items going missing you can blame on a thief.

Isabella, despite not knowing what to do with her life, was smart—incredibly intelligent. She could have done anything.

Isabella was not one to jump to conclusions…so what exactly made her think she was being stalked?

What made her realize?

And not only that…what if I find the answer, and Phoebe won't be there beside me to help me stay afloat in my grief?

"This is the first time I've ordered anything other than a panini," I say, chuckling at the takeout container sitting in my lap from Ruby's Diner.

The hospital hallway isn't comfortable in the slightest but at least Phoebe's door is only two steps away.

"Really?"

Taking a bite of bacon I moan around the food, wondering why the girls and I have never gone there for breakfast.

Xavier snorts. "I think that's about to change."

"Absolutely," I say around a mouthful. "The girls and I usually go to the café on the corner of our block." I shrug. "Usually if we're getting breakfast it's to cure our hangovers and none of us want to drive."

Xavier digs into his breakfast burrito, his own moan tumbling from his lips. It makes my eyes snap to his face, wishing more than anything he was moaning because of me. Xavier clears his throat, and heat crawls across my cheeks at his knowing smile.

I quickly move the subject away from my obvious ogling. "Did you get a chance to read the Merlington file?"

Shaking his head, he leans back, half his breakfast burrito already devoured. "No, did you find anything?"

"I have my theories."

I'm not sure why women love true crime, but I am one of them. Perhaps it's because we know that our safety is always at risk and by indulging in true crime, we're able to work through our deepest fears.

Or perhaps female rage is present within all of us, and we just want to scream *fuck you* to the psychopaths.

Xavier makes a motion with his hand to continue as he shovels in another bite.

"The police reports state that the Merlingtons' bodies were found four days after their deaths. Liam was the youngest son of Arabella and Douglas's children." Taking a quick bite of my scrambled eggs, I go on. "They had four children in total. Alyssa was their oldest at thirteen. She was…" My body stiffens.

"Do I even want to know what was done to her?" Xavier cuts in.

"No," I shudder. Swallowing around the large lump in my throat, my breakfast threatens to rise up as the detailed report I read on her little body forces itself into the forefront of my mind. I try to shake it away. "Their second oldest, Henry, was still brutally attacked, but not as bad as Alyssa and Arabella."

Xavier frowns, his head cocking to the side. "The two eldest women in the family?"

I nod, suddenly hating my breakfast and how it sits in my stomach like a heavyweight.

"Do you think…?" Xavier lets his question trail off.

"With what was done to Alyssa and Arabella…absolutely. There was another girl, Charlotte, but she was nine years old. I think she was too young to have been entangled like the others were." The words taste vile on my tongue.

They were all too young—at no age are you old enough to be forced to endure something horrid like *that*

"What was done to their mother?"

"Same thing as Alyssa, but worse. Her body…it would have been a very painful death," I say sadly, shoving away my food.

"What's your theory?"

"It's stated that Liam was never meant to be in the house. Supposedly he was at the neighbors playing with a friend when he came home early to fetch something. The police think he went up to the attic to grab one of his toys. Apparently that was his playroom."

A cold shiver dances along my spine. I don't know how any child could play in that room; the feeling as I stood in it was atrocious.

"They believe the murders occurred while he was up there, and the attacker didn't check." Blowing out a deep breath, I steel my spine. "This is where…"

"It gets worse?" Xavier asks in surprise.

Nodding, I go on, my gaze avoiding the food. "Liam was found sitting in the middle of his family's dead bodies four days later. He didn't have a scratch on him, but he was in shock." My heart pangs. "The poor five-year-old died on the way to the hospital from dehydration."

Xavier is silent for so long, I fill it with my thoughts as I read the rest of the report and the case findings.

"There was another family member present—their uncle Harvey. His wounds were self-inflicted and by the attack Arabella and Alyssa went through, I think Harvey and Douglas had an altercation." I shrug, hating that the police transcripts seem to agree with my theory. "Douglas found out Harvey was taking advantage of Alyssa and Harvey flew into a fit of rage."

Xavier's face turns ashen, his flesh a green tint. "Why harm Arabella in the same manner? Why harm Alyssa at all?"

My voice takes on a hard edge. "He was a rapist who got caught and I dare say he only went after Alyssa because of the uncanny resemblance she had to her mother."

Xavier's eyes widen. "The police think it was unrequited love?"

"Something like that."

"What a sick fuck," Xavier spits.

"There were rumors around town of Alyssa's sudden change. Apparently, she used to be a ray of happiness, and one day it was flipped like a switch."

Xavier's brows furrow. "They included rumors in the police report?"

I snort despite the subject. "Small town."

Silence grows between us, a pensive one.

A dark look enters Xavier's eyes.

"Why do you think *you* were attacked in the attic?"

I physically flinch at the question.

A hint of pain flashes across his face. He doesn't apologize but patiently waits, leaning against the hospital wall.

"I think that the energy in that attic festered until it no longer resembled a scared little five-year-old boy who no doubt saw and heard his family be butchered." Swallowing thickly, I tear my eyes away. "Who saw how my sister really died and was awoken."

I know I sound insane, but after looking at my body, battered and bruised in the mirror, my mind has opened to the possibility that the afterlife may not be what everyone assumes, and that energy can stick around a lot longer than we think.

The door across the hall flies open. I expect Garret to step out but it's Phoebe's mom staring at me with wide eyes, her chest rising and falling rapidly.

The sight of it has me springing into action.

Before she can so much as utter a word I'm running into the room, my food long forgotten as every horrible scenario that I could face plays on a loop in my mind.

Until I come to a screeching halt at the end of Phoebe's bed to the sight of Garret weeping.

Lying in the bed is Phoebe, with her eyes open wide in terror.

Chapter Thirty-Three

After hours of tests and doctors poking her, Phoebe sends her mom out of the room, her gaze pinned on me in such a veracious manner I know she needs to talk.

"Are the girls on their way?" she whispers when her mom closes the door.

"I texted them. They must be asleep but as soon as they wake I have no doubt they'll race here."

Phoebe's eyes widen. "They're in the house?"

"They had nowhere to go."

Xavier steps forward, placing a comforting hand on my back. "Luke installed the cameras. If anything goes wrong we can see."

Phoebe dips her head but it doesn't appear to bring her any comfort.

"What happened?" I ask quietly.

Phoebe stares off into nothing, her head shaking softly as tears begin to well in her eyes. "I was right… Everything I dreamed has come true and I know how it's going to end."

No wonder she was terrified and constantly choosing

denial. If I was in Phoebe's shoes, I would pretend it wasn't happening, that none of it was real.

The tears that were filling her eyes vanish with a blink and then something akin to rage replaces them.

"I know what we have to do."

Frowning, I look to Xavier and Garret before turning back. "I don't think we should do anything—"

"It needs to leave," she spits.

I'm physically taken aback by the anger simmering throughout her.

"Phoebe, I don't think there is anything we can do."

"There is."

She sounds so certain, so sure of herself.

"What do you have in mind?" Garret asks, his hands clutching hers.

He would do anything for her in this moment, I can see it in his eyes.

With eyes full of fire, Phoebe turns to me. "You need to help me convince my mom to check me out."

"Okay…I don't see how that is—"

"Then I need you to take me back."

"Back…?"

"To the house."

"Absolutely not."

"Blair—"

"*No*!" I snap. "Are you insane? You could have died! I thought you were dying! You are not going anywhere near that house!" I turn on her boyfriend with pleading eyes. "Garret, back me up."

I thought I knew true fear these passing days as I sat beside Phoebe, clutching her hand and praying for her to wake. To flinch. To move…to simply keep breathing.

But nothing haunts me like the idea of letting her walk back into the house that almost took her from me.

Phoebe looks to Garret's bewildered face and something happens, shifts as they have a silent conversation with just their eyes. I know the look because Phoebe and I can talk between ourselves like that.

My back stiffens as Garret dips his head slightly.

"I don't care what you say, you're not stepping foot in that house." My voice lowers, wavering as tears choke my words. "Do not put us in a position where we might lose you again."

Phoebe grips Garret's hand tighter, her knuckles turning white as she grits, "I'm not letting it win."

My arms fly into the air. "It already has! Look around, Phoebe! Look at where you have been lying unconscious for a week!" I snarl at Garret, "Do not let her do this."

"I'm sorry, but if Phoebe thinks—"

I cut off his useless nonsense and pin my gaze on my best friend. "I cannot willingly stand beside you as you walk back into that house of horror."

"Fine, then I'll have Garret drive me."

My head shakes back and forth. "Why are you doing this?"

"Because I'm sick of it controlling my life. I'm taking my power back, B...and you should do the same."

The door bursts open behind me, Phoebe's mom rushing back into the room to be beside her daughter, her presence ending the conversation.

And by the stubborn gleam in Phoebe's eye, nothing will change her mind.

Two days later, Phoebe got her wish.

Rounding the corner into the living room I'm stopped short by the copious number of candles sitting on the coffee table. "Who let Violet go to the candle store unsupervised again?"

Evie snorts as she walks past me. "This was an approved purchase."

My brows rise. "I see…"

Phoebe waves me over to sit next to her as if nothing has happened and she wastes no time. The second my thighs hit the fluffy couch, she pounces.

"Did you read any more journal entries?"

The girls grow silent, still moving about the room doing God knows what, but they're waiting…for something.

Phoebe hasn't spoken to me one on one, she couldn't, not when I begged her to leave the house for her own safety. It hasn't left much room to talk about anything else.

Clearing my throat, I lean back. "Yes."

"And…?"

"Let's just say I don't think she was insane."

I'm surprised when they leave it at that, but nothing shocks me as much as when Violet finally moves all the candles off the coffee table to reveal something that none of us should be touching.

Jumping as far away as I can, I back myself into a corner. "Are you out of your mind?" I scream, more out of fear than anything else.

Violet holds up her hands, treating me as if I'm an animal cornered in a cage. "Blair, take a breath and let us explain before you freak out."

"No explanation needed, Vi, you guys went out and bought a fucking Ouija board!"

The girls look at each other, all seemingly trying to come up with something to say.

I pin my gaze specifically on Evie. "You of all people should know how dangerous this is!" Not only through the horror films she watches but also from her research on getting rid of spirits. I don't doubt that when looking into saging the house it came up to never bring a Ouija board into a haunted house. Even *I* know that.

Evie's eyes grow comically wide, and I can't help but notice the bags under her eyes and how they seem to match mine—dull, purple, and puffy.

I think it's safe to assume that their logical reasoning has flown out the window with the lack of sleep we've all been getting, along with being desperate in our efforts to make *it* leave.

Pinning my hysterical gaze on Phoebe I ask. "Why are you doing this?"

"Because if we do nothing it's never going to leave."

Evie holds up her hands, splaying her palms in a show of innocence. "Sage didn't work, we don't have the resources to get a shaman in here, and I'm out of ideas."

Sputtering, I turn to Phoebe once more. "You can't be serious. Why would you let them bring that in here?"

"I think we need answers, and after what it did to me... I'm willing to do anything."

Violet grabs her laptop, pulling up websites as she throws over her shoulder, "We need answers. We need to try and talk to it, to try and…" She groans. "God, I don't know, tell it to fuck off."

"Shut up!" Evie hisses, her eyes darting around the room. "We don't need a repeat of last week."

I point to the Ouija board, noting how my finger trembles. "Mark my words, this will not help. It will only escalate things."

"I don't think it can get worse than it putting us both in the hospital," Phoebe says hoarsely, her eyes on my scarf-covered neck, hiding the fading bruises.

There's no way in hell I'm taking it off now.

Chewing on their words, I look to the board, then back to their faces—their sunken, fear-filled expressions—and find myself relenting, not because I want to but because they do.

Because I don't want to lose any more people in my life, whether from death or loss of friendship.

My heart can't bear it.

I could swear the scratches along my abdomen burn as I whisper, "When are we doing it?"

"Tonight," Violet says while she counts the candles.

I barely restrain from rolling my eyes. "Do we have to do it in the dark?"

The girls turn to one another before saying in unison, "Absolutely."

Isabella's Journal Entry

I saw them.

After weeks of noting everything—every item that went missing, where my things would be moved to, and the days that the tapping would start—I saw the bastard with my own eyes.

Not that it will do any good because I didn't see anything.

All I saw was a figure running away wearing black clothes.

Usually, the tapping happens every night, except for Fridays...which is odd. I've yet to figure out why but instead of lying in bed, I stuffed it full of pillows and made it look like a person.

And I waited.

For hours.

No wonder Elsie never hears anything. It doesn't start until around one in the morning, and by then, she's dead to the world. It's almost as if the person knows how deep she sleeps and waits.

After the tapping grew louder and I had given myself a pep talk, I yanked back the curtains as quickly as I could.
But I still wasn't fast enough.

The person's reaction time was insane, and all I saw was them sprinting away from my window.

But I did see them.

A person in the flesh, tapping on my window.

I'm not insane.

It was such a relief that I almost didn't process the fact that some random person has been watching me sleep for weeks.

I told the guy I'm dating about it... God, he was such an ass. I really thought my tutor was going to be something promising. We had only gone on four dates but all that pent-up tension from the library really fizzled out outside.

I told him what I saw, and he laughed me off.

What kind of asshole laughs it off when the girl they're seeing tells them they have a stalker?

And the more I tried to prove myself right the more he turned into a sexist pig.

He made me feel as if I was stupid, that nobody would ever stalk me. As if I'm a disgusting person and no one would ever want to peep into my window? "Why would they?" he said.

I never knew someone could make you want to feel worthy of stalking.

Asshole!

To make matters worse, I didn't leave our date when he said that. I stuck around. He truly put the nail in his own coffin when I told him about my professor later that evening.

My skin crawls just thinking about it. My professor approached me the day before with another failed exam. However, this time when he shut the door to his office, he didn't take a seat behind his desk. He sat on it, spread his legs until they grazed mine, and dared to offer me a passing grade while insinuating that I could earn it through sexual favors.

I nearly vomited right there in his lap. I did vomit when I got back to my room after shoving him off me.

Not only did my date—the worst I've ever had—not believe me, but he also asked what I said to initiate it. He claimed, "I must have flirted with him." I was too stunned to speak but as he began screaming at me, calling me a slut and a whore, I broke up with him and ran.

Physically ran out on our date.

I'm ashamed to admit that after that, I lost my nerve to report my professor. The last thing I want to be called is a party girl slut who sent her professor "mixed signals."

I hope Professor Emerson burns in hell.

To: scarter@acmail.com

Re: Inappropriate Sexual Conduct Complaint

Miss Carter,

Thank you for reviewing my complaint. I'm happy to come into the office Monday morning at 9 a.m. I've attached an image below and although I know it may be too late, this was my sister's journal entry from 2022.

Although she isn't here to corroborate her story no longer, Professor Emerson clearly has a history of inappropriate conduct, and I feel as if it is no coincidence that it happened to both me and my sister.

I fear this has happened to many girls on campus.

Blair

🔖Isabella's Journal Confession

Re: Inappropriate Sexual Conduct Complaint

Miss Carter,

Thank you for reviewing my complaint. I'm happy to come into the office Monday morning at 9 a.m. I've attached an image below and although I know it may be too late, this was my sister's journal entry from 2022.

Although she isn't here to corroborate her story no longer, Professor Emerson clearly has a history of inappropriate conduct, and I feel as if it is no coincidence that it happened to both me and my sister.

I fear this has happened to many girls on campus.

Blair

Isabella's Journal Confession

God B, I'm so sorry about Issy

I'm glad they're taking it seriously!

Do you need space or do you want to talk?

Space 🩶

Just down the hall whenever you need me

They won't keep him on the faculty B, I wouldn't be surprised if t headmaster is firing him now

One can only hope

Please tell me you're joking

I wish!

~~Send thoughts and prayers so I don't~~
~~get sucked into hell~~

... too much ?

Not at all

Just contemplating Evie's taste in
movies

Has she never watched a paranormal
movie ?

That's what I said!

I stated for the record that if things go
south I can say I told them so

If it goes horribly call me

I want updates

Check ins to see if I've been possessed? 👻

Should we come up with a code word?

So if I'm still inside you can save me?

Exactly

I feel gummy bear would really drive home the fact there's still a part of you there

What about grizzly bear?

I at least want a badass code word

Gummy bear makes me sound soft

Delivered

Grizzly it is

Chapter Thirty-Four

I've not only experienced tension but I've read about it.

Tension between two people as the slow burn begins to ignite and they're seconds away from throwing out their sorry excuses as to why they can't kiss. Tension between two rivals vying for the same goal. Tension in your heart when you're sobbing through the pain of losing your favorite character.

Tension with the girl that continues to flirt with your boyfriend in front of you. Tension on the biggest test day of your life. Losing a loved one.

I am no stranger to tension and yet I've never felt it quite like this.

It's as if the very air has thickened, making it hard for us all to breathe. So much so I'm shocked Violet is able to light the dozens of candles set around the living room, that the air doesn't suffocate the flame and wink out.

I wish it did.

I wish an emergency would occur to pull us away from this.

I'd put up with anything to get away from the hideous

Ouija board sitting on the coffee table. It feels as if it's mocking us, gleeful and smirking as it waits to feed on our fear.

I'm afraid it's already doing so.

Evie is the first to break the silence that's blanketed us since the moment the sun began to fade. "Does everyone know what to do?"

A bunch of mumbled yeses permeate the air.

Place your hand on the planchette lightly, say hello, and pray you don't die.

No one needed to Google how to use a Ouija board. As stupid as it is we've all watched enough movies to pick up on the dos and don'ts. I feel as if that should prove my point because of how those movies ended...but everyone is set on this.

Swallowing thickly, we come to stand around the coffee table as Violet lights the last candle. She shakes out her arms as if weighed down before plastering on a fake smile, trying to emit her usual confidence but utterly failing. "Are we ready?" she asks shakily.

"Yes," Evie squeaks, sounding anything but.

Phoebe, finally coming to her senses, doesn't lie and stays silent.

I don't look at her as we all take a seat around the wooden coffee table on the floor, each of us taking a respective side. She doesn't say anything either when I bite down hard on my nail. Who knew that over a decade of trying to get me to stop, all I had to do to get Phoebe to be quiet about my nail-biting tendencies was to move into a haunted house?

With Evie to my right, Phoebe to my left, and Violet across from me, I feel like it's impossible to ignore the fear plastered across everyone's face.

"We can't forget to say goodbye," Phoebe says quietly,

finally breaking her silence. "Otherwise, anything can come in."

My frown feels as if it furrows a hole into my forehead. "What if by doing this…it brings something else in here?"

"Like calls to like," Evie chants, a faraway look taking over her features.

CLAP.

"Stop it!" Violet yells, clapping her hand again to push her point home. "We need to go in with a strong mindset and attitude. We are here for answers and answers only."

Clearing my throat, I jump in. "Vi's right, we can't go in thinking it's going to make it worse."

Evie throws her hands in the air, exasperated. "Nobody, and I mean *nobody* here, will be able to go in without a little anxiety. Can we please just get this over with? I want to know what it wants and then get it the hell out of this house!"

Her uncharacteristic outburst makes us all snap our mouths shut.

Evie is breathing hard as she moves to tie up her long blonde hair. I note the tremble in her fingers that she can't disguise.

Reaching over, I lay my hand on hers once it returns to her lap.

"We're all right, we can be both. Strong and scared," I say, trying with all my might to accommodate everyone's feelings. The truth is, Evie is right—no one will be able to put their fear away—but this will require a strong mentality.

Evie blows out a shaky breath. "I'm sorry for snapping. I just really want this thing gone."

"It's okay, Evie, we all do," Phoebe chimes in. Holding out her hand, palm up on the coffee table, Phoebe waits until we're all holding hands around the coffee table before whispering, "We can do this if we are there for one another. If one

of us has hit their limit, then we finish it and say goodbye."
She solidifies her statement with a glance to each of us,
boring into what feels like our souls. She lands on me, brown
eyes on green. "Deal?"

"Deal," we say in unison.

Taking a deep breath we all let go, then reach forward and
lay trembling fingers on the planchette.

It's freezing to the touch, stealing the breath from my
lungs.

Phoebe starts by saying, "We call forth the spirit of this
house. We welcome you to join us."

"We're ready to talk. Come out wherever you are," Violet
sings.

Anyone been possessed yet?

Not *yet*

I'd be more interested watching paint dry

Has nothing come out to play?

Not a peep

Delivered

Maybe Violet hasn't offended it yet today

Chapter Thirty-Five

Two hours later my hand isn't the only thing cramping.

My entire body is locked up tight, screaming for me to run, not out of fear surprisingly but out of sheer *boredom*.

"This is ridiculous," Violet groans for the thousandth time.

Evie stares at the board so intensely her right eye twitches. I'm not sure whether she's praying for it to do something or wishing it away. "I don't understand," she whispers, lowering her head to inspect the board once again.

Phoebe huffs, yanking her hand away. "I can't do this for another second."

"Phoebe!"

"No!"

Violet groans again. "Stop taking your hand off the planchette! This is why nothing has happened."

Phoebe hikes herself up onto the couch, rubbing her lower back as she winces. "No, nothing has happened because it doesn't want to talk. It just wants to continue tormenting us."

Evie scoffs. "If I was haunting someone, I wouldn't come out with my hands raised and leave when they asked."

I narrow my eyes. "Why did you not say that an hour ago? When we all wanted to give up, but you forced us to keep going."

Evie's cheeks flush as crimson as my hair before she shrugs helplessly. "I wanted to talk to it."

"Clearly, it doesn't feel the same about us," Violet grumbles under her breath, being the second to remove their hand.

In doing so it makes me realize Evie and I are the only two still touching the planchette and I yank my hand back like it burned me.

"Well, I call that a success," I chirp, falling onto the couch. No wonder Phoebe was grimacing, my entire back aches.

Evie huffs, the last to remove her hand. "How do you call that a success? Nothing happened!"

"Exactly," I whisper, sarcasm dripping from my voice.

My phone buzzes beside me, another incoming text from Xavier. I couldn't hold back my smile even if I tried.

Violet makes a faux gagging sound before she leans forward, trying to peer at my phone. "What did lover boy say?"

Throwing my head back on a laugh I flip my screen toward her. "Maybe he's right."

Violet scoffs, her eyes rolling into the back of her head. "Tell him to piss off!"

"What did he say?" Phoebe asks.

"That Violet didn't piss it off enough today," I say with a snort.

Evie is the first to chuckle, the sound bursting from her lips. Phoebe cracks next, her breathy sounds joining Evie's now deep belly laugh until we're all cackling. Violet tries to glare, but the twitching in her lips gives her away and before she knows it, she too is laughing.

"In all seriousness, though, it's not funny. The thing hiked Blair into the air like she was a rag doll." Violet says this with a deadly grave face, as serious as they come, and yet it only fuels the laughter in the room. My eyes burn with unshed tears from laughing so hard.

Delirium has officially entered the room.

Evie's hand covers her mouth as she tries to hold her laughter back long enough to say, "Maybe someone threw Blair's voodoo doll out a window."

Phoebe snorts. "Maybe it got Violet's voice confused with Blair's and tried to shut her up."

The longer I laugh, the more tears gather in my eyes. "Did we really just sit here for two hours holding a piece of wood and asking a dead person to talk to us?"

Violet snickers, pointing to Phoebe, imitating her voice as she mimics, "*We welcome the ghost of this house to—*"

A pillow flies across the room, smacking Violet in the face and effectively shutting her up.

Phoebe has another pillow in her hand ready to fly as she wheezes, "You bought the damn thing!"

That sobers Violet up instantly. "Do you think we can get a refund?"

"Hi, our ghost didn't appreciate your board. Can I have my money back?" Evie says, her voice dripping with sweetness.

Another laugh flies from the back of my throat as I stand. "You all owe me food. I said from the beginning it was a waste of time."

The girls stand, Phoebe shaking her finger at me. "No, no, no. You said we would be possessed. Out of everyone here *you're* the one in the wrong." She shrugs, gloating. "I said we would be perfectly safe."

Violet blows a raspberry. "Are you being serious?"

"Phoebe, you were the one giving us pep talks about how strong we had to be mentally." Evie's brows rise, a devilish smirk dancing across her lips as she dares Phoebe to deny the truth.

Phoebe grimaces. "Jesus, I did too, didn't I? Maybe I'm the one who needs an exorcism."

I clutch my stomach as it begins to hurt from all the laughing. "Evie has the perfect background movie to play for—"

Screeching cuts me off.

The sound as slimy as nails scraping down chalkboard.

The laughter that was filling the room abruptly recedes like a tsunami calling back water from the shoreline.

Time seems to pause as the sound grows in the room.

My eyes are bulging out of my head as they lock on the girls in front of me, but none are looking at my wide terror-filled eyes. They're all looking past me.

And as I crane my neck, I find out why.

The sound isn't coming from a chalkboard that magically appeared, it's coming from the Ouija board, the planchette scraping across the wooden board on its own. Coming to a stop over the word *Hello.*

The breath is stolen from me, yanked from my lungs as if the planchette shoved itself down my throat.

"Are you guys seeing…"

"Yes."

"That's impossible," I breathe.

Violet's voice is barely above a whisper. "Coming from the girl who levitated."

Violet has always dealt with things through humor, so her comment doesn't faze me. "What do we do?" I ask instead.

"We wanted to talk…" Evie says, trailing off as if leaving it an open-ended question.

"Why did it wait so long?" Phoebe whispers, a hint of anger in her words.

Staring at the now unmoving planchette where it still hovers over the same word, I say, "Maybe time is different… wherever it is."

Violet groans. "For the love of God can we not talk about philosophy and just figure out what to do?"

I'd feel hurt if it weren't for the noticeable fear coating her words.

"Maybe we should—"

My words are cut off abruptly as scraping fills the air. The planchette is moving again, slowly around the alphabet.

"I think it's ready to talk."

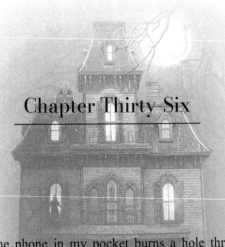

Chapter Thirty-Six

The phone in my pocket burns a hole through my pants, my fingers itching to grab it and respond to Xavier and tell him that I think he's right.

The planchette didn't move until we all began joking about it. Maybe it does need to be offended to lash out. But as we all take up our original seats, our shaking hands resting on the planchette once more, the board feels…soft.

I was expecting it to feel heavy, the air thick with dread, the same way it does every time we interact with the ghost. But this time is the opposite.

"Does it feel different to you guys?" I dare ask.

"It almost feels gentle," Evie answers hoarsely.

Violet rolls her eyes. "Are you guys insane? This thing just moved on its own and you're calling our attacking ghost gentle?"

"No, Vi, I'm saying it feels different."

"Different how?"

I wave my free hand in the space between us. "The air! Every time something happens it usually—"

The planchette moves.

Evie and I squeal at the same time Violet and Phoebe gasp, their shock internalizing while mine seems to crawl up my neck, begging me to continue screaming.

"What is it spelling?" Evie whispers quickly, as if not wanting her words to disturb the movement.

Violet cranes her neck, tracking the planchette.

But there's no need; it stops on each letter, waiting for us to say it out loud before moving on. The girls and I call it out together as it moves.

"I."

My chest tightens.

"S."

Bees swarm inside my lungs, taking flight.

"A."

Sweat beads across the nape of my neck.

"B."

Tears spring into my eyes.

"E."

The girls turn their wild gazes on me, until it moves again.

"L."

It pauses. It won't move on until we call it again.

"L."

A sob flies from my mouth.

"A."

Isabella.

I snatch my hand back, anger rising in me as quick as a whip. "This isn't funny," I practically growl, vibrating with rage. "It's messing with us—with me! Isabella isn't here, it's the stupid fucking ghost messing with my head!"

The planchette moves again, rapidly this time, the movements janky and quick as if whoever is making it do this is trying to speak as quickly as they can.

I don't join the girls in calling out the letters this time. I couldn't even if I wanted to; my throat is burning, my eyes filling with tears.

"P."

"R."

"O."

"O."

"F."

Proof.

Phoebe's brows furrow, a flash of anger and doubt crawling into her features as she chews on her bottom lip. Evie and Violet don't make a sound, their gazes homing in on Phoebe, pleading with her to take the lead.

I don't blame them. I probably look like a crazed bear that's being cornered.

My phone buzzes on the couch and I ignore it, but the sound makes the planchette fly wildly, moving back and forth on the letter *F*, as if urging us to hurry.

"Blair?" Phoebe says softly. My gaze swings to hers just as a tear falls down her cheek. "I completely understand if you don't want to do this but…"

My head begins to shake as I quickly stand, regardless of what I truly want to do.

"What if we hear what it has to say? Let it prove it's her—"

"It's not."

Evie doesn't look at me as she whispers, "But what if it is?"

My eyes slice to hers. I'm about to snap something I shouldn't when Violet saves me.

"You said so yourself, it feels different, not like it usually does."

Reluctantly taking my seat once more I place my hand on

the planchette. "Fine, but if this is it playing some type of sick joke—which it is—we're burning this thing," I snap.

"Deal," Phoebe pipes in before Evie can rebuke me.

The second the word leaves her mouth the planchette is moving again, like it was waiting for the go-ahead. Dread coils in my gut as the girls read aloud the letters it stops on.

"B."

"U."

"M."

"B."

It can't be…

"L."

"E."

I suck in a sharp breath. My head begins to shake.

"B."

Tears spring into my eyes.

"E."

"E."

The final letter rips my heart apart and pieces me back together again as a sob flies from my mouth.

Bumblebee.

My body flinches backward and if it weren't for the couch I rammed into, I'd be sprawled on my back. Another choked sob flies from me, this one full of shock and disbelief.

"Blair, what does that mean?" Phoebe asks.

Even she doesn't know—no one knows what that means. No one besides Isabella and me.

"It's her," I admit with a shaky breath. "It's her."

Phoebe's head snaps to the board as if my sister is trapped inside. "Are you sure?"

"Positive," I say, unable to tear my eyes from the board.

It should be impossible…and yet, the board moved on its

own, revealing my secret nickname. *Bumblebee.* Because Isabella always said I was too busy.

The hairs on the back of my neck stand on end as the left side of my body goes cold, frozen. Gasping, I snatch my hand away, attempting to massage the tingles away. The pins and needles come on so suddenly it's almost ticklish.

"What is it?" Phoebe asks, that wide-eyed horror look still plastered on her face.

"T-the air." Shaking my head in disbelief, I stutter, "I-it's freezing."

Phoebe tentatively reaches out, only to snatch her hand away with a yelp. "What is that?" she exclaims.

"Does it matter?" Violet asks, her voice taking on a hysterical lilt. "Blair's dead sister just spoke to us on a fucking piece of wood!"

"Violet!" Evie reprimands.

"No, it's okay, Vi is right."

I don't blame her, this is ludicrous. If someone told me that this would happen six months ago, I would have laughed in their face but now...I watched the planchette move, watched it spell out bumblebee before my very eyes and I *still* can't grapple with what's happening.

With a pale shaky hand, I reach out and touch the ice-cold planchette.

Urging the girls to follow suit, I say, "We need answers and maybe..." I swallow thickly to utter my next words. "Maybe Isabella can give them to us."

Before the girls can move my arm is yanked forward as the planchette flies to the edge. Hovering over *Yes.*

Squeezing my eyes shut, I try with all my might to hold in my whimper, but it's no use.

A hand lands on my shoulder, so suddenly I scream, flinging my eyes open.

Phoebe raises her hands in surrender. "It's just me, B!"

Nobody tells me I'm overreacting. They don't utter a word, but the color has drained from their faces, making them as pale as ghosts.

"Is this really happening?" I whisper, asking no one in particular.

"I think"—Evie pauses, as if getting a hold of herself before squaring her shoulders and laying a finger on the planchette—"I think Isabella wants to talk and we all need to put our fear and astonishment aside and let her speak."

With a quick glance in my direction, Phoebe lays her finger next to mine on the planchette. Her warmth and presence beside me are the only things stopping me from crumbling.

That, and apparently my dead sister, who wants to talk to me.

I snort.

Three heads snap my way with wide incredulous eyes.

"Sorry," I say, my lip quivering as I try to hold back a chuckle. "It's just…funny."

Violet's brows flick up. "You think this is…funny?"

Evie whispers out of the corner of her mouth but we can all hear her as she says, "Let her be in denial, Vi."

Another snort escapes me, this one louder.

A laugh begins to bubble up and I have no doubt in my mind that Evie is right and that what's happening to me is a type of coping mechanism. I mean, I should know, I'm a psychology major, but the laugh can't escape.

It doesn't have time to.

Because in the next breath, our arms go flying across the board.

Violet squeals before hurrying to join, lightly hovering over the planchette as it begins to move.

"P."

"H."

"O."

"T."

"O."

Photo.

"She wants us to take a photo?" Violet asks.

I deadpan, "Do you really think she wants us to take a photo? No." Turning back to the board, I steady my erratic thumping heart. "Which photo, Issy?"

The nickname is out of my mouth before I can squash it. I haven't said the name since before… I couldn't bring myself to.

Yet it's the most natural thing I've ever said.

After she passed, all I ever wanted was a final goodbye and in a strange arrangement of twisted events, maybe this is my chance.

I'll never want to say goodbye, never stop having questions to ask. But she passed so suddenly, like our parents, taken overnight without warning.

Loss is hard any way you look at it. Either you know it's coming or you don't, and no matter the situation you are *never* ready to say goodbye.

"B."

I know before it moves again exactly what it's about to spell out.

Which photo she wants me to find. And how to find it.

"E."

"D."

"R."

"O."

"O."

"M."

Bedroom.

Phoebe snaps her gaze to mine, a labyrinth of emotions swirling in those chocolate depths, along with unshed tears. Violet and Evie don't have to ask whether I know what she's talking about. One look at my and Phoebe's faces and they find their answer.

"Where?" Violet asks, determination lying in her voice.

"I have a box of Issy's photographs. They were the photos she pinned to her bedroom wall...a collage of her life."

Violet moves to stand, no doubt to race upstairs, but I fling out a hand and yell, "Wait!" She hovers and as the seconds pass, the emotions within me begin to rise, tears springing forth like a tidal wave. "I'm not done speaking to her."

Leaning forward, all I can think of are three words.

Three words that don't mean anything and yet mean so much to me.

For months I've had questions. At the beginning I would text her, asking all sorts of stupid things. It wasn't until the messages delivered did I remember I will never again receive a response.

That her name would never flash across my screen.

So many things I have wanted to say to her ran wild in my mind for two years and in the moment that it counts, all I can ask is, "Are you okay?"

A sad smile, tinged with tears, blooms across my cheeks as the planchette moves to *Yes*.

Silence settles within the room, and I savor the moment.

Savor her answer.

Whether it may be true or not, it brings an immense amount of comfort and peace to my heart.

Then the questions begin to flow, the door within my mind unlocking as the words try to scramble out.

"Who is doing this to us?"

The girls stiffen. The air grows tense, and I'd think my heart stopped beating if it weren't for its incessant thumping in my ears, banging as loud as a drum.

Phoebe is as tense as a board beside me, not breathing until the planchette begins to move. It's slow this time, almost cautious, as if she's scared.

"P."

"H."

"O."

"T."

"O."

My brows furrow as confusion swirls within me. Photo again?

"Why does she keep saying photo?" Violet says slowly, quizzically.

Evie chews on her bottom lip, her gaze full of guilt. "Are we sure it's her?" she whispers.

"Positive, no one else knew about Bumblebee."

"What if it's messing with us?" Violet asks.

Shaking my head almost violently, I say, "I don't think it is, Vi. Unless ghosts now mind read."

"Even I didn't know about it," Phoebe offers.

Her belief that it's Issy is written stark across her face, along with her free hand that hasn't stopped clenching the corner of the coffee table, as if ready to throw herself away from the board at a moment's notice.

"Then what the hell are her photos going to tell us about a haunted house?" Violet pins her eyes on me. Her fringe sticks to her forehead from all the times she's brushed her fingers through her hair. "For you, B, I want to believe. I really do. But this doesn't make sense."

Before I can respond the planchette shoots off, only

pausing as we read out the letters. Each one makes my frown deepen and my heart plummet. The sinking sensation never stops. As if my heart is tethered around a bolder that's been thrown off a cliff.

"L."

"I."

"A."

"M."

Liam.

A spark of recognition ignites within my body. *Liam Merlington.* The little boy from the Merlington attic who was found sitting amongst his butchered family members.

"F."

"E."

"E."

"D."

"I."

"N."

"G."

Feeding.

The more the planchette moves, the more my confusion grows.

"O."

"F."

"F."

Off.

"P."

"H."

"O."

"T."

"O."

Photo.

Phoebe turns to me, a million questions lying in the

depths of her eyes. "Liam feeding off photo?" she says, repeating the words the planchette spelled out.

"I'm just as perplexed as you guys," I say with a shrug.

The planchette scurries again, its movements wild and crazed as it flies around the board.

"F."

"E."

"E."

"D."

"I."

"N."

"G."

Feeding.

"O."

"F."

"F."

Off.

"N."

"E."

"G."

"A."

"T."

"I."

"V."

"E."

Negative.

"E."

"N."

"E."

"R."

"G."

"Y."

Energy.

"Liam is feeding off the negative energy of a photo?" I say dubiously.

"Is that even possible?" Phoebe asks.

The girls start throwing out theories, some valid and others wild, yet all my mind seems to do is sink into the hole of grief my sister's loss left in my heart. Into the black depth of despair.

My back goes ramrod straight.

In all the craziness of tonight, of all the questions to ask, I forgot to mention the most important one. I chastise myself. How could I have forgotten? How could I have been such a horrible sister?

My voice cracks, as if the words don't want to come out. As if they fight against their freedom. Against the answer that I know I need and yet dread to hear.

Leaning forward, as if she's sitting within the board, I lower my voice to barely above a whisper. "Issy…what happened to you? Did your stalker…?"

I can't finish the question, can't utter the words that I so desperately need to voice.

But it doesn't matter; it never has with Isabella. My sister could read me like a book, knowing things before even I did.

The planchette starts moving, slowly at first, as if tentative with her answer, until a chill goes down my spine and the planchette pauses in its wake.

BANG.

A door slams upstairs.

Our hands are flying in an instant, the planchette whizzing across the board as something that is not my sister enters the house.

Thump.

Thump.

Footsteps sound upstairs.

"M."

BANG.

The girls squeal as another door slams.

"U."

"R."

BANG.

"D."

"E."

The hairs on the back of my neck stand.

"R."

Murder.

Ice fills the room.

The planchette moves faster, hurrying to get the message out before whatever is in the house overpowers her.

The hallway light switches off.

"P."

"H."

"O."

"T."

"O."

The planchette is ripped beneath our hands as it and the Ouija board fly across the room, slamming into the wall and smashing into a thousand pieces. Splinters and wood sail throughout the room.

My scream pierces the air, along with the girls' as we jump off the floor and round the coffee table and huddle together.

Just in time for all the candles in the room to be blown out at once. No air conditioning or open window in sight.

When my sister entered the room, it felt warm, as if her calming presence filled the space, her rays of brightness heating the otherwise frigid temperature. Now that's gone and we've been plunged back into hell.

Standing huddled in the living room, shaking head to toe in darkness so vast I can't see my own hand, the situation terrifies me beyond repair. Especially as our wheezing breaths fill the empty space.

It takes several moments for our eyes, and as they do, no one dares to utter a word.

Violet's silence is deep within our bones as her fear tinges the air. The last time she spoke with this thing in the room, it choked me.

I don't think she wants to make the same mistake twice.

Although, I don't think it matters what anyone says. The room is electrified, its frenzy and anger felt in the air.

"I think it's pissed we brought the Ouija board here," I whisper, the image of the board flying into the adjacent wall and smashing into small pieces attesting to that.

Phoebe's voice quivers. "I don't think it liked that Issy told us about—"

Violet's eyes widen. "Don't provoke it!" she snaps.

Flailing my hand around in the air, I say, "Clearly it's already been provoked!"

We wait for what feels like hours in the living room. Not daring to whisper anything else. Not even a whimper.

But nothing else happens.

No doors slam shut, no footsteps stomp around, and nothing else flies across the room.

It simply just stops.

I don't say anything until the room feels as if it's back to normal, until the awful energy retreats just as quickly as it arrived.

"I think it's gone," I dare to say around my sharp exhale of relief. "Does anyone have their phone for a light?"

Evie's phone light illuminates the room, lightly showcasing the smashed Ouija board but I quickly avert my gaze away, fearful of its return.

"So odd," Phoebe whispers.

"It certainly didn't want to talk." My hand instinctively reaches for my neck. "I'm just glad it left."

"That's what's so strange," Phoebe says, and I can't help but agree with her.

But I don't dare voice it.

"We need to find that photo," Violet urges.

My heart sinks as a groan rises in my chest.

I put off looking at those photos for a reason. It encompassed everything she had lost—the person I lost. The happiness that was always present.

And I miss it so terribly I know that looking at those photos will be my undoing. But I fear if we don't look, we won't get answers.

And I'll die just as my sister did.

Chapter Thirty-Seven

"Do you want us to come with you, B?" Phoebe asks.

Turning around on the banister with the lights now fully on and the dreadful feeling of the ghost no longer lingering, I face the girls.

"I don't think I can do it alone," I confess.

Not a moment later, they join me up the stairs, their support felt through the marrow of my bones. Especially as dread and fear slice through my heart as I step into my bedroom and find all the lights glowing bright.

"I don't suppose you turned them on before the Ouija board?" Violet asks, although it sounds like she already knows the answer.

With a simple shake of my head, the girls visibly recoil. I can feel a shudder wanting to make its way through my body, but I don't let it—I can't. I have to be strong, especially as we do this.

Phoebe takes a seat on my bed, leaving a spot open for me beside her as Evie and Violet take the two bean bags.

Retrieving the box from my closet, I'm surprised it feels

heavier, as if a fifty-pound weight was added. While trying not to look at the photographs directly, I sort the photos into four piles, handing the girls one each, leaving a pile for myself.

Swallowing thickly, I peer down at the pile in my hands only to see my own face smiling back at me.

Costa Rica, the year before my parents' accident.

It's a photo my mom took of Issy and me. In the photo we're sitting on the beach, staring at the waves. Talking about God knows what but the look on our faces…carefree, happy, and peaceful.

I can't help but sigh. I look so happy. *Isabella* looks happy.

Little did we know that just a short 173 days later, our parents would be taken from us.

And two years later, my sister would join them.

"What exactly are we looking for?" Evie asks gently.

Emotion clogs my throat, my fingers trembling as I quickly scan a few images before pulling out a group shot of Issy and her friends.

"The blonde is Anna Marie, then Juliette, the redhead is Carrie, and the three brunettes are Lucy, Cleo, and Natasha." I show the image, urging the girls to pass it around. "They'll be in a lot of photos."

I'm surprised my teeth don't snap by how hard I'm clenching my jaw trying not to cry. "I think whoever was stalking Isabella is in these photos, and for one reason or another, she wants us to find who it was."

Violet has the decency to wince as she asks, "How exactly will we know who it is?"

"I honestly have no idea." I shrug helplessly. "But she was incessant on us looking through these photos. Maybe someone is acting suspicious in the background of one?"

Phoebe jumps to my rescue, scanning the image in her hands. "Blair doesn't know anything more than we do. Let's just take a look and see where it gets us."

Following Phoebe's lead, the girls start sorting through the images, albeit reluctantly.

As I flick to a photograph of Isabella standing in a lecture hall with her arm wrapped around a friend, I pause. My eyes narrow behind her shoulder to a familiar face. One that is usually full of charism and charm yet narrowed with hatred here, glued to my sister's back.

Holding out the image to the girls, I voice my thoughts aloud. "Professor Emerson made a pass at Issy... What if it was Emerson who was stalking her? Look at the hatred in his gaze. She shot him down so thoroughly, it probably wounded his ego."

Phoebe's furrowed brow deepens further. "Did she report him?"

I never showed the girls her journal entry and the thoughts of shame she felt. I know that although Issy loved Phoebe, she wouldn't have wanted anyone else to know.

"No, some stupid guy she was dating made her lose her nerve."

"Prick," Violet hisses.

Evie bites her lower lip. "What does Professor Emerson have to do with this house though?" She rushes on before anyone can speak. "I'm not doubting you or your sister; he's a sick pervert and I hope he gets fired and charged. But are we sure this is the photo she wants us to find?"

"Evie's right, set it aside. We should look at them all first."

With grim faces the girls turn back to their piles.

It's hard to go through what feels like someone's entire life. One that was cut too short.

Every smile spread across my sister's face slashes my heart, as if it's chained to a whipping post.

What I didn't realize, however, is the amount of frat parties my sister attended. She truly wasn't lying in her journal entry; nearly every image I find is her at some type of party, a red Solo cup in hand with her arm wrapped around what I'm assuming are her friends.

Or people she met while she was drunk.

What is up with everybody becoming best friends when they're drunk?

My eyes are opening to a whole new side of my sister that I never saw. Of course, she'd told me about the frat parties, but she downplayed it, saying she went once a week. There are simply far too many photographs for it to be a weekly occurrence.

I know because she's wearing a different outfit in each photo.

No wonder she was failing her classes. She may look happy, but she also looks intoxicated. I wouldn't want to wake up at the crack of dawn and go to a lecture with a splitting headache.

I don't realize how tight my chest is until a deep breath whooshes from my lungs as I stumble upon a set of photographs that were taken outside of a party.

This is the sister I knew.

The one who had sleepovers with her friends, attended bonfires, and was a dedicated student. Flipping through the photos of the friends I know, pulling goofy faces, a smile of my own spreads across my cheeks.

She looks so incredibly happy in these photos.

The smile vanishes from my face the moment the thought pops into my head. Whether she did take her own life, her journal paints a different picture. Not of a smiling, carefree college girl—the sister I adored. But one with secrets, fears, and terror running through her blood at every waking moment.

Evie's sudden gasp makes me drop the remaining photographs in my hand.

I lean forward to see what's made her face ashen, but she quickly snatches the photo out of view, squashing it to her chest.

"Evie, what is it?" I ask, sounding desperate to my own ears. "Show me the photo."

"No," she squeaks.

Violet frowns, her eyes cutting my way quickly before settling on Evie again. "If it's a nude just put it face down."

Scoffing out a laugh, I say, "Isabella would never take a photo of herself naked, let along tape it to the back of her bedroom door."

Violet must see something in Evie's eyes that I don't because all humor fades as she rises onto her knees. "Evie, give me the photo."

Suddenly appearing like a cornered animal, Evie clutches the photo tighter. "No!"

My heart sinks as tears well in her eyes and her bottom lip begins to tremble.

"Evie, please," I plead.

Shaking her head, her long gold locks swish side to side as the tears that were pooling begin to roll down her cheeks. Before any of us can move Violet pounces, pushing Evie to the ground as she snatches the photograph.

"Don't, Violet!"

Violet sits back and the moment her gaze lands on the photograph, it isn't fear I see but pure, undulated rage. One so fierce I flinch backward, afraid of the war path that's promised within her gaze.

Phoebe, seeing the reaction in our friend, lurches to Violet's side and grabs the photo. She gasps, her brows furrowing so deeply that ice settles into my stomach.

Phoebe lifts her gaze to mine, confusion no longer present, but tears.

I don't want to ask. I don't want to see.

Because I know without a shadow of a doubt that whatever they saw is going to break my heart beyond repair.

Then my eyes track downward, to the word scribbled on the back of the photograph.

A nickname that I thought was only for me.

Isabella's Journal Entry

I can feel his eyes on me.

They're always on me. Leering at any inch of skin he can find.
Everywhere I go, anything I do, I can never escape him and those eyes.
But that ends tonight.

He doesn't know that I know. He hasn't realized that I didn't run to my
building out of fear. Instead, it hums in my blood, chanting a word that
fuels the anger.

Revenge.

Instead of him watching me sleep, change, and eat—no doubt perving on
me while I shower too—I will be the one to watch him. I will be the one
to torment him. I will be the one to make him second-guess everything. I
will be the one who puts fear in his eyes as he looks over his shoulder for
the thousandth time.

And I am going to nail his balls to the wall for this.

Confronting him won't be enough. I want to humiliate him, I want him
arrested, and I want everyone to know what he's been doing to me and no
doubt to others in the past.

Sneaking into my room and stealing my underwear, stealing lipsticks and
hairbrushes, watching me sleep—I want them to know the psycho that
lies beneath the mask he's created.

But first...I want him to know that I'm not afraid.

Isabella

The moment my bedroom door handle twists, horror thunders through me. But only for a second because as he steps into my room, a greedy smile full of anticipation dancing across his lips, anger takes hold.

Barging out of the closet, I throw the heaviest book I own at his head before quickly flicking the lights on.

"You sick son of a bitch!" I scream.

He doesn't have time to recover from the whack to his head. As he rubs the tender spot where it landed, I kick him in the back with all my might, sending him sprawling to the floor. My hand clutching the baseball bat trembles violently, and no matter that I'm white knuckling it, my hand is slicked with so much sweat it slides down the length of it.

I don't want to hurt him. Not physically, at least. I just want to scare him before I make his life a living hell and burn his world to the ground.

It takes him a moment to turn, as if he's grappling with what to do and doesn't want to face being caught.

I kick his shoe. "Look at me," I spit through gritted teeth.

Blue eyes snap to mine, full of so much rage I take a step back, lifting the bat in my hand higher.

I point it at him. "Stand. Up."

He's slow at first, wincing as he rights himself, no doubt feeling a sledgehammer of a headache coming on. The book was a 1201-page hardback... It would have hurt like a bitch.

"What will it take to keep you quiet?"

My brows flick up in surprise. Does he really think he's getting out of this unscathed? That he can throw Daddy's money around and shut me up?

"You tormented me for months!" I sneer. "Nothing will fix this. Money doesn't make all your problems go away, and certainly not this time."

A muscle feathers in his jaw.

His body exudes tension. I've never seen him stand so still. Every fiber of his being seems to be focused on control-ling himself—leashing the rage simmering in his depths.

"You put on a good mask, I'll give you that. You have everyone fooled—me included." I scoff out a laugh devoid of any humor. "I wish I saw through you the moment I laid eyes on you. I wish I never spent time with you, let alone touched you."

I cannot believe I ever went out with him. That I kissed my stalker...

If I had stayed away from alcohol and partying, I would have never failed my classes. I would have never been propo-sitioned by my professor. I wouldn't have had to go through any of this.

"What do you want, Isabella?" he asks, his voice devoid of emotion.

It's as if a switch has flipped and the golden boy persona has dropped.

His true self is hideous.

The way he's looking at me right now sends a chill down my spine and I clutch the baseball bat just a little tighter. Something tells me that if I told him I'm going to expose him, it would be the last thing I ever did.

So, I don't.

"I won't tell anyone, so long as you never look at me again." My back straightens, steel inflicting my tone. "I mean it. If I so much as feel your gaze on me again or find you anywhere near me or my room, I will not only tell everyone, but I will castrate you myself."

His eyes narrow, his neck flushing red as that anger boils over. When he takes a menacing step forward, it takes all my restraint to hold my ground, to not allow him to see the fear that makes me want to cry and scream.

"I'm not done with you," he says, deadly low, ice in his voice. "We are not done."

"Yes, we are." Gently placing the baseball bat against his chest, I start to push, surprised that he allows me. No doubt he thinks he still controls me. That I didn't lie before and am going to keep his secret.

Not anymore. I will never let him get away with this.

Taking one last look at the boy who captured my heart, only to play with it like I was his prey, I say with all the anger and strength I can manage, "Walk away, Xavier."

Chapter Thirty-Eight

The photograph of Isabella kissing Xavier on the cheek falls from my hands.

I think someone is calling my name, maybe jostling my shoulder, but…I can't feel anything. I can't hear anyone either. My brain cannot handle this, especially as the photograph lands upside down on the ground, showing me the blue scrawl on the back.

The nickname that stole my heart…only to smash it into a thousand pieces.

Sunshine.

I turn to the side and hurl.

"Grab a bucket!" Phoebe calls, bending down to rub soothing circles on my back.

I can hear again. It's as if the bile rising in my stomach jolted my body from shock.

But I don't want to hear.

I don't want to be in a world where Xavier dated Isabella.

I don't want to be in a world where he lied to me.

I don't want to be in a world where he betrayed me.

Phoebe hisses beside me, "What are you doing?"

"Seeing if that scumbag was the one to stalk her." The anger in Violet's voice is like no other.

Evie rushes back, the pad of her steps hurried before she shoves a bucket under my mouth.

I shake my head. "I don't want to know, Violet. I can't—" Bile rushes to the surface.

"I do."

"For the love of God, Violet, can you just give her a moment to process—"

Evie and Violet gasp.

My eyes slide to them for a second, there and gone, but it was enough to see the object they hold in their hands.

My sister's journal.

"It was him," Violet says, her temper rearing to the surface, moments from explosion. "That son of a bitch!"

"Did he hurt her?" Evie asks in a small pained voice.

A whimper tumbles from my mouth a second before I vomit more. I clutch my gut as I begin to dry heave, the contents of my stomach empty though my body isn't done purging.

As if my body is trying to rid the cells that came into contact with Xavier.

I wish it was that simple.

I wish betrayal didn't feel like the photographs reached into my chest and yanked out my heart.

I wish it didn't hurt as much as it did.

And I wish I never fell for the man who murdered my sister.

BANG.

The girls and I freeze. Horror and dread curls around us as we wait…and wait…and wait.

A soft buzzing fills the otherwise silent house.

"Is that a phone?" Phoebe asks.

We quickly search. Violet finds hers on the bed, Evie's is on the desk, and Phoebe pulls hers out of her back pocket. The only phone not accounted for is mine.

I curse under my breath. "I left it downstairs," I whisper.

BANG.

BANG.

Violet snaps her gaze to my open bedroom door, only to sigh in relief. "It sounds like the front door."

"Thank God," Evie breathes.

Knock, knock.

"Blair?" a male voice calls.

The sound of it sends ice down my spine and makes my stomach cave in.

Violet rises. "What the fuck is he doing here?"

The moment the question leaves her lips my eyes snap to the red blinking dot in the corner of my bedroom. The terror and fear and dread over the last few weeks can't even compare to the feeling as my eyes connect with the camera blinking back at me.

Turning away, I lower my head and wheeze, "The cameras!"

Gasps and curses follow until someone is pulling me away and we're suddenly all huddled in the bathroom.

"He knows," Violet declares.

Phoebe clicks her tongue. "We don't know that."

"Yes, we do! He's banging down our front door right now!" Evie whines, fear in every word.

"Is that why he installed the cameras?" I ask no one in particular. "To watch me?"

Everyone falls silent. The already small room fills with tension.

Violet suddenly grabs my arms, turning me to face her.

The seriousness in her gaze, the steely reserve, snaps something within me, making me cling to every word she utters.

"You need to go and send him away." She shushes the girls as they protest. "This man stalked your sister for months and most likely…"

"Killed her," I find myself saying for her.

The severity of the situation hits us all, cutting us deep.

Violet's grimace is full of sadness and grief. "We need to be smart. It's no coincidence that you two are dating and despite our fucked-up circumstances, he put cameras throughout the house."

Phoebe nods. "She's right, and he probably saw you find the photograph. You can't lie about that."

Evie doesn't take her gaze off the closed bathroom door. "How is she going to make him go away?"

"Tell him you found it, let him weave whatever bullshit excuse he's going to come up with, and let him think you believe him." Violet ducks, catching my gaze. "You need to make sure he believes you, Blair."

She doesn't say why. She doesn't have to.

I need to make sure he doesn't turn on me…that he doesn't try to hurt me the same way he hurt my sister.

"How do I pull this off?"

"Be angry," Evie says, her gaze still glued to the door as if she expects Xavier to barge in here any moment. "Let him know that it's not okay but let him speak and let him persuade you."

"Then ask for space," Violet chimes in.

"Can you do this, Blair?"

The question comes from Phoebe, who looks just as angry and guilt-riddled as I am. I could have known two years ago. I could have read her journal and given it to the police. Then none of us would be in this situation.

My own grief stopped me from finding answers, and I will never forgive myself for that. But now is a chance to make up for it.

"I think so," I say finally. "I have to be."

"Then we cut the cameras," Evie whispers as quietly as a mouse.

Violet pulls out her phone. "Already on it."

Phoebe's gaze lingers on mine before she grimaces and turns away. "Should we maybe leave them on?"

Evie frowns. "Why? I don't want him watching me."

"No, she's right," Violet admits, pocketing her phone. "He is the lesser of two evils."

"How?"

"In case he barges in here, we need it on camera."

The thought makes me woozy, stars shooting into my vision before Violet's voice draws me back to the here and now. "Okay, we all go down, let him know that we know too, and won't leave you alone. The second he's gone, we come back here and call the police."

"That sounds wise," Phoebe mutters under her breath.

She sounds sarcastic, but her eyes say anything but, fear shining clear within them.

Steeling my spine, I move to open the door. "Let's get this over with before I lose my nerve."

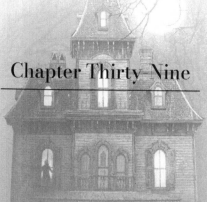

Chapter Thirty-Nine

Trepidation hums through my bloodstream, fear pulses in my heartbeat, and rage ricochets off every step I take toward the front door.

He's still knocking, calling my name as a desperate plea.

It makes me sick.

I can't stomach the emotions I'll feel once I face what we were to each other. How easily he manipulated me. How he infiltrated my life.

What he took from me—what he *did* to my sister.

I can't face it. Not now, especially as I wrap a shaking hand around the doorknob and yank it open.

Xavier stands at the door in light-wash baggy jeans and a white T-shirt—panting, as if he's just run a marathon.

I suppose that's what fear does to a person. So I guess I'm surprised my own chest isn't rising and falling rapidly.

He heaves a deep sigh. "Thank God! I thought something terrible had happened."

Something terrible did happen.

My brow furrows. "Why are you here, Xavier?"

I can't keep the ice out of my voice, and I chastise myself

for it because he looks at me—truly looks at me. At the anger brimming in my gaze, the way I'm clenching the door, not opening it fully.

Then his gaze moves behind me and his face plummets.

He takes a step forward, devastation pouring off him in waves. "Oh, Blair."

I hold up my hand. "Stop. Don't take another step."

He clutches his chest as if pained.

Is this real? Is the loss I see on his face real or is this all an act?

"You know."

As if my heart needed him to confirm it, it splinters, cracking into a million tiny pieces. Effectively killing the infatuation that beat for him.

"Yes," I say simply, trying not to sneer.

His eyes bore into mine. "Let me explain—"

Anger rises. "Sunshine?" I spit. "Ran out of creative ideas, or were you just too lazy? Felt like recycling?"

He looks as if I physically slapped him.

"Please, Blair, you have no idea—"

"You dated my dead sister and never told me about it!" I scream, erupting like a volcano that's laid dormant for thousands of years. "You *actively* pursued me. *What is wrong with you?!*" I bellow.

He leans back, his brows furrowed deeply as he shakes his head. "I *never* dated your sister."

I pause. "Don't lie to me. There's a photo of her kissing you."

"On the cheek."

"Like that makes a difference," I scoff.

He raises his hands in surrender. "I swear to you, Blair, I never dated her. It was a friendly kiss on the cheek. We used to party together, but we were never more than two drunk acquaintances."

He truly is a fabulous liar, a professional. If it weren't for the journal entries, I'd believe him. Just like it seems he believes his own lies.

Sticking to the plan, I begin to close the door. "I need time to think."

He shoves his foot between the door, jamming it before I can close it. The movement makes my heart lurch.

This is the last face my sister ever saw. The last person she laid eyes on.

This is the man who stole her from me.

With that piece of truth in mind, my eyes narrow, my jaw clenching as I spit, "Remove your foot, Xavier."

"Please, Blair, don't do this. I know I should have told you that I knew her, but I thought it would be too painful and I didn't want you to know about that side of her. You thought so highly of her—"

"*Do not blame this on Isabella!*" I roar. "Do not pin your guilt and blame on her! She is innocent!"

Tears well in his blue eyes. "Please don't shut me out, Blair. I can't lose you."

The plan, B, think of the plan.

I can hear Violet's voice in my head as clear as day, as if she was telepathically talking to me.

It's what gets me through my next words as I take a deep breath. "I'll call you Xavier...I promise. I just need space to work through this." Swallowing past the lump of disgust, I force myself to say, "To process."

It looks as if I sucker punched him. "Okay." Taking a slow step back, he whispers, "I'll wait for you, Blair. I always will."

I wish I could scream but instead, I say nothing and let the door slam shut before I turn the deadbolt.

"What exactly did the journal say?" Phoebe asks, turning to Violet the moment we enter my bathroom again.

She shrugs helplessly. "That she saw Xavier leaving her place when no one was there."

The small sliver of hope that blossomed in my heart when Xavier pleaded his case, when he looked *wounded* by the fact that I didn't believe him, disappears the moment the words leave Violet's mouth.

Evie holds up her hand to stop the chaos that no doubt was about to start. "What I don't understand is how this photo ties into our haunting problem."

The girls mirror my frown.

"The board—Issy—whatever spoke to us—said that Liam was feeding off the photo's negative energy." My gaze darts around the girls' faces full of despair. "What if Liam is somehow feeding off Xavier?"

"It's possible?" Evie says but it comes out more like a question.

Phoebe rubs her temples. "I can only deal with one problem at a time and so far, we only have a solution to one, so can we please just focus on calling the police and nailing this sick fucker?"

My head rears back at her language. Phoebe never swears.

Violet pulls out her phone without another word and Phoebe doesn't reprimand me as I begin to bite my nails.

Violet's swallow is audible as she says, "Police please."

Her eyes flash to mine. "My friend is being stalked and I'm concerned about our safety."

After explaining everything in detail to a very grouchy 911 operator the girls and I were surprised when she said to hang tight and that they'd send a patrol car when they could. I had to bite my tongue to stop myself from sneering. We had just encountered a possible murder and that the suspect was no doubt lingering outside our house and she simply told us to *wait*.

That was two hours ago.

We haven't left the bathroom out of fear and shock.

But as Evie's stomach grumbles loudly, I sigh. "We need to leave the bathroom."

Violet lets her head fall back to the wall. "We didn't check if everything was locked. I'm not leaving until the police are here."

"Why don't we just check the cameras?" I suggest, making the girls perk up. "We can see that it's all clear, go downstairs, and eat some food while we wait for the police on our very nice and comfortable couch."

Phoebe's brows rise. "Could you eat right now?"

"No," I answer honestly. "But Evie needs to."

Her cheeks tint pink with a fierce blush. "I didn't eat lunch! I was so nervous about the Ouija board!"

"That feels like weeks ago." I can't believe that was just mere hours before now.

"I can't believe I actually forgot about it," Phoebe says. Then she bursts out laughing. "I forgot about a ghost throwing a Ouija board across our living room."

Violet doesn't raise her head from her phone as she snorts. "I think we're all going to need Blair to put us through therapy after this."

Evie gives me a small smile. "No offense, B, but I think you might need it more than us."

"You're not wrong about that," I grumble.

My mind still hasn't caught up to the fact that Xavier was the one to stalk Isabella and the one to— I can't go there. I can't face it, not yet.

"It's clear," Violet declares suddenly. Pocketing her phone, she stands, opening the bathroom door and hurrying down the stairs. "I'm starving!"

While Violet and Evie rush to the kitchen I veer left into the living room, surprised when Phoebe trails behind me.

"You're not hungry?"

Her eyes are red-rimmed and puffy. "No."

She doesn't have to say it. I know how she felt about Issy, how much she admired her. We all felt like sisters and this betrayal is no doubt slicing its way through her heart as much as it is mine.

Her entire body sags as we take a seat on the couch.

"How much longer do you think the police will be?" she asks after a moment.

"I thought they would have turned up hours ago, if I'm being honest."

Phoebe shakes her head, tears welling. "I can't believe I encouraged you to date him."

A sob flies from her throat and the second the sound permeates the air I lean forward, wrapping my arm around her. "You couldn't have known, Phoebe."

Her shoulders shake, silent tears rolling down her cheeks.

"I'm supposed to be comforting you, not the other way around."

"Oh, you will, and I expect you to, but…" I shake my head. "I feel numb."

I don't want to feel it. Not yet.

Chapter Forty

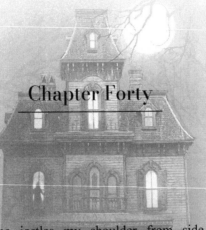

Someone jostles my shoulder from side to side, shaking me without reprieve as they scream my name.

"Blair!"

My eyes feel as heavy as boulders as I try to lift them through my sleepy haze. It's dark, incredibly so, and yet there's a shadow standing over me.

It isn't until I see the red hair, identical to my own, do my eyes flare.

"Issy?" I whisper in astonishment.

She covers her lips. "Shh!"

Scrambling to sit up, I look around to find I'm still in the living room. The girls and I fell asleep. They're still all where I last saw them sitting.

Shaking my head, my eyes fill with unshed tears as I come face-to-face with my sister.

"Isabella," I sob.

She kneels before me, putting her hands on my shoulders. The moment I feel her warm touch on my skin once more, I crumble, tears wracking my body.

"I thought you died!"

Pity fills her green eyes, identical to mine. She smiles down at me with such sadness. She strokes my hair, leaning forward to plant a gentle kiss on the top of my head. "Oh, B. I did."

Pulling back, my jaw goes slack. "But you're standing right in front of me, Issy. Don't tell me that you're dead."

She leans forward. "This isn't real, B."

I can't help but frown. "What are you talking about?"

She looks over her shoulder. I follow her sight to see nothing but my living room, yet when she turns back to me, fear is etched across her face. It wracks her body as she shakes like a leaf.

"Please wake up, Blair."

"I am awake…"

"No. Wake up, Blair!"

"Stop it, Issy! You're scaring me!"

She shakes my shoulders harder this time, so hard my head goes flying back. "*Wake up, Blair!*" She looks behind her again, a whimper flying from her mouth. "He's in the house!" she screams. "Wake up!"

Chapter Forty-One

I jolt awake with a gasp.

The living room is plunged in darkness and if I hadn't awoken with a start, I'd think I was still dreaming. The girls are sleeping in the same position as they were in my dream. The only thing that's different is that my sister is no longer here.

Issy... My heart pounds in my chest so frantically I place a hand over it and push, hoping the movement will slow its beat and yet knowing it's fruitless.

I don't even remember falling asleep. The girls came to join Phoebe and I as we waited for the police to arrive and then...nothing.

Violet's sound asleep beside me, her phone clutched in her hand face up with the camera's live feed still on her screen. I gently pry the phone out of her hand and look around the living room quickly, the dream playing in the corner of my mind.

I inspect each live feed of the thirteen cameras Xavier installed and come up empty, nothing amiss.

It isn't until I'm putting the phone back down that I realize each room was pitch black.

And we never turned the lights off.

Quickly snatching the phone again, I rewind the tapes instead of watching the live feed.

"*No.*"

The phone tumbles from my hand, landing quietly on the plush couch as I slap my hands over my mouth to squelch the scream that wants to tear free. Scrambling, I force myself to pick it up and watch, despite how much it shakes in my hand.

The camera feed shows the living room twenty-three minutes ago, where I and the girls were fast asleep—while a tall, dark hooded figure stood over me.

Tears spring to my eyes as my entire body feels as if it was plunged into thick oil.

I have never in my life felt as violated as I do in this moment.

Without taking my eyes off the phone I reach out and begin to shake Violet. The moment a grumble falls from her lips, I shush her and give her one hard shove.

"Violet!" I hiss.

The moment her eyes open, I'm shoving the phone in her face. She can't look away, even as her face turns paler and paler. She reaches down and picks up the bat she left on the floor.

"When was this?" she asks quietly.

"Over twenty minutes ago."

A full body shudder overtakes her before she closes her eyes quickly. When they fly open a second later, she has to blink away tears. "Call the police."

I glance down at the phone in my hand.

3:13 a.m.

Speaking of police, *where are they*?

Violet quietly jostles Phoebe and Evie awake while I dial 911 and lift the phone to my ear.

"He's in the house," Violet whispers and the second the words leave her lips the girl are springing into action, sleep and drowsiness long forgotten. Phoebe reaches forward and plucks the carving knife off the coffee table that Evie brought into the room with her.

I press the phone against my ear harder as no ringtone sounds. Frowning, I pull it away to check the volume only to find it has no signal.

"What the fuck?"

The girls are next to me in an instant, and once they see the no-signal icon flashing at the top right of my phone screen, they all pull out their phones to check.

"How do we not have a signal?"

"Do you think he used a signal jammer?" Evie offers, the true crime buff within her coming out.

My eyes widen. "He's watching us. He knows that we know he's here."

Before I can even finish my sentence the camera on the phone screen cuts out, the screen turning dark as the signal is jammed.

"Fuck this shit, I'm out!" Violet announces, grabbing Evie's wrist and pulling her toward the front door.

Not needing any convincing, Phoebe and I follow, hurrying to catch up.

Violet wraps her hand around the door handle, jostling it this way and that.

"Violet, open the door!" Evie cries.

"I'm trying!" Violet yanks it side to side, twisting and tugging in every which way. "It won't open!"

"What do you mean it won't open?" Phoebe asks. Shoving Violet out of the way gently with her hip, she tries the door. Her hand wraps around the knob, twists and pulls. Her brows furrow as she gives it another hard yank.

It won't open.

"Has he locked us in somehow?"

My voice silences them and the hairs on the back of my nape stand up as fear like no other consumes me.

Hurrying back to the living room, I try the windows, tugging upward with all my might but they don't move an inch.

"*Ughhh!*"

Tears fill my eyes as the very real possibility of being trapped inside, with no cell service in a haunted house and a psycho on the loose, weighs on my consciousness.

I spent weeks researching sociopaths and psychopaths, pouring over the differences, and all along I was dating one and never saw the signs.

"No, no, no!"

At my frenzied cries, the girls rush over, trying the windows again and again.

They never give an inch.

"We need to hide from the cameras."

Violet comes to stand beside me, the bat still clutched in her hands. "He cut them. He can't see us."

"We don't know that." Evie chews on her bottom lip, her eyes darting from the bat to the knife in Phoebe's hand. "He could have disconnected it for us, not him."

"I think either way, you two need to get something sharp and pointy."

My head snaps to Violet. "I can't stab him!"

"If you don't, he will," Phoebe says gravely. "Us or him, Violet."

"Are we really talking about murdering someone?" I

whisper hoarsely, my fear taking over and making my words crack. "Do we really think he will hurt us?"

Did he truly kill my sister?

The pity that fills my friends' gazes has my stomach lurching. "Okay, fine, but we don't split up though."

"Slasher film 101."

We've taken a hesitant step out of the living room when the door to the basement slams shut.

BANG.

We couldn't hold back our screams even if we tried.

Clutching Phoebe's arm, unshed tears burn my eyes as I try to see through the darkness. I reach over and flick on the hallway light switch. The switch clicks, the sound filling the hallway, but nothing turns on. Not even a flicker.

"The bastard cut the power," Violet growls.

THUMP.

THUMP.

THUMP.

My head snaps upward toward the ceiling as three more heavy boot steps fall.

THUMP.

THUMP.

THUMP.

My eyes widen. If he's upstairs...who shut the basement door?

With one hand wrapped around Phoebe, I reach over and grab Evie too, pulling them down the dark corridor toward the basement.

I'd rather run toward the doors that slam on their own than the psychotic stalker who killed my sister and no doubt is hunting us like his prey. Why else would he seal all the doors and windows?

Before fear can scream at me to not enter, I open the

closet door beneath the stairs and shove the girls inside, quickly shutting it behind us.

THUMP.

THUMP.

THUMP, THUMP, THUMP.

He's running.

Slapping a hand over my mouth out of fear he will hear us breathing, I squeeze my eyes shut tightly as the thumping ensues, sprinting down the stairs.

THUMP, THUMP, THUMP, THUMP.

He pauses and my heart stops.

"Where's Violet?"

Phoebe's question is answered by a high-pitched scream and a crash so loud the floorboards reverberate beneath me.

A whimper flies from my chest as it constricts. My heart feels like it's dying.

"I thought she was behind Evie!" I cry.

The loud crashing noises stop.

Phoebe slaps her hand over my mouth. Her body is shaking so violently I'm surprised it doesn't make a sound.

Thump.

One step toward us.

The screaming has stopped.

Oh God, what has he done to Violet? How stupid could I have been to not check that we were all inside the closet?

THUMP.

Another step.

THUMP.

Glass suddenly smashes.

Before any of us can react, the closet door flies open.

My throat burns as a scream tears from my throat, only to die as my eyes land on Violet, with blood pooling from her temple.

Without saying a word, she reaches in and yanks me out. I'm quick to grab Phoebe, and look back this time to ensure Evie is following as she urges us up the stairs.

But the moment I'm plunged back into the darkness of the hallway, my eyes trace out a large silhouette crumpled on the floor, a vase of flowers shattered around his head.

My arm almost pops out of its socket as Violet latches on and pulls. "Blair!" she reprimands, yanking me out of my shocked stupor.

But it was the wrong thing to say. The wrong name to call.

At my name, Xavier's eyes flare and lock on mine.

"*Run!*"

Taking my own advice I sprint up the stairs as fast I can. I push Evie in front of me, urging her and the girls to go faster.

I make it ten steps.

Ten measly steps before a hand wraps around my ankle, taking me to the floor.

I plant my hands on the stairs, catching myself a second before my face smashes against the corner of the step. The relief is short-lived. Before I can try to fight off the hand around my ankle I'm being pulled.

Yanked down…down…down…down.

Every corner of the wooden stairs assaults my stomach and ribs, smashing into the bones like someone's taking a baseball bat to my body.

I never knew being dragged down the stairs could hurt so much.

"Blair!" Evie screams.

My hands shoot out blindly, frantically trying to latch onto anything to stop me from being pulled farther. My nails claw into the wood, splinters burying themselves under my nails until my hand finally wraps around something warm.

My head snaps up as my body is jolted in two directions. Evie, clutching my hand with a tight grip, pulls me up.

But gravity is on Xavier's side, and all it takes is a menacing growl and a swift tug until I'm falling again.

"We're not done!" he roars.

Screaming, I pull my free foot back. "Yes. We. Are!" With all my might I kick out, relief filling my entire body as my foot connects with his face and a sickening crunch follows. His hand instinctively lets go of my ankle.

Clambering to my feet, I rush for the girls. "Hurry!" I cry.

Xavier slides down the stairs, clutching his nose. Blood pours from beneath his hand, a river of red running down his shirt as he roars in pain.

Rushing into Violet's room, Evie locks the door behind us as Phoebe and Violet begin sliding furniture in front of the door. Not caring for what breaks or smashes along the way.

"Put the heaviest furniture in front of it! Quickly!" Phoebe urges.

We slide Violet's desk in front of the door while Phoebe begins to stack her bedside tables on top. Heaving and panting not only with exertion, but fear.

I'm lifting Violet's ottoman from the foot of her bed when a chill snakes down my spine.

"*Blair*," Xavier sing-songs.

I freeze, the ottoman midair as Xavier calls my name again, eerily singing it from the bathroom next door, just one wall separating us.

"*Blairrr.*"

He's gotten as close as he possibly can.

Evie whimpers, scampering back into the farthest corner from the wall.

"What a shame it had to come to this."

He almost sounds remorseful, but I know it's an act. The

only reason he felt any emotions toward me and my sister is because of his obsessive attachment, but those feelings aren't real. They're fleeting, and the only ones that stick around are his rage and temperament over controlling what he believes belongs to him.

"Go to hell!" I scream.

He tsks, "That's not the way to speak to me right now."

Tears spring into my eyes. "Why did you do it?"

I have to know. I need answers.

"What? Stalk your sister or slash her wrists?"

My body sways. My vision blurs. My heart drops.

Phoebe's hand snaps down on mine, squeezing tightly as I begin to wheeze. I couldn't hold back my tears even if I wanted to. Deep sadness and yearning bubbles up within me, my heart breaking in two for the sister he stole from me.

The life he cut short.

I didn't know I needed to hear it from his mouth. That I needed the confirmation, but now that I have it… Guilt, strong and swift, slashes my heart.

I knew she didn't leave me. She would have never left me.

And yet, I believed it. I didn't go searching for answers.

I should have, and that will be the biggest regret of my life.

The guilt of knowing that I could have locked Xavier away years ago with Isabella's journal makes me sick to my stomach, the weight of it suffocating.

"Why are you doing this, Xavier?" Violet asks, deadly calm. Yet I see through it—her anger is bubbling over the fear. The loss of control we're all feeling, the helplessness— she shoves it aside and allows the fury to come forth and fuel her.

"Violet…" He says her name as if he's tasting how he will

make her blood spill again. "Are you going to hold me to your promise?" he taunts.

Her brows furrow before snapping sky high.

She promised to make him wish he was never born, along with a colorful explanation of cutting his balls off and shoving it down his throat.

"I hope you do," he sighs. "These things get rather tedious when no one fights back. People always think we don't want the struggle, but on the contrary...it's exactly what we want."

Fear gives way to rage as memory after memory floats through my mind of all the times he betrayed me. "You held me while I cried over what happened to my sister...while all along it was *you*."

A dark rumbling laugh bursts free. "Blair, if this is going to work, you have to let go of the past."

"If *what* is going to work?" Phoebe demands, taking a protective step closer to me.

He sighs deeply as if exasperated. "This is what's going to happen. You're going to give me back *my* Blair. If you do so, I'll let you three go, but make no mistake, if you don't give her back to me, I have no qualms killing every last one of you to get to her."

"Did he say *my Blair*?" Phoebe whispers, dumbfounded.

"He doesn't own me."

"He thinks he does," Violet says, her gaze locked on the wall that's shared with the bathroom. "He's never going to give up."

"Ahh, finally someone has a fleck of intelligence. Well done, Violet."

Violet snatches the knife out of Phoebe's hand. "We need to kill him."

"Vi!" Evie cries.

"Did you not just hear him? He just announced that he's going to kill us!"

My eyes slide to the window. Cupping my hand around Violet's ear, I whisper, "You go out the window and down the drainpipe and find help. I'll distract him."

Violet pulls back, already shaking her head as tears spring to her eyes. The sudden emotion in her shocks me to my core. Violet never shows vulnerability, only anger.

"I'm not leaving you with him," she sniffles.

"You have to." I grab her arms and plead, "Get us help, Vi."

Before she can protest, I turn to the wall. "What do you want from me, Xavier?"

"You."

Coldness seeps into my bones.

Violet is right, he will never stop.

"You had me…and then you lost me."

A thump against the wall startles me.

I turn to the girls, pushing them to the window as quietly as I can as I plead with my eyes for them to try. I start talking again to cover up the sound of the window sliding open. The fact that it budges almost makes me cry with relief.

"It wasn't enough that you took my sister away, but you had to have me too. Why, Xavier? How can you do that to someone you love?"

"That's what men do to women."

"No, they don't."

He chuckles darkly. "It's what my father did. You never did ask how my mother died. It seems to be a running tradition in our family."

My eyes widen. "You're sick."

"You don't get it. You will never get it," he spits.

Craning my neck, I find the girls whispering under their

breaths with their heads out the window, no doubt trying to figure out the safest way to get down the two-story drop.

"Explain it to me, then."

Anything to distract him.

A sick, slimy sensation crawls over my skin as his voice takes on a whimsical pitch. "Isabella was perfect... *We* were perfect. I didn't see how smart she was, though. I knew there were brains behind the party façade but not to her extent. It truly did shock me when she caught me in her room." He scoffs. "The stupid bitch was so paranoid, she wasn't in her right mind when she broke up with me. I knew it was a lapse in judgment."

I clamp a hand against my stomach as if I can stop the nausea churning through me.

"I loved her... I could have given her a beautiful life, but she had to ruin it." A loud bang slams against the wall, making me scream with a jump. "*Nobody leaves me!*" he roars. "We're done when I say we are done!"

A sob rises but I stuff it down.

No matter what he says, no matter how much it makes me want to scream and cry and rage, I have to keep going. I have to get us out of this.

It's my fault, after all. The girls don't deserve this.

"You killed her because she broke up with you?" I ask, allowing my need for answers to fuel me.

"No, I killed her because she wouldn't do as I said. She was disobedient and had to be put down."

A humorless laugh bursts free from my chest before I can stop it. "She wasn't a dog!"

"Clearly not, because she was untrainable." His voice loses the hardness, growing impossible soft. "That's when I saw you, Sunshine, at her funeral." He sighs whimsically. "Oh, it was like you were heaven-sent. My very own ray of sunshine gifted from the universe. The moment I saw the uncanny resemblance, I could barely restrain myself, I wanted you so much. I thought, here's my second chance! To make things right!" His voice changes, taking on a light tone as if he was smiling at the memory. "That's when I knew Isabella was sent to me as a test. A trial run, if you will."

I can't stop the vomit from rising this time. Snatching Violet's trash can, I hurl, the sound of his voice making my stomach roll relentlessly without an end in sight.

"I waited for you, Blair. I saw how sad you were and although I wanted to comfort you, I knew you weren't open. You weren't quite ready for me. I needed my sunshine to glow." He groans. "It was painful, watching you day in and day out for two years. I had plans for us, but fate intervened. Our run-in wasn't planned, but when we met in that hall-way… I felt the sparks fly, Blair. I knew it was fate bringing us together."

Wiping my mouth as soon as my stomach settles, I lift my head to find the girls tying sheets together.

"I just needed…to give you a little push."

My brow furrows. A push? As much as I hate myself for it, I was head over heels for him the moment I met him. What sort of push—

Suddenly, a gasp escapes me. The sound drives a laugh from him.

"Putting the puzzle pieces together now?" He clicks his tongue. "The car battery…" he groans, yet it almost sounds like a moan. "It felt so good to have you at my mercy."

"You son of a bitch," I spit.

"I don't think *bitch*. The devil, perhaps. Satan does have a nice ring to it, but do you want to know what sounds better, Blair?"

"What," I say through gritted teeth.

"Ghost."

The blood drains from my face. My entire body plunges into a cold so frosty I'm surprised I'm not drowning in the ocean.

Out of the corner of my eye, I see the girls pause.

"What did you just say?"

"You won't understand this now but, in the future, years from now when we start a family of our own, you will see I did this for us." I can hear the smile in his voice, the breathy quality it's taken, almost as if he's turned on. "When I followed you to that haunted house in Campbellton and watched your terrified face as you ran out of the house screaming, I saw you run directly into Phoebe's arms, clinging to her for dear life. It got me thinking…I needed you to *need* me. Not want. Lust comes and goes, but dependency? *Fear?* That sticks around."

My knees threaten to give way and Phoebe rushes to me as I sway.

"What are you saying, Xavier?"

"That it was far too easy to spike your morning caffeine with psychedelics. Guess I got lucky you were all too stupid to question *who* made the coffee."

The girls faces' turn grim and ashen. Phoebe whispers, "Is he saying that…?"

There's a tense moment of silence before Xavier's laughter floats through, having apparently heard Phoebe's sickening question. Only, he suddenly pauses. The silence stretches for what feels like hours until he says darkly, no emotion in his voice, "What I'm saying is that there was never a ghost roaming these halls."

Violet cranes her neck, listening to something I can't hear from the other side of the room.

BANG.

The sound ricochets from within the wall, shocking Violet so roughly she falls to the ground, taking Evie with her. It's so deafening that when there's a pause, I can hear my own heart thumping in my ears. Until a bang breaks the silence once more and the very walls shake as an axe slashes through it.

"He's in the wall!" Violet screams.

Chapter Forty-Two

Chaos erupts as Xavier pulls the axe out of the wall and strikes again.

He's inside the wall.

Furniture flies as we all struggle to clear the doorway, not daring to go anywhere near the open window.

"Where the fuck did he get an axe from?!" Violet exclaims.

"I don't care! Push!"

Throwing the ottoman to the side it almost collides with Evie, who is pulling with every ounce of strength she has to move the desk.

BANG.

"*Ahh!*" A sob flies from me as a piece of the wall gives way and Xavier smiles from within.

"Come here, Blair."

My shoulders shake with silent sobs. I can't even muster an ounce of relief once we clear a crack in the doorway. Not when he slashes his axe again.

BANG.

The sound of the metal hitting the wall makes Phoebe

drop the knife in shock.

Violet shoves her way through the small crack open in the door, hurrying Phoebe. "Just leave it!"

Phoebe is next as Evie doubles back to pick up the knife, right as Xavier begins to step through the large hole he created in the wall.

I scream as loud as I possibly can, praying that the neighbors soon wake from their drunken stupor. Throwing myself through the crack I reach out, my fingers skimming Evie's arm to pull her with me, but I'm not the only one who reaches for her.

Her golden blonde hair splays in all directions by how quickly Xavier wraps his hand around the back of her neck and yanks.

A yelp of surprise is all that leaves Evie's lips before Xavier pulls the knife out of her hand and plunges it into her abdomen.

Evie's blue eyes widen in shock, locking on mine as blood begins to pool around the knife wound. With a sickening sound of tearing flesh, Xavier wrenches it out, stealing her breath.

"I told you what would happen, Blair."

My body grows numb as fingers wrap around my arm and pull me the rest of the way. Evie's haunted eyes follow the movement until I can no longer see her, and Xavier is running for the door.

Violet practically carries me down the hallway.

Phoebe cranes her neck as she runs. "Where's Evie?"

My mouth opens and closes, but no sound comes out. Violet stops at the top landing. "Blair, what happened to Evie?"

"H-h-he stabbed—"

Violet lets go of me, running down the stairs to meet

Phoebe, only to grab the baseball bat out of her hand and run back.

"No, Violet, don't!"

She lifts the bat as the sound of crashing furniture comes from within her room. "I'm not leaving her!"

Phoebe and I run after her, trying to grab her and stop her. Phoebe sobs, her body shaking uncontrollably.

Violet's bedroom door swings open, making Phoebe and I come to a halt.

"You don't have a choice," Xavier growls.

Phoebe and I let out a deafening scream as Xavier brings the back of his axe down upon Violet's head, making her crumble to the ground with the force.

Sobbing isn't the right word for the sound that tears from me. It's like a dying animal, wailing in grief and pain.

Phoebe is no different.

We huddle together, and despite my numb body, it seems to know what to do as it subconsciously flees for my bedroom. My steps are wobbly, my mind hazy. It's as if I was the one hit in the head.

But the ten-second head start that we needed, the moment we needed to pounce and run, is taken away as Xavier charges into the room and snatches Phoebe, pressing her back to his front. He holds the knife to her neck.

Evie's blood drips down Phoebe's neck.

"Let her go, Xavier!"

A devilish smirk dances across his lips. "Come with me or I kill her."

Phoebe sobs, the working of her throat making the blade slice her skin, sending droplets of blood down her throat. They mingle with Evie's.

The sight is enough to allow true panic to engulf me and common sense to leave.

"I'll come with you!" I cry out. "I'll come with you. Just please put the knife down."

Phoebe starts to cry, no doubt a protest about to leave her lips, but Xavier pushes the blade farther into her neck, cutting off whatever she was about to scream.

She tries to plead with her eyes, begging me not to go with him, but all I do is smile, one full of sadness and sorrow.

He already took one sister away from me. I'm not letting him take another.

"It's okay, Pheebs," I say gently.

She tries to shake her head but the blade stops her.

I look to Xavier, relief in his gaze.

"Pack a bag, Sunshine."

My stomach recoils at the nickname and before I can stop myself, I flinch.

"I'm not doing anything until you let her go."

He cocks his head, those blue eyes that I once adored boring into mine. And then he moves, ripping Phoebe away and pushing her so forcefully she goes flying across the room. The resounding smack of her head as it collides with the wall makes me sob.

"Phoebe!" I scream and rush for her.

I'm inches away, my gaze connecting with the blood trickling behind her head on the wall, but then fingers wrap around my bicep and I'm yanked backward so suddenly the wind is knocked from me as Xavier pins me to the ground.

With my wrists above my head and the blade digging into my wrists, his face hovers above mine. "Our deal was I let her go and in return you pack a bag." He shakes his head as if disappointed with me. "I never said anything about going to her." A smile flashes across his lips. "You should have bargained a better deal, Sunshine. Where's the girl who loves to negotiate?"

My lip curls back in a sneer. "Get. Off. Me."

His face drops, a hair's breadth away from my lips. "What's the magic word, Sunshine?"

"Fuck off," I spit.

Before I can blink his hand whips out, smacking my head to the side and making stars shoot into my vision. He roughly cups my jaw, whipping my head back to his and shaking me until my vision clears.

"Don't you ever speak to me with such disrespect again!"

I realize with stark clarity that this was the training he was talking about.

Everything he has done, his beliefs and his ideologies, have stemmed from his father. He even killed Isabella the same way his father murdered his mother.

All of this is normal to him, and as I peer into his rage-filled eyes, I know without a shadow of a doubt there will be no reasoning with this man.

So, I play the part he wants me to. It takes no effort for me to allow fear to seep into my eyes and fill with tears as my gaze flicks to Phoebe's unmoving form. "I'm sorry, I'll never speak to you with such disrespect again. I'm just worried Phoebe hurt herself."

Herself, not him.

And as his eyes clear and soften I know I chose my words wisely.

Xavier has to believe he's in control, calling all the shots, and that I'll do whatever he says. He needs me to play the part of a doting girlfriend, one that is madly in love with him and not sick at the sight of his very face.

For the first time, I'm beyond thankful that I went down the road of psychology and studied sociopaths all these weeks, especially as Violet's words rush to me, those she spoke to me in the bathroom before everything went wrong.

I have to make him believe me.

He smashes his lips to mine and I'm grateful for the shock that courses through me. If it weren't for that, the disgust that is raging beneath it would have reared its ugly head and I would have messed up my chance before it even began.

Relief fills me once he pulls back and stops kissing me. He smiles. "I knew you were perfect."

"W-where are we going to go?" My voice cracks and I have to clear my throat, willing the tears back down. "You k-killed Evie, most likely Violet too… They'll look for you."

Phoebe, I'm praying, is just unconscious. This cannot be for nothing.

He leans back, letting go of my wrists. Only now do I realize how tightly he was gripping them. My hands have turned numb.

He rolls his eyes. "That's what happens when you come between soulmates. Stupid bitches," he spits. "That's why I need you to pack a bag. My father's cabin isn't registered in our family name and it's so far from civilization, no one knows it exists besides us two."

My lip quivers and it takes every single ounce of strength within me not to cry.

I can't let him take me; I cannot get into his truck.

If I do, I fear it will be the last time I'll ever see this world.

"W-what should I pack?"

He begins to get up and yanks me to a stand, leading me away from Phoebe and toward my closet. "Just the essentials. We should get a move on."

With shaking hands, I move to open my closet door but pause and turn to Xavier, who's watching me like a hawk. "Where are the police, Xavier?"

His eyes darken. "What?"

"We called the police hours ago—"

"You owe me for that. It was one thing to convince them it was a prank, it was another to call my dad and get him to cancel the officers to your house."

All the blood within my body feels as if it rushes for my head, making me sway as my legs threaten to buckle beneath my weight. "Y-your dad's a—"

"The sheriff."

And then it all clicks, like a lightbulb going off inside my brain. It's how he got away with it, how Isabella's death was ruled a suicide, why no one questioned it. How Xavier's father got away with it too, not only once with his mother but twice by covering up Isabella's murder.

It also clicks just how much danger I'm in. Xavier and his dad can make me disappear without a trace. Gone within the blink of an eye. Even if Phoebe wakes up and manages to get help…it could be too late. I could vanish forever.

He frowns, taking a menacing step forward. "Pack, Blair, or I'll keep to my word about Phoebe."

His words snap me into action and I push my closet door open, surprised that he allows me to shut it behind me. I yank a duffel bag off the floor and grab whatever clothes I can, not caring or focusing on what I pack so long as I put items in the bag.

I need *time*. I just need more time to *think*.

Surely I can get out of this. There has to be some way. Maybe I can run before he puts me into his truck. It's parked on the str—

BANG, BANG.

"What's taking so long?" he exclaims.

The lie flies from my mouth before it fully forms. "It's laundry day, I barely have any clothes. I have to search."

"Just pack whatever you can, I'll buy you the rest."

Like hell you will. I'd rather chew off my own arm than—

A box in the back left corner pokes out as the long coat I just pushed sways, giving way to my crafting box. My eyes alight with excitement as I quietly pull the lid off and rummage through the copious amount of beads, papers, and stickers. A sob flies from my mouth as my hands wrap around a pair of fabric scissors that I used when helping my mom create my figure skating costumes.

The door swings open, the hinges squeaking as I quickly shove the pair down the front of my pants and spin. I can only hope the baggy jeans hide the sharp blades.

Xavier's eyes narrow on my face, no doubt locked on my puffy red-rimmed eyes. He says nothing, until his eyes flick down and my heart stops beating.

Thump, thump.

He takes two steps forward and, with it, my will to breathe.

Swallowing thickly, I tip my head back, unwavering determination filling me as I'm prepared to lie through my teeth to make him—

He snatches the hat out of my hand that I didn't realize I was clutching. "You won't need this; I said essentials only."

My entire body deflates. Using the movement and relief I bend down, quickly picking up the surprisingly light duffel bag. I don't even know what I shoved in here, I was too flustered to pay attention.

"I'm done."

In more ways than one.

It feels as if the scissors burn my skin, begging me to yank them out and plunge them into his flesh like he did Evie. To make him stop hurting my friends. To claim vengeance for what he did to Isabella. To claim revenge.

I've never hurt anyone before, never had a thought cross

my mind so dark and poisonous toward another. But now, standing here looking at the man that took so much from me, all I can think about is ruining him to save myself.

His heavy hand comes down upon my shoulder, squeezing tightly as he steers me out of my bedroom, away from Phoebe's unmoving body and into the hall, where I find Violet lying unconscious.

My eyes burn with the tears that roll down my cheeks, and each step I take down the stairs feels like I'm walking to my death.

Thump.

My heart drops into my stomach.

Thump.

Sound evades me as I'm pushed into a tunnel without an end, cornered like a wild beast.

Thump.

My life flashes before my eyes, everything that I will never accomplish, the world I'll never travel.

Thump.

Then all Xavier has done, all he has taken from me, the deception he weaved—it explodes into my vision.

Thump.

The scissors call my name, marking me a killer as I reach for it.

Thump.

The attic rushes through my mind, what it showed me and how I'll die the same fate as Isabella.

In one swift motion the rage I've been holding back rises without reprieve and before Xavier can blink, before he moves to clear the last step, I spin, relishing in the way his eyes flash with shock as I lift the pair of scissors in one fluid motion, and plunge it into his chest.

Chapter Forty-Three

Crimson blood spurts across my face, droplets of it spraying, then leaking, out of his chest. Before my mind can catch up with what I've done, before it can register the flicker of fury in his eyes before hurt and betrayal take over, I run.

Past the front door that he's sealed shut and for the kitchen. I run so fast that once I make it to the kitchen island I slam into it, not being able to stop myself in time and grunt at the impact. But the burst of pain I expect to fill my body never comes.

Instead, I rear in shock as I reach for the kitchen bar stools and find both my hands covered in blood. It smears on the chair, but I don't have time to care.

This is my shot, my one chance to escape my death. That's what would happen if Xavier took me away—a life of abuse and a slow, torturous end.

With every ounce of strength I can scourge up, I lift the bar stool and pull it back, screaming with fury as I hurl it at the kitchen windows overlooking the front yard.

Glass explodes in all directions, littering the floor and my hair. I rush for the opening, reaching for the freedom I've created, a sob of relief bursting from my lips. I haul myself up onto the frame, without a care for the glass still jutting from it.

"Help me!" I scream at the top of my lungs. "HEL—"

A hand fists a chunk of my hair and yanks my head back, cutting off my pleas for help and pulling me back into the horror.

"You stupid fucking bitch," Xavier spits in my ear.

A second later he roars, and I begin to fly forward, too fast to stop anything as he smashes my head against the window frame with a sickening crunch. Glass impales my skin, followed by a blast of pain that engulfs my entire body. Stars shoot into my vision.

I cannot scream. I can't even cry. The pain is so demanding that no sound leaves my lips as I simply fall to the floor.

With darkness creeping at the corner of my vision, waiting to take me, memories assault me—terrifying ones.

It's the attic and what I suspect was Liam showing me my fate. The shadow that I now know was Xavier and how he killed my sister. Perhaps a part of Liam came back, a part of the little boy he used to be, one who saw the evil lurking in the shadows around me and decided to stop being a monster himself for a moment to show me.

It plays on an endless loop in my mind, especially as Xavier kneels beside me with a tinge of worry in his voice.

"Why would you make me do that to you, Blair?" His hand strokes my face but I can't stop it, still paralyzed by pain. "You made me bruise your beautiful face!" A sob tears from him. "My poor sunshine."

The nickname pulls a disgruntled groan from my chest.

Blood trickles into my eye as I feel more than see Xavier lean closer to me. "Blair, are you awake?"

My fingers twitch beneath me, flinching as I come in contact with a piece of broken glass.

"You can never run from me again, Blair." His voice lowers, that tinge of worry disappearing as anger takes hold. "Do not force me to hurt you."

My eyes flutter open for a moment, a split second, and yet it's enough to see how he caught up to me so fast. I plunged the scissors between his shoulder and chest.

I missed.

My one chance—gone.

A sob tears from me as something other than physical pain begins to consume me.

Despair.

Xavier wraps his hands around my shoulders as he maneuvers me onto my back, surprisingly gentle despite him causing the damage to my body.

"You were meant to be better than Isabella, Blair. You were meant to be the good sister."

My eyes flash, connecting with his blues that seem to sparkle above me with glee. He wanted this; he wanted me to be as "bad" as Isabella.

"Now that I see you're not dead…" His smile drops, wiped away in an instant. "Shut the fuck up before someone calls the police and get in the truck." He rises, clutching the area where I stabbed him. "Get. Up."

But I can't. I can feel every bone in my body, can wiggle my toes and my fingers, but I can't move. As if every instinct within me is protesting, fighting in the only way it can by refusing to obey him.

I watch the anger come over his face, the way his fists curl and his teeth grit.

But his fingers aren't the only ones to curl.

He drops beside me, spitting with venom, "I said get the fuck up, you stupid bitch!" He lowers his face to an inch above mine as he teases against my lips, "Or will you end up being like Isabella after all? For all her stupid meekness, she was tough. Do you want to know the last thing she said before I dragged that blade across her wrist?"

My breath is coming in hot pants now, every word that spews from his mouth fueling the fury within me, overriding the pain that was consuming me moments before.

He leans closer, the warmth of his breath puffing across my face. "She begged, not for her life, but for *yours*. She knew I'd find you, that with how similar you two looked I would never let you go. She knew I would claim you…so she begged for your life. What do you think she would say if she could see you now?" His eyes darken, the blues disappearing almost entirely. "I think she would wish for her last breath back. I think she'd regret wasting it on some pathetic, stupid little bitch—"

Xavier's words are cut off by the shard of glass that I plunge into his neck.

Surprise fills his features, followed by crimson blood as it pools into his mouth and drips onto my face, but I don't care. I keep my gaze locked on his, wanting to watch the very life drain from his eyes. "*That* was for Isabella," I sneer.

He makes a choked gurgling sound as he tries to speak, his mouth opening and closing until I rip the large shard of glass out of his neck. The flesh tears, more blood than I've ever seen in my life pouring from him.

Then his eyes turn unseeing, and Xavier crumbles, his weight crashing atop me.

Tears stream down my face, my body wracked with anguish as I drop the shard of glass.

My entire body is drenched in his blood as he lies motionless above me.

I'm not sure how long I stay like that—I'm not aware of anything but Xavier's dead body—until sirens blare in the distance. Red and blue lights flash through the shattered window.

All I can do is sob beneath the man who took my sister from me.

This time, when heavy boot steps thump against the patio, when their reverberations vibrate beneath me, I don't quiver in fear but cry in relief as the police knock down the front door.

Chapter Forty-Four

Two long days later, thousands of questions asked and answered with the police, an abdominal surgery for Evie, concussions for Phoebe and Violet, and many, *many* stitches for me, I sit with the girls around Evie's bed.

The relief that swept through my body as the police called out that they had a pulse was one I will never forget. That, and when they wheeled Violet and Evie out on stretchers into two separate ambulances and threw a white blanket over Xavier after the police photographed the crime scene.

I killed someone.

No matter that he killed my sister and attacked us...my hands took a life. Stopped someone's heart from beating. Every time I try to close my eyes I either see him stabbing Evie, hitting Violet unconscious, throwing Phoebe across the room, killing my sister, or coming for me.

I don't regret it, not in the slightest. I just feel changed, haunted in another way entirely.

"Did the police tell you about the crawl spaces?" Evie's hoarse voice asks.

Our gazes roam each other before we nod. "Yeah, they told us about the walls. How it was a maze of hallways just wide enough for Xavier."

Violet's jaw clenches. "The holes in Blair's wall, giving him a view to look in."

Evie's voice is scratchy as she speaks but whether that's from the ordeal she suffered or emotions clogging her throat, I don't know. "They said he had an entry point for every room."

Phoebe shakes her head. "He fooled us all."

Evie's hands wring. "What about the toxicology report?"

"What about it?" Violet says tightly.

Her entire body is guarded, her emotional walls locked tight as the vulnerability we all unknowingly were put in no doubt wreaks havoc on her mind.

"Are we going to talk about it?" she asks, her voice so small my heart pangs.

"There's nothing to say," Violet snaps.

Phoebe grimaces. "I know you don't want to talk about it, Vi, but the man claimed to have drugged us…except the doctors found nothing but high dosages of B12 vitamins in our—"

"I know," Violet cuts off, her jaw grinding.

"Does that mean that all of it…?" Evie clears her throat and tries again. "Xavier thought we were scared of a ghost because he assumed he was spiking our coffee with psyche-delics…but he wasn't." Evie's blue eyes flick between us all. "Was it all…real?"

The question hangs between us.

The ghosts.

The *need* that Xavier wanted to inflict upon me.

He thought he created it all…

"Whatever may or may not be true," Phoebe interjects,

cutting the tense silence, "I'm just grateful that his supposed dealer ripped him off. Could you imagine the side effects we would have gone through having psychedelics in our system for weeks?"

Violet visibly shudders.

"I'm not saying I'm not grateful, I'm just wondering—"

"Yes, everything that happened truly did happen," I cut in, *needing* to say what no one else can.

"We don't know that," Violet interjects. "He could have been the one slamming the doors, the lights... We know he was the one breaking in, so why couldn't it have been him doing the rest?"

Evie frowns. "Because there's so much that doesn't make sense that can't be explained. What about when Xavier saw the door—"

"Don't say his name," Violet says, deadly quiet.

I physically wince. If it weren't for me, Xavier would have never stepped foot in that house. Would have never stabbed Evie or came after the girls. A sob rises in my throat and I'm unable to stop it before it flies. "I'm so sorry."

Vi's head snaps to me. "You have nothing to apologize for," she swears vehemently.

Evie chews on her bottom lip. "Please, Blair, don't take the guilt for what he did. You didn't know."

"None of us did," Phoebe chimes in.

No matter what they say I'll always feel it.

I'm permanently stained red.

Evie frowns. "I'm sorry, but I just don't get it."

"What?"

"If you guys believe there was no ghost...how did he do it? Most things I can understand the logistics of; it would have been easy to mess with us. I mean, he had access to everything whenever he wanted but..."

Phoebe grimaces. "He was there for some of it."

Evie dips her head, a small nod of confirmation.

Not to mention how none of us can answer for how Phoebe and I ended up in the hospital.

"You should have seen his face when the door opened on its own. It was fear and horror but also…surprise and delight." Shaking my head, I feel a hot dose of self-loathing come on. "I can't believe I didn't see it until now."

"The police said he was sleeping in the closed-off attic. He had access to the house during the night so he could have set up traps," Violet suggests, her normally shiny black hair now dull after the ordeals of the past few days.

Evie's eyes flick to mine, pity in them. "Did the police tell you what they found?"

My mind flashes through the images the police showed me. Ones that I wish I never saw. "He had dozens of photographs of me, taken over the span of two years since the funeral. I saw most of them." What's left of my heart weeps. "He watched me for years."

It's how he knew so much. My favorite flowers, my coffee order. He never had to ask what classes I took and where because he already knew. It was the first thing I asked Phoebe when we were reunited… She never told Xavier all my favorites.

Something must flash across my face because the girls lean forward and place their hands on my leg in support.

"It explains the intruder," I say, sniffling. "How he came and disappeared so quickly. I also never realized how fast Xavier showed up after I texted him… I was in so much shock I wasn't thinking straight." I can't believe I feel for him and his manipulation…all the while learning about sociopaths and psychopaths.

"No matter what happened—ghost or Xavier—I'm never stepping foot inside that house again," I vow.

It's haunted for another reason entirely now. I killed someone in that house.

The girls murmur their agreements. Violet's mom is no doubt searching for a new place for us now, a more secure one with house plans that don't include walls large enough for a man to live within.

Phoebe's gaze flicks to the door, to the two silhouettes of police officers guarding the room. "Did you hear about Xavier's dad?"

Evie gasps, leaning forward. "No."

Phoebe and Violet exchange a glance. "He's been taken into custody. Apparently one of his deputies has been secretly investigating him for years."

My eyes widen as Violet lowers her voice and adds, "The sheriff's former wife wasn't the only one he abused and murdered. There's whispers that his camping trips were when he…"

Violet can't finish the sentence, but she doesn't need to. We all know where Xavier learned to kill.

"Like father, like son," I murmur.

Phoebe's eyes glisten. "At least Isabella is finally getting justice."

In a sick twisted way, I'm glad my parents aren't here to see all of this; it would have broken their hearts. Still, I would do *anything* to be wrapped in their warm arms of comfort.

"When is Garret coming back?" Evie asks.

Garret refused to leave Phoebe's side ever since the police contacted him. The only reason he left was because Phoebe begged him to get her things, saying she never wanted to go back in the house, let alone see it. He offered to pack a bag for us all.

The horror that overcame his face when he learned what Xavier had done... The image will never leave my mind, as if it branded my soul.

"Should be soon," Phoebe says.

Evie groans, sliding farther down into her hospital bed. "This is not what I had in mind when I said I loved horror movies."

A bark of laughter fills the room, one of surprise and shock that we're joking so suddenly. Although humor sometimes is the best coping mechanism.

Violet snorts. "Nice one, Evie."

She shrugs, a coy smile dancing across her lips. "I told you guys we should have gotten a German Shepherd."

Three Weeks Later

Jasper, Evie's ten-week-old German Shepherd, is glued to her side, practically nipping at her heels as she walks around our new living room space, unpacking too many boxes for just four girls.

The second we left the hospital, Evie began her search for Jasper. She's fallen in love with him like no other, and with her parents deciding to move closer due to the events that occurred, she now has a dog sitter available whenever she needs.

Her parents also couldn't say no when their daughter hadn't slept a wink in a week and would jump at the littlest of sounds.

Since then, we've all chipped in on training, taking Jasper to intense self-defense training on the weekends. We all love him, but he's Evie's soul dog.

We were also reluctant to move into a new house considering everything but after numerous inspections and checking the walls and city copies of floor plans, we moved into our new house today. The house is closer to campus, security installed by a state-of-the-art company, and Garret now lives with us. We've all felt safer since he made the decision to move in.

That, and the fact that Xavier is dead.

Although, in some twisted way, my nightmares now include Xavier running my parents' car off the road...my brain's creative way of torturing me. Along with the vivid nightmares of him killing my sister, to only then run after me with a large butcher knife, I've barely slept since I plunged that shard of glass into him, stealing Xavier's last breath.

The nightmares where I relive that moment are the most horrendous.

There was no one to tell about my sister. No parents, uncles, or aunts. Besides Phoebe and her family, the only other people I was able to share the truth with were her friends, giving them that sliver of peace that it wasn't her mental state that took her. I'm almost glad I didn't have to tell any family members; it was hard enough telling her friends.

I haven't returned to classes yet, although, I did receive an email informing me that Professor Emerson was fired. No, he wasn't the one stalking Isabella, but if he propositioned my sister and me, I have no doubts he was inappropriate with other girls.

In fact, I know he was. The moment gossip spread about the school board and police looking into him, women came forward...dozens of them.

Knowing I can walk into my psychology lecture Monday morning and not see his face brings such immense relief, it makes me excited to go back to classes. When I get to that point again.

"Housewarming anyone?" Evie grins.

"No!" we call in unison.

"I never want to hear the word *housewarming* again. It feels like the catalyst for everything."

Evie shrugs. "Fair enough. But I want a movie night."

I waggle my finger at her. "I've had enough of scary movies."

She scoffs out a laugh. "Once you've lived in a slasher film, you find the movies barely scare you anymore." She beams. "I say we watch *Barbie*."

Jasper prances away as we laugh, throwing out our movie suggestions.

"How about *The Notebook*?" Phoebe offers.

My brow quirks. "With my love life history? Not a chance."

Violet winces. "No thriller, no horror, *and* no romance… We're screwed."

Jasper's sudden bark has us turning. He's standing at the beginning of the hallway, his head tilted with his hackles raised.

Evie frowns. "Jas, it's okay, it's just the dark."

He crouches down low, another warning growl leaving him.

"Jasper, what is it?" I ask.

He's young and he's only attended training for two week-ends, but that's his cue that something is amiss—the low crouch and verbal growl of warning.

It has the hairs on the back of my nape standing on end. Everyone puts down whatever they are unpacking as we stand behind the small fur ball and assess the dark corridor.

"Jasper, what—"

Music.

Deadly, chilling, bone-jarring music begins to play.

One that makes stars shoot into my vision and my body sway.

It can't be.

"Is that…?" Phoebe trails off.

Violet sucks in a breath. "The vinyl I threw out at the old house."

A blood-curdling scream tears from our throats as the door at the end of the hallway flies open on its own and the music that's haunted us for weeks rises in volume.

Jasper whines, hiding behind Evie's leg, trembling, until she picks him up. "We were right... Xavier wasn't the only one roaming the halls at night."

The music stops abruptly.

My swallow is audible as I feel his phantom blood on my hands. "Or he's come back to finish what he started."

Screeching fills the halls, fills the room, fills our ears.

"What is that?" Evie whispers, horror in her voice.

My eyes narrow as something in the room catches my eye.

Taking a tentative, wobbly step forward, my eyes flare as shock and disbelief crash through me.

"It can't be..."

The girls gasp in unison as the scratching ceases and one word is left embedded in the hardwood floor, shining like a beacon of terror.

Hello.

Those final hours in the house come crashing into me, slamming into my consciousness so forcefully I stagger backward as the reality of one of our greatest errors becomes apparent.

My voice is small, hoarse, and coated with dread as I whisper, "We didn't say goodbye on the Ouija board."

The music starts again.

Rising and swelling, the classical music reaches a crescendo, one so chilling my body breaks out in goose bumps.

The lights flicker, the door sways, and then we're plunged into darkness.

"Liam?" Evie dares call out.

Cold air scuttles down my spine as a breath puffs across my ear and growls.

"Hello, Blair."

Remember… secrets don't stay buried with the dead.

Acknowledgments

In every book, I put a piece of myself in it, and while this one isn't as heavy as my other's it was just as special.

Truth be told I didn't have the easiest childhood growing up. Yes, I may have had a roof over my head and food in my belly—both of which I'm eternally grateful for—but my life was filled with the worst type of chaos.

I didn't have many friends growing up and I was bullied for years. Only to then go home to a very unhealthy, toxic household.

I wish someone put a book in my hands to help me escape (that came later in life) but all I had was TV shows.

I used to get lost in them, absolutely throwing myself into the fictional world in the hopes of distracting myself from what felt like a never-ending depression.

One of those shows was Pretty Little Liars.

I'm not going to bore you with the details of how much I loved that show—perhaps it was because it gave me a glimpse into what it felt like to have friends.

Nevertheless, that show holds a very special place in my heart because those characters gave me something to look forward to in my life.

It made me hold on just a little longer.

And so to be sitting here writing to you—those who do read the acknowledgments—after reading a thriller I wrote at the age of 26.

I'm just grateful to be alive.

And I'm amazed that a story can be inspired by a dark time.

I can now bore you with how much I love psychics and the paranormal but perhaps I'll save that for the next spooky thriller I write.

From the bottom of my heart, thank you for reading my books.

You all give me a reason to wake up, a purpose, and a will to continue moving forward. Because what is a story if no one reads it?

And of course a huge thank you to all those who helped me on this project. To Makenna my beautiful editor. Thank you for your wit, open mind, and brilliant brain.

To Thea for your astonishing artistic talent. It truly blows my mind every time I see your artwork.

Thank you to all the BETA readers and to Bec for proofreading for me. (I'm sorry for scaring you)

Last but certainly not least...to my Charlie, thank you for falling asleep to the sound of Barbie movies after I've written, read, or watched something scary.

I love you endlessly and most importantly, I love you the most.

Made in the USA
Middletown, DE
23 October 2024